PENGUIN BOOKS

Hungry Ghosts

Praise for *The Fourth Queen*:

'A sumptuous historical hybrid that gallops through romance, adventure and sheer horror . . . a lush, sinister book, which I enjoyed tremendously' *The Independent*

'Intelligent and gloriously romantic' *Eve*

'Astonishing . . . A fascinating story' *Tatler*

'An enchanting tale' *OK!*

'Enthralling . . . an unputdownable story of murder, sex and true love. Gripping and very moving, with some unforgettable characters. *The Fourth Queen* is strongly recommended' *Sunday Tribune*

'Not just bodice-ripping but thrillingly erotic, sensuously evoked and quirkily intelligent' *Amanda Craig*

'An exciting and original historical novel, a real page-turner. The book offers a compelling twenty-first-century take on a secret world of murderous scheming and exotic sensuality. It's fabulous' *Barbara Trapido*

'Marvellously evocative and highly readable' *Good Book Guide*

'A fascinating read' *The Big Issue*

'A rip-roaring, atmospheric story' *Woman and Home*

ABOUT THE AUTHOR

Debbie Taylor is the founder and editor of *Mslexia*, the national magazine for women who write. She has been writing and travelling ever since she abandoned her career as a research psychologist. She has worked as editor of *New Internationalist* magazine and co-edited *The Virago Book of Writing Women*. Her non-fiction book, *My Children, My Gold* (Virago), was shortlisted for the Fawcett Prize for women's writing and her regular *Heat and Dust* column ran in *The Sunday Times* for most of 2003. She lives with her partner and daughter in a disused lighthouse at the mouth of the River Tyne and in an old farmhouse in Crete, where *Hungry Ghosts* was written. Her previous novel, *The Fourth Queen*, is published by Penguin.

Hungry Ghosts

DEBBIE TAYLOR

PENGUIN BOOKS

PENGUIN BOOKS

Published by the Penguin Group
Penguin Books Ltd, 80 Strand, London WC2R 0RL, England
Penguin Group (USA) Inc., 375 Hudson Street, New York, New York 10014, USA
Penguin Group (Canada), 90 Eglinton Avenue East, Suite 700, Toronto, Ontario, Canada M4P 2Y3
(a division of Pearson Penguin Canada Inc.)
Penguin Ireland, 25 St Stephen's Green, Dublin 2, Ireland
(a division of Penguin Books Ltd)
Penguin Group (Australia), 250 Camberwell Road,
Camberwell, Victoria 3124, Australia (a division of Pearson Australia Group Pty Ltd)
Penguin Books India Pvt Ltd, 11 Community Centre,
Panchsheel Park, New Delhi – 110 017, India
Penguin Group (NZ), cnr Airborne and Rosedale Roads, Albany,
Auckland 1310, New Zealand (a division of Pearson New Zealand Ltd)
Penguin Books (South Africa) (Pty) Ltd, 24 Sturdee Avenue,
Rosebank, Johannesburg 2196, South Africa

Penguin Books Ltd, Registered Offices: 80 Strand, London WC2R 0RL, England

www.penguin.com

First published 2006
1

Set in 11/13 pt Monotype Dante and Formata Light
Typeset by Rowland Phototypesetting Ltd, Bury St Edmunds, Suffolk
Printed in England by Clays Ltd, St Ives plc

ISBN–13: 978–0–141–01243–8
ISBN–10: 0–141–01243–9

For Andrea Badenoch (1951–2004)
and Julia Darling (1956–2005)

Acknowledgements

My love and thanks to Bill and Izzie, to Bill senior and Dorothy, and to everyone at *Mslexia* magazine, for allowing me the space and time to work on the book. Thanks also to Margaret Wilkinson, Gillian Allnutt and Andrew Crumey for inspirational writing workshops that sowed the seeds of the story; to Andrea Badenoch and Julia Darling for whisking me off to retreats in Scotland, where the seeds germinated; and to Mari Evans, Judith Murray and Lisanne Radice, for invaluable comments on the first draft.

I am also grateful to David Taylor for information about treatments for depression; to Mark Hussmann for help researching the hippy community in Matala; to John Lambert for access to the laboratories at the Royal Victoria Infirmary in Newcastle upon Tyne; to Russell Baston for teaching me about film developing and hand-tinting; and to Sirkka-Liisa Konttina for introducing me to the delights of cold-water swimming. And to all my Greek friends on Crete and Karpathos, especially Georgia Kourounakis and Aphrodite Delagrammatica, for making me feel at home.

Martin's story was sparked by a short newspaper report about a boy who was discovered 'living with dead animals' in a leafy Home Counties suburb. However, I did not research the background to that story before writing *Hungry Ghosts*. All the events concerning Martin in the novel are entirely from my own imagination.

Of course you know what is meant by a magnifying glass – one of those round spectacle-glasses that make everything look a hundred times bigger than it is? When anyone takes one of these and holds it to his eye, and looks at a drop of water from the pond yonder, he sees above a thousand wonderful creatures that are otherwise never discerned in the water. But there they are, and it is no delusion.

From 'The Drop of Water' in *Fairy Tales Of Hans Christian Andersen*
by Hans Christian Andersen, 1872

Chapter 1

The Man Spoon

Martin's mother told him that horses got pregnant by standing with their tails raised and their rumps to the wind. He'd seen them doing that in the field by the Cherwell. When the wind was fierce and made the river smack at the bank, the mares would snort and buck and wave their tails like flags.

She'd said that was how she'd got pregnant with him. That she'd stood on a rock by the sea and opened her arms, and he'd come to her on the wind.

Another day she'd said that he'd come riding towards her on a white horse. They'd been at the seaside in the middle of winter. In a grey café overlooking a wide bay. Their anoraks had been on the backs of their chairs and their noses were red from the freezing wind. He remembered drinking hot chocolate from a purple mug with *Cadbury's* written on it in gold. The wind was making the door rattle.

The waves seemed to start out by the horizon, running in low and fast then rearing up. with the wind whisking white flecks from their crests. 'When they're like that, we call them white horses,' his mother told him.

There were things she told him when she was being serious, and other things she told him as a joke. Only he didn't always know when she was joking. She'd confessed later that horses didn't really get pregnant like that. But she never told him anything about his father.

Martin was seven. Sometimes he thought he was part of a story that someone else had made up.

He'd been three when the oven was last used. He remembered kneeling on a chair by the table and helping his mother tip and mix ingredients. They were going to bake a cake. The kitchen window was all steamy. He could smell the oven warming up, its hot smell of old roast chickens.

He remembered his knees hurting. There was a red weal across each at the front where the edge of the chair seat had cut in. He'd been concentrating so hard he hadn't noticed.

He was using two cups – the thin white one with the yellow rose on, and the thick blue striped one. One cup was for wet things, like butter and milk. One for dry things: sultanas, currants and flour; and the special brown sugar that kept moving after you'd touched it.

Now he was seven he wondered if he'd dreamt that day. They still had the cups, but they never used them. They were in the larder with the paint tins and brushes. His mother kept plates in the oven, stacked on the wire shelves; and there was a Chinese tray on the hob with a bowl of hyacinth bulbs. She looked at secondhand cookers sometimes, in Fast Eddie's House Clearance on the way to the chip shop, but 'it's not a priority' she said.

He remembered poking a hole in the sugar and watching the crystals tumble slowly down into it. His mother had been feeding him sultanas. They were named after a beautiful woman in a harem, she'd told him, because she was sweet and juicy and her skin was exactly that colour. A harem was a house full of princesses, she'd said. They were all married to the same king and he made them take turns.

He'd liked looking at the long red dents in his knees. He'd sprinkled them with flour to see if it would stay in the creases. They were hot compared with the rest of his leg. They hurt, but it didn't matter. He supposed he was wearing shorts. Or maybe just underpants.

Maybe it had been so hot he'd taken off his trousers. But he'd been wearing a red tee shirt. He could see it now, with her big floury handprint in the middle of it, on his tummy, and his little one beside it.

He had no image of the cake, though there must have been one. Perhaps he'd been in bed when she'd taken it out of the oven. Or maybe they'd eaten all the raw mixture as it was. He remembered his chin covered with sweet grease and his knuckles shining; cleaning sugar gravel from his nails with his teeth.

Later he'd lined up all the spice jars like paint pots and spooned misty colours on to the blue Formica. He'd used his Man Spoon with the tiny figure on the handle. He remembered mixing milk into the little heaps and smearing a brown rainbow on the table with his fingers. She'd taught him the names of each colour: turmeric yellow, nutmeg brown, cinnamon pink. Her cheeks had been red and her hair tied up with green string. When she'd bent to kiss him she'd smelt of sultanas.

When Martin thought of the word 'happy', this was what he thought of.

There were some things that he remembered; and some things that he dreamed. He tried to keep them apart, but when a memory was very old it sometimes felt like a dream. And if he asked his mother, she sometimes said something completely different, or changed his version so her memory got mixed up with his.

Did the cooker ever work as a proper cooker? He thought so. He thought the dents in his knees proved it. You wouldn't dream a detail like that.

That day's tea was a tin of cold rice pudding in the cold kitchen. 'You can eat it with your Man Spoon,' his mother smiled at him. 'Like when you were a baby. Do you remember?' And she rifled in the drawer for the tin-opener.

Martin smiled back. He didn't know what he remembered. Because it was the same every week: the silver spoon with the little man on the handle; the tiny reflected blue table in the spoon's surface; the pinch of nutmeg.

That night he dreamed he was leading a brown mare through a forest. The path was muddy and her hooves made a squelching sound; her brown breath was on the back of his neck. He was barefoot and the mud felt warm. His bare legs were splashed with brown. In his dream he could smell nutmeg on the mare's breath, like the steam from a newly baked fruitcake.

He woke suddenly and found his bed bathed in blue moonlight. There were big patches of brown paint on his wallpaper, where his mother had been experimenting with one of her colour schemes. 'Earth tones', she called them, or 'autumn shades', splashing spice on the dingy sprigged wallpaper.

Every week she brought books home from the library. She said some of the books were 'fact', which meant real. And some were 'fiction', which meant that someone had made them up. Fiction was different from lies, she said. Fiction was when you wanted someone to tell you a story and you both knew it wasn't real. A lie was when someone tried to make you believe a thing that wasn't true.

Chapter 2

Sylvia parks the car and sits back for a moment against the doughy upholstery. It's six a.m. on Valentine's Day and she's been speeding down the Coast Road with the heater blasting. The streets are dark outside. Her swimming costume feels slithery inside the fleece of her tracksuit. Is she really going to do this?

She turns off the engine, the heater, the headlights. This is Bennet's car, really. Long and solid, like him: a safe cocoon, with air conditioning and quad sound. Rollbars and air bags. Even switched off, the engine ticks and hums.

A gust of sea wind buffets the window and rocks the car slightly. The shop windows on the seafront are black. The pavement glitters with frost.

Scooping up her towel, she gets out and slams the door. Out in the open, the cold hits her face like a slap and her lungs fill with the smell of the sea. She exhales an orange cloud in the glow of the streetlamps. Everything is murky orange: the white walls of the pub, her winter-pale skin, her new trainers; the chip wrappers cartwheeling past her down the street. It's like the inside of her aunt's darkroom.

She crosses the road and looks down into St Edward's Bay, a faint curve of sand fringed by rocks, far below in the darkness. She can see a blur of waves crashing, and a fraction later their sound reaches her: the suck and sneeze of the North Sea. Her cheeks are scuffed by the wind and her eyes are smarting. Swathes of seaweed are strewn like tresses across the beach.

Walking down the steps, she feels the handrail icy under her fingers. The weeds on the bank are stiff and frosted. A dark pipit flicks away as she submerges, away from the orange light. There's a beer glass upended on the bottom step.

Down on the beach the roar of the sea fills her head. Ghostly grey in the darkness, the waves rear up, curl over, smash down like a tennis serve. They flail at the shore, claw at the tumbled rocks below the ruins of the Priory. Cod-cold, the black water stretches all the way to the Arctic.

Underfoot the sand is crisp as snow, peppered with the blow-holes of invisible worms. She finds a rock and starts tugging off her trainers and socks.

Unzipping her tracksuit top, she notices what looks like a lump of driftwood lying in a niche between the rocks. When it blinks at her, she realizes it's a seal: its head perfectly round; its body a dense tapered sleeping bag. Has she woken it?

The seal gazes at her with calm eyes as she folds her clothes neatly on the rock. When she's finished, it turns and makes its way unhurriedly down the beach towards the clamouring waves.

Sylvia watches it go, the wind biting into her bare shoulders. Shards of icy sand prick her bare feet. Her arms are smocked with goosebumps. She thinks of the tiny muscles raising each hair on her forearm. She thinks of the capillaries in her skin squeezing shut to push her blood deeper into her body, to keep her heart warm, her lungs, her liver. Her wounded ovaries, cratered by the technician's needle. Her empty womb.

Her feet are numb by the time she reaches the water. As she walks in, the numbness spreads up her legs: a burning numbness, like electricity and strong peppermint. Her knees, her thighs are disappearing, her skin shrinking like silk under a hot iron.

Suddenly the sand drops away beneath her feet and a wave hits her like a closed door, knocking the breath from her lungs. The door opens and gulps her down into a room of ice bubbles. There's freezing mercury in her armpits. It's squeezing her chest until she can't breathe. A polar noose is closing around her neck. Her thighs are compressed in an armour of ice. She's in a straitjacket padded with snow. Her limbs are disconnecting from her body: frozen meat, numb as skittles.

For a moment she panics, thinking she's paralysed. This is how

6

people drown, she thinks. Then it begins: the fizzing feeling she's been longing for: red sherbet buzzing in her fingers and toes. Weeping hot tears, she starts to swim.

'The sand was actually crisp,' Sylvia tells Bennet when she gets back to the house. 'It was like walking on crème brûlée. Only freezing, of course.'

'My wife's a nutter,' he mourns, buttoning his white shirt.

'When I got into the sea I thought I was going to die. Everything went numb and I couldn't breathe. Then this amazing tingly feeling started spreading through my body, like a zillion electric shocks.'

'And this is supposed to cure infertility.'

'Infertility, heart disease, cancer, you name it.' She unlaces her trainers. 'And boost the immune system. When the surface vessels contract there's a surge of blood to the core organs.'

'That's what Mengele did with the Jews. Immersed them in cold water. I didn't realize he was doing them a favour.' He's rummaging for socks; his hair's damp from the shower.

'Baptism used to involve total immersion,' she remarks, walking into the en suite and turning on the taps to run a bath.

'That was in the Sea of Galilee, not the bloody North Sea. Christianity wouldn't have got very far if it froze all its converts half to death.'

'It's supposed to increase libido too.'

'Now you're talking.' He stands watching her from the doorway. There's a lopsided smile on his face. 'Maybe I'll test out that theory tonight.'

'But I'm not —' She stops herself.

'We don't have to make love only when you're ovulating, you know.' His eyes are hurt. His collar is up, his silk tie hanging loose like a stethoscope.

'I know. It's just – I don't seem to feel like it in between.' How can she tell him? That she feels dead when he touches her. That knowing she's ovulating is the only thing that makes it possible.

7

'I'm sorry,' she says, clutching a white towel to her chest. 'Maybe I'll feel different this evening.'

'I'll be there if you will,' he says softly. Then, caressing her cheek with the back of his hand, 'Happy Valentine's Day, you daft bint.'

Why doesn't she tell him the real reason she's been sea-bathing? That she hoped the cold water might jolt her out of her numbness. That she sometimes picks up his razor and rests the blade against her wrist, imagines slicing into herself, to prove she can still feel something.

Why doesn't she tell him about the seal?

These days she goes to work on the Metro. After the first miscarriage, she stopped riding her little Honda scooter. Though she didn't really believe that bumping over drains and potholes could dislodge a foetus, sitting astride the saddle made her feel vulnerable. So she wheeled it round to the back yard, tucked it up in a tarpaulin, and stashed her crash helmet in the cupboard under the stairs.

These days when she leaves the house, she wears a narrow black wool coat instead of her creaky leather jacket: nurses' lace-ups in place of her black steel-toed boots.

She isn't a nurse, but she likes their standard-issue shoes. She thinks they're rather elegant: neat and understated. Though she doesn't have to wear a uniform in the lab, she's created one anyway to wear under her white coat. Plain black tee shirt and tailored black trousers; no jewellery; fob watch pinned to her top pocket.

She's in the cutting rooms today. In Histology the teams are rotated through the various sections every three months – cutting, embedding, mounting, staining – so their skills stay up to scratch. The other women say this makes it less boring, but Sylvia's never found her work boring. Repetitive, yes. But so is eating, sleeping. She can't understand the women – it's mostly the younger women – who say they're bored. She thinks it must be because they aren't doing the job properly.

When people ask her how she stands it, chopping up bits of body all day, she shrugs and says, 'You get used to it.'

What she doesn't say is how much pleasure she gets from her work: from slicing ten-micron-thin slivers of wax-embedded tissue and floating them on to a pristine glass slide; from immersing them in the stains and seeing the translucent cells blossom red and purple under the microscope. It's so precise and intricate. So satisfying. It's so *beautiful*.

She loves the row of fat brown bottles the special stains are kept in, and the recipes for combining them; the alchemical names: Sirius Red, Alcian blue, Masson's trichrome, heavy Giemsa.

Seen up close like this, the human body is an entire planet of seething life: white blood cells squeezing through capillary walls and squirming after bacteria; giant microphages scavenging debris; microscopic cell hairs waving. All this from the fusion of ovum and sperm.

Of course she never sees anything alive. It's all dead and dunked in formalin by the time it reaches the labs. Today she's early and the night samples are waiting to be taken to the cutting benches: blood vessels in jars with red lids; lung in grey; breast biopsies in pink; urinary in yellow.

The other women did ask, after her first miscarriage, whether she wanted to stop working on the gynae tissues for a while. But she'd shaken her head.

'I don't want to start avoiding things,' she'd said. 'Where would I draw the line? What about placentas? What about breasts? The only thing that would be left would be cleaning up the wax in the embedding room.'

It wasn't as if she didn't know what a foetus looked like – at four weeks, eight weeks, twelve – though it's rare to see an undamaged foetus in the lab. They're usually in pieces; odd brownish fragments floating in formalin. The 'products of conception': you can shake them up and watch them settle, but they never fall in the shape of a baby.

*

The Valentine's banquet at the restaurant is all in shades of pink. Bennet orders pink champagne while Sylvia contemplates the unlikely food combinations: smoked salmon with pink grapefruit; red mullet with a beetroot coulis; rhubarb and tomato cheese-cake.

'How did you find this place?' she giggles as her raspberry taramasalata appears.

'Blame Val. I asked her to recommend somewhere with white tablecloths and decent cutlery. She was here with one of her Desperate Dateless men last week.'

'Are you sure you didn't specify high camp?'

'Not guilty, your honour. Bone-handled knives and starched napkins were my sole criteria.'

Sylvia lifts her champagne and lets the bubbles tickle her nose. 'God, I love this stuff,' she sighs, taking a sip. 'Don't let me drink more than one glass.'

'I suppose it's not worth me pointing out that the link between moderate alcohol consumption and infertility is tenuous at best?'

'You should cut back too, you know.'

'And put on my underpants backwards. And sleep with a badger's paw under my pillow.'

'Seriously, B. I found an American website last week that said—'

'Seriously, Syl. I'm going to chuck your PC in a skip when we get home.'

'I just want to make sure we're doing everything we can.'

'How about two glasses?' He grins at her. His grey eyes look tired. His suit jacket is rumpled.

She smiles back. 'Is that your idea of a compromise?'

'How else am I supposed to get you into bed?'

It's in bed, with his warm hands roaming her skin, that the numbness is worst; when she can feel his friendly weight on her and taste the Courvoisier on his tongue.

It's not that she can't react to what he's doing. Her body's as responsive as it ever was. There: the nipples puckering as he sucks them; the answering drag in her uterus; the wetness starting to seep out of her. But it's happening in pieces that won't hold together, to a body that's nothing to do with her. She's an android with its sex programme running. She's Pavlov's dog, salivating to the bell instead of the bone.

Tonight he's ready to come quickly, but he's waiting for her. She can feel him unclenching his buttocks and slowing his breathing. She lies motionless beneath him, her hands resting lightly at the base of his long back: a freeze-frame from *Come Dancing*.

She can feel his stretch marks with her fingertips, scars from when he grew six inches in six months when he was fifteen. Now he's moving again, building up to a steady rhythm. It's time for him to kiss her. His mouth is hot; his cheek clamped against her nose. They're panting, mouths mashed together. Closing her eyes, she can see them: the contorted faces, the damp hair.

Now's the time for her to move her hand down to her clitoris and press the button that releases her orgasm. In her mind she sees her fingers slipping quickly side to side; sees the spasm, the padded red walls pulsing. Perfectly timed, after years of practice, to coincide exactly with his ejaculation and suck his semen deep inside her.

Then his laugh of satisfaction, that they've come together yet again. And her surge of sadness that it's left her feeling so empty.

'No sense wasting it,' says Bennet, reaching for a pillow with a long arm. He pushes it under her buttocks and eases out of her. 'They say the act of mating stimulates cats to ovulate, so who knows? Stranger things have happened.' He hands her a wodge of Kleenex. 'Anyway, I like to see your fanny displayed on a cushion.'

'Do you think it makes any difference?'

'Brightens up my life no end.'

'Lying propped up like this afterwards, you dope.' She stretches her lips into a smile, to match his mood.

'I don't know,' he says, standing up to close the curtains. 'There's a kind of logic to it, I suppose. But then I used to think that if a girl jumped up and down after sex she couldn't get pregnant.'

'I don't think anything can stop a sixteen-year-old girl from getting pregnant. It's thirty-eight-year-old primigravidae who have the problem.'

'It just takes longer, that's all.' He lies down again and pulls up the covers. 'At least we're "unexplained". It could be worse.'

'"Unexplained". That's such a cop-out. Everything can be explained if you look closely enough. They're just not trying.'

'So we'll have to try harder ourselves.' He nuzzles her neck. 'Tomorrow's good for me.'

'"Unexplained" makes me think it's my fault. That I should stop drinking completely. Or give up working at the lab. Stop exercising.'

'Now you're being daft,' he says. 'You saw those Indian women on TV. Twelve hours breaking rocks in that quarry and a thimble of rice for supper. Didn't stop them having babies.'

Five years of tests and they'd found nothing. The odd slow-swimming sperm among millions of sprinters; a partially blocked fallopian tube, now flushed clear. Sometimes she wishes they would find something. Even if it meant she'd never have a baby. At least then she'd know.

It's the not knowing that makes her want to scream. If she knew what was wrong, she could do something. Take a hormone or a vitamin. Drink less coffee. She could do that thing she's so good at: worrying at a problem, trying different solutions and recording the results; working systematically through every alternative until it's solved.

Later, when Bennet's asleep, she slips out of bed and goes to sit by the window. Their bedroom is at the front of a big Victorian terrace, overlooking a stretch of city allotments. Pulling back the curtains, she can see the orange streetlights lining the Great

North Road beyond; and car headlights slowing, shunting at the junctions, then speeding away.

She pictures clouds of orange exhaust settling on the kale and winter cabbages, the parsnips and sprouts. She'd given up her plot after reading about the pesticides people used years ago, that persist in the soil for decades. All the old men shuffling between their rows of potatoes with rusty tins of banned poison. Nothing, she thinks grimly, is ever unexplained.

She thinks of her latest miscarriage. Its heart was beating at eight weeks. She saw it on the monitor, like a glow-worm blinking. By twelve weeks it had stopped, so they'd sucked it out of her. It had been male, they'd said. Normal as far as they could tell, but macerated.

Out beyond the Coast Road, in the Arctic water, night fish are mouthing the ice pebbles. Midnight mussels are opening and fanning themselves. Tomorrow she'll go swimming again.

Chapter 3

The Blue Lace-Ups

Martin's mother was always buying magazines about houses.

'We could have yellow in the hall,' she'd say, 'like butter or dandelions.' And she'd tear out a picture and hurry into the hall to Sellotape it next to the others. Then she'd close the magazine and stack it on one of the piles on the staircase. There were so many there now that they had to edge upstairs through the narrow passage between them.

The walls of every room were covered with torn-out pictures of other houses. The hall was full of hall pictures; the bedrooms full of bedroom ones. Some of the pictures were so old the Sellotape was brown and brittle.

Sometimes she woke up restless and excited and rushed out without any breakfast. He'd sit eating his muesli and banana while she locked him in and called 'Be careful!' through the letter box.

Half an hour later she'd be back with some more paint tins. Then she'd paint half a wall, or maybe a window frame. As though she was in a hurry; as though she was a match that would burn out if she didn't finish quickly enough.

Painting always involved moving things out of the way. One day it was bags of clothes from when he was a baby. They were like photos, she said; only better, because you couldn't touch photos. Or smell them. And anyway she didn't have a camera. There was a bag for every year of his life.

'All the baby clothes in the shops were pale pink or pale blue,' she said, slurping arcs of deep orange on a wall in the spare bedroom. 'But I read somewhere that babies can't see pastel shades. So I dyed all your Babygros the brightest colours I could find.'

The one she'd kept was cherry red, like a teeny Santa outfit. Martin spent ages working out how the poppers fitted together. When he'd finished it looked as though he'd just dressed an invisible baby.

She'd finished the whole wall before she realized she was hungry. By that time he had all the clothes out of the bags and had lined up six pairs of little shoes in a row.

'I remember those,' he said, pointing at a pair of blue lace-ups from the third bag. 'I remember polishing them and getting the blue polish on my hands. And it wouldn't come off. D'you remember? And it got on my nose too, so I had to go all day with a blue nose.'

'This wall's making me fantasize about baked beans,' she said, dunking the brush in a tin of water. 'I must have chosen this colour because I didn't have any breakfast. Maybe all the paint I buy looks like food because I'm always starving when I choose it. What do you think?'

'You came back with a real eggy yellow last week,' he agreed, hiding the blue lace-ups in a heap of old coats. 'But it was the turquoise for your room before that. You couldn't have been thinking about food when you bought that.'

'OK, clever clogs.' She yanked him to his feet. 'So it's not such an insightful theory after all.' They began bundling the clothes back into their bags. 'No, wait a sec. That was the day we went to the Botanical Gardens and we got the paint on the way back. We had Bars Mars by the alpine beds, don't you remember? So I couldn't have been hungry when we were in the paint shop.' She cuffed him triumphantly. 'So my theory does work.'

She shooed him on to the landing, where every door was a different colour. Pictures of other staircases lifted and subsided as they clumped downstairs.

On the half landing the window frame was bright pink. When he was younger he'd imagined each coloured window looked out on a different world. The pink world was full of pigs and strawberry milkshake. That must have been when he was five. The privet hedge was already up to his bedroom window by then and you couldn't see into the house from the street.

One afternoon last winter he remembered looking into other people's living rooms and realizing his house was different. He'd been walking home from the library with his mother. It wasn't time for tea yet but it was already dark. He remembered the shock of seeing all those normal living rooms lit up; just like in the magazines. He'd assumed that everyone else's house was like his inside.

It was around that time that he'd started asking about his father. He thought he remembered being carried by a big soft man with a green canvas coat. He could remember the material, stiffer than anything his mother wore, and the two little brass-lined holes in the collar, like rings. He'd tried each of his fingers in them to see which fitted best.

He remembered looking down and seeing the blue lace-up shoes. They were new; that was why he kept looking at them. No, not new. Polished. They'd been grey and scuffed but now they were like new again. They'd never been polished before.

He'd hidden the shoes because he remembered now when he'd seen the blue smudge of polish on his nose. He'd been in a bare hallway and a man had been lifting him under the arms so he could look in the mirror. Being lifted that way made his duffel coat bunch up around his face like a tortoise's shell. The man's face was behind his face, to one side. His eyes were smiley and he had long bushy sideburns.

After cold baked beans, bread and butter and milk, they came back up to the spare room and moved a chest of drawers, seven cardboard boxes and two deckchairs, so she could get to the far end of the wall. While she tied a purple scarf over her hair and levered the lid off the baked-bean paint, Martin opened the biggest of the boxes they'd moved.

Sticking out was something long and rolled up. 'Oh, you've found the Crete box,' she said as he unrolled the grass mat as far as he could in the space. It smelt of hay and sun. After he'd unrolled it there was sand on his fingers.

'We went there for a whole summer when you were little, and camped in a cave by a lovely sandy beach. It was like we were cavemen.'

He had a vague memory of peeing with no clothes on in the sunshine; standing up and not even holding his dick. The pee had made a little puddle in the sand, then disappeared. He had an image of flapping material. 'Were there lots of tents?'

'A few little ones, but it was mostly awnings. People suspended saris and bedcovers from the rocks to make it shadier. We kept all you kids out of the sun when it was hot. Actually, I think we probably all went to sleep in the middle of the day. We arrived in April, but by the beginning of August I'd had enough.'

Then he remembered lying on his tummy at the water's edge and the sea like a giant dog licking him. There was a yellow cliff above him, covered with a patchwork of billowing colour.

'Can we go back there, Mum?' he asked, lifting a small blue bucket out of the box. It was full of shells. It smelt salty and fishy.

His mother stopped painting and looked at him. 'You know I haven't thought about Matala for years.'

'What's this?' He held up a knobbly pink-and-brown striped object, the shape of a ball.

'That's a sea-urchin shell. When they're alive they're covered with black spines. You can see the rows where the spines used to be.'

There was a necklace of little mauve shells, each with a hole in exactly the same place, threaded on a piece of black cotton. And another kind of necklace made from a shoelace, with two pink shells, a little brass bell and a bundle of white feathers lashed together with red twine.

His mother squatted beside him. 'God, I used to wear these all the time. Just shells and a bikini, and a wrap-around Indian skirt. And bare feet. In those days we all went barefoot, even in the street.'

Now she was delving into the box too, and unzipping an embroidered purse. 'Here are my toe rings! I'd forgotten all about them. And my silver pipe – I thought I'd lost it.'

But Martin had picked something else out of the shell bucket: a stiff little sea horse. Corrugated and dry; pursing tiny lips at the end of a blowpipe snout.

Looking at the sea horse made him feel funny, like being in the lift in Debenhams when it went down fast. The feeling put the sea horse in the same cupboard in his mind as the blue lace-ups.

*

There was a big glass tank in a green room somewhere, with a light and bubbles in the corner. The room was empty but the tank was full of fish. Even now he could see them clearly: nippy little ones with blue stripes, and slow round white ones with feelers. The blue stripes made the little fish seem lit up from inside. You could actually see their intestines.

In a smaller tank beside the big one were two tiny sea horses. Their tails were coiled around a piece of branched pink stuff and they were swaying slightly, fanning the water with ears like moths' wings.

When he first remembered the fish tanks, and asked his mother about them, she said he must have dreamt them. But they were so real, he began to wonder if he was really two boys: one who lived with his mother in the full house; and another who lived with his father in an empty house with an aquarium in the living room. He thought maybe that was why he had odd eyes: one green and one smudged with brown.

Then he read about some Americans who said they'd been kidnapped by aliens from another planet when they were asleep, and had tiny machines put into their brains through their ears. They had woken up the next morning and thought they'd been dreaming, but when a doctor examined them he found little puncture marks where the machines had been inserted.

He wondered whether something like that had happened to him, only in reverse: and he was really an alien who'd been kidnapped and put in his mother's house. He examined his body sometimes for fresh puncture marks, but he never found any.

One night the previous year he was woken up by the record player. It was playing 'I can't get no satisfaction' over and over. He got up and discovered all the lights were on, even though it was four in the morning. Thinking maybe it was the aliens coming to take him home again, he ran into his mother's bedroom.

She wasn't there, so he rushed downstairs. He found her in the kitchen. She was on the floor by the cooker and there were three bottles of wine on the table. She was trying to crawl into the oven.

He stood by the door and watched her try to go in head first, doubled up in her pink dressing gown with her bum towards him. Then, when she couldn't get her knees in, coming out and trying again. She bent over sideways this time, until one hand was on the floor, and tried to ram her bum inside, pushing up with her hands and feet and grunting with the effort. She looked like a huge floppy Christmas turkey with her dressing gown open and her head lolling down.

He wanted to ask what she was doing, but he thought she might be sleepwalking – and she'd said you should never wake someone when they're sleepwalking, because the shock can kill them. So he went back to bed and put his fingers in his ears until he fell asleep again.

Next morning the bottles had disappeared and when he asked his mother about them, she said he must have had a bad dream. It was around then that he started pretending he was really a horse in a boy's body.

Chapter 4

The seal is on the beach again the next morning, its mottled face glimmering at Sylvia from the darkness, its eyes huge as a bushbaby's. This time she feels surer about what she's doing. She puts on a swimming cap to keep her head warm, and tests the sand more carefully as she wades out. The sky is clear and pricked with stars; the sea molten black ice, blades of silver glinting on the surface from the light of the half-moon.

She splashes water, a soup of plankton, on her arms and face before submerging. Again, that primal gasp as the air is forced out of her lungs; the deadness in her legs, her feet; the electric fizz as the blood is cut off from her skin and channelled into the depths of her body. That intense series of sensations, like whole-body ECT, that parachutes her back into her flesh, is worth it all.

It doesn't last, of course. Yesterday it was gone by the time she arrived at the lab. Standing up in the Metro, she could feel her body receding like a passenger left behind on the platform. Maybe today the effect will last longer.

Sometimes she's surprised when she catches sight of herself in the mirror, to see how whole and normal she looks. Glossy wings of dark hair either side of her small oval face; clear brown eyes; cheeks pink as ever. When she feels so fragmented and wooden.

It's still dark when she gets back to the house. The postman's been and the door opens on to a slither of shrink-wrapped medical journals and junk mail. Absently sorting through them, she wanders into the kitchen and switches on the light. Halfway down is a brown Jiffy bag with her name on it in small hand-written capitals.

A package from her mother. She puts it on the table by itself and looks at it. What can her mother have sent her?

She takes a pair of white-handled scissors and places them next to the Jiffy bag. She fills the kettle with filtered water and spoons decaff into the cafetière, then walks to the window to stare out into the back yard. She can hear a trickle of robin's song, but everything outside is still black. All she can see is her own face staring back at her, grave and ghostly, silhouetted against the floodlit white kitchen like an alien peering out of a spaceship.

When the coffee's ready she pours it into one of the big French *mélange* cups they brought back from Languedoc. She heats a small jug of organic milk in the microwave, then sits down at the table.

She picks up the Jiffy bag and cuts it open. Inside is a sheaf of assorted letters in her own handwriting, pinioned in a big rubber band. And a separate folded sheet of the old-fashioned pale blue vellum her mother always uses, because 'I like to see a proper watermark'.

Sylvia unfolds the sheet and reads what her mother has to say.

My dear Sylvia,

I was sorting through Marjorie's papers and found these in the bureau drawer.

I've got a man coming next week to clear the place out, see if the furniture's worth anything. And some of her friends have been in for the paintings. It seems she left a list, saying who should get what. There's a painting for me, too, though God knows what she thought I was going to do with it. It won't go with anything in the house.

She wanted you to have her camera. It looks a terrible battered old thing, but one of the friends said it's rather valuable. Some kind of classic, apparently, so there you are. I'm sending it by Parcelforce this afternoon, so it will probably reach you before this little lot.

The will's due to be read next week. I imagine the cottage will be worth a pretty penny. The estate agent said Devon prices have gone through the roof. I did think of getting someone to slap a coat of

magnolia on the walls before selling it, but he said the plaster's so bad
it would only draw attention to it.

Anyway, I'll stop now. Try to take it easy, darling. I thought you
were looking a bit peaky at the funeral. Tell that husband of yours to
look after you.

Your loving,
Mother

Sylvia picks up the sheaf of assorted paper and weighs it in her hand: every letter she's ever sent her aunt must be here. *Not much to show for thirty-eight years*, she thinks with a stab of shame. They are in date order – had her mother done this? – with the most recent, in her own small slanting script, on the top.

Seeing it there gives her a jolt. She remembers writing it four months ago: a quick note to enclose a birthday present of purple fingerless gloves to keep her aunt's arthritic knuckles warm while she painted. It had seemed such a silly little present at the time, far too garish for Sylvia's taste. But her aunt had been over the moon, had actually telephoned to say she'd been looking for something like them for years, how clever Sylvia had been to think of them. Just a few weeks before she died.

Leafing down through the pile, she can see the handwriting change, growing clumsier and rounder as the writer grew younger. At the bottom is a hotchpotch of donkey postcards and forget-me-not notelets.

Sylvia tries to envisage the child who'd written these wobbly little thank-you notes. Her hair was always short, because her mother was obsessed with nits; and fleas, too, which was why she wasn't allowed any pets.

There was always sand in the sheets at her aunt's cottage, and kittens on the stairs. Every summer, until she was twelve, she'd gone to stay with her aunt in Devon for four weeks while her parents worked in the surgery. And every summer she'd come home with flea bites on her ankles and her mother's mouth would purse as she dabbed them with calamine.

She remembers waking to the rasp of a tiny tongue on her earlobe and a purr like a bee inside her head. There was a scab on her left knee one year that never healed because she kept falling off the secondhand bicycle her aunt bought her. She remembers scratches on her arms from blackberrying in the hedgerows; bruises on her legs from rock climbing.

'OK, Cinderella,' her aunt would always say on the last day of the holidays, 'time to tidy you up before your mum sees you.' And she would run a bath and lay out a clean summer dress, and pumice her feet and scrub the dirt from under her nails until she was 'fit to go to the ball'.

The bath was a huge chipped enamel one with brown stains under the taps. Sylvia can see herself crumbling a musty cube of lavender bath salts into it. Did they still make bath salts like that? She would step into it grubby and salty, and emerge pink and scented with the summer washed away.

At the very bottom of the sheaf of letters is a yellowed piece of lined paper torn from an exercise book, folded around a single black-and-white photo. It's a photo of herself, aged about ten, on a wide deserted beach. Her hair's wet, plastered to her head. She's wrapped in a stripy beach towel, her lips thin with cold. She's grinning triumphantly at the camera.

Sylvia remembers suddenly: the 'rainbow towel' she always used at her aunt's house, how cold the sea was, her aunt laughing at her, daring her to go in.

She turns over the photo. On the back, in smudged turquoise ink, her aunt had written: 'New Year, 1976. Hartland Bay. S faces death and survives!'

She'd been swimming in the sea in the middle of winter. She's done this before. For a moment she feels giddy. How can she have forgotten something so intense, so vivid?

She picks up the piece of lined paper and flattens it out. 'When I Grow Up' is printed across the top in big pencilled capitals and decorated with crayoned flowers. Beneath it is a list of statements in careful joined-up writing.

I will have a cat and a horse and a monky.

I will never drive a car. I will always go by horse or moterbike.

I will be a vet or a photografer or work in a cercus.

I will never wear high-heled shoes or make-up.

I will never live in a city. I will live on a houseboat, or a jipsy caravan, or a house by the sea.

I will never cut my hair. When I am an old lady I will have a long white platt.

I will never wear a skirt. Only trowsers or shorts.

I will have two lots of twins, two boys then two girls.

I will grow all my own food and never watch television.

I will always do good to others.

'I love that last one,' says Bennet when she shows it to him later over breakfast. 'Just in case God's peering over your shoulder.'

'It's so strange reading it. I was such a tomboy in those days.'

'You were spot on with the motorbike, but where on earth did the monkey come from?' He butters toast and reaches for the marmalade. 'And that wonderful long white plait. I can just see you as an old biddy in your shorts, planting parsnips with your monkey on your shoulder.'

'Do you think working in Histology is a combination of being a vet and a photographer?'

'You're forgetting about the circus.'

'I loved being there – once I got used to everything being so messy. It was such a relief to be neglected for a change. We went whole days without seeing each other. Then she'd emerge from her studio at supper time with paint in her hair and a fag hanging out of her mouth.' Sylvia stirs her Earl Grey. 'These days she'd probably be arrested for child abuse.'

'That's not the only thing she'd be arrested for. Lucky there weren't any sniffer dogs at that funeral bash. Talk about passive smoking. I felt quite mellow by the time we left.'

The funeral had been months ago, before Christmas. Bennet had insisted on booking them into a four-star hotel 'to escape the folk music and felafel rissoles' at her aunt's cottage.

'I was very fond of your dear aunt,' he'd said, 'and I'm more than happy to give her a good send-off, but when the ear-pulling starts and the soggy roaches are being passed round, I want to be sitting in a nice deep leather armchair miles away, sipping a single malt.'

Sylvia gets up to put her cup in the dishwasher. '"Mr Bennet" she always called you. D'you remember?'

'One of the few people to use my correct title.'

'Except she was using it in the Jane Austen sense. I don't think she realized you're supposed to address surgeons as "Mr". "Your Mr Bennet is a very good provider," she used to say.'

'Meaning I was a male chauvinist plutocrat.'

'No, she liked you. You know she did. But I think she always had a secret yen for me to end up as an artist in a commune of Aran jumpers.'

' "What shall it profit a man, if he shall gain the whole world, and lose his own soul?" '

'She thought working for money was a kind of slavery.'

'I'd say that entirely depends on the wad of money on offer. Since I signed on with the partnership, even scrubbing up has gained a fascinating fresh allure.'

The funeral service had been held in a tiny grey church. It was crammed with people in bright scarves and red Doc Martens, with open-air faces and dirty fingernails. The church smelt of wet dogs and rolling tobacco. Afterwards, back at the cottage, there was lots of hugging and laughter; wine boxes squirting into plastic cups; tea bags squeezed into thick pottery mugs. Loaves were sawed on the wooden table; saucers were used as ashtrays. Sylvia sat in a corner in her black coat with her feet together while Bennet made her a mug of camomile tea.

'She had a point,' Sylvia says now, clearing the last of the breakfast things and steering toast crumbs into her hand with a square of kitchen roll. 'If you don't enjoy what you're doing, no amount of money can give you those hours back.'

'I do enjoy what I'm doing.'

'Not you. I'm talking about me. Anyway you said you hated those private laser ops; that you preferred working with the transplant teams.' They're in the hall now, jostling for a look in the mirror. She's brushing her hair; he's tousling his forwards at his receding hairline.

'I thought you liked your job.' He takes his coat from the cupboard and puts it on.

'I do. It was just seeing all her work, all those weird people she knew. Who obviously thought she was wonderful. Her paintings sold for quite a bit, you know. And her photos.'

'And your point is?'

She puts down the hairbrush and turns to look at him. 'I was just wondering what I'll leave behind when I die.'

'So that's what this is all about.' He rests his big hands on her shoulders and gives her a little shake.

'I used to get so excited about things, didn't I? Doing up the house, getting the allotment going. Now I just go to work and come home and sit at the computer. I'm like a hamster on a wheel, running round and round the same little circle.'

'You could have applied for that research job.'

'Not when we were just starting IVF.'

'They wouldn't have minded. People get pregnant all the time.'

'I just feel I can't get on with anything. It's like someone's pressed the "pause" button on my life and it won't start again until I have a baby.'

She collects the camera from the depot on her way back from work and unpacks it on to the kitchen table: the body, with its worn leather strap, and all the attachments. She sets them out in a geometric pattern on the bleached oak: the long lens, the wide-angle and the close-up; the coloured filters; the flash; the spare lens caps. The leather case that her aunt never used, with the little pack of desiccant still inside.

The case used to hang behind the door to the darkroom; along with the tripod her aunt could never get the hang of. She used volumes of the *Complete Oxford English Dictionary* instead, balanced on a chair: A–M for standard straight shots; all the way up to the *S–Z Supplement* if she wanted to tilt the camera down towards something.

The darkroom smelt of potatoes and was always freezing. It was the old scullery, with a Belfast sink and a long slate shelf where her aunt kept the developing trays and enlarger.

Sylvia remembers standing on tiptoe in the orange twilight, watching her own face materialize on the blank sheets in the developing trays, like a swimmer surfacing from a long dive. It's this alchemy that she relives every day in the Histology labs, immersing slices of translucent tissue in the dyes that will make them visible to the human eye.

Bennet bought her an enlarger after their first IVF attempt failed. He'd come home one evening to find her crying in the spare room, sitting on a dust sheet in his old shirt, with a new roller and a tray of paint beside her.

'I thought you were going to wait until we knew whether it was a boy or a girl,' he said, kneeling down and folding her into his arms.

'I know. But then this morning I just couldn't bear it like this any more. With the bare boards and that awful wallpaper. Like a bad tooth, niggling at me. I thought if I painted it white, it wouldn't seem like a room waiting for a baby.' Sobs shook her as she buried her face in his chest.

'So you went haring off to B and Q—' He fished a folded handkerchief out of his pocket.

'Then I realized that having it white would be even worse. Like an admission of defeat. A blank white room, with nothing to put in it.'

'Well, I think it's a very good idea,' said Bennet, mopping her eyes and tucking her hair behind her ears. 'Why don't you turn it into a darkroom? You've always said you wanted to get back into photography. We can make it into a nursery when the time comes.'

The IVF doctor had given her a photograph of the three fertilized embryos they'd put back inside her. And a form to sign, giving permission for the rest to be used for research. The three they'd chosen to put back into her looked like three rock cakes on a plate.

'Peter, Paul and Mary,' Bennet called them, joking about whether he'd be able to cope with a trio of singing prodigies. But Sylvia hadn't wanted to give them names. She didn't want to look at the photograph. She wouldn't think of them as children. They were seeds of children, no more. And they had fallen on stony ground. She never asked what they were going to do with the embryos they didn't use.

A week later Bennet had come home with rolls of blackout material for the window and an enlarger. But Sylvia never unpacked it. She couldn't bring herself to go into the echoey little room with its dusty grey floorboards and chipped paintwork; the only room in the house she hadn't decorated.

And soon they were embarking on their second IVF attempt, and she was inhaling from the Buserelin puffer, to switch off her natural cycle ready for the surge of synthetic hormones that would swell her ovaries with a fresh batch of eggs for the technicians to harvest.

They gave her a photograph of the second trio of embryos too. She handed it straight to Bennet and he put it into his wallet. This time he didn't talk about giving them names.

Sylvia picks up her aunt's camera. It feels familiar in her hands; her forefinger rests naturally on the shutter release as she moves the viewfinder towards her eye and frames the black coffee maker against the white tiles; the vase of creamy lilies beside the antique Bakelite telephone.

*

'Can't you just go swimming at the gym like a normal person?' asks Bennet.

Sylvia is laying out her swimsuit and jogging suit in the hall, ready for the morning. 'I've been swimming at the gym for three years and where has it got me?'

'Some pretty nifty biceps and the thighs of an Amazon warrior. Come to bed, Sylvie.'

She ducks out of his embrace. 'I just want to check something first.'

'This is getting silly.'

'Please, B. I had to leave something in the middle when you came home.' Walking into the study, she switches on the computer.

'Well don't forget the time.'

'OK.'

'I mean it, Sylvie. You must know all there is to know by now.'

But she's not listening. She's checked in and gone through to a departure lounge where he can't reach her. The screen lights up, she clicks 'Internet' and steps inside. A page of possibilities presents itself, like a road junction, with ten blue underlined roads. And soon she's wandering through a maze, following a trail of fragmented blue cotton.

Some nights the search is soothing. She feels she's moving smoothly forwards, reeling in fertility drugs, risk factors, side effects. Other nights are full of dead ends, or routes that circle round and end up where they started.

She's been through all the main medical sites now, but is retracing her steps to check studies she'd ignored the first time round. Reports from Brazilian research institutes and Egyptian foundations; papers from Finland and India. Sri Lanka. China. She can hear Bennet getting ready for bed: locking the front door; switching off lights.

She's reading a research paper from Hong Kong, about the use of acupuncture to treat infertility. It's written in the odd formal English Bennet calls 'medico-pidgin'.

They accepting to receive treatment, she reads. The results were

23 per cent successful more than when placebo. The researchers were doing it with electrodes instead of needles. *The guanyuan, zhongji, sanyinjiao and bilateral zigony sites were stimulated*, she reads. She imagines serious doctors with slick black hair bending over green-gowned women somewhere in Shenyang. How could an electrode make you pregnant?

The central heating goes off and the radiators begin clicking and cooling. Once inside the medical part of the maze, there is no getting out. All the links lead to other medical journals; other doctors, research fellows. There was a joke she'd heard as a child about a Muslim in Heaven being shown around by St Peter. 'What's that?' he asked, pointing to a high wall. 'Shush!' hissed St Peter. 'That's where the Catholics live. They think they're the only ones here.'

Once, by mistake, she keyed in 'endometriosis' on Google instead of logging on to Medline first. There was a pause, then the first of eight hundred thousand links she'd never seen before filled the screen. Societies and support groups; helplines and alternative therapies; personal testimonies. And she caught a glimpse, suddenly, of all the other infertile women all over the world: in waiting rooms and chat rooms, churches and temples; questioning, praying, being counselled; counting the days, filling in charts, shaking down ovulation thermometers.

Or simply sitting at their computers like she was, maybe late at night, like she was, following the trails of illuminated blue cotton they hoped would lead them to a baby.

She exits Hong Kong and types *infertility spontaneous abortion*. 'Spontaneous' makes it sound quick and impulsive, when in reality it was anything but: more a long tenterhooked time of sharp cramps and faint bloodspots before the inevitable steady expulsion. She'd been watching *The West Wing* when her first one started.

She clicks on to a report of some research in Japan. The house is getting chilly and she wanders through to put the kettle on, draping one of Bennet's big jumpers around her shoulders.

Cupping her hands around a mug of camomile tea, she goes back into the study.

Induced abortion is the most likely type of family planning in Japan, she reads. She'd been to Tokyo once with Bennet and had hated it: the mausoleum slabs of the city-centre buildings; the gardens of dense conifer and rock; solid traffic shimmering in hundred-per-cent humidity. Out of the centre it was awful in a different way, like an anthill broken open, with everyone hurrying, smoking, carrying things.

En route to some ancient site they'd visited a little Shinto shrine. Inside, leaning at all angles in the corners and against the walls, were scores of wooden poles etched with Japanese characters. A doctor friend told them later that they'd been placed there by women who'd had abortions; each one represented the spirit of an unborn child.

The weeks meander by. Sylvia gets up, drives to the beach, swims, showers, skims the newspaper, takes the Metro to work. Says 'I'm fine' to the women in reception; 'No, really, I'm fine' to the women in the lab.

Her period comes and goes. There are daffodils in Sainsbury's.

It's taking her longer and longer to do the shopping. She's made a list of teratogenic food additives and has started reading the labels on everything she buys. She searches for certified GMC-free oats, and coffee decaffeinated with water instead of chemicals.

One Saturday she's away so long Bennet goes looking for her. He finds her at the dairy counter with an empty trolley, picking up one pack of cheese after another, trying to remember which are possibly infected with listeria.

'Do you know what time it is?' He takes a slice of brie from her hand and puts it back on the shelf. 'You've been in here for three hours.'

'I wanted some cheese for tonight.'

'It doesn't matter. We can have something else.'

'There weren't any organic carrots, so I can't do that casserole. I asked the fish man about the salmon and he's gone to ask someone where it's from.'

'Come on. Let's go home.' He puts his arm around her and draws her away from the trolley.

'But Val loves cheese.'

'Val won't even notice.'

'I need to go to the garden centre to get something to keep the cats away from the tubs in the front where I planted all those bulbs. There's all that research about toxoplasmosis. And some proper gloves that don't —'

'We'll go tomorrow.' He steers her towards the exit, edging past the trolleys that snake up the aisles from the checkouts.

'But I haven't got anything for tonight.'

'We'll get a takeaway. Val will understand. And all Bill wants is a chance to get out of that awful flat. We'll get them drunk and fill the house with flowers instead. I'll go and get some wine and you stay here and choose some flowers. OK?'

He gives her a hug, then yanks up a wire basket and heads back into the crowded store.

'OK.'

People are nudging at her with heaped trolleys. How can they eat all that stuff? Emulsifiers and stabilizers. Hydrogenated fat. Permitted colourings. Aspartame. Her scalp feels hot, as though she's wearing a tight beret. Has she really been here for three hours?

She turns towards the flower display. Lilies from Turkey. Roses from Malaysia. Everlasting chrysanthemums. How do they make them everlasting? Carnations guaranteed for a week. A pot of jasmine in full flower at the end of February.

She opts for tulips and fills her basket with pallid creaking leaves and bullet blooms of scarlet.

'Someone told me the other day that tulips keep on growing in the vase,' remarks Bennet later as she slits cellophane and fans the first bunch on the kitchen table.

'What do you mean?'

'Maybe they spray them with something to force them into flower. You're the gardener. You tell me.'

She picks up a red tulip and pulls off its lower leaves. The stem is wet and hollow. Each torn-off leaf trails a thin hangnail from the mother stem.

'So they're still alive.' The thought makes her shiver.

'Do you want coffee?'

'Please.'

'Leaded or unleaded?'

'Unleaded – there's an open packet in the fridge.'

Of course, in a sense all cut flowers are alive. Otherwise they wouldn't open, or fade. But the idea of the tulips actually growing disturbs her. Severed from their bulbs, but still pushing their red fists towards the light. As though life were a substance that leaked out gradually.

She picks up another flower and stares at it, unable to rip off the leaves.

'Sylvia?'

It's been cut, but it's still growing. Drops of water are landing on the table.

'Sylvie? Oh, sweetheart. Why are you crying?'

'I don't know. I didn't know I was.' She touches her cheek. Fat warm tears are rolling down her face.

'I'll phone and cancel supper. I'll say you're sick. We can do it another time.'

'It's Mother's Day next week,' she says.

'I know.'

'There were signs up everywhere.'

'I know.'

'Oh, B,' sitting down and laying a heavy head on her arms. 'I'm so tired of pretending to be fine.'

That afternoon he sits her down beside him with a mug of peppermint tea while he searches the Internet and books two return flights to Crete. Then he prints out a letter for her to sign requesting a leave of absence from work.

'Three months is too long,' she objects.

'I'd have made it six if I thought for a second you'd sign it.' He hands her a pen.

'Crete'll be deserted this time of year.'

'I imagine there'll be some Cretans there.'

'It's practically in Africa.'

There'll be wild thyme on the hillsides. The air will smell of olive wood and fennel. She'll be able to swim in the clean blue Aegean sea.

Chapter 5

The Jay's Feather

Martin was galloping down to the river, across the open acres of wood-land and scrub behind the house. Brushwood hands were clutching at his tee shirt. They were trying to catch hold of his mane but he was too fast for them. It was dawn and the air was sweet and cold. Dew-wet grass whipped his bare legs. He shook his head and pranced sideways.

At this time of day it was only him and the Dog People: the bobble-hat woman with the Labrador; the jogging blonde with the Afghan; the red-shiny-face man with the chow. His mother said chows had blue tongues and came from China, but he'd never seen this one open its mouth. It just trotted stiffly along with its plumy tail coiled like a pig's.

His mother had said not to talk to anyone, but if a Dog Person waved at him he couldn't not wave back. He kept his distance, but he liked them seeing him. They made him feel visible.

Why would a dog have a blue tongue? It couldn't be from eating blue food. Perhaps all Chinese dogs had blue tongues.

His mother said that there were some Official People who wanted to take him away from her. That was why he shouldn't talk to anyone except her. The Official People thought that because she was sad sometimes, and couldn't always get up in the morning, that she shouldn't be allowed to have a child.

'When I found out what they were planning,' she told him, 'I bundled you up in a blanket and ran away with you.'

'How big was I?' Martin loved this story.

'Big enough to walk, but not too big to carry. Just the right size for running away with. I threw some things into a suitcase, grabbed my passport and rang for a taxi.'

'What about me?' He knew the answer, but he wanted to hear it again.

'It was the middle of the night and you were fast asleep. I scooped you up in your 'jamas and you didn't even open your eyes. You stayed asleep all the way to the airport.'

Martin's mane and tail were chestnut. He was a young stallion fleeing from men who wanted to lock him up in a stable. He shied at an empty Tizer bottle, then cantered to the lightning tree and jumped over it. The men wanted to race him, like the horses at the betting shop. They were wily, but he knew how to outwit them. He could leap right over their heads if he had to.

The betting shop was always full of men smoking and staring at a television on the wall. His mother said watching television made your brain go woolly, so you couldn't read books any more.

'We took some honey and plenty of money,' she'd say and he always chimed in: 'Wrapped up in a five-pound note.'

In the rush to leave, she'd packed silly things: 'I remembered your sun hat, but left your swimming trunks behind. I had skirts and tops for me, but no underwear. I put in your wellies, for some reason, but not your sand shoes.'

She hadn't wanted people to realize they were running away, so she'd left a note saying they were going on holiday. 'They thought we'd be away for a fortnight, but we sneaked back after a week and came here.'

She'd used some of the money to buy the house, and put the rest in a special bank that paid you to keep your money there.

The Official People who wanted to take him away were in the city where they used to live, so he was probably safe now. But she didn't want to take any chances. That's why he shouldn't talk to anyone. They'd take him away if they found out she still had him.

Sometimes he wondered whether the Official People were really his father.

A glint of silver made him veer sideways; he snorted and tossed his head. It was a supermarket trolley on its side in a patch of brambles. He hauled it out and righted it. It was a new one; not rusty and bent like the ones in the river. He could put things in it and carry them home. If he got some rope, he could make a harness to pull it with.

In the old days, when there were no cars or lorries, people used horses to move heavy things and the streets were ankle-deep in horse poo.

Martin had asked his mother what had happened to all the horses. His mother had explained that horses were domesticated, which meant they were owned by people. When the owners didn't want any more horses, they just cut off their testicles.

But some of the stallions had escaped before they could be operated on, she'd said. There were herds of wild horses on Dartmoor and Exmoor, and in a place called the New Forest near London; and some beautiful blonde horses on the windy plains of Norfolk. She brought a book back from the library for him and he'd stared for ages at the photographs of wild horses: American mustangs, Australian brumbies and the white horses of the Camargue.

There was a riding school across the river by the main road. He cantered down to the paddocks every day and trotted along the perimeter fence. He was a mustang stallion planning how to free his herd. His favourite was a dark brown mare. She was Arab, he thought, because of her dished face and small ears.

'Intelligent and fleet of foot,' the book said. She came right up to the fence and blew soft grassy breath on his face.

Her lips were grey and silky; she let him kiss her on the soft place between her neat nostrils. There were glossy black hairs growing from her chin. Her hot folded ears fitted into the palm of his hand. He'd seen her with a bit in her mouth and a schoolgirl on her back, in a line of other horses. Trotting around and around a small enclosure, knees bent like a roundabout horse – when she should have been galloping flat out across the deserts of Arabia.

Martin had a den where he hid sometimes. It was a green cave in the middle of a shaggy thicket swathed in old man's beard, up against the chain-link fence that surrounded the school. In the school yard there was a man with a limp who clipped off the shoots that twined in through the diamond-shaped holes, so the thicket was flat and neat on the school side.

Martin had put a piece of plastic sacking on the ground inside, to stop stones and twigs hurting his knees. And he had a tartan biscuit tin there to keep his things dry: his *Observer's Book of Birds* and the empty shell of a thrush's egg; two owl pellets crammed with fur and tiny mouse bones; the blue striped feather from a jay's wing.

When it was fine he sat hidden there for hours. If he was early, he watched the children arriving. All dressed identically, in navy-blue skirts and trousers, they poured into the fenced yard. They were all shouting; their noise filled Martin's ears. Sometimes they crashed against the wire by his hideout, making the leaves tremble. Then all at once they were inside the building and Limping Man was locking the gates.

Then it was quiet again and he could hear the blue tits calling from the clump of silver birch. It was just him and the Dog People again. Through the leaves he saw rabbits grazing and a jay strutting along the path. He knew where the green woodpeckers were nesting.

When the Dog People walked by, the rabbits dived into their holes. The jay jumped into the air with a squawk and wood pigeons clattered in the treetops. The Dog People never saw what the woods were like when they weren't there.

Martin had seen a fox scent-marking an oak tree and had sniffed the place himself afterwards. When he read that animals did this to mark their territory, he started copying them: pissing outside his secret places to keep them safe.

He had a secret place by the school and another by the riding stables. When he wasn't a chestnut stallion, he'd decided he was a red fox.

Except for his mother and the Dog People, nobody knew he existed.

Martin wasn't allowed into the centre of Oxford on his own, but he did go there sometimes without telling his mother. He liked to look at the women in the make-up department at Debenhams. He liked their stiff hair and red lips. They looked like the women in his mother's magazines. He went to the television department, too, and watched for as long as he dared.

The first time he went into town by himself was the previous winter. He'd gone into Debenhams in daylight, but when he came out it was getting dark. He'd been cold, because he'd left his anorak at home. It was too small for him and he was worried it would make people look at him.

Above the noise of the buses on Broad Street he'd heard a twittering sound. When he looked up he saw the starlings coming in to roost on the trees and window ledges of St Giles. Filling the sky with movement, they swirled round the spires, clattering in to land high above the winter shoppers. No one else seemed to notice them. All the other people were looking at the pavement, at the windows, in their handbags.

Martin had read somewhere that there were no birds in China. They had eaten them all, he read; swathed that huge country in nets and caught them like fish. He imagined silent trees and bare rooftops; a deserted sky with clouds slowly patrolling.

He imagined warblers and finches laid out in rows in the butchers' windows; and billows of plucked feathers on the floors. He pictured a pie to feed all of China, full of tiny stewed corpses. He saw them sizzling in deep-fat fryers until they were crisp, then being crunched by black-eyed children with sharp square teeth.

That evening he'd sat on the steps of the Ashmolean for an hour and watched the birds arrive: thousands and thousands of them. It was freezing sitting there without his anorak, but he hadn't cared. He'd been up in the sky with them, swerving and fluttering like tea leaves in water, quarrelling about where to perch, fidgeting and twittering in the dark branches.

He'd hugged his knees and shivered in his green jumper. From where he was sitting there was no horizon. The sky was small and dingy, stained orange by the streetlights. But out there in the fields, where the birds came from, it was huge and dark blue, hanging over the river like a circus tent.

He'd thought of the river going there and had sniffed the air for the fox's scent. He'd lifted his head and had blown a cloud of orange breath into the darkness. He was a horse standing in bruised grass by the river, watching birds stream away towards an orange glow in the distance.

Chapter 6

Bennet is loading their cases into a taxi to take them to the airport when the post arrives.

'Do you want these?' the postman asks, thrusting a handful of mail at Sylvia as she opens the door of the taxi. She makes a face: 'Go on then, but it's probably all junk.'

'They're all for you,' she says, as Bennet gets in beside her. 'Catalogue, bill, catalogue, boring, boring, boring. Why do you get such uninteresting letters?' She dumps them in his lap.

'Not so fast, missy.' He extracts a long cream envelope and taps her on the nose with it. 'This exciting-looking one is for you. Can we interest you in a new kind of credit card, madam? Are you thinking of remortgaging your house in the near future?'

The taxi jolts forwards as she tears it open and scans the contents. She reads it again, then silently tugs Bennet's sleeve. Her mobile shrills while he's reading.

'Has the post come yet?' It's her mother.

'I'm just looking at it now.'

'So how much did you get?'

'I'm not sure. Bennet's trying to decipher it.'

Fifty thousand pounds. It's written in numbers in the second paragraph, then spelt out in words, in brackets, as if the writer had known she wouldn't be able to believe it.

'I've phoned the solicitor, but he won't tell me anything. All he'd say was that she left a "substantial sum" to charity with "individual bequests" to her family and friends. If she's left it all to her dope-smoking cronies I'll spit.'

'Mum, it's none of our business what she does with her money.'

'All she left me was her jewellery. The bits she got from Gran when she died.'

'But that's wonderful. Aren't you pleased? You loved that necklace.'

'So, have you read the letter?'

'Look, Mum, I'm on my way to the airport. We're off to Crete for a few weeks.' Fifty thousand pounds! If she forwards her details they'll arrange a bank draft immediately.

'Well, what did you get?'

'I'll call you when I get back. Bye.' She clicks the disconnect button, then switches the phone off and subsides back against the seat.

'Why didn't you tell her?'

'Because she'd go apeshit. She'd think it was all about her. That Marjorie gave me the money as a way of getting at her.'

'It says here you're supposed to "spend it on something that will make you happy".'

'What do you think she meant by that?'

'So much for all that "money can't buy you happiness" crap. The old duck obviously came to her senses before she pegged it.'

Sylvia thinks of the money appearing on her bank statement. All those zeros, sitting fatly among the modest sums that usually went into and out of her account. Her small salary. The weekly Sainsbury's shop. Cheques for stamps and envelopes; for underwear; for another black tee shirt. All the big sums are in Bennet's account.

Fifty thousand pounds. Of course she doesn't need it. Bennet pays for almost everything: the kitchen extension; the Italian bathroom; all the new furniture; the decorators; anything she wants. Still, she can't help the flash of guilty glee as she thinks of the money in her account.

'Let's have champagne on the plane,' she says. 'It's on me.'

'According to this book, they'll be burning an effigy of Zeus at the port on Sunday.' Bennet is sitting on a tiny wrought-iron balcony overlooking Chania harbour while Sylvia unpacks. 'It's the climax of some kind of pre-Lent carnival that's been going on here since the seventh of February.'

'So they get three weeks of carousing and all we get is one measly Pancake Day.' Sylvia arranges her neat piles of black and white clothing on the shelves in the hotel wardrobe.

'Everyone wears a mask and they're not supposed to speak until someone recognizes them. In the old days half the men used to dress up as women because it was forbidden for women to dance. It's supposed to be a hangover from the Venetian occupation in the sixteenth century, but it's obviously because the Greeks are all closet poofters.'

'Are you going to change before we go out?'

'Into a nancy boy or the Phantom of the Opera?'

'Into a clean shirt, before I put them all away.'

'It's supposed to ensure the fertility of the animals and crops, so we've come to the right place. Leave out that beige one on top.'

'I can't believe we're here,' she sighs, stepping out on to the tiny balcony beside him. She can see a horse in a straw hat pulling a red cart over the cobbles below, and a clump of old men fishing from the harbour steps. 'I can smell the sea, and garlic and chargrilled sardines.'

'I can hear "Never on Sunday" playing in every bar.'

'I don't care. I love Greek music. The tackier the better. I think we should get masks. Do the whole tourist thing. Hurry up and get changed. I'm starving.'

She pushes him towards the bathroom and goes back to staring from the balcony. The paint has peeled away from a knot of wood on the balustrade. She strokes it absently with her thumb. It's warm and slightly sticky. If she bends closer, she knows it will smell of dust and pine resin. The numbness recedes for a moment and she feels connected to her thumb, to the balustrade, to the sun-warmed planks of the balcony.

★

Wandering the streets of Chania that evening is like being in a limbo between the living and the dead. Half the ancient Venetian buildings are in ruins; fig trees sprout from fourth-storey windows and cats stalk abandoned rubble-strewn courtyards. Others are partly inhabited, with pink or red geraniums cascading from isolated balconies on cliffs of blind windows and broken shutters. Some of the carved wooden doors are open, and old women in black sit crocheting on the doorsteps with blankets over their knees. Other doors, with dusty jasmine tangled in their gratings, seem to have been locked for decades.

Between bright shop windows and restaurants, like missing teeth, are the shuttered facades of tourist shops closed for the winter. A few of the open shops have masks hanging outside, and carnival costumes on racks inside. In the darkness the masks peer down like gossipy gargoyles, jostling together in the breeze. Beneath them, blue glass evil-eye charms stare out balefully from stands of keyrings and bracelets.

They go into a shop selling enamel jewellery and posh women's clothing. Some child-sized puppets are hanging on the wall and there's a display of exotic handmade masks.

Bennet chooses a glum Pierrot, which looks oddly sinister above his languid beige body. Sylvia can't decide between an angel with white ringlets and a mermaid with iridescent scales on her cheeks. She prefers the mermaid, but it looks odd with her own glossy bob swinging either side. Then another mask catches her eye.

It's a cat, with fur made from black and chestnut feathers that flare out into fans of unlikely whiskers. She strokes its feather cheeks, then puts it on and looks in the mirror. The whiskers hide her hair, and the mask covers her face but leaves her mouth and chin exposed.

'What do you think?' she asks.

'Very nice, provided you don't start picking fish heads out of the gutters.'

'I think it makes me look rather glam.' She strikes a pose and looks in the mirror again. She can see her eyes glittering through two tiny holes.

'Do I get to call you "Pussy"?' he asks, handing over his gold Visa card.

'You get to be grateful I'm not a violent woman.'

By day three they've lost their winter pallor. Bennet has burnt his forehead slightly and bought a Panama hat, which makes him look even taller – and even more English, in his chinos and cashmere cardigans. He's rather formal with the waiters at their favourite taverna, and they call him 'Dr Bennet' and put a 'reserved' sign on a table in a sunny corner, where he takes up residence, drinking tiny cups of *gleeko* Greek coffee and puzzling over two-day-old *Guardian* crosswords.

Sylvia roams the streets alone, with her aunt's camera around her neck and reels of black-and-white film in her pocket. The sun's hot and the buff-coloured walls radiate warmth down into the narrow streets. Though her limbs still feel disconnected, she can sense heat seeping into her torso, loosening knots in her neck and shoulders. It's as though she's been crouched for a long time in a dark cupboard.

At first she wants to photograph everything, and frames fragment after fragment of the old city: chipped carvings and rusty ironwork; small-footed cats and brimming window boxes; an old man carrying a sack of potatoes; a crow silhouetted against the sky.

Then she puts the camera away and begins to look with her eyes. At the way the people here live with what they have: patching bits of furniture and propping them up lovingly like old relatives. Painting them over and over. Using an olive-oil tin as a plant pot; a plastic crate as a stool; an oil drum and a scrap of bright cloth as a table. And flowers, flowers, everywhere.

She begins to feel out of place in her tailored monochrome clothes: too sharp-focus in a place where everything is colourful and crumbling. A two-dimensional cartoon in a three-dimensional world.

After a while she starts taking pictures of windows. She thinks: each one is a portrait of a person. There are faded shutters, dimmed by decades of sunshine, and stone sills, worn and sagging as old sofas; bold red or blue oblongs against fresh whitewashed walls. And ghost windows, creaking in the breeze, swinging open on to empty space.

'I thought I'd be itching to dip my toes in the sea,' she tells Bennet over supper on day five. 'But I love just walking around soaking up the atmos. I spent all afternoon looking at the boats in the marina.'

'Aha. Another set of fascinating photos for the archive. So what is it this time? Masts or fishing nets?'

'Philistine.' Sylvia sticks her tongue out at him then pours a long dribble of olive oil on to a bowl of white cheese and tomatoes. 'Actually I was trying to decipher the names from the Greek lettering, and wondering what it would be like to live on them.'

'The houseboat from your "When I Grow Up" list?'

'I was thinking about having everything you own in one tiny space.'

'I don't think I'm a boat kinda guy. I'd get hunchbacked from stooping in the cabin and keep banging my head on the boom.'

'We've got so much *stuff* at home.'

'May I remind you that most of that *stuff*, as you put it, was purchased by you and is – or so you assured me at the time – in the best possible taste.'

'I don't mean just lamps and ornaments. I mean things like the juicer and DVD player. Electric toothbrushes.'

'Are we still talking houseboat, or have we gone on to banning TV and growing our own food?'

'Being here just makes me aware of how little someone needs to be happy.'

'And are you happy?' He picks up her hand and cradles it in both of his. His mouth lifts hopefully at one corner.

'Yes,' she says slowly, surprising herself. 'In a sad kind of way. I mean there's still that big baby-shaped yearning inside me. But there's something about this place that makes me – oh, I don't know, just grateful to be alive.'

He kisses her palm and lays the hand gently back on the table. 'Good,' he says. Then, 'How about hiring a car on Monday and finding you somewhere to swim?'

Late on Sunday afternoon the town starts to fill up in anticipation of the evening's carnival festivities. The streets are full of cars hooting and motorbikes revving as gridlock spreads outwards from the town centre. Every car seems to have its windows open and its radio turned full on, blaring competing blasts of loud music.

Bennet has staked out his favourite table, but they are soon hemmed in by a large family group shouting for coffees and elaborate desserts.

'There must be at least four generations here,' says Bennet. 'That old fellow's ninety if he's a day.'

'There was a queue of three old women in the loo,' says Sylvia. 'They seemed to be arguing about the toilet paper.'

A waiter brings them a towering ice cream concoction in a tall glass. 'A present for you. To make you in the carnival mood,' he says, handing them two long-handled spoons.

'When does the burning of Zeus take place?' Bennet wants to know.

The waiter looks puzzled. 'What you mean about Zeus?'

'I thought there was supposed to be a fire tonight, to burn Zeus.'

'Maybe in the old days. But now, no.'

'So why the carnival?'

The waiter laughs and spreads his arms. 'I don't know why. It is just things we do. Peasant things. I don't know why we put the masks, the funny clothes. We like it. Anyway, enjoy your ice cream.'

Later, when it gets dark, they don their masks and set out for the old market, where according to their waiter, 'is everything Greek – music, dancing, fireworks'. It rained briefly while they were changing and the cobbles are shiny and slippery underfoot. Along the quay, the streets throng with people in masks or full costume.

'Pity about the Zeus thing,' Bennet remarks, steering Sylvia down a side alley. 'I thought we'd stumbled on to a really juicy bit of living mythology.'

The fireworks have started, and the lofty ruins of the town are illuminated every few seconds by starbursts of cerise and green.

'Bang goes our fertility rite,' she says.

'As the actress said to the Greek Orthodox bishop.'

Sylvia slips her arm through his and rests her head briefly against him. 'It's weird the way people forget why they do things, isn't it? Like bringing fir trees and mistletoe into the house at Christmas.' The smell of grilled lamb fills her nostrils, along with the sour tang of cordite.

'I tried reading up about Zeus in that Graves tome I bought yesterday,' Bennet's saying. 'But the man is so clearly batty, it's hard to extract a sensible narrative.'

'I thought Zeus was supposed to have been born in the Dictean Cave.'

'Ah yes, but did you know that his mother hid him there to prevent his father from gobbling him up? Apparently she gave the old man a rock to swallow instead. Cunning minx. And naturally he never even noticed. Then later, when Zeus had grown up, he gave his dad some kind of poison that made him vomit up the stone, along with all his older brothers and sisters. Who were eternally grateful, as you might expect.'

'The cave's in a village near Heraklion,' she says. 'I thought we might drive over there next week.' She looks down at their feet, at his beige deck-shoes and her black leather loafers, miles away, sauntering along in time with each other, like the two policemen on *The Bill*.

47

'Anyway, the Cretans, who Graves says are "notorious liars" – can you believe that? I mean, what a cheek the man has! As if the Cretan version is any more unlikely than the rest of it. Anyway, according to the perfidious Cretans, Zeus is reborn every year in that same cave, along with a flash of fire and a stream of blood.'

'Hence the burning of the effigy, I suppose.'

They reach the main street, joining the crowd moving towards the market. As they near the centre, the crowd presses tighter. Everyone is talking at the tops of their voices, hailing one another, shaking hands, exclaiming over their costumes. There are cars parked on the pavements; pushchairs rammed into knees; toddlers passed overhead like beach balls and hoisted on to shoulders. A high-pitched motorbike revs suddenly behind Sylvia and she stumbles and lets go of Bennet's arm. Someone steps on her heel and her shoe comes off. She bends to retrieve it and when she looks up again, the crowd has surged on, taking Bennet with it.

With one shoe on it's impossible for her to follow him, so she hops over to a taverna and sits down on a chair just inside the door.

'So, Cinderella!' A man in a bull mask detaches himself from the crowd and whisks the shoe from her hand. 'And this must be the magic slipper.'

Sylvia stands and tries to grab it back, but he lifts it out of her reach, so she'd have to jump to retrieve it.

'Can I have my shoe back, please?' she says stiffly, feeling foolish.

'But how do I know that it is truly your shoe?' The man's voice is faintly accented. There's a ring on his wedding finger. 'There may be another maiden in the city whom it might fit.'

'But I have the other one here.' This is ridiculous. She takes a deep breath and forces herself to sit down. The bull mask is quite an elaborate one, made of black velvet, with a gold ring through the nose.

'This is true,' the man concedes. His English is so good. Is he some kind of academic? He's shorter than Bennet, and more muscular. His hands are brown and his nails short and clean. 'But perhaps you have stolen this other shoe too. Perhaps you have cut off your toes to fit into it.'

'No, look—' She holds out her shoeless foot indignantly. 'This foot is exactly the same size.'

He drops to his knees suddenly and grasps her stockinged foot in one hand. 'So it is. I am so sorry to doubt you. This is clearly the foot of a princess.'

He strokes the arch of her foot with his finger. 'Or perhaps it is just the cat, purring.'

The feel of his finger caressing her foot through her stocking is electrifying. She tries to jerk away, but he holds her tighter.

'Please, let me go.' Her voice sounds small and frightened. Her foot is tingling. Part of her wants to run away. Another part wants to kick out at him with her free foot. Her cheeks are ablaze with confusion beneath her cat mask.

'Please. Let me have my shoe back,' she says again.

'Very well.' And he places her foot on his knee and slips the shoe expertly on to it. 'There, it fits. You will marry the prince after all.'

'Thank you. But I am already married.'

With both shoes on, she feels more secure. She can run away now, if she needs to. Push through the crowds towards the fireworks, or loop back to the hotel where she guesses Bennet will have gone to find her. Or she can stay sitting here and flirt with a man with the head of a bull.

There's a crackle of fireworks and a distant cheer from the crowds. 'Where did you learn to speak English so well?' she asks.

'The Minotaur is a creature of many tongues,' he says, sitting opposite her at the table and gesturing to a waiter.

'Do you live in Chania?'

'Why do you have so many questions? This is a night of disguises. We do not have to answer questions. I am an astronaut.

49

I am an archaeologist. I am an alchemist. I am everything you can think of that begins with the letter A.'

'Someone told me today that all Cretans are liars.'

'He was lying,' he laughs. A tray with two beers on it arrives. 'And what about you, Catwoman?'

'I work in a circus,' says Sylvia, and it feels true. She looks at the beer. She never drinks beer. 'I have a cat and a horse and a monkey. I live alone in a gypsy caravan and tell fortunes.'

As she picks up her glass, she sees Bennet pushing through the crowds towards her.

Chapter 7

The Expired Passport

'I can't believe they're still there!' Martin's mother burst into the kitchen with a postcard in her hand. 'Rachel and Greg. I wrote to them weeks ago – when you found that box of seaside stuff, d'you remember?'

She put the card on the table in front of him, picture-side down. There were a few lines of zigzag writing; the green stamp in the corner had a bald man on it.

'I found the address of a taverna in the box and remembered that was where we used to get our letters from. I never thought they'd still be there. But look – they want us to come and stay.'

While she was talking, Martin turned the card over. There was a yellow cliff in the distance, like a wedge of layered sponge cake tilting into a blue sea. In the foreground was a row of red and green fishing boats.

'Can you see the caves?' his mother asked, and he looked closer. The cliff was covered with black holes: some small, some larger, with sandstone arches and tiny people sitting outside. 'The awnings are down,' she was saying, 'so that photo must have been taken in the winter. See that big cave? That's where Rachel and Greg used to live. You won't remember, but they were nearly the first people there, so they had one of the biggest caves. Ours was higher up and tiny, because we weren't there for very long. But you loved it. I couldn't stand up in it, but you could. There was a little Martin-sized passage to the cave next door and you were always crawling through it.'

He thought he remembered that: rough sandstone under his hands and knees; a dark tunnel with a blare of sunlight at the end of it; guitar music; the smell of smoke. He looked at his mother. Her cheeks were flushed and her eyes shining.

'I'll see if I can find my passport,' she said.

*

They had two kinds of money: Day Money for things like toilet paper and bread; and Blue Moon Money for big things and emergencies. Day Money was what the bank paid you for letting them look after your money – 'like apples from the apple tree' she explained. Blue Moon Money was when you had to chop off a whole branch of the tree, which was why she tried not to do it.

She'd bought their bicycles with Blue Moon Money, and paid the man who unblocked the drains. She used Blue Moon Money for the plane tickets too. 'So we can't have any emergencies for a whole year,' she said, kissing him. 'And the roof will have to wait until next spring.'

She'd been making the roof wait for as long as he could remember. There was a leak above the bath, and one wall was completely coated with mossy green stuff. It smelt like the woods in there; he quite liked it.

'It's the best place possible for a leak,' she always said. 'Whoever heard of a dry bathroom?'

There was a leak on the landing, too; just a little one. She kept a yellow bucket under it, and you could tell how hard it was raining by the speed of the drip-drip into the bucket. Last week a new stain had appeared on the ceiling in his bedroom, and the spriggy paper had started peeling off the wall in one corner.

At the airport a week later, he looked at his mother's passport.

'What does "expiry date" mean?'

'That's when I die,' she said. Then, seeing his face: 'I'm joking, silly. It's the date the passport runs out. You have to get a new one every ten years because your face changes. Mine runs out at the beginning of October.'

The photo showed her with rounder cheeks and a smoother fore-head. Her long heavy hair was tucked behind her ears and she was wearing big complicated earrings. Her solemn eyes were outlined in black and she had pale lipstick on her wide mouth.

'Miss Theresa Elizabeth Stevens,' he read. 'You look like a doll.' It was funny to think of her as 'Miss Theresa'. It was funny to think of her before he was born.

He flicked through the pages, looking at the few smudgy visa stamps from different countries. At the very back he found a printed section with his name and date of birth written on it: Master Martin Paul Miller.

Why did the passport call him 'Miller'? He'd always assumed he was a Stevens like his mother. When she'd taught him to write, it was always 'Martin Stevens': M and S, like the shop on the High Street. His tummy did that thing, somersaulting and kicking the air from his lungs: Miller must be his father's surname.

He wanted to ask her about it, but didn't dare. She was so happy, he thought it might spoil her mood. So he squirrelled the knowledge away in the box he'd labelled 'father'; he'd take it out later and think about it when he was alone.

The food on the plane was hot and there was see-through orange cutlery. They flew so high the ground looked like a map; they flew right through the clouds. There was a bag to be sick in and a mint chocolate in gold paper.

At Heraklion airport all the luggage came out of a hole in the wall and circled around on a huge black conveyor belt. They got on a turquoise bus and ate sugar doughnuts bigger than his head, and swigged water from a clicky plastic bottle. There were donkeys on the road and the letters on the signs were all back to front or upside down. Everyone on the bus spoke Greek and one woman was carrying a live turkey in a wicker basket.

The bus reached Matala after dark. It was one of the last stops, so there were only three other passengers left when they alighted. A fat woman with a moustache insisted on taking them home with her, and fed them on salt-cheese and sweet tomatoes before showing them into a tiny storeroom, where she unrolled a thin stripy mattress on the floor.

Next morning they emerged to the scene from the postcard. Whoever had taken the photo must have been standing right outside the little room where they slept. Every detail was the same; even the colours of the boats. When they packed up their things and started towards the yellow caves, it was as though they were walking into a dream.

*

Martin's skin went brown and his shoulders peeled. His soles grew hard as leather from scrambling barefoot along the narrow cliff paths. At night, sometimes, his tummy ached from laughing so much.

There was a Brazilian boy called Juan, who was ten, and a French boy, Pierre, who was a bit younger than him. And an English girl called Sacha, who was twelve. And three babies, but he didn't know their names. Sometimes Sacha pretended she was too sophisticated to play, but most days she was even wilder and funnier than the boys.

The first few days Martin had to stop himself staring at them. Juan had a broken tooth and big knees. Sacha's breasts were little hills under her tee shirt. He couldn't get used to being so close to other children. They smelt of dust and hay. They tugged on his arm and smeared his back with suntan lotion. They shouted all the time in a mixture of languages. They splashed him and wrestled him in the water.

On the third day he moved his sleeping bag to the boys' cave further down the cliff. After that he only saw his mother at group meals under the trees on the beach, or when she tracked him down to exchange his filthy tee shirt for a clean one. He got used to digging a hole to do his poo in. He got used to seeing women's bare breasts and men's dicks. He got used to eating with fifty other people, dunking warm bread in green oil and picking morsels of white flesh from little charred fish.

From a distance he watched his mother change too. Her breasts went brown and her hair coiled into salty black ringlets. She laughed a lot and wore things he'd never seen her in before: filmy scarves draped around her hips; bracelets around her ankle. From the way the men looked at her, he could tell they thought she was beautiful. Everyone called her 'Terry'. Seeing her dressed like that, hearing her called by that name, made her seem like a stranger.

She spent hours with Sacha's mother, Rachel, a busy brown woman with eyes like chips of green glass. They brewed sweet coffee on a little Primus stove and smoked big fat cigarettes that Rachel rolled herself on a special flat stone. They hugged each other and told him they were sisters, but he knew they weren't really.

Sometimes it was all just too noisy and touchy, and Martin had to sneak off by himself over the rocks beyond the caves, with a bit of thread and some bread in his pocket. He'd say he was going fishing, but really he just wanted to be on his own for a bit. He'd keep going until he couldn't hear anything except the sea, then edge right down to the base of the cliff and squat there looking at the lapping water.

Most days there was a big blonde man there too, further along, with a proper fishing rod. His name was Karl and he slept in a small green tent under the trees on the beach. Usually they ignored each other, but one day Martin found himself clambering over the rocks towards him.

There was a wet cloth on the rock, and jerky movement underneath it.

'Only two fish today,' said Karl in his sing-song foreign accent. 'But I have caught a nice something with my net.'

Martin peered at a tussock of seaweed in a bucket of water. All he could see was a little grey prawn with waving feelers.

'I can catch prawns like that from the beach,' said Martin – more rudely than he intended.

'You are not looking hard enough.'

Gingerly, Martin started parting the fronds of weed. Then he saw it: a live sea horse, delicate and perfect.

'Now I will tell you something,' Karl said, propping his fishing rod in a cleft in the rocks. 'A man should discover one piece of new knowledge each day. So this will be yours for today.'

He sat down and stretched furry blonde legs out in the sunshine. He was wearing baggy beige shorts with lots of pockets and he took out a red penknife and started cleaning his nails with the blade. Martin noticed that the third finger of his left hand was missing.

'The sea horse is the only animal where the father is pregnant instead of the mother.'

Was he joking? Martin stared at him, but he just went on cleaning his nails.

'The babies come out of a little hole in the father's belly. They say he even seems to be in pain when the babies come out.'

'What about the mother?'

'She mates with the father and lays her eggs inside his belly. The eggs hatch out and stay there until they're big enough to be born.'

'And the mother just swims away?' He still couldn't believe it.

'Oh, she doesn't care what happens to her babies. If she swims past she could even eat them without knowing it.'

Martin looked at the sea horse again. The belly did seem swollen. 'Is it a male or a female?'

Karl laughed. 'I think you must be a sea horse to know that,' he said. 'Now, you tell me something I don't know.'

Martin tried to think of something to match what he'd just heard, but he couldn't.

'What about your name?' Karl's pale blue eyes had white lines at the corner where he'd been squinting into the sun. His eyebrows were yellow on top and darker underneath.

'My name is Martin Paul Miller,' said Martin.

Chapter 8

Next day Bennet hires a car and they go exploring. He buys a detailed German map of the island and a set of worry beads to hang from the rear-view mirror. Sylvia wraps her swimsuit in a hotel towel and slings it in the back seat.

They head out of Chania after breakfast, then turn off on to a side road that skirts the winding coastline. The sun through the car window is warm on Sylvia's arm, on her lap. She sees herself looking at her arm, at her hand splayed on her white linen knee. She tries to feel the blood in her fingers, to feel it flowing up her arm to her heart.

'I was thinking of growing a moustache,' Bennet remarks, peering at the reflection of his upper lip. 'Becoming a fully paid-up member of Greek manhood. What do you think?'

'I think a moustache is the perfect culture medium for bacteria that thrive on snot and Mythos,' she says tartly.

'Nothing twee, you understand. Something rather bushy and brutish.' He looks sideways at her. 'Are you sure it will be cold enough to swim?'

'Ha ha. For your information, the hotel man said it snowed here last month. One metre fell overnight and decimated the olive groves.'

'I'm sure he didn't say "decimated".'

'He said it was "a catastrophe". The branches weren't used to having any weight on them.' She imagines the flakes fluttering down silently, billions of white feathers settling gently on the leaves, and branches groaning and cracking like gunshot.

'Presumably that's why our trees lose their leaves in the winter,' he muses, steering the car into a wide hairpin above the glittering sea. 'Look down there. Half the cypresses are bent over at the top.'

'I blame the Americans.'

'All those burgers changing the world's weather systems. Why can't they sup gruel like the rest of us?'

'It says here that Kalives has a good beach.'

The beach is long and white, the sand coarse as granulated sugar. It shelves steeply into a crystal sea, each wave rising like a sheet of green glass with foam whipped from the crest by a biting wind.

Sylvia looks down at her legs wading, in slow motion. Under the green water her skin seems translucent, sheathed in tiny bubbles. Small silver fish flick around her white ankles chasing shoals of invisible diatoms. Flecks of icy foam whip past her cheeks. It's like immersing in iced champagne.

She swims out past the waves and floats on her back, looking back at the shore. The skin on her cheeks is stinging with salt. There are five kites flying above a village in the distance. The air's so clear she can see the wild broom flowering on the hillside. She imagines bees landing and probing the yellow throats for nectar.

'You should try it, B. It's so fresh. I wanted to take off my cozzie and swim naked.'

'That would really give the natives something to talk about. They think you're mad enough as it is.'

They're drifting down the main street of the village in the sunshine, munching pockets of bread stuffed with chickpeas, salad and tzatziki. Bennet had asked for lamb in his, but the vendor had said '*Ochi arni!*' and had shaken a finger at him, though there was meat clearly visible in the fridge at the back of the shop.

'You were right about it not being cold enough, though,' says Sylvia.

'Bloody Roman Catholics. Never happy unless you're atoning for something. Shall I beat you with twigs instead?'

'You've never really bought this cold water theory, have you?' After her swim she's ravenous. The flavours of mint, garlic and tomatoes explode on her tongue; rich yoghurt and olive oil fill her mouth.

'If you're happy, I'm happy, my sweet.'

'Seriously, though.' She wipes her greasy chin with a paper napkin.

'Seriously, though, I think you're doing it as a kind of penance. Sackcloth and ashes to bend the ear of a jealous God. Trying to get a handle on something that's outside your control.'

'It's not outside my control. Don't say that. I bet if we lived here I'd conceive in two minutes. Away from the lab fumes and the Ring Road. Eating fresh fish and zucchini from some little old lady's back yard.'

'Go on then, money bags. There's an estate agent on the corner. Let's see what fifty thousand smackers can buy you in Crete.'

They wander over and peer in through the window. There's a poster showing a new development of toytown white villas with faux traditional terracotta roofs, above a set of doll's house floor plans. Further along are some photographs of building plots – scrubby land with distant sea views – and a few older houses. Sylvia's eye is caught by a small stone house with green shutters. There are pots of geraniums by the door and two wooden chairs flanking a small table beneath a vine pergola.

'So? How about it?' Bennet is saying. 'I've been wondering how to launder my ill-gotten gains.'

'Could we really buy a house here?' Suddenly it's all she wants to do.

'Don't see why not.'

'But what about the attic?' They've been planning their attic conversion for years. Do the nursery first, then create two new bedrooms and a shower in the attic for when the second baby arrives.

'My dear girl, have you any idea how much I will have earned by the end of this financial year? Thanks to the furred arteries of the Arab World we're going to have spondulix coming out of our ears.'

Sylvia looks at another old house in the window: bare grey stone and terracotta tiles; a prickly pear thicket and an orange tree in the garden. She could paint it white and plant jasmine and marguerites. She could go jogging by the sea. She could dig into red earth and feel the sweat pouring off her. She could swim every day in the teeming glassy water.

'You could stay here to charm the builders,' he's saying. 'And I'll fly out every four weeks to impregnate you.'

'But I've only got three months off.' She's arguing, but she wants him to convince her.

'So take another three. As your doctor, I insist. It has to be better than moping about in Newcastle, getting into a tizz about particulates.'

She grips his arm, excitement bubbling in her throat. 'But we don't know where to start. We don't know where the best places are. We don't know what we want.' She wants the smell of the sea wind. She wants lizards and scorpions and cicadas. She wants the tang of fresh goat's cheese on her tongue, the gritty sweetness of ripe figs warmed by the sun.

'What's wrong with starting right here?' Bennet chucks the remains of his lunch into a bin and shakes out a white handkerchief to wipe his hands. 'There's a nice beach and a few decent shops. And – most important, this – it's not too far from the airport. A man shouldn't have to schlep to the other side of the island every time he swoops in for a bonk with a fertile woman.'

'I love you.' She snakes her arms around his neck and tiptoes to kiss him on the mouth. His lips open and his tongue touches hers. He tastes of garlic and cucumber. She thinks of the Minotaur's moustache and his soft leather jacket. She thinks of a silver fish whisking around her white ankles.

She opens her eyes and looks up at the clear blue sky. Dancing high above them, like a dog tugging at a lead, is a hexagonal kite, with rainbow panels radiating from the centre, and a double tail of swooping red ribbon.

Once the decision's been taken, Bennet gets the bit between his teeth. They visit four estate agents one after another, 'to get the lie of the land', and set up seven viewings for the next day – of every property that grabs their imagination: three old houses and four building plots.

That evening he orders an ouzo and unfolds the map in his favourite corner. Sylvia takes a photograph of him squinting at her in the evening sunlight, with his Panama hat on the table beside him and both hands splayed on the map like a military strategist.

'I reckon that third plot's a bit close to the main road,' he says. 'You don't want juggernauts thundering past when you're communing with nature. Rather defeats the object. But the first one looks good. Village outskirts. Five minutes' walk from the beach.'

'I like the look of this old olive press,' says Sylvia wistfully, tracing a stone arch with the tip of her finger. 'But it needs so much work.'

'More a ruin than a house, really. I reckon we're better off starting from scratch. Buy the land with your dosh, then sort out a euro mortgage with mine. Use one of those architects they were all so keen to push at us.'

'I wasn't that taken by any of those new developments,' she says doubtfully. 'But if we're hiring an architect, I suppose we could ask him to design something a bit less obvious. I can't stand all those fake wooden pergolas and carports.'

'At least we'll know that the wiring works and the sewage is going somewhere legal.'

'When I was little I used to draw pictures of my ideal house. It was always just two rooms and a kitchen and bathroom. Just room for me. And maybe a husband. I can't remember.'

'Husband, horse, monkey – we're all the same really.'

'I used to draw a ground plan with all the furniture, and paint designs for the different wallpapers.'

'Obviously a vain bid to escape from your mother.'

'Are we really going to do this?' She picks the slice of lemon from her glass and nibbles at the rind. Her mouth floods with saliva.

'It's your money, sweet pea. You tell me. Perhaps you'd rather spend it on negligées and pamper days – whatever they are.'

'It's just so sudden. What if the builders cheat us?'

'What if they don't? There is always that possibility, you know.'

'We can't just go on holiday for two weeks and come back with a house.' She's grinning now. She can't stop.

'Why not?'

'Because that's what mad people do.' Her cheeks are aching from smiling so hard.

'Look, I haven't seen you this excited since I took you for a spin on the Harley fifteen years ago. That has to be worth fifty grand of anyone's money.'

The viewings the next morning are with an elegant young Australian Greek, with dyed auburn curls and red fingernails. She takes them to two building plots and an old house in the middle of a small village along the coast. Bennet is quite taken with one of the plots, but Sylvia doesn't like anything.

Over lunch she's despondent. 'Maybe this wasn't such a good idea.'

'Don't be so negative. We've hardly started.' He's digging into a plate of lamb chops, squeezing lemon over a dish of fried aubergine.

'I can't even have an ouzo to drown my sorrows,' she mourns, pouring fizzy water into a glass.

'We're just establishing what we don't want.'

'Right. No sixties' pine panelling. No salmon-pink bathroom tiles. No fields of boulders. No main roads. No building sites next door.'

'Look, if we can't find anything we like here, we'll try the other side of Chania. It ain't over till the fat estate agent sings.'

The fat estate agent in question is an older Greek man with a sprightly mop of grey hair and a carefully trimmed moustache. There's a crumpled red camper van with British number plates parked outside when they arrive at his office, and a small blue pick-up behind it. In the front seat of the pick-up is a sheep, with its nose pressed against the windscreen; in the back is a yellow cement mixer and a stack of purple plastic chairs.

'Mr Bennets!' cries the estate agent as they walk in. 'It's good you are here.' He's sitting on an ancient leather swivel chair that creaks enthusiastically as he waves them to sit down. 'This is the builder who works for me.'

He resumes counting out fifty euro notes into the paint-encrusted paw of a burly man in a dusty checked shirt. 'He is a very good builder. He is working for me for many years. Argyrakis is his name. Leonidas Argyrakis.' The builder nods at them briefly. He has a nicotine-stained white yardbrush moustache and a blue baseball cap.

A younger man with long dark hair tied back in a ponytail sits against the wall with his lean hands resting quietly on denim knees.

'Argyrakis will be good for you, because he has this new boy working for him. Martin, he speaks English, so my English families like him very much.'

The young man lifts a hand in the ghost of a salute and smiles shyly. His eyes are odd-coloured, Sylvia notices, like David Bowie's. When he looks at her, she has the fleeting impression that there are two people regarding her instead of one. Now he's watching Bennet, who has gone into hail-fellow-well-met mode and is shaking hands and slapping shoulders with the two older men.

'They have just finished one job for me,' Nicos the estate agent is saying, 'so if you find something you like, they can start straight away. The job they have finished is a very good quality work. A house for a Swedish family. We can go there if you want to see.'

The burly builder folds the sheaf of notes and stuffs it into his back pocket, then takes a softpack from his shirt and offers it to Bennet.

'*Ochi, efharisto*.' Bennet shakes his head. 'Cigars are my bag.' He turns to the young man. 'Can you explain, mate?'

'Leonidas understands more than he lets on,' Martin says. His accent is unplaceable. 'And I understand less than I seem to.' He spreads his hands in a take-it-or-leave-it gesture, softened by an apologetic smile. 'Together we manage.'

The builder gets up to leave. Cue more hand-shaking and back-patting. The younger man hangs back, as though distancing himself from the show. Sylvia watches him. She wonders if he's gay. The long hair and mild manner make her think so, and there's something about the way he stands, relaxed but alert, back to the wall, as though he's used to defending himself.

As the older men move towards their cars, Sylvia finds herself smiling ruefully at him. *Don't mind them*, she says with her eyes, then turns away suddenly, annoyed with herself.

Five minutes later she's back in the passenger seat beside Bennet and they're hurtling down narrow lanes behind Nicos's dusty white car.

Their first stop is another boulder-strewn field with a distant view of the sea. After tramping around it for just long enough to avoid seeming rude, they wend their way down more tiny lanes to the old olive press Sylvia was so excited about.

In fact the building is in better condition than they'd expected, but it has no land whatsoever; just a tiny courtyard with a couple of cracked clay pots in one corner.

Bennet catches her eye. 'Goer?'

She shakes her head. 'It's sweet, but a garden's really important. I didn't realize how much until now. Even if it's just a little piece of land. I want to grow things, B. I don't know why. I want to be able to put my feet on my own soil.'

'Sorry, mate—' Bennet turns to Nicos. 'The lady says she needs a garden. What else have you got?'

'I have a very good feeling for this next place. It is a big building plot with planning permission, at the edge of a nice village. There is a taverna and a *kafenion*, and two shops. And there is a bus from the square to go to Chania.'

'Sounds just the ticket. Lead on Macduff.'

'There is no sea view, but you can see the mountains. And the owners say there is an old path somewhere in the village that goes to the sea. I think you can take a donkey down there.'

'What do you bet it's another field of rocks?' says Sylvia as they set off once more.

'Chin up, sweetness. The guy did warn you about the olive press.'

She peers at the map. 'It's in Arkassa, that nice village we passed through this morning. Where we had to back up to let that lorry past.'

'So Argyri-whatsit and his boys will have a good audience when they try to get a JCB to the site.' The streets were so narrow they'd had to snake backwards all the way into the main square. Two old men from the *kafenion* had hobbled out to shout instructions.

They follow the white car through the village and up a winding hill on the other side, coming finally to a halt beneath a massive walnut tree. Pushing open a rusty gate, Nicos conducts them past a tiny stone cottage then opens his arms to embrace the expanse of land beyond.

The plot is huge: a series of terraces overlooking the village, leading down to a wide flat area at the bottom.

'The old woman was growing vegetables down there, but it will be perfect for your new house.'

'Is the little house included in the price?'

'Of course. But it is small for you. The old woman was living there by her own. Old Greek womens don't need a lot of room. Just for a bed and a small table. I don't think there is a bathroom.

But there is electricity and water on the site. And lots of garden for your wife.' He winks conspiratorially at Bennet.

Sylvia walks down the overgrown path to the edge of the plot, where the land falls away suddenly above a grove of grey olive trees. There are fig trees and another big walnut tree; orange trees decked with winter-wizened fruit. There's an empty hen-house with some kind of purple flower growing through the rusty wire. The wide vegetable plot is littered with the imploded shells of last year's melons punctuated by exclamations of gone-to-seed onion flowers. When she tugs one tall dry flower head out of the ground, the smell of earth and fresh onion fills her nostrils.

At the back of her mind she can hear Bennet asking about square footage and bedrooms; about how much it costs to fit air conditioning.

She can see it all: a neat white house with a long veranda overlooking the valley. A fragrant filigree of jasmine draping the bedroom windows. White hens laying brown eggs. Fresh basil in a pot by the kitchen door. She can almost smell the clove perfume as she tears the leaves over a dish of tomatoes.

She walks back to Bennet, trying to control her excitement. 'How much was it again?' she asks casually.

'Sixty-five thousand euros,' says Nicos, consulting his details. 'But there are taxes to pay, and the lawyer's fee, so maybe seventy thousand altogether.'

'So, about forty-five thousand sterling, give or take,' says Bennet.

'I see that your wife likes it,' says Nicos.

Was it that obvious? Sylvia thinks of the letter in her handbag. She could get a bank draft today. This piece of land could be hers.

'I know the owners will be happy to go ahead straight away. There are two nieces who are waiting for the money. The old woman didn't have any children. I think she was the young daughter who looked after the old parents. So when they died—'

he shrugs. 'This is traditional in the village. At least she got the house. Anyway, if you buy I am sure you will find out the whole story.'

'Can we check out the little house?' Bennet asks.

'If I can find the key.' Nicos leads the way back to the little stone cottage. 'The owners said it was hanging somewhere – yes, here it is!'

He reaches down a large iron key from a hook beneath the eaves. It matches a keyhole in a faded turquoise door with a wrought-iron grille over a glass panel. The iron is rusty and the glass broken, but the lock is well oiled and the key turns smoothly.

Nicos pushes open the door and the pungent smell of goat dung billows out. 'Someone has been keeping animals in here,' he says apologetically. 'It is always like this. People leave their houses and the neighbours come in. But anyway, you can see – it is more a stable than a house really.'

Sylvia follows him in. The room's tiny, maybe seven foot by ten, ankle-deep in soiled straw.

'What do you think, Sylvie? We could buy a goat and get the neighbours to milk it for us.'

She could clear out the rubbish; brush down the walls and spread sweet yellow hay on the floor. She hugs the image to herself.

'Here is the old sink,' says Nicos, lifting a plastic fertilizer sack from a stone drainer with a knot of grey rag in the plughole. 'They have been using the tap for the animals' water.' There's a length of green hosepipe attached to the single cold tap, and a metal bucket on its side in the dirty straw.

'I think the main room is through here.' He pushes open another turquoise door, stretching spiders' webs and scuttling two tiny brown lizards across the wall.

'Greek old ladies are smaller than English mens,' he chuckles as Bennet ducks his head under the jamb.

Inside the second room it's much darker, the shuttered window muffled by cobwebs. Nicos picks up a broken broom handle and winds them on to it like grey candyfloss. Flakes of plaster and fly husks rain down over his arm; spiders hunch and scatter.

This room is piled high with broken furniture and bales of rusty wire netting; oil cans; a crate of empty Metaxa bottles. 'All the rubbish the relatives don't want,' says Nicos, touching a stack of aluminium pans with the toe of his shoe. 'The owners live in Heraklion. They can't use these village things.'

'That's a point,' says Bennet. 'If we buy the place, would all this gubbins be ours too? All the bits and pieces?' Sylvia's lifting a tiny leather bridle from a hook on the wall and opening it out like a cat's cradle; she imagines easing it over the furry ears of a grey donkey.

'Sylvie's a whiz at interior decor, aren't you? Has a real knack of hanging junk on the wall and making it look like art.'

'Is that supposed to be a compliment?' She reaches for his hand and squeezes it tightly, trying to communicate how much she wants this place. There's an old wooden saddle on the back of a broken chair, and a tall terracotta pot in the far corner; a metal milk churn; a tiny crooked walking stick leaning against a rusty bedstead. She's picturing the white walls of the airy new house; its wide tiled floors and plain wooden windows. The old pot could go on the veranda; she could polish the saddle and prop it next to a wood-burning stove in the sitting room.

'What's through there?' she asks, spying another door in a dark alcove, half hidden behind a pile of paint tins and cement sacks.

'Another small room, I think, or maybe a cupboard,' says Nicos.

Sylvia tries to get closer, shifting a pair of upended broken chairs. There's a faint rhythmic squeaking, like a rusty hinge, coming from the other side of the door. 'Can you hear that?' she asks. 'I think there's something in there.'

'Rats,' pronounces Bennet. 'There'll be hordes in a place like this. Probably come and go through that hole at the bottom of the door.'

She crouches for a closer look, then stands up again quickly and backs away. There's a definite movement on the other side of the door; a pair of eyes staring, then whisking away.

'Come on,' she says, heading back out into the sunshine. 'Let's look at the building plot again.'

'They're going to think we're horrible and rich, muscling in on their village,' whispers Sylvia, glancing around nervously. They're sitting in the village taverna waiting to be served. On the sign outside is a friendly-looking butterfly with the word *Petaluda* painted in pink beneath it.

'We are horrible and rich, but I'm sure we'll make up for it in entertainment value. You saw the excitement me parking the car caused. We're talking serious sensory deprivation here.'

The woman proprietor emerges from the kitchen with a sheet of clean white paper, which she spreads over the red tablecloth and secures with clips at the edges.

Bennet smiles at her and orders an ouzo and a dish of olives. 'The unfortunate truth is that we're part of an inevitable process. Old people dying, leaving their property to young trendies in Heraklion. They want smart flats in the city, not rat-infested hovels in the sticks. You could say we were doing them a favour.'

'What if they hate us?' An old man sitting at the back of the taverna eyes them curiously: out-of-season tourists ordering lunch in the middle of the afternoon.

'We don't have to do this, you know,' Bennet says.

'Do you trust me to deal with the architect?'

'As long as there's a decent shower and a shady place for me to do the crossword, I don't care. You're the Jasper Conran in this relationship. Or is it Shirley Conran? I can never remember.'

'Idiot.'

'We forgot to check out the beach.'

'You want to swim?' The proprietor sets oil and vinegar on the table and a basket of thick crusty bread.

'We heard there was a beach near here,' says Sylvia.

'There is, but it is a difficult walk. It is really for the goats. And when you get there it is only peebles. Do you say "peebles"?' She's plump, about Sylvia's age, with a man's denim shirt loose over skin-tight pink pedal pushers and strappy silver sandals. Her mop of soft black curls is threaded with white.

Sylvia smiles. 'Pebbles,' she says.

'I can never remember,' the woman grimaces. 'Pebbles, pebbles,' she repeats, tapping the side of her head with her finger. 'And is it "peesants" or "peasants"?'

'Peasants.'

'*Orea*. So, the peebles on the beach, they are hard on the feet. I prefer to swim from the rocks. There is a good place I can show you. But it's too cold to swim now.'

'That's right. You tell her,' says Bennet. 'My wife believes that swimming in cold water is good for her health.'

The woman laughs, a big laugh that shakes her small breasts like apples on a tree. 'You make me think of my mother,' she says. 'She was a very hard worker but very fat. So when she finished weeding the *horta* in the summer, she went to that rocky place and swimmed in her clothes. In those days it is not permitted for an old woman to wear a swimming suit. Her clothes used to float up around her, but she didn't care. She said the cold water calmed her blood.'

'We're buying a house here,' blurts out Sylvia suddenly.

'*Bravo!*' The other woman claps her hands. 'They said some English people were looking at Kokona's old place. *Kalostine*. It's not good for that place to be empty. A house is like a dog. It needs people. If you leave a dog tied up on its own, it will be miserable. Every time someone passes, it will jump up and wag its tail, or it will bark.'

She plucks three pink geraniums from a pot in the window and pops them into a little pottery jug. 'A garden is different. A garden is like a cat. It can look after itself. If you have the right kind of ears you would be able to hear Kokona's poor little house howling.' Then, seeing Sylvia's look of dismay: 'Oh, don't listen to me. I am always talking too much. It is because my husband is so quiet. My tongue has to play on its own. Do you want to eat? Come to the kitchen to see what I have.'

Sylvia follows the other woman through a bamboo curtain into a small room dominated by a big modern stainless-steel range. A pretty teenage girl is washing some greenery in the kitchen sink.

'This is my daughter, Maria,' says the plump woman. 'She wants to be at the Internet café in Vamos, but I have chained her to the kitchen.' Maria makes a face at her mother and starts piling the wet leaves into a colander.

'The house is really being sold as a building plot,' says Sylvia. 'We're going to build a new house on that level bit of land at the bottom of the slope.'

'That is a good space, yes. So: we will be neighbours. I can wave from my terrace and shout up to you like a peesant.' She takes the lids off two large saucepans and invites Sylvia to look inside. The first contains chunks of meat and translucent leaves of onion; the second a clutch of chubby meatballs in tomato sauce. 'And we have Greek salad, of course; fried zucchini, potatoes, tzatziki, *skordalia*, *horta* . . .'

Sylvia orders one of each meat dish, both of the dips, and a plate of *horta*, which turns out to be the rosettes of dark leaves the reluctant Maria was washing.

'I was going to clear out the little house,' Sylvia explains, 'and use it as a darkroom – a room for making photographs.' Now where had that idea come from?

'So, you are a photographer? *Oraya*.' She lights the gas and tips the *horta* into a saucepan, then picks up a lemon and slices it in two.

Sylvia watches as the other woman lifts one of the cut surfaces to her nose and closes her eyes for a second, as if in prayer, to inhale its bright yellow scent. She wonders whether to correct the assumption that she's a photographer, but decides to let it lie for a while. The woman's quick intimacy is slightly unnerving;

71

Sylvia's not ready to talk about her real job yet; her real life; her real reason for being here.

'You are lucky you were not here yesterday,' the other woman is saying. 'The taverna was full of families coming to fly kites in the mountains. It is a special day we call Clear Monday, when we tidy everything and purify our bodies to prepare for *Pascha*.'

'Was that why they wouldn't serve us meat in Kalives?'

'Of course. Many families will not eat meat again until the Lamb of God is killed. But some of us only become vegetarian for one day.'

'Her name's Aphrodite,' says Sylvia when she returns to their table. 'Can you believe it? The goddess of love owns a taverna in Crete.'

'I wondered what had become of her.'

'I was thinking, maybe I should use one of the rooms in the old house as a darkroom. What do you think?'

'If it stops the howling, I'm all for it.'

'I'll bring the enlarger with me when I come back. It'll give me something to do while I'm waiting for the architect to come up with the goods.'

'We haven't bought the place yet, you know.'

'The food looks wonderful. I ordered one of everything. And a bottle of retsina to celebrate.' She grins at him. 'I thought I could stay here in the taverna while they're building the house. Aphrodite says she has rooms to let.'

'Fine with me, so long as she allows conjugal visits.'

Chapter 9

The Peasant Cup

When they got back home, it was as though the trip to Crete had never happened. It was just Martin and his mother again, like before. Except a big bit of ceiling had fallen down on the landing while they'd been away. And it must have rained every day for three weeks, because the plants outside the house completely covered his bedroom window, and the whole house was bathed in shimmering green light inside, as though it was underwater.

Even though it was chilly and muddy outside, he still went barefoot. He was proud of being able to gallop over the rough ground without his shoes on. It made him feel like a boy of the woods.

Once it started pouring with rain while he was out, so he took off his tee shirt too, then galloped as fast as he could across the open ground and over the bridge to the horse field, where the brown mare stood waiting for him with a film of raindrops on her mane.

His mother had been quieter than usual since they'd been back. She'd cleaned up the landing, and ripped up the wet carpet, but it was obvious one yellow bucket wasn't enough to hold the drips any more.

She sat on the wet floorboards with a dustpan and soggy brush in her lap. Martin sat beside her and gazed up through the ragged hole in the ceiling. You could see right up to the rafters; it was huge up there, like the inside of a church. There was a small square of grey sky near the top where the slates were missing. He could hear sparrow chicks squeaking and wheezing for food.

'It's my punishment for blowing so much of the Blue Moon Money,' she said. There were three different drips now, at the edges of the hole, and a steady patter of rain directly beneath the patch of grey sky.

'Can you fix it yourself or do we have to get a man?' Martin asked.

'We can't afford a man, Marty. It costs hundreds of pounds for a new roof.'

'Shall I get the ladder? We can go up and have a look.' He wanted to see the sparrow's nest. He thought there might be bats up there too. 'Please, Mum.'

'Not now. I can't face it.'

'Let me go by myself then. I'll report back what I find.' He got up, but she grabbed his leg.

'I said "no".'

'Why not? You don't have to do anything.'

'Because I'm tired and sad and I don't want to think about it.' She released his leg and let her head flop back against the wall. Her eyes were shut, but a couple of tears had squeezed out on to her eyelashes.

'Are you getting a Bad Sad?' he asked.

'I don't know.' The tears dropped. 'Maybe.'

'How bad?'

'Only a four so far.' She opened her eyes and smiled up at him. 'It's being back here after all that sun and companionship. And having to be careful again, and knowing I can't talk to anyone in case they start asking questions. And then the fucking ceiling collapses.' She wiped her eyes with the back of her hand. 'And I'm sad about you, Marty,' stroking his bare leg. 'You should be at school with other children, not playing by yourself all day.'

'I don't mind. I like being on my own.' A four's not so bad, he was thinking. She could sometimes get herself out of a four.

'But wouldn't you like to go to a proper school, with a uniform and a school bag, and a proper mother to pick you up in her car at the school gates?'

He was speechless for a moment. This was so completely removed from the way they lived that he'd never even considered it.

'I'd rather go back to Matala,' he said eventually.

She dropped from a four to a ten in just five hours.

He'd seen it before, and she'd explained all about it, but it was still really frightening when it happened. One day you could look into her eyes and she'd be in there, looking back at you. Then she'd be gone, and her eyes would be empty.

This time she'd prepared a list of instructions, with notes in red biro to cheer him up. 'There's £20 of Day Money in the spoon drawer. Use £5 to buy a treat for you.' 'Remember our picnic last month. It proves I'm not always like this!' 'If you really can't stand it, go to the phone box, dial 999 and ask for an ambulance. They'll know what to do. I love you!' 'Try to ignore me. Remember: it never goes on for more than two weeks.'

By teatime she was rocking backwards and forwards on the sofa in the front room, bent over with her arms crossed as though her tummy was hurting. She was in her old tracksuit bottoms and her pink dressing gown, as though trapped somewhere between waking and sleeping.

They didn't use this room very much. The privet grew right over the window so it was always gloomy, and the fireplace was blocked up. There was a birthday card on the mantelpiece from when he was six and some brown carnations in a vase of green water.

Noticing that her feet were bare, Martin went upstairs to fetch her slippers. As an afterthought, he dragged the duvet off her bed and brought that down too. The evening was warm, but her big feet were icy as he eased them into the slippers. Brown from the sun, her scuffed toes were still decorated with silver rings. Draping the duvet around her shoulders, he went to make her a cup of tea.

She wouldn't drink it, he knew. When she was like this she could go whole days without drinking or going to the toilet. But it was something to do and he hoped it might cheer her up.

The light was going and he realized he was hungry. While the kettle boiled, he opened a tin of corned beef and sliced onion for a Dogbreath Sandwich. Raindrops started to pit-pat the window as he ate and he thought about the hole in the ceiling. Tomorrow he'd get the ladder and see how bad it was.

He thought of the bats, wrapped in their wings in a dry corner of the attic. He thought of big Karl's tiny green tent. 'A full stomach and a place to sleep, and a piece of new knowledge each day. That's all a man needs,' Karl had told him. The thought made him feel important and grown-up.

When he'd finished eating, he retrieved his mother's favourite mug from the pile on the draining board. It was made of rough brown pottery; he couldn't understand why she liked it so much. She called it her Peasant Cup. 'It's pleasant to sup from the Peasant Cup,' she said. It should have been 'sip', really, but that wouldn't have rhymed. And it was a mug, not a cup.

He stirred in sugar then carried the mug carefully through and placed it on the floor in front of her, where she could see it. Then: 'Goodnight, Mum. I'm going to bed now.'

He left the door open when he went upstairs, and the light on in the hall – in case she needed something during the night.

Looking back on that time, they called it the Great Flood because, including the time they were in Crete, it had rained for forty days and forty nights. Martin felt as though they were on a ship, with sodden floorboards and portholes lashed by wet clematis and ivy. He was the Ancient Mariner, sailing alone into the storm; his mother was a dead albatross in her dark cabin across the landing. It went on for so long it became normal to hear the pit-pat on the landing and the gutters running. It went on for so long he forgot how to speak.

Then one morning it stopped. The drips slowed and stuttered; the sun blazed in a blue sky; the thickets around the house were full of darting birds. Outside in Argyle Street steam began to rise from the tarmac. Pouring the last of the milk on to his muesli, Martin heard movement in his mother's bedroom above his head.

'Martin?' She was calling down the stairs.

He cantered up to her room, where she'd pulled back the curtains and was trying to wrench open the painted-shut turquoise window.

'It stinks in here!' she was saying, banging on the frame with her fist. The sun was shining through the creepers covering the glass, sending green-and-white ripples over the blue walls.

'Are you better?' He hardly dared believe it. A part of him had begun to think she would never get out of bed again.

'Can you switch on the immersion?' she asked. 'I smell like a bag lady.'

The window came open at last, letting in a blast of sweet air and birdsong. She sat down and took his hand. 'How long was it this time?'

'Nineteen days,' he said. 'I've been counting them up. I thought when it got to twenty-one I'd call nine-nine-nine.' Her hair was lank and her breath smelt, but her eyes were smiling.

'Was it awful?' She was back and looking at him.

'When it got to fourteen days, I started getting worried.' He was finding it difficult to speak. His mouth and chin felt wobbly and his throat ached.

'Did the money last out?'

He nodded. 'There's fifty pee left. I had to buy a new tin-opener.'

When the old one had broken, he hadn't known what to do. There was only five pounds left; he was sure a new one would be much more than that. He'd eaten bread and peanut butter until he was sick of it; then bread and Marmite; then bananas and muesli; then chicken paste and tomatoes and ice cream. He'd tried opening a tin of tuna with a screwdriver, but only managed a little jagged hole. Finally, in Tesco, he'd seen a new tin-opener on a little stand by the checkouts. It only cost sixty pee.

'How's the Swamp?' This is what she called the wet on the landing. 'Have the alligators moved in?'

'Not yet, but there's slugs in the sitting room.'

When it had been too rainy for him to go out, he'd opened the French doors and rigged up a covered play area on the terrace just outside, with one of the plastic sheets she used sometimes when she was painting. He'd cut back the bushes with her secateurs and tied the sheet to the overhanging trees. It had taken hours: a whole day when he managed to forget about his mother lying unmoving, staring at the wall upstairs.

Afterwards he couldn't shut the French doors properly. There was a hinge loose on one side and the left-hand door had tilted away from the frame. But the plastic sheet had given him an idea.

'I fixed the ceiling,' he told her proudly. 'Not properly, but so it only needs a bucket again.' He'd gone up through the trapdoor and used bricks to secure another plastic sheet across the hole. Then he'd made a small opening in the middle for the rainwater to drip through.

She admired the pallid shape bulging through the hole in the ceiling. 'I must have walked underneath it to the loo without noticing,' she said. 'But I was aware of the dripping in the bucket. It was like a clock ticking, or a water torture. In Japan they used to drip water on the heads of prisoners to drive them mad.'

He looked at her in alarm. He'd liked the dripping noise; it reminded him he'd fixed the ceiling by himself. He'd never thought it might be driving her mad. 'Is that why you're better now?' he asked. 'Because the dripping's stopped?'

She understood immediately what he was thinking and pulled him into her arms. 'No, silly. I'm better because I'm better. Because I've been sad long enough.'

But the thought stayed with him: if he'd managed to fix it properly she might not have been sad for so long.

Two weeks later they were packing to go back to Crete.

'What about the roof?' Martin asked. It felt like his roof now. He'd seen the thick layers of old sparrows' nests along the purlins. He'd traced trickles of rain along the rafters. He'd felt the chimney stack vibrate with the cooing of wood pigeons. He'd watched a bat unfurl like a tiny brown umbrella.

'Bugger the roof,' she said, stuffing purple espadrilles down the side of the suitcase. 'I worked out we could have four holidays in Crete for the money it would cost to get the roof fixed properly. So I sat down and thought about it for – oh, about three nanoseconds.'

'If we get another leak, I'll fix it again,' Martin volunteered.

'That's exactly what I thought,' she said. ' "Gather ye rosebuds while ye may." We'll mend the roof another day.'

Chapter 10

Back in Newcastle, Sylvia is preparing for what is now her six months in Crete. She polishes her nurse's shoes and lays them side by side on their shelf at the bottom of the wardrobe, below the row of freshly ironed lab coats. Two days ago she took a box of cream cakes to work, for the lab girls, and two bottles of bubbly, and received a good-luck card in return, in the shape of a giant Bluebird of Happiness. Opening the card, seeing all the little messages in all their different handwritings – the kisses and exclamation marks, the 'i's dotted with flowers – made her feel panicky. As though she might never come back.

The following day she drives to Wickes on the Coast Road and buys a pair of navy-blue overalls and some tough builder's gloves in the smallest sizes they have. She displays them to Bennet when he gets home.

'I feel like I'm in the middle of someone else's sexual fantasy,' he comments, lolling in the hall as she rummages for tools in the understairs cupboard. 'Naked woman in men's overalls wielding monkey wrench. Be still my groin.'

'This is like when I was little, packing to go away for the summer,' she says, sitting back on her heels. 'I'd be all goody-girly for the train, but my case would be full of jeans and wellies. And my camera and all my insect books. God, I'd forgotten about them. I'd take a photo of some fab green beetle and all you'd see was this teeny little speck in the middle of a photo of a tree stump.'

'Didn't your aunt give you any guidance?'

'I expect she thought I should learn from my mistakes. She had a very hands-off style of childcare. My mother would have been horrified if she'd known what I got up to on those holidays.'

'Smoking rollie-ups and snorting coke . . .'

'More like falling off rock faces and swimming out of my depth. Having the cat in the bed. Hanging out with the local farm kids. Staying up till all hours. Going to bed without washing.'

'From the state of the house, I'd say cleanliness was never very high on her agenda.'

'It was filthy, wasn't it? But close to nature, she'd have said. An owl fell down the chimney one year, and the kitchen was invaded by flying ants.'

'They do say after the first four years the dust stops getting worse. Apparently it stabilizes into a felt-like layer over everything.'

'Do you think I should pack the snorkel?'

'Indispensable for clearing out Greek hovels, I'd have thought.'

'What about this?' She holds up a large box. 'Do you mind if I take it?'

'Ah, the virgin Black and Decker. I knew it would come in handy some day.'

'You won't be needing it then?' It had been her present to him one birthday.

'Why do something yourself when you can pay through the nose for some toiling artisan to do it for you?'

'I'd have thought drilling and screwing would have been right up your street.'

'That's dentists, my dear, not surgeons. Quite a different kettle of squid. Have you got the extension lead? I suppose they do have the same kind of electricity as we do?'

She packs the rest of the tools into a smaller box. 'I wonder if I need some kind of licence to travel with this lot,' she says, scrambling to her feet. Then, meeting his eyes: 'Will you be all right without me?'

'With no one to enforce the organic regime? Listen, lady, I'm planning a serious junk food bender.'

'Are you trying to get rid of me?'

'Now promise you'll come home if you get lonely. Don't stick it out for the sake of an air ticket. I'll visit whenever I can. And Val said she'd try to grab a week in May.'

'I'll be fine. Really—' she insists, responding to his raised eyebrows. 'This is just what I need. I haven't thought about my hormone levels for – oh – at least three hours.'

'Speaking of which, don't try to do too much. Remember, this is supposed to be rehab. As your doctor, I advise plenty of sitting in tavernas reading about serial killers.'

'I thought I might buy a Greek grammar.'

'As long as you leave time for a good relaxing dose of rape and murder. And no sneaking the laptop into your hand luggage. No faddy detox books. And no checking out the Internet when you're there.'

'Yes, doctor,' demurely.

'That's "Mister" to you.'

Her ticket's booked for 8 April. Bennet is called to theatre, so their friend Val gives her a lift to the airport. Val is posh and languorous, like one of those glossy blonde dogs with too much hair. She shared a cadaver with Bennet when they were medics at Cambridge and they discovered a similar sense of humour and a passion for crosswords.

'What have you got in here?' she grunts now, helping heave the luggage on to a trolley.

'The big square one's the enlarger. The black zippy one's mostly tools.'

'I thought you were getting a builder.'

'They're for the outhouse. I thought I'd turn it into a darkroom. Something to keep me busy on those long lonely evenings.'

'Very enterprising and arty. Provided you don't expect me to get involved in any DIY when I come out. The only thing on my agenda is sea and sun, plus the odd steamy siesta with a few of your hunkier locals.'

'You're incorrigible.' Val's extracurricular activities are notorious. After a long day zapping gliomas – she's a neurosurgeon –

she has a habit of cruising bars on the Quayside. 'Any special requirements?'

'No beer guts, slapheads or hairy backs.'

'I'll see what I can do. Anything else?' Sylvia wheels the trolley into the airport.

'Nothing under seventeen or over seventy. Nothing smelling of goat. And no funny moles or warts. Apart from that, I'm easy.'

'That goes without saying.'

'Excuse me. I am simply leaving no stone unturned in my search for Mr Right.' This is a well-rehearsed routine. Despite her penchant for Lonely Hearts and computer dating, they both know Val likes her life as it is. Her Quayside flat is full of leather armchairs and heavy glass tables. She has underfloor heating and underground parking for her silver two-seater.

'Look after Bennet,' says Sylvia, giving her a hug. 'Take him out somewhere exotic. He's quite capable of spending every night watching *Football Italia* on Sky.'

Bennet likes to take charge of their tickets and passports, so it feels strange to be going through passport control without him. Sylvia keeps checking her shoulder bag, her aunt's camera case, thinking she's left something somewhere. Then realizing it's his arm that's missing: the crook of his elbow she'd normally link into, his big hand on her shoulder in the queue at the bookstall.

The other passengers in the departure lounge are all low-season travellers: earnest young couples with preschoolers and elderly people in knee-length shorts with binoculars slung around their necks.

She tries not to look at the babies: their faint eyebrows and folded strawberry hands; in slings and babyseats, jiggled on knees. She tries not to notice the delicious creases at the backs of their necks or feel the *whumph* of envy, that hits like a fist under her ribs when she sees one mother bending over her infant, and pressing her mouth to the top of its head, to that secret place where the skull hasn't formed yet; seeing her eyes close as she inhales the smell and glories in the sensation of warm down against her lips.

Sylvia gets up and walks over to stare out at their plane instead, at all the folded buggies and rucksacks being loaded. She pictures herself standing there – the only woman of her age, the only woman on her own – and is glad she's put on one of her natty little jackets over her black 501s. Maybe they'll take her for a businesswoman; or a photographer, with her camera over her shoulder. *I could be anyone*, she thinks as she hands her boarding pass to the attendant.

'So the room is OK?' Aphrodite calls out from the kitchen as Sylvia appears downstairs at the *Petaluda* after unpacking.

'Lovely, thank you.' There were red blankets on the twin beds and a froth of purple bougainvillaea in a terracotta jug on the side table. The tiny shower room smelt of lemons; the old wooden wardrobe of lavender.

'You are the first visitor this year. I thought maybe for your English Easter, but nothing. So, you will bring me luck. I like it when the foreigners come. It's good to talk something that is not peesant rubbish.' She's spooning coffee and sugar into a little stainless-steel jug and setting it on a tiny burner. 'By the end of winter I feel like screaming. Who is insulting who. Who is the daughter who is wearing too much make-up. Who is the sheep walking on the *melanzanes*. I want to pack up and go back to Athens.'

'Isn't this your home village? You said your mother used to swim—' Sylvia pictures the old woman's clothes billowing in the water, the stately paddling of big feet beneath.

'I was at the university in Athens,' Aphrodite stirs the brown liquid, watching a scum of brown bubbles form on the surface. 'I am very cultured. I have my mother's big brain. Her father kept her in the village with the chickens so she pushed me to go to Athens. I was working on a thesis about the Minoan script when I met my husband.'

The brown scum begins to heave and she lifts the pot off the heat and pours it into two small white cups. 'So now I am a cook,' she says, setting them on a tray with two tall glasses of water. 'I like to make nice food, nice rooms. But my daughter wants to move to Chania. She says the village is for dead people.'

'But it's so lovely here.'

The smell of sweet coffee fills her nostrils. The tray has a design of pink roses on it. Aphrodite adds a saucer of small biscuits and carries it through to a sunny table by the door. 'Anyway my husband was suffocating in the city. "Suffocating" – is this the right word? He was studying linguistics, lecturing at the university, but he had to stop work.' She nods her head outside, to a middle-aged man forking manure from a wheelbarrow. 'Really he is happier with the potatoes.'

Sylvia watches the man bend to pull up a weed. His shoes are caked with red mud, his round face bland and serene. She wonders if he's on medication.

'It was in the summer and we were in a heatwave,' Aphrodite continues. 'Of course it is always a heatwave in Athens in the summer, but this time the air is so bad they are ordering people to stop driving their cars. But no one complied. Then the old man in the apartment below us died, so Vasilios took a hammer and began hitting all the cars parked in the street outside.'

She shrugs and perches her ample bottom on a chair. 'So we came here,' she concludes. 'Now, sit. Tell me about your life.'

Talking to Aphrodite, Sylvia feels like an orange, peeled and split into segments. The other woman pounces on each gushet of information as though it's edible, sniffing it, tasting it, asking unexpected questions. What did she feel when she met Bennet for the first time? Isn't he worried she will have an affair with a Greek man, like in that film? Does she take photographs of people or churches?

Sylvia keeps expecting questions about her job, but they never come. Aphrodite simply assumes she's a photographer; and Sylvia is content to let the lie hang there for a while, like a coat she might put on if it gets chilly.

She'd planned to fend off questions about her infertility with something pat about starting a family next year. But she has no responses prepared for the kinds of thing Aphrodite wants to know – 'Do you ever dream about the babies you will have?' 'Is your husband a man who will play with his children?' – or for the way she leans forwards in delighted anticipation, with her plump forearms on the checked tablecloth. And soon Sylvia's spilling out the details of her two IVF attempts, her two miscarriages and her decision to come here to purify her body before trying to conceive again.

'So these are your troubles,' Aphrodite sighs, leaning back like someone who has just eaten a satisfying meal. 'Everyone has these heavy things they carry in their hearts. For me they make these white hairs.' She fingers her curls. 'For you, the sad lines at the corner of your mouth. My trouble is a husband who does not speak any more. And this restaurant that is always too empty or too full. And a daughter who wants to be a hairdresser.' She rolls her eyes. 'A hairdresser! She wants to buy a pink van and a special hairdryer to take to rich women's houses. And paint their nails. Toes and fingers, both, with black-and-silver designs. She thinks it is Art. She thinks this is a good career for a woman.'

Sylvia laughs. 'What would you like her to be?'

'I don't know. Something with a brain. Something that will make her rich. A psychiatrist or a lawyer. Maybe an architect for all the new English houses. There are fortunes to be made in that business.'

'We're going to use an architect.'

'There, you see? And you will listen to this architect with respect. And pay a big cheque at the end of it. Not five euros to have your toenails polished.'

'I don't suppose you know of someone you'd recommend? The estate agent's very keen for us to use a man called' – ferreting in her bag for a card – 'Broudakis.'

Aphrodite shrugs. 'I have heard this name, but I don't know his work. I just tell the builders myself what I want. The pergola was made by a man who arrived here last year with no money. I paid for the wood and cooked for him at the taverna until he found a job. Now I just ask him when I need something.'

'My husband's hopeless at that kind of thing,' says Sylvia. 'I bought him a drill, but he's never taken it out of its box.'

'Oh, my Vasilios has very masculine hands. But after the trouble of the cars, we decide he should not use those tools any more.' Sylvia doesn't know what to say. Together the two women look outside, to the garden, where Vasilios is feeding water tenderly to a row of transplanted seedlings.

After supper that evening – an unctuous stew of lamb and potatoes – Sylvia takes out her mobile and texts Bennet.

Aphrodite nutty but nice. Hubby mentally ill, but seems harmless. Will pick up deeds from Nicos and see architect Monday. Lovelove.

Clicking 'send' she feels like she's a small boat on a big sea, and the phone is the rope that tethers her safely to the jetty.

Next day, after a breakfast of thick yoghurt and fresh oranges, she pulls on her new overalls, lugs the tools to her hire car, and drives up to the plot of land everyone refers to as '*to spiti tiss Kokonas*' – Kokona's house.

For a while, she simply stands with her back to the old cottage and gazes down at the shallow terraces that make up the garden, at the tumble of red-roofed houses below her, at the craggy swell of the mountains opposite. A chilly wind is chasing fat clouds across the expanse of pale blue, stirring up the scents of woodsmoke and pine resin.

The village sprawls up both sides of a small valley bisected by a narrow river bed. Over the bridge, on the other side, she can see Aphrodite hanging a red shirt on the line; and Vasilios slowly uncoiling a length of yellow hosepipe. Above them, labouring faintly up the mountain road in the distance, a turquoise bus is on its way to Chora Sfakion, far away on the other side of the island.

As she wades down to the building plot, thigh-deep through clumps of wild flowers and grass feathers, butterflies flap raggedly into the air and the trees around her bristle with busy finches.

She spends a happy half-hour pacing out the plot, imagining where the different rooms will go, to take best advantage of the view. They've decided on three bedrooms: one for themselves, one for guests, and a third, by unspoken agreement, for the baby. Two bathrooms; kitchen-diner and living room. Nothing imposing: single-storey; something to blend in with the rest of the village.

There's a boulder where the kitchen door will be and she sits down on it, thinking: *This is where I'll sit in the early morning when I'm pregnant, sipping peppermint tea and feeling the baby kicking*. The image is so strong, it makes her catch her breath.

Filled with sudden energy, she wades back up to the cottage and reaches down the old key from its hook. As before, it turns easily and the door rasps open over dry straw and dead leaves. For an instant, as she stands on the threshold, there is movement everywhere: skittering on the walls; rustling in the straw; dark shapes whisking into the shadows. Then silence.

Pushing the door open as far as it will go, she makes her way to the window. Both panes of glass are missing, so she reaches through to unfasten the shutters. They creak open on rusty hinges through a curtain of vine leaves, admitting a river of dappled sunlight that eddies around the small room prompting another wave of invisible scuffling.

She does the same in the other little room: unbolting the door to the outside and wrenching open the shutters to let buttery light flood in over dusty heaps of oil cans, mattresses, barbed wire.

For a moment, standing there surveying it all, she quails. She hadn't remembered this room being quite as full. There are things here that she can't even lift, let alone dispose of. A television the size of a dishwasher; a chest freezer full of metal window frames.

'So what are you going to do with that little lot?'

She whirls round, the sun in her eyes. The young builder – Martin? – from the estate agent's is in the doorway behind her.

'God, you startled me!' she says. Where had he appeared from? She hadn't heard anyone approaching. 'I was just wondering vaguely if there was some kind of official dump,' she says. 'A landfill site or something.'

His long dark hair is wet, slicked back from a brown forehead. His clean white tee shirt has a small rip in the side. 'Argyrakis would hire a brace of Albanians to pile it on a truck and tip it down the mountain on the Sfakia road.'

'But that's illegal, surely?'

'The deal is they take the rap if they're caught. But they never are.'

'I thought I'd try and burn most of it,' she says doubtfully, 'and put the rest in bin bags.'

He hoists a big rusty gate with two hands and looks at her with his eyebrows raised.

She grins sheepishly. 'Bury it in the garden? Maybe your boss could get his Albanians to dig a grave for it.'

What's he doing here? She feels embarrassed, as if he's caught her stealing something. She wishes her overalls weren't so obviously new, still starched and creased from the shop.

'It seems a pity to chuck it,' he's saying, rotating the gate in the air. 'Mounted on its side, like this, it could form the basis of an interesting sculpture.' He eyes her speculatively. 'Or you could give it to an old man I know who's building a pen for his goats.'

'Great. He'd be doing me a favour. There's some netting in the other room he could have too,' she says. 'But he'll have to collect it himself – there's no way it'll fit into my hire car.'

Martin carries the gate outside and rests it against the wall. 'He was keeping them in an empty old house, but he had to move them out when it was sold,' he says casually.

'Oh God.' Suddenly she understands. 'They were his goats in here, weren't they? Is he furious?'

'More philosophical than furious. If you give him the netting, he'll be your friend for life.' He wipes rusty hands on the back of his jeans. 'But I'd get a lock fitted on that toilet if I were you.'

What's he talking about? 'I didn't even know there was a toilet.'

'It's round the side, but you might want to brace yourself. I'm not sure your standards of hygiene are the same as his.' He hefts the bale of chicken wire out into the sunshine. 'He's one of those men you get in every village. A bit dim, a bit smelly, never married. You passed his house on the way up here. It's just a shack really, with half a roof.'

She shudders. A few goats in the cottage is one thing, but a filthy old man using the toilet makes her feel slightly nauseous.

'How do you know he's been using my toilet?'

He shrugs. 'I hang out at Aphrodite's, fixing things for her. People talk. I listen.' He's unearthed a box of rusty bolts and hinges and is rummaging through it. 'There are some good things in here, you know.'

'Aphrodite's great, isn't she?'

'Is she?' He looks at her as if to say, *How would you know?*

'Don't you think so?'

'I think so,' he says simply.

'Is that man still using the loo?' She can't stop thinking about it. She's wondering if they sell rubber gloves in the village.

'I expect he's gone back to squatting in with his goats, but I've got an old lock in the van if you want me to sort it for you now.'

Without waiting for her reply, he strides off down the track to where his pockmarked red camper van is parked behind her pristine white Corsa.

When he's gone, she ducks under the shaggy fig tree at the side of the house and discovers another shuttered window buried in the leaves, and a stone lean-to with a wooden door hanging half off its hinges. Gingerly, with one hand over her nose, she pushes the door open. The toilet bowl is caked with brown smears; a pool of murky water glowers inside. There's a sliver of grey soap on the grimy basin and a long green stain under the single tap. On the wall is a small mirror in a pink plastic frame; on the floor a shaggy heap of soiled leaves.

She backs away, nausea nudging at her throat, and flails back through the fig tree to the front of the house. What on earth made her think she could use this filthy old ruin for anything?

'Did you discover the alfresco shower?' Martin asks when she emerges. 'Right at the back, beyond the toilet. Great for sluicing yourself down on a hot day and completely private.' He has a screwdriver in one hand and an old mortice in the other. A leather tool-belt is slung low around his narrow hips.

'Listen, thanks for offering to sort the loo and everything. But I think I've changed my mind—'

'If it's the toilet that's bothering you, I can easily—'

'It's not just that—' To her dismay, her eyes are filling with tears. 'It's just too difficult. The goat man, the loo, all that stuff to get rid of.' She rakes her fingers through her hair. 'I'm sorry.'

She'd stuffed a wad of loo roll in her overalls before leaving the taverna, but now she can't find it. She can feel her nose running as she digs feverishly into one pocket after another.

'I bet you feel a right prat in that get-up,' he says.

His tone is teasing, but his eyes, when she looks into them, are gentle. And suddenly she's sitting on the doorstep with her face in her hands and crying properly: big jerky sobs that shake her shoulders and squeeze hot tears down her cheeks.

'It's only a bit of dirt, you know,' he says matter-of-factly, sitting down beside her and fiddling with the lock.

'What?' She's found her loo paper and is blowing her nose.

'The shit in the toilet. Flies love it.'

'There are over a hundred different kinds of bacteria in human excrement,' she sniffs sullenly. 'And at least ten can be fatal.'

He's squirting oil into the keyhole from a tiny can. His long fingers are covered with rust and oil.

'What doesn't kill you makes you strong,' he says.

The village shop she enters first is a dim brown cave on the corner of the square, opposite the *kafenion*. Part gift shop, part ironmonger's, it's run by a man so fat he can barely stand. Wedged, morosely sweating, behind a till on a low table at the back, he flaps a doughy hand at Sylvia to help herself from the shelves.

'*Oraya*,' he comments as her purchases pile up on the table in front of him. Bleach and scouring powder; a toilet brush and a pack of pan scourers – he taps the prices into the till: 'Is need clean *to spiti tiss Kokonas*,' he says. Fly spray and ant killer; rubber gloves; black bin liners; dustpan and brush; light bulbs and toilet paper; a bar of Lux soap and a small yellow towel with a green puppy on it; more rubber gloves.

Opening her purse to pay, Sylvia hesitates, then adds a bread knife she discovers on a rack with the chisels and screwdrivers.

When she gets back, Martin has removed the toilet door and laid it on the ground to fit the new lock. Inside, the fetid leaves are gone and the floor and walls have been swept. With the door off and fresh air circulating, it doesn't look quite so daunting.

'I turned the water on and flushed it a few times,' he says. 'I'll give it a scrub later if you want to steer clear of those deadly bacteria.'

She looks at him sharply. Is he getting at her?

'I think I can cope,' she says stiffly, upending one of her two carrier bags.

'People in some countries pay good money for a barrow full of shit,' he remarks as she rips open the first pack of rubber gloves.

'Yes, and that's why they're all infested with worms,' she retorts.

'In India people squat in special fields set aside for the purpose, and shit systematically in rows, so there's no risk of stepping in someone else's mess.'

She stares at him. 'I'm not sure I need to know this.'

He's finished the lock and is sawing off the bottom of the door, where the planks are rotten and splintering. 'Did you realize that there's a special kind of white blood cell in human blood that has evolved specifically to combat parasitic worms?' he asks, looking up and meeting her eyes.

'I did actually,' she says. 'I've seen them through the microscope at the lab.' Stained violet with Giemsa, they're spherical and grainy as muesli. Their twinned nuclei look like the two halves of a broad bean.

'So what are they doing now our flush toilets have put them out of business?'

'I don't know.' She's never thought about it.

'If eczema's caused by obsessional mums washing their babies all the time and fucking up the skin's natural immunity, what are those special white blood cells up to in our guts?'

'Eosinophils,' she supplies automatically.

He's bending over, sanding the blonde cut edge of the door. She can see the long ridges of muscle either side of his spine through his tee shirt.

'D. H. Lawrence used to carry a golden spoon for tasting the shit of his mistresses,' he remarks after a while.

'What?' Is he trying to shock her? What does a builder know about D. H. Lawrence? She shakes Vim around the basin and starts scrubbing, cutting a satisfying swathe through the green and grey layers.

'I mean, coprophagy is a lot more common than most people think,' he goes on, lifting the door and propping it against the frame. 'Can you hold this steady while I line up the hinges?'

The door's heavier than she expects. It takes all her strength to hold it straight.

'And rimming's something gays do all the time,' he says. 'But they're not all dying of botulism or whatever. I mean, how could man have survived all this time without some kind of defence against the bacteria in his own shit?'

'Are you trying to get me to stop cleaning the loo?' She's joking, but he takes her seriously.

'No way,' he says vehemently. 'Aesthetics are really important. But I don't think people realize how powerful their bodies are. As long as they're fed and exercised properly. And not messed about by neurosis.'

She bridles. Is he calling her neurotic?

'Sorry,' he says, abashed by the expression on her face. 'I didn't mean to lecture. It's a bit of a thing with me.'

'Have you always been a builder?' she asks later over lunch. They're sitting cross-legged on a patch of concrete in front of the house, with salami, bread and tomatoes spread out on a plastic bag. The toilet and sink are sparkling; the floor's washed; the door, with its new lock, is back on its hinges.

'You mean what's a bright boy like me doing fixing up other people's houses?'

'I suppose so, yes.'

'People always ask that. They think you need more brains to be an accountant than a joiner.'

'I work in a hospital, preparing pathology slides for the doctors,' she says, offering him a fat red tomato. 'People are always asking me why I didn't become a doctor.'

'So you understand.' His eyes lose their wary expression. It's as though she's pulled back a curtain.

'I like cells,' she goes on. 'And I like working with my hands. There's a real knack to finding exactly the right place to cut a piece of tissue, to show a particular kind of cell in all its beauty.' She stops, embarrassed, but he's nodding.

'Like a sculpture,' he says. 'Or a painting.'

'Maybe.' She looks away. The intensity in his strange-coloured eyes is unnerving. She shrugs. 'Maybe I'm just not very good with whole people.'

She's conscious of him watching her as she kneels up and starts clearing away the remains of the food.

'Argyrakis has a trailer I can borrow if you want to get rid of some of that stuff,' he says after a while.

'What will you do with it – or shouldn't I ask?'

'Let's see how much there is before we worry about that.' He brushes crumbs from his jeans and rises to his feet in a single sinuous movement.

They start with the mattresses. 'These'll burn right down to the springs,' says Martin, dragging them into a clear space away from the trees, while Sylvia starts sorting through the sacks and boxes underneath.

'Hey, look at this!' He's back and edging past a heap of old chairs towards the rear of the room. 'It's the old sleeping platform.' There's a little wooden ladder leading up to what looks like a wooden stage with a neat balustrade along the front edge.

'It's collapsed at the back, but the boards are still here.' He's climbing up the ladder and jumping down into what seems to be a small cellar. 'Wow! They must be twelve-inch at least. And solid oak. You can't get wood like this any more. The old woman would have slept up here. And underneath, can you see where the firewood was stored?'

Sylvia climbs up the ladder and peers down. Beneath the tent of fallen timbers is a careful heap of sawn logs, with an axe laid neatly across it. For a second she can see a woman's hand grasping the handle and setting it there, like a knife on a plate.

'Some kind of beetle must have got to the beams,' he's saying. 'But those boards will last you forever. So – I reckon I'll need about five hundred for materials to fix the platform. Plus bits and pieces for patching the outside doors at the bottom where the rain's rotted the wood. But the roof looks fine and the windows can be sorted in two ticks.'

He looks up at her. 'Plus labour, it'll be about three K for the lot. What do you think?'

Sylvia gapes at him. What's he talking about?

'Aphrodite said you wanted the house sorting out.'

She laughs suddenly. 'Oh I see. No, I don't want to live in it. I just want to clear out the rubbish and use one of the rooms as a darkroom. The first one probably, because of the tap. All I need is some glass in the window and blackout panels to stop the light getting in.'

'What?' He seems shocked.

'We're going to build a new house on that flat bit of land overlooking the village,' she explains.

'What's wrong with this house? There's three rooms, a toilet and shower. What more do you need?'

'Well, hot water for a start,' she says, feeling needled. What business is it of his what she does with the bloody place?

'Why do you need hot water? Are you planning to be here in the winter?'

'And a proper bathroom.'

'There's a shower outside, I told you. I can rig up a screen if you're worried about old Spiros getting an eyeful.'

'What about kitchen units?' *This is absurd*, she thinks. *Why are we having this conversation?*

'Well unless you're an Ikea freak, there's any number of old cupboards in here you could use. And tables and chairs. I could sort out all the furniture for another 500 euros. A new mattress and a fridge and you could have the whole house habitable for under five grand.'

His eyes challenge her.

She stares hotly back. How dare he dictate what she does with her property?

Suddenly he backs down. 'Sorry,' he says, hoisting himself up out of the cellar. 'I just hate to see things thrown away when they can be mended.'

'It's not really big enough for us.' Why is she justifying herself to this young man?

'Obviously it's your decision. I'll do whatever you like. Evenings and weekends, ten euros an hour.'

She stares down at the axe, thinking about the old woman who laid it there, so carefully, before she died. 'Aphrodite said the house was howling,' she says.

'That's what I mean,' he says.

Chapter 11

The Yellowy-Grey Stone

There was someone staying in their cave when they got back to Matala, but Juan's family were just leaving, so they took over their space. His mother liked it because she could stand upright in the middle. Martin liked it because there were two alcoves in the walls to use as sleeping spaces, with pillows carved out of the rock.

'Do you think they were made by cavemen?' he asked, unrolling his sleeping bag.

'Greg says the caves were used by Roman soldiers when they were in charge,' said his mother. 'But I bet there were cavemen here before that.'

'Why don't the Greek people live here?' Martin has wondered about this before: the white village houses were all stacked up the slope on the opposite side of the bay.

'I don't know,' she said, shaking out a long scarf and winding it around her hips. 'Maybe it's easier to build on that side; not so steep. Maybe they think the caves are haunted.'

It was late June by then and very hot. Everyone woke early, when it was cool, and slept through the afternoon heat. The awnings Martin remembered were back: reeds from the dry river bed, woven into loose trellises; grass mats tied to wooden frames; Indian bedcovers and saris, knotted to branches and outcrops, billowing in the warm wind that rose up the face of the yellow cliff.

He spent most of his time in the water with the other children. There was a new Swedish girl called Ingrid, who was nine, and her brother Soron, who was eleven. They spoke English and their hair was almost white from the sun. When Sacha was in charge they played Olympics or Pirates. When Soron was in charge they went exploring. Martin thought it was strange to have someone telling him what kind of game to play, but he didn't mind.

The evenings went on forever. No one told the children to go to bed. They just slept and got up when they felt like it. Sometimes they ran off to play after supper, but usually they ended up lolling against their parents, listening to music and conversation, watching red cigarette-tips pulsing in the darkness.

Big blonde Karl had taken down his tent and replaced it with a mosquito net, which he tied up in a white knot during the day. His space under the trees was more defined. There were some flat rocks there to sit on, and a wooden beer crate lashed to a tree, where he kept his things. He had a tall clay pot that he filled with drinking water from a standpipe on the beach, and a white goat, which he milked every morning.

Soron's parents had set up a wide shelter nearby. They'd come overland, all the way from Sweden, in a rusty mustard camper van with a special rack for their four bikes on the back. Soron's father, Jan, was a carpenter and the inside of the van was full of cunning shelves and alcoves. He'd taken control of the toilets and dug a long pit, away from all the shelters, and set up bamboo screens and a platform with holes to squat over.

Martin loved to watch Jan working, fashioning unlikely bits of drift-wood into something useful. All his movements were strong and precise. When he planed a piece of wood, the curls peeled evenly away in blonde ringlets. His chisel bit deep and clean as a silver tooth. He countersunk every screw. He kept his tools in a special box that opened out in three layers, with a black oilstone to keep the blades sharp. Martin liked touching the tools: the bulbous handle of the plane; the clicking ratchets of the screwdrivers; the cross-hatching on the little bradawl.

Jan was scathing about the skills of Greek carpenters. 'Do you know what this is?' He held up a heavy claw hammer. 'It's a Greek screwdriver,' he said. 'They use five nails here instead of one screw and bang them in until the wood splits.'

Martin grinned, pulling out the metal tape measure to a hundred centimetres exactly, then letting it snap back into its case.

'You can make a good box or a bad box,' Jan told him. 'They will both hold your things, but the good box will make you smile every time you open it.'

Wading back to the shore one day after a swim, Martin felt suddenly that he belonged there. So much about Matala was like their life in Oxford: not having a normal house, mending things yourself, not going to school or the doctor, living in the open air.

'It's like being at home,' he told his mother later. 'Only hot and with lots of people like us.'

'And no sluggy carpets or falling ceilings. Our house would be fine if the weather was like this all the time.' They were washing the lunch dishes in the sea with a brick of green soap and an unravelling yellow pan scourer. Her hair was a black tangle in the wind; a red silk scarf was clinging to her wet thighs.

'No one here worries about me going to school,' said Martin. 'Karl says school makes you stupid. It gives you some answers but makes you forget how to ask questions.'

His mother laughed. 'He's probably right. But I'd still send you to that navy-blue school if I could.'

'Karl says a man has to teach himself about the world. He thinks I'll learn more in five weeks here than I would in five years at the navy-blue school.'

'What are you learning, Marty? I hardly see you these days.'

'If we stayed, you could marry Karl and I could look after his goat,' he said. 'Or one of the others,' he added quickly as her eyes widened in alarm. 'All the men here think you're wonderful.' *And I would get a new father*, he wanted to add.

She put a wet brown arm around his bony shoulders. 'Why would I want one of these men when I've got you?' she asked. 'You're the only man I need.'

By then Martin had realized that most of the Matala people were there because they didn't like the way things were run in their own countries. Drowsing with his head in his mother's lap, he heard them talking about bombs that could blow the world to pieces, and a long war that they wanted to stop. They talked about travelling to India, where there were thousands of different gods; and about ancient Greece where the gods turned into animals and mated with the people. They talked about different kinds of families, where the women mated with all the men and no one knew which fathers went with which children.

They talked about lots of other things he didn't understand, but he liked to listen, because it felt as though they were discussing his life. It felt like they were planning a future which would be good for someone like him, who couldn't go to the navy-blue school.

'What I really like about Matala,' Martin told his mother, 'is being with everyone and feeling normal.'

'Do you believe in one god or lots of gods?' he asked Karl one day.

They were taking the goat to a new bit of grazing, half a mile inland along the river bed. Martin was holding the goat's tether and wearing a straw hat. Lizards whisked out of sight as they wandered along the warm path.

'That is a very good question, young man.' Karl always called him 'young man'. 'Of course I was taught to believe in the Christian God, but now I don't like him so much.'

'Why?' Martin had never thought of God being someone you could like or dislike.

'He was so mean to send Adam and Eve out of the Garden of Eden. And I didn't like his Ten Commandments. If he is so good, why do we have to be commanded to love him?'

'My mother says that God is a woman,' said Martin. He'd known she was joking but he wanted Karl to keep talking.

'In the old days everyone thought God was a woman,' said Karl. 'They didn't know that fucking creates babies, so they believed that women had magic powers. And the most powerful person they could think of was a big fat mama god.'

'I tried to pray once,' said Martin, 'but I couldn't get a picture of someone to pray to.' He'd borrowed a book of Bible stories from the library and read about John the Baptist praying in the wilderness. He'd liked the word 'wilderness'; it made him think of the land between Argyle Street and the river.

'In Australia the Aborigines believe that God is in the rocks and trees,' Karl was saying. 'And in Africa people believe in animal gods. I think they have both got the right idea.'

This was something Martin wasn't expecting. God in a stone? In a goat? God in a horse?

'No one really knows if there is a god, so you have to decide for yourself. Do you think the universe just appeared – poof! – out of nothing? Or do you think that a god made it? Maybe a god made it by accident, by sneezing, and has forgotten all about it. Maybe we are all gods, but we don't realize it.'

'I'm not a god.' Martin was pretty sure about this.

'How do you know?' They'd reached a patch of thick yellow grass and Karl tied the goat's tether to a tree. 'Maybe you just haven't developed all your power yet.'

They stayed for four weeks this time, then went home for a fortnight; then came back to Matala for another four weeks. Each time they went home the leaks were a bit worse and the house a bit more overgrown. A tom cat had been into the sitting room and sprayed the sofa. The yellow bucket had overflowed on the landing and there was chickweed growing in the gaps between the floorboards.

'It stops being our territory when we're away,' Martin said. 'The woods start taking over again.'

'Maybe we should keep chickens in the hall,' said his mother. 'Chickweed's their favourite food and they could eat the slugs in the sitting room.'

She was joking, but he thought it was a good idea. 'What about a goat?' he suggested. 'For the garden. We'd have free eggs and we could make cheese like Karl does. And grow tomatoes and cucumbers under the plastic sheet.'

'Have you had enough of being away?' she asked. 'Do you want to stay at home for a while? Just the two of us?'

*

Looking back, they called them Rainbow Days: the warm autumn weeks after their long summer in Crete.

'Let's have a Green Day to cheer ourselves up,' said his mother after she'd scoured the scummy bath and hung their clean sheets out to dry. 'I'll get out some Day Money and we'll have a feast.'

They ate watercress sandwiches and cooking apples and stalked crickets on the overgrown lawn. Later she found a single grasshopper in the middle of her clean duvet: a small lime-green one with spindly legs.

The next day was a Blue Day. She brought the ladder into her bedroom and pulled snakes of clematis in through the window. 'Letting the sky in,' she called it, reeling in great coils of green, until there was an expanse of clear blue at the top.

A dead butterfly had fallen on to the window sill: velvet-brown with blue eyes on its wings. 'It's a peacock,' she said, stroking its downy thorax. Her eyes were dark as the peacock's wing; her hair glinted in the blue light. Martin was glad to be alone with her again; glad to be away from all the Matala men.

Later, dressed in denim, they went on a quest for blue food and bought food colouring and potatoes.

'Why do chows have blue tongues?' he asked as they tucked into blue mash.

'I don't know,' she said.

So they did what they always did when he asked a question she couldn't answer: walked to the Central Library to find out. They set out just as the schools were closing and suddenly the streets were full of children in grey uniforms.

Martin pulled on his mother's arm. 'Let's have a Grey Day tomorrow,' he said.

At the library they discovered that the only other creatures with blue tongues were bears and a special kind of Australian lizard. They read that chows might be related to bears, because they had the same number of teeth, and walked differently to other dogs, with stiff back legs. But that might have been because the Chinese ate them – the word 'chow' meant 'food' in Chinese – and they had been bred like that, because the hind leg was where the tastiest meat was.

According to a Chinese fairy tale, they read, when the stars were first set in the sky, they dislodged fragments of blue, which fell to the ground. And the chow lapped them up; that was why its tongue was blue.

The next morning his mother packed Ryvita and liver pâté and they rode to the gravel pits on their bikes. At Abingdon Road they dismounted and pushed, walking slowly and staring at the pavement. It was browny-grey, they decided, whereas the road was more bluey.

'Why are clouds grey?' he asked as they turned off the main road.

'Because they're full of rain,' she said. 'The really dark storm clouds are called "cumulo-nimbus". "Nimbus grey": that's a good name for a paint colour.'

'But the sea's blue. Why aren't clouds blue too?'

'Most of them are blue,' she said. 'But we can't see them because they're the same colour as the sky.'

At the gravel pits it was deserted and still. The sky was perfectly reflected in the expanses of water, loaded with slow fat white clouds. 'Can you see that big blue one over there?' she asked, pointing. Martin blew a raspberry at her.

They slithered down scree and crumped over pebbles, collecting as many different greys as they could. Then they laid them out on the wooden jetty and poured water over them to make them shine. They counted thirty-five different shades: yellowish and pinkish greys; browny and creamy; blueish and blackish. Martin sorted them into separate groups.

'I don't think grey is a colour at all,' he said when he'd finished. 'I think it's just people being lazy and not looking hard enough.'

'It's the same with blue clouds,' she said. 'People are just not looking hard enough.'

When it was time to go, he wanted to take all the grey stones home with him. 'You can't,' she objected. 'It's cruel to keep a stone in captivity.'

'I'll keep them out in the garden,' he argued, though he knew she was joking. 'They can run around all they like.'

In the end he chose just one: a smallish flattish yellowy one. He wasn't sure why. Something about it reminded him of the day they'd just had: solid and warm and golden.

'Maybe they are running around,' his mother said later. 'But in stone time rather than human time. And we are just flashes of light.'

'Why can't we just stay in Matala all the time?' Martin wanted to know. It was cold at night and his bed felt damp. He thought it was probably warmer and drier in Crete.

'Because there's no library there and I can't teach you properly. Anyway, we can't go back now until I get a new passport. And I daren't send off for one, because if I do they'll find out where we're living.'

'So we've expired.'

'Yes, Marty,' she said with a sigh. 'I'm afraid we've expired.'

She'd brought a pile of books home about depression, which was the proper name for her Bad Sads.

'Winston Churchill called his depression "the Black Dog",' she told him. 'Other people call it "the blues". Isn't that weird? Blue is one of my favourite colours.'

Martin agreed. He thought of the blue on his jay's feather, and the patch of sky at the top of her window; the glitter-blue of the sea at Matala; the milky crinkle of Karl's eyes.

His mother told him that blue was also the colour of something called 'the unconscious', which was where all the things we knew but couldn't remember were kept. 'All your dreams are there,' she said, 'and what it felt like to be in my tummy before you were born.' Martin thought of the blue lace-up shoes he had when he was three, carefully hidden in the tartan biscuit tin under his bed.

'Our brains are much more powerful than we realize, full of power and knowledge we don't use,' she was saying. 'Sometimes I think depression is my brain trying to get in touch with all that power. And that's why I can't move when I'm in a Bad Sad. It's my brain making me slow down and pay attention to my unconscious.'

There was a kind of music called 'the Blues' she told him, which developed from sad songs sung by black slaves in America.

At the library they found a book about Winston Churchill and another one about slavery, and an LP called 'Lady Sings the Blues', which they borrowed to play on their record player.

The lady was Billie Holiday, who killed herself because she was so depressed. Martin wondered if it was because she spent her whole life singing sad songs, but his mother said it was because she drank too much wine, which can make people concentrate on the bad things in their lives.

Winston Churchill had lived to be a really old man, though. He smoked big cigars and went to war against Germany and only needed four hours' sleep a night. And he painted pictures; the book showed some of them: big bright views of the countryside. You couldn't be sad looking at them.

One of the songs from the record made Martin shiver, even though the bars of the electric fire were burning his legs. He thought at first that it was about the jungle, then his mother explained that the 'strange fruit' in the song were dead black people who'd been hung by their necks from a special tree.

There was a damson tree in the garden and the fruit had dusty purple skin and reddish flesh. When he found out what the song meant, he thought of the damson tree.

'Do you think you'd be happier if you painted your bedroom yellow?' he asked his mother when she kissed him goodnight.

Chapter 12

Sylvia asks Aphrodite to show her the path down to the rocks.

'I'll take you,' she says, untying her apron. 'Let me escape from this kitchen before the Saturday multitudes arrive.'

She leads the way down a narrow lane winding along the backs of a street of whitewashed houses, then another, skirting a clump of ruined farm buildings and a field of chickens, turning right past a little church, eventually emerging beside a graveyard overlooking the sea.

'How lovely,' says Sylvia, looking down.

'We like to bury our relatives with a nice view.'

'Is your mother here?'

'Of course! Where else would she be? Come. We go down here.' There's a path, quite clearly demarked, zigzagging down the side of the cliff. 'Vasilios keeps the thorn bushes cut back for me,' she says. 'These men do have some good uses.'

The air fills with the scents of thyme and hyssop as they descend. The sea is boiling around the rocks. Beyond the fringe of waving weed, it's a deep, deep blue.

'You climb down to the water over there,' Aphrodite says, pointing to a sloping ledge of rock. 'There are places for your feet, but you must be careful for the echinoderms.'

'The what?'

'These round spiny animals. They are called echinoderms, yes?'

Sylvia smiles. 'Yes, that's their technical name. Most people call them sea urchins, because they look like the heads of scruffy little boys.'

'Anyway, take a stick and wiggle it in the algae before you put your feet.'

Sylvia starts to change into her swimsuit. 'Thank you for sending Martin up to the house,' she says.

'I didn't send him.' Aphrodite seems surprised.

'Oh.' Sylvia's puzzled. 'I thought—'

'So he going to work for you, is he?' The Greek woman's lips press together.

'He's trying to persuade me to do up the little cottage and live in that instead. He seemed quite put out that we were going to build on the land.'

'He is always arguing something like that. He was angry with me for paving over the cobbles in my yard. Saying about the skill in getting them in that pattern. But they were impossible to sweep, and my customers were complaining that the tables are wobbling. He would like to keep everything the way it is.'

'Where does he live?'

'It depends. In his van. In his small tent. On the floor of the house he is working. He doesn't care. When he was building my pergola, he was staying in your room.'

Sylvia digests this information as she folds her 501s and tucks her socks into her trainers. Martin's head on her pillow; his bare feet on the tiles in her shower. She feels a flush of embarrassment, as though he's been in the room with her: watching her brush her hair; watching her sitting on the toilet.

'Your husband is right,' laughs Aphrodite as Sylvia stands up in her swimsuit. 'You are crazy to swim in this weather.' Though in fact it's a beautiful evening, with the sun low in the sky, pouring honeyed light over the rocks.

'In England I used to go swimming in the sea every morning. Even when there was ice on the sand. So this seems warm to me. And it's so much cleaner here. Where I swim in England it's all murky, and the sea's polluted. There's a big chemical factory just up the coast, and a nuclear power station further up.'

'So why do you do this, crazy English lady?'

'It's supposed to be good for the circulation, the blood. It makes me feel fresh. Like a new person.'

'So you are baptizing yourself. Washing away your sins, like Jesus in Galilee.'

'That's what my husband says.'

'So your baby will stay next time.' Aphrodite nods as though this makes perfect sense. 'The vegetables from Vasilios are very unpolluting. He refuses to use any fertilizer or insect killer. He even squashes the bugs with his fingers.'

'That's good. I was wondering whether I could get organic food here.'

'He talks to the *horta*, but not to me,' Aphrodite shrugs, watching Sylvia edge gingerly over the rocks towards the water. 'Did you find the pictures when you were clearing Kokona's house?' she asks suddenly.

Sylvia dips a toe in the water, scanning the weed for black spines. 'I haven't really looked properly yet. We were just shifting the big stuff outside. Why?'

'No old pictures of children?'

'I thought she didn't have any children.'

'People used to give the photographs to her as a reward. She used to help women in the village, but she always refused to take money.'

'Oh? Why?'

Big shrug. 'I don't know. Maybe she was scared of bandits. Years ago, they used to come up the road from Sfakia and rob the villages. There were many guns left over from the Germans. A lot of people were killed. It's the Albanians you have to watch out for these days.'

Sylvia pushes herself off into the water. It slips up over her shoulders like a chilly silk dress: cold but not shocking, not heart-stopping, not ECT cold. She swims away from the rocks until she's surrounded by blue and gold; the evening sky, the copper sun, the inky sea.

'Look out for a picture of little Aphrodite!' Aphrodite calls, waving from the rocks. 'I am wearing a big yellow ribbon in my hair!'

Sylvia swims until the sun sets, her white arms gliding through the gold-spangled water. She thinks of Aphrodite's mother swimming here, with only the graves to see her big body buoyed up by a billow of black skirts.

On the way back to the taverna, she passes Vasilios in the garden. He's squatting beside a freshly dug trench.

As she approaches, she thinks she hears him say something.

'*Parakalo*? Did you speak to me?' she asks.

He looks up and opens a muddy palm to show her a small freckled bean. 'I was just asking this little one where she wanted to be planted,' he says in perfect unaccented English.

The *Petaluda* is packed that evening with two noisy family parties; the tables have been pushed together into long rows laden with oil lamps, glasses and bottles, ashtrays, dishes of olives and pickled octopus. A little boy is pushing a plastic car between the plates; a baby's bashing the tray of its high chair with a teaspoon. Aphrodite is clattering pans and crockery in the kitchen, shouting at Maria, and a ruddy round-faced musician is rattling out traditional reels on a kind of lute in the corner.

Sylvia sits at her table-for-one nursing a soda water and pretending to study her book of Greek grammar. She's feeling hungry and forlorn. She's ordered *briam* – a vegetable stew with potatoes and garlic – but after plonking down her drink and a basket of bread, Maria seems to have forgotten about her.

She imagines people are talking about her, the English woman who's bought *to spiti tiss Kokonas*, the woman with no children. The musician keeps sashaying over to her table and a litre jug of red wine has appeared – a gift, apparently, from the tall man with beetling eyebrows at the head of one of the tables – delivered by one of the old men who seem to live here. She looks up, flustered, and smiles her thanks. The tall man nods cheerily and raises his glass to her, and all the heads in the taverna swivel in her direction.

To cover her confusion, she takes out her mobile and keys in Bennet's number.

'What on earth's that racket?'

'Half the village is crammed into the taverna and I'm playing wallflower in the corner.'

'Poor poodle. How's it going?'

'Well, I think. I've hired that English builder guy on an hourly rate to help me sort out the cottage. He's a bit weird, but seems to know what he's doing.'

'What kind of weird?'

'Sort of hippy leftie traveller.'

'Dog on a string, animal lib?'

'More martial arts vegetarian, though he was fine with the salami at lunch. He's very disapproving of the new house, though. He thinks we should renovate the hovel instead.'

'Bloody cheek. Trying to undermine our imperialist enterprise.'

'How are you? How's the football?'

'Lazio are crap as usual. Del Piero's as flaky as ever. Your mum rang this morning to give me an earwigging about abandoning you in a foreign country with, and I quote, "antediluvian plumbing".'

'Tell her I spent most of today cleaning the loo.'

'I didn't know we had a loo.'

'Neither did I, but you could eat your dinner off it now.'

'I'd rather not, if you don't mind. I've got a date with a Meat Feast Pizza and a vintage *Columbo* video.'

'I miss you.'

'Me too, Boo Boo.'

'I just wanted to say hello.'

'Hello, Boo Boo.'

'Hello, Mr Smarter-than-the-Average Bear.'

Next day she's up at the cottage before nine, parking under the walnut tree, walking down what is already a familiar path. Everything is just as they left it yesterday afternoon: the freezer and TV by the gate, waiting to be taken away; the mattresses propped in a fat wigwam in the garden, waiting to be burned.

She unlocks the toilet and looks inside. Apart from the gecko on the wall, and a new leggy spider in one corner, it's as spruce as it was the day before. Martin's put up a little shelf for the Vim and toilet paper. *I could paint the shelf red*, she thinks suddenly. *Or sugar-pink to match the mirror.* She giggles, imagining it. *And the door, too. I could have a Barbie loo.*

When she opens the doors and shutters of the cottage this time, it feels different. More welcoming; less musty. There's space to move, to look around. She feels like Goldilocks at the cottage of the Three Bears. Yesterday everything was too big or too small. Now it feels the right size.

She starts by clearing out the stable, sweeping the soiled straw into a heap, then ferrying it over to the mattress wigwam in the tin bath.

I'll start a compost heap, she thinks and starts to prowl around for a suitable site. She finds one behind the old chicken house, where a flush of green weeds shows where someone in the past has been piling up chicken manure. Without thinking, she unbolts the rickety door to the chicken house and reaches inside. There's an old pitchfork there, as she knew there would be. She brings it out and looks at it. The handle's been cut down to a woman's height. The grey wood is smooth and brown in two places, where a woman's hands would grasp it.

By eleven the stable is cleared and swept and the old stone sink scoured. On the terrace outside is a wooden saddle, a tangle of bridles and a big empty Calor gas container. Sylvia stands in the doorway and surveys the empty room with a sigh of satisfaction.

Under all the goat shit and straw, the floor's tiled in a checker-board pattern of white and terracotta. And there are two little turquoise cupboards recessed into the wall either side of a greasy black stain, where some kind of cooker must have stood. Above the sink is a length of turquoise wood with hooks for utensils;

beneath it a shelf behind a scrap of curtain on a length of rusty wire.

She walks around the little room, guessing, from scuffs on the walls and floor, how the kitchen must have been arranged. A small table and two chairs; some kind of cupboard; and something large and square hanging on two big nails on the wall. There's a circular mark in the corner behind the door which she puzzles over for a while, then remembers the big terracotta pot in the other room. The old woman must have stored her water there before the tap was fitted.

Feeling like a detective, she goes into the next room and begins dismantling the towers of old furniture, trying to identify the pieces that might have inhabited the old kitchen. Soon they're all back in place, including a set of carved shelves which fit exactly over the odd square outline on the wall, and a little enamel gas hob perched on the cupboard beneath the greasy black stain.

A growling in her stomach makes her glance at her watch. Two thirty. And she's due to meet the architect at three. Ripping off her overalls and grabbing her car keys, she quickly closes up the house and drives down the hill.

Apostolos Broudakis is a small brisk man with a big nose and bulging Filofax. He has two mobile phones, which both ring within minutes of his arrival – they've arranged to meet at the taverna – and a portfolio of photographs and ground plans which he quickly spreads across three tables as though dealing from a pack of giant cards.

Sylvia sips sweet Greek coffee and tries to concentrate. Her stomach's still grumbling and her hair's damp from the shower, but she's put on lipstick and a black linen dress.

Broudakis visited the building plot last week to measure up, he tells her, and has some ideas about what they can do. Lighting up a Marlborough, he starts pointing out features on the houses depicted in the various plans.

He seems to favour wide arches and open-plan living areas;

enclosed patios with steps up to tiled roof terraces. It's all much more tasteful and individual than she'd expected: minimalist and Turkish-looking. Just the sort of thing they'd had in mind, in fact.

'How much for something like this,' she says, picking out a sturdy three-bedroom house with a vaulted fireplace in the living room. Looking out of the taverna window, she tries to imagine it on the hill opposite: white and pristine, framed by froths of jasmine and bougainvillaea.

The faded turquoise shutters of the old cottage stare back at her; the mattress wigwam to one side; the glint of white freezer by the gate.

'Of course it depends on the budget,' Broudakis is saying. 'Tiles can be ten or ten hundred euros per metre. Bathroom suites, fitted kitchens, the same.' He slaps a pile of coloured brochures on the table, scattering ash.

Sylvia picks up a bathroom catalogue and opens it, at random, on an oval wet room with green mosaic tiling and twin aqua glass basins with stainless-steel fittings.

'Yes! This is the one for me!' Aphrodite snatches the catalogue away and displays it to two old men playing backgammon over a glass of raki by the door. They ogle it, turning the pages in hushed amazement. Sunken baths and jacuzzis; glass bricks and slate flooring. Sylvia can almost hear the speculations later, about the expensive bathroom the English woman is building.

'I thought we could turn the old house into a garage and storeroom,' says Broudakis, tapping ash and exhaling blue smoke. He unfolds a ground plan of the cottage in front of her, with the existing walls shown in faint dotted lines and the new layout superimposed in darker ink. 'Create a driveway to the patio and knock through the door and window openings here —'

'You can't do that,' she blurts out without thinking.

'I'm sorry?'

'That's the kitchen,' she explains. 'You can't turn it into a garage.'

'But there will be a kitchen in the new house,' he says, obviously confused.

'I'm sorry.' She feels flustered. 'I meant I was going to turn it into a darkroom. For developing photographs,' she explains.

'OK,' he shrugs mildly. 'If that is what you want. We can use the other room as a garage. See it is bigger, so perhaps that would be better. Or maybe you could put your black-room here, in the third room.'

'What third room?'

She looks at where his finger's pointing on the plan. At a narrow room opening off the room with the sleeping platform. And remembers the shuttered window hidden beneath the big fig tree at the side of the house. And the door she assumed led to a cupboard. The eyes she thought she'd seen through the hole in the door, the sense of being looked at, the eerie squeaking.

As soon as he's gone, she's off up the hill in her overalls, hauling sacks of cement from the recess in front of the mysterious turquoise door. The hole's there, just as she remembers, and she keeps thinking she can hear a kind of scuffling on the other side. But every time she stops dragging sacks and stacking paint tins it's silent.

When she's cleared a path she tries the handle, but the door's locked. Sighing with frustration, she begins casting around for a key. But there's nothing: not on the top of the door frame or on the floor; not under the apron and cardigan she finds hanging on the wall beside the door. Not in the apron pocket, with the box of matches and candle end, and the knotted plastic bag of corn the old woman must have scattered to entice the chickens in at the end of the day.

Taking out her secateurs she goes round to the side of the house, where she begins cutting away the branches of the fig tree covering the window. When she's cleared a space, she tries the shutters. But it's hopeless: they're shut tight, fastened snugly on the inside.

She cuts back more branches, to clear a route around the side of the house, and discovers the shower, just as Martin described it, completely concealed from view behind the lean-to toilet: a sloping square of concrete beneath a heavy-duty iron shower head, with a row of hooks on the wall for clothes and towels. There's a plastic soap dish in a little alcove in the wall, another candle end and a piece of pumice stone. But no key.

Sighing, she wanders back round to the front of the house and sits down at the kitchen table. With the door open, she can see right into the taverna, to the table where she'd sat earlier looking up at the house. For a moment she fancies she can see herself sitting there: leafing through bathroom catalogues in her black linen dress, discussing what kind of house could be built with the €200,000 mortgage Bennet's arranged with his investment broker.

And the thought strikes her that right now this place belongs to her alone. The house, the land, have been bought with her money. But as soon as they start building the new house with Bennet's money, it will belong to him too.

She lets the thought settle into her mind and tastes its unfamiliar flavour – then jumps up guiltily as she hears footsteps.

'*Kalispera*!' Martin knocks briefly on the open door and walks into the room. 'Hey, this is amazing,' he says, looking round.

'Welcome to my Greek heritage site.'

'These old tiles are beautiful.' He kneels and scrapes at them with a fingernail. 'There's some stuff I can get for you, if you like. To get the dirt off. They'll come up brilliantly.'

He's in his work clothes and his hair's dusty. There's sawdust on the back of his shirt and his arms are splashed with mortar. 'I've brought the trailer for the freezer,' he says. 'There's a hole we can use at a site in Kokkino Horio.'

'Are you any good at breaking and entering?' she asks.

'What?' He looks startled as if to say, *How did you find out?*

'I need a door opening and I don't have a key,' she explains.

'To the other room, you mean?'

'Am I the only one who didn't realize there was a third room?'

'It's because you're a woman,' he says.

'Excuse me?'

'The female brain can't work in three dimensions. I've seen it over and over with clients. If there's a turn in the stairs they get confused in their own houses. Can't work out where the down-pipe will come out or which bedroom's over the sitting room.'

'Can you open it or not?' It comes out more testily than she intends.

'Have you looked for the key?'

'I checked all round the door, but there's no sign.'

'I mean, have you really looked for it?'

'Well, no. I haven't gone through all the old cardboard boxes and yoghurt pots, if that's what you mean.'

'Try thinking where the old woman would have left it. That's what I always do if I want to get into a house. Close my eyes and imagine that person locking the door.'

'You're mad.'

'Go on,' he insists. 'Close your eyes and feel your feet on the floor where her feet were.'

She stares at him.

'Go on,' he says again. 'Have a go. What harm can it do?'

Feeling self-conscious, she closes her eyes. *Why am I doing this?* she thinks. She tries to picture the door and the apron hanging next to it. She tries to think of the old woman tying the apron around her waist.

'It's no good,' she says. 'I can't see the door at all. I keep thinking of that old axe under the platform.'

He's grinning at her. 'Go on, then.'

'What do you mean?'

'Obviously that's where the key is.'

And it is: hanging on a hook hidden under the ladder. Without looking, she puts her hand on it straight away.

She takes it out and stares at it, feeling slightly giddy. She hasn't eaten since breakfast, she remembers, fitting it into the keyhole.

She's expecting some resistance as she pushes the door open: more straw, perhaps, more piles of rubbish. But the door swings open cleanly. Inside it's womb-dark and warm; just razors of light at the joints of the shutters. She moves towards the window to let in some light, and the room suddenly springs alive with movement as dark shapes explode in front of her, and brush hard against her, knocking her off-balance, then whisk out through the open door.

She comes to to find Martin kneeling over her with the puppy towel in his hand. His strange eyes are dark with concern. There's a fresh graze on his forehead, she notices, and a smudge of dust on his cheek. She feels swimmy and weird.

'I think you fainted,' he says. He hands her the towel. 'I wet this, but I'm not really sure what to do with it.' An awkward smile.

'I forgot to have lunch,' she says, struggling to sit up. 'What were those things?'

'Cats,' he says, getting up to open the windows. 'A mother and two young ones, scared shitless. Flew out of here like bats out of hell.'

He pulls open the shutters and light floods in like an embrace, quivering with leafy shadows.

'Dear God,' she breathes, gazing around. 'It's like some kind of chapel in here.'

The far end of the narrow room is taken up by an enormous ornate sideboard, covered with all manner of objects: vases and bowls, dolls, plates, bottles of oil, an oil lamp and candlesticks, framed photographs of children. Above it, suspended from big hooks on the ceiling, are bunches of what look like dried herbs. On the walls, running around the room like the Stations of the Cross, are more photographs of children.

There's a low bed against the wall, with a stool beside it. Another stone sink, like the one in the kitchen, on the opposite wall, with a tin bath and a pink plastic potty beneath it. A flattened fur-felted pillow shows where the cats have been nesting. Apart from that the place seems untouched.

'Do you think this was her bedroom?' Sylvia whispers, awed by the odd solemnity of the little room. The children's eyes seem to follow her, as she scrambles to her feet. Smiling, serious, defiant.

'I don't know.' Martin's whispering too. 'It looks more like some kind of shrine.'

The photographs have been hand-tinted. The effect is other-worldly, as though ghosts were looking down from the walls.

Sylvia goes over to the sideboard and opens one of the cup-board doors. Inside it's more of the same: jars and bottles; bunches of crumbling vegetation; spoons, dolls, little metal cars, packs of candles, a tin of sweets.

'Aphrodite said there were photos here,' she says quietly, moving to the faces on the walls. 'Here, look. This has to be her.'

The girl in the photo is decked out in formal frills. A yellow ribbon droops over her forehead. She's grinning at the camera, but she looks mutinous, as though she'll leap up and run out of the room at any moment. Sylvia takes down the photo and shows it to Martin.

'I think you should put it back,' he says. There's something odd about his voice, an urgency.

'She said she wanted it,' Sylvia objects.

'Please, leave it.' His eyes are pleading. 'You don't know why these things are set out like this.'

'What do you mean?' She's beginning to find this irritating, his constant interference with what she wants to do.

'You can't just come into a place like this and rearrange things.'

'Why not?' She props the photo of Aphrodite against the wall and starts taking down the other photos. How dare he tell her what she can and can't do with her house? 'Anyway I'm not rearranging things.' She raises her voice deliberately. 'I'm clearing them out so I can turn the place into a darkroom.'

She surveys the space again. 'In fact it's perfect. Much easier to lightproof than the stable, and a sink for mixing the solutions. And I can hang the print lines from the hooks above the sideboard.'

She reaches up to tug one of the herb bunches down, but he grabs her wrist.

'Stop it,' he says.

She tries to twist out of his grip, but he's far too strong. She glares up at him. He's very close. She can smell his sweat; the doggy smell of his dusty hair.

'Please,' he says. 'Listen to me first.'

'Oh, all right,' she says crossly, too embarrassed to keep resisting. 'But this had better be good.'

'Look, I know this is going to seem strange to someone like you. But you can't just pay out X-thousand euros and think you own a place. Houses can't change hands just like that. They're not just stones and mortar. They're history, memory. Something very important went on in this room. Don't pretend you can't feel it.'

'So what am I supposed to do? Lock it up like Tutankhamen's tomb?'

'Maybe,' he says stubbornly. 'If that's what it takes.'

'If that's what *what* takes? This is ridiculous.'

'If that's what it takes to appease the hungry ghosts.'

'I can't believe we're having this conversation.' She's laughing now, exasperated. 'And what do you mean, "someone like me"?'

'Oh, *reasonable* people,' he says scathingly. 'People who believe in causality. People with a proper education. People who think there's an explanation for everything. That everything has to fit into the knowledge we have – when we know so bloody fucking *little* about the world.'

He's almost shouting. His face is blazing with anger.

'People who think telepathy's a trick and that it's impossible to move objects with the mind. People who think there's no such thing as ghosts. I mean, look at that sideboard? The size of it. How did a great thing like that get into a tiny room like this?

Check out the doorway. There's no way it could have got in through there.'

'So what's your explanation?' she says, feeling the hairs bristle slightly at the nape of her neck.

'That's what I mean. There's no obvious explanation. But that doesn't mean it didn't happen. Sometimes you just have to let something be unexplained.'

'So you think it arrived there by telekinesis.'

He sighs in irritation. 'You don't get it, do you? I'm saying I don't know. I'm saying that maybe sometimes it's *good* not to know. I'm saying we have to recognize the limits of our understanding.'

'I reckon it was an Ikea flatpack,' she says, trying to make him smile. Then, when he doesn't: 'So, what are these hungry ghost things then?' she asks.

'Do you really want to know?' He's defensive now; quieter. The wary curtain's back over his face. She nods and he goes on: 'They're desperate sad spirit entities, stranded between dimensions. The Buddhists depict them with stick limbs and starving bloated bodies, like famine victims. And tiny sucking mouths. They're always hungry, always thirsty, because they didn't get what they needed when they were alive. In Tibet when people set the table, they always put out a bowl of food for the hungry ghosts.'

He's wandering around the room as he speaks, staring at the photographs.

'The idea is that every house contains the spirits of the people who once lived there. And that we have to acknowledge them, even if we never knew them. Because we are standing on their shoulders.'

'Right,' she says. 'I see.'

She stands in front of a photograph of a gurgling baby clutching a huge fluffy horse, and aches with the urge to hold its dimpled sweet weight in her arms.

'I'm unexplained,' she says quietly, not looking at him. 'I mean, my infertility. The reason I can't have a baby.'

Chapter 13

The Front-Door Key

Soon after his eleventh birthday Martin started wondering how long they had to stay in hiding. The threat of being taken away seemed more and more remote. Also he was beginning to think it might be quite exciting to be taken away.

Some days he longed to be like other children. Other days he couldn't imagine ever living in their world. The gap between them seemed to widen every day. The boys his age carried heavy bags now and wore ties. The girls did funny things with their hair. He couldn't imagine how he'd speak to them.

He thought of Sacha, Soron and Pierre in Matala and tried to remember what they talked about. The only people he spoke to were the women on the checkouts at Tesco, the Tweedy and Lacy Librarians and the young assistant at the aquarium shop on Magdalen Road.

He talked to the Dog People, too, sometimes, even though he wasn't supposed to. There were two new Dog People that year: the Pug Woman who carried a walking stick she never used; and the beaky grey man with the Bedlington terrier. When he told his mother about Bedlington Man, she said he'd discovered a new kind of ancient human.

They got a book out of the library about evolution, with pictures of hairy men with dangly arms and overhanging brows. Martin stared at the pictures for ages: Cro-Magnon, Australopithecus, Neanderthal. It said that humans were descended from monkeys and lemurs in Africa. It said that people were more closely related to chimpanzees than dogs were to foxes. The knowledge made him feel funny, as though he was walking down an escalator that was going up, passing cavemen and gorillas; mandrills; capuchins. He looked at his hand and imagined it holding a flint tool, scraping flesh from the hide of a woolly mammoth.

The book had another series of pictures showing a little doggy creature turning into a horse, with its legs and neck growing and its toes
disappearing. And another set of pictures showing the embryos of
different animals developing: a dog, a chicken, a fish, a human.

He stared at these pictures for ages too; because at the early stages
they all looked exactly the same. 'Ontogeny repeats phylogeny,' the
book said. He liked the sound of the phrase and repeated it over and
over. He looked the words up in the dictionary, but he still wasn't
sure he understood what they meant. Something about every creature
going through the whole evolution of its species before becoming an
adult.

The Pug Woman offered him a toffee one day and he walked all the
way to the river with her while she told him about her husband, who
was in hospital with his knees, and her son who had an ostrich farm in
South Africa.

Martin liked the idea of an ostrich farm. He thought it might be
nice to live in South Africa. He thought there might be lemurs and
chimpanzees there. He wondered how you went from being an invisible
boy in Oxford to being a man with an ostrich farm in South Africa.

There was never a good time to ask about his father. When his mother
was depressed he was afraid asking would make her worse. When she
was happy he was worried about making her depressed again.

But there had been long periods recently – four, five months at a
time – when his mother had been free of her Bad Sads. 'I'm curing
myself,' she told him. 'So I'll be ready for the next Great Flood.'

She'd planted herbs in a sunny corner of the garden: sage, basil and
lemon balm; wild oats and wood betony; St John's wort, valerian,
hypericum. Some she'd bought from the garden shop on Windmill
Road; others they'd had to search for in Iffley Fields. She brewed them
into fragrant green teas that she drank all through the day now. She
called them Grasshopper Tea to distinguish them from the Factory Tea
(strong with two sugars) that she used to drink. She said that the
Grasshopper Tea 'stabilized the neurotransmitters' in her brain.

She'd been ordering brain books on interlibrary loan and they'd studied them together. Martin now knew exactly what it looked like inside her head: a pink cloud inflated by something called a neural tube; except he knew the brain was actually more rubbery and quite solid, crackling with synapse sparks. When he pictured it 'unstabilized', he saw it as a fireworks display inside her skull, with long dark pauses and intermittent explosions.

She said the sparking was from a kind of energy called chi, that sparks all round the body. She'd been going to a class at the Old Fire Station, where they were learning to fight in slow motion. She said the movements helped the chi move through the body properly; it was clogged and stuck in most people, she explained.

When she'd come back from the first class, she'd unearthed an old manual lawnmower from the shed and cleared a bumpy patch where the lawn used to be. Then she sculpted the air every morning in bare feet and pyjamas, carving out an invisible ball with her arms and moving it gracefully around the small green arena.

Everything in the universe was space and energy, she said, with hardly any matter at all. If you had a powerful enough microscope, you'd see that even something as hard as a stone was mostly empty space: tiny blips of energy whizzing around minute particles, with great chasms of nothing in between. 'Like the stars and planets, only in miniature,' she said.

'If you put your finger under that microscope,' she told him, 'it would look exactly the same as that yellowy-grey stone you brought back from the gravel pit. Millions of teeny-weeny solar systems with moons and comets looping around them.'

Martin was not convinced. 'So why do they look so different?'

'Because of the way all the bits are joined together.'

They were sitting in the middle of the bumpy patch, eating bananas. She was supping from the Peasant Cup and he had chocolate Nesquik in the Oxfam glass with the red and yellow circles on.

'Do you remember us reading about the different forms of carbon last year? How the lead in a pencil and diamonds and coal are all made of the same substance, even though they look completely different? It's the same with me and this mug, or you and the grass.'

Or a boy and a horse, Martin thought. If he looked hard enough he'd find they were exactly the same.

His mother told him that Hindus believed that everything that died was reborn in a different body. So a lizard could come back as a goat; a cat could come back as a woman. What you came back as depended on how good you were in your last life. So a really good bat might come back as a man. But a lazy woman might be reborn as a slug.

'I think I was a horse,' he said. 'Like you.'

His mother laughed. 'Ah, but were we good horses or bad ones?'

'Good ones.' Martin was sure about this.

'I've always wondered why it's considered an advance to be reborn as a human being,' she said. 'I think being a dolphin might be much more fun than being the Lacy Librarian.'

'What do you come back as if you're a good human?'

'If you're good enough they say you don't come back at all. You become a part of God.'

'What if you don't want to be part of God?' Martin thought he'd rather go back to being a horse.

'Maybe you have to do something really bad as a human.'

None of the neighbours could see them when they were in the garden. There were trees and bushes and climbers all round. The shed was a mass of jasmine and bindweed. Clematis had reached the roof of the house and was twining out along the telephone wires. The damson and walnut trees wept swathes of ivy and honeysuckle. Bramble and raspberry vines shot prickly arches up over the shaggy shrubs in the borders.

Martin had created a green tunnel between the bumpy patch and the French doors. The doors were open all the time now, ever since a robin had built a nest on the bookcase the previous year. The sitting room was part of the garden now. There were snails on the skirting boards and heaps of dead leaves in the corners. The carpet was covered with silver slime trails and mice had burrowed into the back of the sofa. That spring the room had been invaded by tiny frogs on their annual migration from the river.

His mother called it the Jungle Room. 'It's Gaia reasserting herself,' she said. Martin liked the idea of the earth being a woman god with the power to heal her own wounds.

'Little buggers behave as if the town doesn't exist,' his mother complained as she crawled around on the damp carpet with him, catching the frogs and putting them in the washing-up bowl. 'They swarm through here every year and get splattered on the Cowley Road. I don't know where they think they're going.'

'Maybe there was a swamp once where Tesco is,' said Martin.

He liked to imagine how Argyle Street used to look millions of years ago: covered with conifers and giant ferns, and animals making their way down to the river to drink. He pictured blue-tongued bears shambling through the undergrowth; wolves weaving through the trees. And before them, the dinosaurs: hopping bird ones and great munching buffalo ones.

There was moss on the window sill in the bathroom and fingers of ivy edging through cracks in the window frame. There were toadstools growing on the hearthrug in the Jungle Room. The house was becoming more and more like the woods.

'Maybe the frogs are going shopping,' he said, keeping a straight face. 'I'm always finding trolleys in the river.'

The Jungle Room was really Martin's room now. It had become his during the Great Flood, when his mother had taken to her bed for three weeks. She was still allowed in, but she didn't come unless she was invited: when he'd got a new animal to show her, or when he wanted help with something, like catching all the frogs.

Martin thought it was wrong to keep pets. He hated the way the Dog People's dogs followed their owners with their eyes all the time, and chased sticks and came when they were called. He'd read that in prehistoric times wild dogs ran in packs beside human hunters, and shared the kill. He'd seen the foxes patrolling the woods: lean and alert. He thought there was something wrong with an animal that sat when it was told to.

There was a young rabbit in a box in the Jungle Room that he'd saved from one of the cats. The cat hadn't been hungry; it was just gnawing on the rabbit's ears and batting its head to make it move. All the pet cats were like that: bored and cruel. With ten Cat Women in one street, birds and mice didn't stand a chance.

There had been a point, about two years before, when getting a man in to mend things had stopped being a possibility. The house had just become too different from ordinary houses.

The magazines on the staircase had soaked through during the Great Flood and had welded themselves together like bricks. The hall was crammed with bits of wet carpet from the landing and two broken chairs the binmen wouldn't take away. There were paint tins in the pantry and a lawnmower in the downstairs loo. There was a bird's nest in the sitting room and every window was covered with clematis and ivy.

'I suppose we could clear things up a bit,' his mother said doubtfully one day. 'Then maybe I could call someone in to do the roof. Not properly. Just patch it up where that big hole is.' She bundled up her hair in the purple scarf, made herself a mug of Factory Tea 'to fire me up', and strode into the front hall.

'We can start by piling all this rubbish up in the front garden,' she said. 'Behind the hedge so no one will complain.'

She reached the key down from its hook and put it in the lock, but it wouldn't turn. She jiggled it a bit and tried again. Then took it out and looked at it, then rubbed it with her finger, but it still wouldn't turn. She fetched some cooking oil from the kitchen and spooned a little into the keyhole. She went out through the kitchen door, and down through the long garden to the gate at the bottom, and out along the footpath to the end of the terrace and up the passage and back along Argyle Street and tried to unlock the door from the outside. But it still wouldn't budge.

Standing in the hall, Martin could hear her pummelling the door and shoving at it with her shoulder. She came back along the street, and down the passage and along the fences at the bottoms of the gardens and in through the kitchen door and through to the hall and pummelled and shoved from the inside too.

Then she kicked the door and threw the key at it. Then she sat down at the bottom of the stairs and burst into tears.

Martin sat down cross-legged on a patch of floor at her feet and waited. It could go either way, he thought. Either she'd go droopy and sad and go to bed, or she'd tug him to his feet and start laughing.

He squeezed his eyes tight and waited.

'Come on,' she said at last, reaching for his hand. 'Let's go and buy a hammer and some roofing felt. We'll try to patch the damn roof ourselves.'

When the front door wouldn't unlock it felt like a link with the normal world was severed. They couldn't go straight out into Argyle Street any more, on to the beige pavement, beside the flat blue-grey road where the cars were parked. They had to be skulkers, whether they liked it or not, slipping out through the overgrown garden where no one could see them. Although the electricity still worked and the plumbing, and his mother paid all their bills on time, they'd slipped out of society completely.

Chapter 14

Sylvia is swimming from the rocks in the early morning. The sun is just rising and the sea is still, heavy as oil, rainbow-skinned. She slips through it without splashing, like a seal, and rolls on to her back to float, letting the living water fill her ears and filter through to her skull: cold and calm.

High above her specks of swifts are diving silently for insects through skids of cirrus. She feels like the first woman at the dawn of the world.

Turning back on her stomach to scythe through the flat water, her ears fill again with the sounds of the morning: a round of cocks crowing; the clonk of goat bells; the wheeps of little finches on the thorn bushes bristling the cliff face.

There's a sudden clamour of bells from the little white church, and she looks up at the graveyard at the top of the cliff, at the gravestones honey-pink in the rising sun. And imagines a jostle of ghostly old faces staring down at her: Kokona, Aphrodite's mother, all the old people from the village. And wonders how it would feel to know, all your life, the place where you would be buried; how that would root you and pull you home, like a compass needle swinging towards north.

Climbing the path later, she wanders among the graves: all beautifully tended, with white pebbles, fresh flowers, little photos in frames. So unlike English graveyards with their forgotten bones and sad leaning stones. She looks down at the sea, caressing the shore like a satin sheet, and pictures herself floating there minutes earlier: face upturned, hair sleeked to her head, limbs a drifting milky star.

Then she pictures that body in the ground; the slow disintegration of cells as the myriad microscopic creatures of air and soil consume it. She's seen necrotized tissue under the microscope, and knows how the cell membranes fragment, how the contents liquefy and seep out.

When she lost her faith as a teenager, it was not a knee-jerk rebellion against the Irish priest's hectoring sermons at their local church, nor the Pope's inane stand on contraception: it was after her grandfather's cremation, when her mother collected the ashes. Then she knew, with a jolt of dismay, that he had really gone. That there was no soul or ghost, no spirit smoke floating above the urn; just a little heap of ash and bone fragments, like the scrapings when a bonfire's burned down, the tippings from an ashtray.

Vasilios is staking runner-bean seedlings when she reaches the taverna. The stakes he's using are gnarled and brown, years old; the bones of felled saplings.

'The flowers will be red,' he says quietly. 'Soon everything will be red.'

Is he talking to her? It's hard to tell.

'It's the red season,' he continues in his measured scholarly voice. 'There is blood. There is death. There is rising from the dead.'

'Oh, you mean Easter!' It's strange to hear Oxbridge English issuing from a man with earth-stained hands and an unravelling straw hat.

'There will be blood on all the eggs,' he says, selecting another stake and angling it into the earth. 'And sweet bread. Body and blood. Amen.' He crosses himself and reaches for another stake.

'Vasilios was talking to me in English just now,' she tells Aphrodite at breakfast. 'I thought you said he never spoke to people.'

'Oh, he can speak when he wants to,' she says crossly, polishing glasses with a scowl. 'He can speak six different languages. He can read Sanskrit and Urdu. But he doesn't listen any more. You ask him a question and he ignores. His words are like the weather. They happen by themselves.'

'He was talking about red eggs.'

'Yes, it is Easter soon. *Pascha*. We will be dyeing the eggs and making *koulourakia*, *kalitsounia*. And the children will be carol-singing.' She sets a basket of fruit on the table, and a small knife; a dish of creamy yoghurt. 'That is what you call this door-to-door begging for sweets, yes? You will hear it, the week before Easter, the song of Lazaros, about that dead boy Jesus brought back to life.'

Sylvia picks up a nectarine and cuts around it, slicing through to the stone and pulling the two halves apart. She knows this story; the horror at the heart of it. That the body was already in the tomb; had already, after three days in the heat, begun to putrefy.

'You must tell your husband to come,' Aphrodite is saying. 'This is the best time in *Kriti*. When the hills are green and you can eat *gigantes* straight from the pods. We have lambs and baby chickens. The tourists always come in the dry season, when the wild flowers are finished and we are just hosing the streets for the dust.'

Sylvia slices sweet yellow fruit into white curds and thinks about red eggs. Then realizes with a sudden pang of – What? Horror? Guilt? – that her fertility thermometer is still where she put it when she unpacked last week, in a little drawer with her mosquito repellent and suntan lotion; that she hasn't taken her temperature once since she arrived; that she has no idea when she might be ovulating.

She decides to walk up to the cottage, instead of driving, and arrives out of breath, with burning calves and a handful of flowers the disgusting old goat man gave her as she passed. She arranges them in a small terracotta jug she'd discovered in one of the kitchen cupboards and sets it on the kitchen table.

She's brought her camera with her, and four rolls of black-and-white film. She wants to photograph her reconstruction of Kokona's old kitchen, and the strange displays of images and objects in the 'secret room', as she finds herself calling it. As she frames each shot, it's as though the rooms have been embedded in wax; and she's slicing through them, floating off slivers of time, and fixing them forever.

She concentrates steadily, as though this is a job of work she has been assigned: opening and closing doors and shutters to alter the subtleties of the light and experimenting with lenses; taking close-ups of individual objects on the big sideboard and flash exposures of the contents of cupboards and drawers, like a crime-scene investigator. Afterwards she stands at the kitchen window to capture views of the village below; then walks down to the building plot to frame the house itself.

By the time she's wound off the last roll of film, it feels as though the cottage has imprinted itself on her brain: a face she'd recognize from any angle. She stands in the middle of the building plot, with four finished rolls in her pocket and the last frame still in her mind: of the cottage with its shutters and doors wide open, and the shaggy old fig tree nodding to one side, the fresh vine tendrils dangling down over the patio. And she realizes something that's been gradually dawning for days now: that this is the house she wants to live in. Not the chic new building with its tasteful arches and bespoke bathrooms, but this scarred old cottage, with its memories and history. This is the place where she wants to root herself.

Martin arrives to find her sorting furniture on the patio.

'Are these mendable?' she asks abruptly, indicating two splayed wooden chairs with frayed rush seats.

'Everything's mendable, if you're prepared to go far enough,' he says with a grin, upending one of them and testing the struts. 'My van's been patched up so many times there's almost nothing of the original van left. Just the steering wheel and a bit of the chassis. And the cooker inside.'

He's looking tired; there's a fresh cut on the back of his hand and his forearms are peppered with white paint.

'Where have you been working today?' she asks.

'We're on a new job, in Drapanos. Load of dinky little rabbit hutches for English people.' His face is brown; his forehead smooth and unlined. She finds herself wondering how old he is.

'Did you tell Aphrodite you were working for me?' she asks. 'I got the distinct impression she was pissed off about it.'

He seems taken aback. 'Is there something she needs doing?'

'No, it's not that.' She looks at him through her lashes. 'I thought maybe she wasn't keen on you working for another woman.'

'Like we were having sex, you mean?' The strange-coloured eyes stare straight at her. 'And I was being unfaithful to her?'

Sylvia feels herself blushing. 'I wouldn't have put it quite like that.'

'Aphrodite knows there's nothing like that going on with me.'

'What do you mean?' Sylvia's furious with herself. What was she thinking of, trying to flirt with the builder? He must be at least ten years younger than she is.

'I never have sex with women I'm working for,' he says.

'I didn't mean—' she says hotly.

'Yes you did. But that's OK. I'm used to it.' He's pulling the chair apart, and placing the pieces in a neat row on the ground. 'That's why I'm celibate. It solves a lot of problems. No one can speculate about me, and I never have to turn people down.'

'God, you're arrogant.' It bursts out. He's behaving as though she's just propositioned him.

'Not arrogant, just practical.' He starts unwinding the old rattan from the seat of the chair. 'Clients used to fall in love with me all the time. Because I sorted things out for them, no questions asked. They didn't have to nag. I'd just turn up when I said I would and fix whatever it was. They'd forget they were paying me. All they'd focus on was how I fixed whatever it was that was bugging them.'

'You make them sound so shallow.'

'Do I?' He looks genuinely surprised. 'I was just trying to be straight with you. So you could relax.'

'So you used to have sex with all your clients?' Why does she find this so disturbing?

'Not all of them, no,' he says matter-of-factly. 'Just the ugly ones.'

'What?' Is he joking?

'Well obviously I didn't think they were ugly. I'd never make love with a deeply ugly woman. But I've never really liked having sex with pretty girls.' The rattan's off and he's holding up the bare frame of the seat. 'There's an old guy in Vrisses who does restringing. Do you want me to drop them off?'

'How much does he charge?'

'About ten, fifteen euros. But you won't get them back straight away. He can only work on the days his arthritis eases up.'

She's thinking about the ugly women he's slept with, imagining curtains drawn in the middle of the afternoon, and dowdy middle-aged women shyly shedding their Crimplene. And him naked on the bed propped up on one arm, appraising them with those unsettling eyes.

'If I give you the money, can you get the wood you need to repair the sleeping platform?' she says.

'What about the architect? I thought he wanted to turn the kitchen into a garage, and fill the bedroom with sunloungers and sit-on lawnmowers.'

'Who told you that?' Of course, Aphrodite and the two old men at the taverna. By now the whole village must know about their plans for the new house.

'Have you changed your mind, then?' He's standing with his legs apart and his arms loose at his sides, just looking at her.

'I haven't decided yet,' she says, not wanting to let him think he's persuaded her. 'Maybe we'll rent it out. It seems a shame to waste it, if it can be done up for as little as you said.'

'You're going to live here, aren't you?' Again, she has a sense of a curtain being pulled back from his smooth oval face, of a much younger man being revealed: alight, eager, unguarded.

'I've photographed the little room,' she goes on, ignoring him. 'So I've got a complete record of what it was like. I'm going to start clearing it out tomorrow.' She narrows her eyes and faces him, waiting for him to challenge her.

'Right, here's the deal,' he says, squaring up to her. 'I'll help you with the house if you let me decide how to clear the secret room.' He raises a hand as she starts to object. 'No, don't go all middle-class madam how-dare-you on me. This is a take-it-or-leave-it situation. Either we clear that room my way, or you find someone else to fix your platform for you.'

She glares at him. He stares her down.

'Deal?' He holds out a dusty brown hand and she looks at it for a long moment. It feels as though he's on the other side of a ravine she has to cross.

'Deal,' she says, putting her hand in his.

That evening she takes out the thermometer and lays it on the bedside table with her temperature chart, where she can reach for it first thing, as she did in Newcastle. Then she picks up her mobile and calls Bennet.

'How did it go with the architect?' he asks.

'Fine, I think. I've told him what we want and he's coming back to me with an outline proposal next week.'

'Make sure he includes the gold taps and jacuzzi.'

'I've asked him to quote for a gym and plunge pool too.'

'How's the argumentative artisan?'

'Ornery but controllable. He seems to know everyone on the island. He's getting some old guy to restring all the broken chairs and has found a hole where we can bury the freezer.'

'Great stuff. Talking of holes, when do you need your next squirt of spermatozoa?'

'You really know how to charm a girl.'

'My bags are packed, as the bishop said to the actress.'

'No sign of a temperature blip yet,' she lies, looking at the blank spaces on her temperature chart. 'But you know how travel messes up my cycle. How much notice do you need?'

'Twenty-four hours should do it. I've warned people I might have to dash off to sign papers for the house.'

It's easy to lie, she thinks, *when your conversation's full of jokes. Easy to skate over things*.

'It's Easter here the week after next. Weird isn't it? Nearly a month later than the UK.'

'That's the mañana culture for you.'

'*Avrio*'s the word you're after. Apparently so many lambs are roasted on Easter day, the whole island disappears under a pall of barbecue smoke.'

'I feel like a spot of rising from the dead myself.'

'Is that all you can think of?'

She smiles at the phone as she switches it off and sets it down next to the thermometer. She'll surprise him with the house, she decides. Get the platform fixed and the rooms cleaned in time for his visit. It will be easier to tell him if he's got something to look at; easier to see the house's potential.

She doesn't need to swim every morning – the water's not cold enough to have the effect she was getting in England – but she likes the ritual of rising with the sun and being part of the village as it eases itself into the new day. She likes pushing her arms through the water. She likes shivering and rubbing herself dry. She likes the chafing feeling, the warm feeling, the numbness slowly receding.

She imagines herself tracking the seasons like this: seeing how the flowers wax and wane on the cliffside, how crops of fruit and vegetables ripen in their turn, how the sun moves across the horizon.

She greets the dour shopkeeper with a grin as she pays for two more packs of bin liners, then strides back up the hill, nodding briefly to the old goat man as she passes. She wants to clear everything out of the bedroom before Martin arrives, so he has space to get on with the platform.

Clouds mount up, threatening rain, as she works through the heaps in the middle room. Soon the mattress wigwam is inhabited by ripped blankets, old cardigans and bales of straw; and a row of black bin liners – crammed with rusty paint tins, plastic shoes, empty jam jars – is building up by the gate.

On the patio is a sparse collection of furniture: an iron bedstead, in three pieces, and a rickety wardrobe; a small bedside table and a three-legged stool; a second kitchen-type table and another empty Calor gas canister; three white plastic garden chairs and the large terracotta pot.

She drags the kitchen furniture out, too, then checks every item, brushing off spiders' webs and bits of straw, to see if it's serviceable. Apart from the splayed chairs and some loose joints on the wardrobe – plus a peppering of woodworm on everything – the haul is surprisingly sound.

I could sand it all down and paint it, she thinks. And as her mental list grows – sandpaper and paintbrushes, white spirit, paint stripper, wood filler – she finds herself getting excited. *If I can pay for everything with the money Auntie M. left me, then the house will be all mine*, she thinks.

Martin arrives late afternoon with a load of wood on a trailer attached to the back of the camper van: lengths of blonde new pine and a collection of smoke-blackened beams that look like fossilized tree trunks. As Sylvia runs to help him unload it, the first spots of rain begin to splat on to the patio. By the time they get to the beams they're both soaked and rain is running down their faces and into their mouths.

'These are really heavy,' he warns as she takes hold of the end of a beam with wet hands. 'I can ask Vasilios to come up if it's too much for you.'

'I'm fine,' she says, bracing to lift it. The wood's as dense as iron and her shoulder muscles are screaming, but she doesn't want to let him see. His middle-class-madam jibe still rankles.

'Are you sure?' Tendons tauten in his neck as he hefts his end with a grunt.

'I said, I'm fine,' she says through gritted teeth, shaking back her hair and trying not to slip in the mud.

By the time they've shifted all the beams into the bedroom, her legs are trembling and her face is red with exertion.

'If this was England we'd break for a cup of tea about now,' he pants, surveying the neat stacks of damp wood. Water's dripping off the end of his ponytail and he's licking the rain from his lips. Outside heavy drops are battering the young vine leaves and sluicing dust from the fig tree.

'This is great,' he comments, surveying the empty room. 'You'd make a good builder's mate.'

'Not too bright, but able to follow simple instructions?' she asks, wiping her face with the back of her hand.

'I was going to say: careful, systematic, not afraid of hard work.'

'Oh.' She blushes. Then, to cover her confusion: 'Thanks for getting the beams. Where did you find them?'

'Over in Vamos. Someone ordered a job lot for a trendy bar and these were left over.' His black tee shirt's plastered to his bony chest; she can see the small points of his nipples.

'You're soaking,' she says. The tang of new pine fills the room, combined with the older smoky scent of the beams. The rain is purring steadily outside, a grey curtain over the windows and doors, sealing them inside the little house.

She's aware suddenly of what she must look like: with her face red and her hair flat and dripping; her sodden overalls and squelchy trainers. She can feel sweat dripping down her back and between her breasts, smell its vinegar in her armpits. 'I should have brought something to change into,' she says. 'I didn't think.'

'There are dry clothes in the van if you want to borrow something. Why don't you test-drive the shower while I look out a shirt and some jeans?' She hesitates. 'Go on. You'll have to try it out sometime. I promise I won't peek.'

She showers in the rain, under the glowering sky, behind a green screen of rustling bamboo. The water runs away into a stone trench that leads to the base of the vine. The wet earth smells rich and brown as she reaches for the puppy towel. The row of hooks, beneath the overhang of the roof, is in exactly the right place for her clothes.

'Is that Martin's shirt?' Aphrodite asks when she gets back to the taverna.

'And his jeans,' Sylvia says, demonstrating the rolled-up legs. 'We got soaked in that rain, so he lent them to me.'

'Don't let him become involved with you.' Why does she seem so annoyed?

'According to him, he never gets involved with his clients,' Sylvia says.

'So he told you his no-sex story, did he?' Aphrodite snorts. 'That is just his method to keep women away from him. Until he decides it is the right time.'

The idea that he might have lied about it makes Sylvia feel hot; uncomfortable about wearing his clothes, about showering with him just around the corner. 'Are you saying he does have affairs?' she asks.

'I am saying sex is not the only way for a man and a woman to become involved.'

When she takes off his clothes, she wants to fling them away from her. Not because she's angry, but because she'd enjoyed wearing them. The threadbare cotton of the shirt was soft and smelt of sunshine. And she'd liked cinching the jeans tight around her waist with a length of rope; because she had a woman's shape and he had a man's.

She puts on her nightdress quickly and avoids standing in front

138

of the mirror in the bedroom: because he has slept here and breathed this air; he has looked at his reflection in the mirror.

First thing after breakfast next day she's in the corner shop buying sandpaper and a hard brush.

'For the furniture and doors,' she explains to Dimitri as he drops them dolefully into a plastic bag. He nods and shrugs, as if to say, *Why are you telling me this?* Then, as she turns to leave, he reaches down a flowery scarf from a stand on the wall behind him, and hands it to her.

'For the hair and the dust,' he grunts brusquely, waving her money away.

By the time Martin arrives in the afternoon, she's brushed down all the loose plaster in the kitchen and has begun sanding the bigger of the two tables.

'It's coming on,' he says approvingly. 'I'll get you some white-wash if you like. Emulsion just peels off old walls like this.'

He goes into the secret room and she hears him opening the drawers of the sideboard. 'Can you find something we can make a noise with?' he calls over his shoulder. 'Spoons and hammers. Oil cans, pan lids. That kind of thing.'

'What on earth for?' She follows him in and finds him easing open the knot in a plastic bag.

'I'm going to create a ritual,' he explains, picking up what looks like a tiny ornate metal urn. 'To greet the ghosts and let them know we're here.'

Before she can stop it, her laugh explodes like a sneeze. 'You're mad,' she says.

He faces her. 'Look, I'm not asking you to believe any of this,' he says. 'It's for me, right? So I feel OK about working here. I was going to do it just in the secret room, but I think it would be good to do the whole house. Just to be sure.'

'To say hello to the ghosties.' She can't help the teasing tone in her voice.

'You can leave me to it if it makes you feel uncomfortable.'

'Why should I feel uncomfortable?'

'Because you don't believe in ghosts.'

'How do you know what I believe in?'

'OK, then. Do you think it's possible that rocks, walls, caves can act like photographic film, and record what happens in a particular place?'

'No, of course not.'

'Why not?'

'Because such a process isn't possible.'

'How do you know it's not possible? Maybe you're just not able to see it. Or maybe you're not looking properly.'

'I know how photographs are made,' she says stubbornly.

'OK, how are they made?'

'By a series of chemical responses to different light intensities and wavelengths.'

'What if thought waves act like light waves?'

'There's no such thing as a thought wave. What people experience as thoughts are just the frontal lobes observing the operation of other parts of the brain.' She's rather proud of this explanation.

'And you'd know all about that, wouldn't you?' he says. 'Because you've sliced up a brain and seen exactly how it works.'

'Well, no. I only look at dead tissue in the lab. But MRI scanners can show what happens in a living brain.'

'So what you see depends on what instrument you're using to look with.'

'Oh, very clever, very quantum.' She sticks out her tongue at him. 'But the squeaking proves those cats were in the room before we unlocked the door.'

'How do you know it was those cats that were squeaking? It might have been some other cats. It might have been something else altogether.'

'Rats, for example,' she suggests, trying to make him smile.

'The first thing we do is make a noise in every room, to signal our presence,' he says, ignoring her. 'Then we sprinkle salt and burn incense to banish any bad memories, images, feelings.'

'Vibes,' she supplies with a giggle.

'That's what these burners are for,' he continues doggedly, opening one and putting a little cube of greyish powder inside. 'Then tomorrow, we'll leave gifts.'

'What kind of gifts?'

'Flowers, bread, oil. The kind of thing an old Greek woman might appreciate.'

'The kind of thing those rats might appreciate, you mean,' she quips.

'Obviously, it doesn't matter what happens to the food,' he says with exaggerated patience. 'It's the gesture that's important.' Then: 'Why do you always make a joke when you feel uncomfortable?'

'Why do you keep telling me I feel uncomfortable?' she parries.

'Stupid people get angry and clever people make jokes. But they're both doing the same thing: batting something away before it can touch them.'

She sighs. 'You can be very tiring to be with, do you know that?'

'Sorry,' he says with a grin. 'My social skills are a bit rudimentary. I missed out on some of the niceties when I was a kid.'

'So, how many of these ghostbusting percussion-type thingies do you need?'

To start with she feels self-conscious, stomping behind him with her saucepan and tin spoon, banging them and shouting *Yia sas!* and *Ela!* into the corners of each room. She feels wooden and stiff; her mouth won't open properly. And she keeps thinking of the sound bouncing down into the valley like a bright football, of everyone in the village looking up and wondering what's going on in Kokona's old house.

But after a while she gets caught up by the rhythm of the ritual and finds herself shouting as loudly as him, until she fancies she can see spirits flapping up out of the corners like pigeons and whirling around their heads.

When they stop, the house echoes for a long moment, then is

silent, like grey feathers drifting downwards. They stand breathless and elated, beaming at each other.

'Did you feel them?'

'No, of course not,' she says. Then, after a beat, seeing his face begin to close up: 'But I know what you mean.'

'I'll come back tomorrow evening to finish it off,' he says. 'Then you can start clearing out the secret room.'

Next day he arrives with an armful of flowers: marguerites, geraniums, wild chrysanthemum, roses. He tumbles them on to the kitchen table: a silent clatter of colour.

'Can you look out something to put them in?' he says. 'Jam jars will do, or coffee cups. Whatever you can find. And some plates or saucers for the bread and oil.'

As she washes the crockery in the sink, he begins dividing the flowers into separate bunches.

'The other day,' he says. 'You started telling me about your infertility.'

'I'm sure you don't really want to know.'

'No, really. I'm interested. But only if you're OK talking about it.'

'I just keep having miscarriages, that's all.' She dries three small retsina glasses and hands them to him. 'Are these big enough?' Then: 'Well, that's not quite true. To start with I couldn't conceive at all, so we started having IVF. That's where—'

'—they take the eggs out of the woman and the man has to wank in a room full of porno mags.'

She smiles. 'That's one way of putting it.'

'But it didn't work.' He starts stripping the lower leaves off the stems and arranging them in the glasses.

'No. Well, it did in a way. I mean, they were able to fertilize the eggs, and they developed lots of good embryos, but they couldn't get them to implant.' She thinks of herself stripping the leaves off the tulips back in February, of her tears dripping on to the table. 'Then I got pregnant naturally. Probably because they'd had to stimulate my ovaries so much to ripen all the eggs for IVF. Usually only one ripens at a time, so you have to be injected with hormones if they want to harvest more than one.'

'"Harvest"? Is that what they call it?'

'Yes, but it's done with a needle, so it's not like picking apples.' She wants to see him wince; she wants to impress him with what she's had to go through. 'Anyway, I miscarried that embryo at six weeks. Then a few months later I got pregnant again. That foetus lasted a bit longer, until the twelve-week scan.' She can hear her voice talking, as though she's part of a documentary on *Woman's Hour*. 'That was six months ago.'

'Why did they miscarry?'

'They don't know. They don't know why I didn't get pregnant earlier. They don't know why the IVF embryos wouldn't implant.'

'But what do you think?' He's stopped fiddling with the flowers and is staring intensely at her with an expression she can't fathom.

She shrugs. 'I think lots of things. I think my body's not as healthy as it could be. I think I've messed it up with the pill and the coil. I think I'm too old and my eggs aren't as viable any more. Getting pregnant is a whole chain of events; any one of them can go wrong. The egg, the sperm, the fallopian tubes, genetic abnormalities in the embryo, the balance of hormones, the condition of the womb. People who've had abortions sometimes miscarry because the neck of the womb doesn't close properly afterwards.'

'Why don't you call them babies?'

'What?'

'You keep saying "embryo" and "foetus".'

'That's what they're called.'

'Maybe if you called them babies you wouldn't keep losing them.'

'What did you say?' She can't believe what she's just heard.

'I'm sorry. I didn't mean to say that.'

'What could you possibly know about it?' She wants to slap him, but she keeps her voice even.

143

'Nothing. You're right. Ignore me. It was a daft thing to say.'

'You keep talking about "people like you", but you don't know anything about me.'

'Sylvia, please—' It's the first time he's used her name. 'I was just trying to—'

'What?' She rounds on him. 'Fix it for me? *Sort it out?* Like the lock on the loo door?'

'Look, I'm really sorry. I didn't mean to upset you.'

'I'm not upset. I'm angry,' she says, knocking hot tears from her cheeks.

'Do you want me to go?' His face is a mask of anguish. He's holding a pink rose in one hand.

And suddenly her anger dissolves. 'Is that for me?' she asks, smiling through her tears.

She starts on the secret room the next day, beginning with the sideboard. She intends to throw most of the stuff away – the brittle bunches of herbs and yellowed exercise books; the little toys and kitschy ornaments. But when she picks up the first of the little dolls, something makes her hesitate. Maybe it's the silly rituals Martin made her go through, but she finds herself wondering about the child the doll was intended for, and going back down the hill instead, and begging a heap of cardboard boxes from Dimitri. And laying the little objects inside them with something like reverence.

She leaves the photographs until last, lifting them down one by one and dusting them with a cloth. She imagines the photographer hunched over his tripod, with his flashgun raised; and invisible parents looking on with encouraging smiles.

The hand-tinting has been lovingly done. She had thought the effect was unnatural and crude when she'd first seen them; now she likes the way the pastel tints seem to float the images against the background, as though they're in three dimensions. *I'd like to try that with my photos*, she thinks.

By the time Martin arrives she's stacked all the boxes in the centre of the room and is brushing down the sideboard.

'I don't know why I'm bothering to clean it,' she says. 'When it's got to be broken up.'

'Maybe you like it,' he suggests.

'You're joking! I hate it. Great ugly thing. I'm just an obsessive-compulsive.'

'It could be useful for storing things.' He pulls open a drawer to demonstrate. 'It's very well made.'

'It's horrible, Martin. And it takes up half the room.'

'Maybe you could paint it.'

'Maybe you could take an axe to it.'

'You take an axe to it,' he says. 'I've got work to do.' And disappears into the next room, where she hears him beginning to wrench the rotten beams away from the collapsed floorboards.

From now on the pattern of her days is set: swimming at sunrise, breakfast with Aphrodite, dropping into the grocer's to buy something for lunch on her way up the hill, then working on the house until Martin arrives. She always walks up these days, and has begun recognizing the faces that greet her as she plods up the lane winding up to the house.

Sophia, watering the pots on her veranda; Georgia tipping veg peelings for her chickens; the other older Sophia, crocheting in her black scarf; old Costas in his polished black boots, cracking sunflower seeds under his mulberry tree. And Spiros, the goat man in his ruined house, barefoot in his brown raincoat, tying the wire netting she's given him to a framework of metal posts.

She's begun exchanging pleasantries with them in her rudimentary Greek. Yes, she is working hard on the house. Yes, the weather is fine. Yes, her husband will be visiting shortly. And soon they start handing her small gifts as she plods past.

Georgia presents her with a plastic bag of eggs swathed in serviettes. 'For *Pascha*,' she says. '*Kokkino*.' And mimes putting them into a pot to dye them red. Old Sophia gives her a little cross made from palm leaves and tells her to fix it above her bed. Spiros, the goat man, offers her a little bundle of oregano soaked in oil. 'Grossartig,' he says in German, placing it in her hand and closing his own filthy palm over it. His stench wraps itself around her like a blanket: warm and foetid. 'Der kinder,' he says, yanking her nearer and pointing a blackened talon at her belly.

Aphrodite shows her how to dye her eggs. It seems the whole village is preparing for Easter.

'We will crack them together on Easter Sunday,' she declares. 'And the one that is last to break will bring good luck for the whole year.' She piles warm red eggs like apples into blue bowls, and sets them out on all the tables. 'In the old days we believed that the person with the last unbroken egg would have a baby before the next Easter,' she says.

She's plaiting sweet dough into heart shapes and embedding the eggs in them. 'There,' she sighs. 'So lovely. I will give them a shine of sugar and sell them for ten euros to husbands who want to make their wives happy.'

'I wish you were here to see it,' Sylvia tells Bennet on the phone a few days later. 'There was a procession this afternoon through the village, with a statue of Jesus on a funeral bier covered with flowers. And everyone dressed in black, singing and scattering petals on the road.'

'Very charming and bucolic. I assume you took lots of photos.'

'Two whole rolls. They're piling up waiting for the darkroom to be ready. Aphrodite's making a special kind of soup for tomorrow, out of what she calls "sheep gizzards", which is presumably all the unmentionable bits they hoick out of the carcass before they roast it.'

'Yummy. Pancreas and penis. My favourites.'

'It's the first meat some of these people will have tasted since Clear Monday. We're supposed to eat it when we come back from Midnight Mass.'

'Don't forget to say a little prayer for me.'

She walks to the little church with the rest of the village, carrying a candle Aphrodite has given her as a present, with a red ribbon tied around it. She's tired from scrubbing the tiles on the kitchen floor, and slightly drunk on the wine people kept pressing on her at the taverna. Filing in through the church door, she thinks longingly of her room at the taverna, its plump white pillows, its pristine sheets.

It's the first time she's been inside the church and she's unprepared for the beauty of the simple ceremony: the hypnotic chanting of the stately bearded man at the pulpit; the banks of white candles casting an oily glow over the gilt and icons; the smoky hush as they're doused to denote the death of Jesus.

In the darkness, she can feel the press of other bodies; all waiting, all breathing together in the small space. Then the single flame appearing from behind the screen, wavering and guttering as the priest bends to touch it to a candle in the front row; the glow building as the flame is passed around the church, from candle to candle, until the whole church is ablaze with yellow light.

Aphrodite is on one side of her, Martin on the other. She feels her fingers slipping on the wax as she holds her new white wick in Aphrodite's flame. It seems an age before the flame catches, and she holds her breath, after-images dancing red and green around the central yellow tongue. As she turns to pass it to Martin, it gutters uncertainly for a second and she cups her hand around the flame to steady it.

When every candle is alight, and the little church is a fragrant blur of gold and incense smoke, they file silently outside where the bell ropes are untied and the quiet is shattered by the wild joyful tolling of two big iron bells. The sound echoes across the valley, adding to the sudden cacophony of bells, explosions and fireworks that fill the night.

Then everyone, friends, relatives, strangers, are turning to one another, and smiling, kissing cheeks, shaking hands, saying almost conversationally: '*Christos anesti*' – Christ has risen! – and replying. 'Alithos anesti' – Yes! He really is risen. And for a second Sylvia feels that in this church, in this place, perhaps it could be true.

Afterwards each person carries a lighted candle back to their home; slowly, in cupped hands, with flesh glowing red around the bones, along the lanes, one after another, appearing and disappearing through the trees like glow-worms. Sylvia carries her candle towards the taverna with Aphrodite and Maria, then changes her mind and joins the winking trail of her neighbours making their way up the hill.

The cottage squats waiting, a friendly shape in the moonlight, as she forms the sign of the cross beside each door as she's seen the others doing, to bless each room and keep it safe for another year.

A sharp sound from around the side of the house makes her jump. It's Martin, carrying his candle. 'I thought I'd do it for you,' he says. 'I didn't think you'd be coming.'

'Shouldn't you be doing it at your place?'

'I don't have a place,' he says. 'Just the van, and I don't think that counts.'

'What are we supposed to do with the candles now?'

'Keep the flame burning until Good Friday next year. Some people set up little shrines in their houses, with oil burners on them. And they transfer the flame to that.'

'There was an old oil burner amongst all that stuff I packed away,' she says, handing him her candle. 'Hold this, will you, while I try to find it.'

She finds it easily, and washes it by candlelight, then fills the blue glass reservoir with olive oil and watches it soak slowly up the wick.

'Christos anesti,' he says quietly as she lights the wick with her candle.

'Alithos anesti,' she replies as she sets the little burner in the centre of the empty sideboard and blows out the two candles.

'I still don't believe it,' she says, looking at him apologetically.

'But you did it,' he says, his eyes glinting in the light of the little lamp. 'You took it seriously. You treated it with respect.'

'What do you believe?' she asks, watching their shadows dip and quiver against the wall.

'I believe everything,' he says. 'I believe stones have souls. I believe plants feel pain. I believe people are kidnapped by aliens from outer space. I've never heard a single argument that convinces me not to believe.'

'You're mad,' she says.

'I wish I could persuade you,' he sighs. 'Sometimes when I see you working away, sanding something, or scrubbing at those damn tiles for hours on end, I want to make you stop and just put your hands flat against the wall, on all those old stones, or on the trunk of the walnut tree.' The passion in his voice takes her by surprise. 'Or on this piece of furniture that you hate so much.' He takes her hand and places it on the sideboard.

'Why?' His hand feels strong on hers, pressing it against the smooth grain of the wood.

'To make you feel what I feel. Because you're so determined and *busy* all the time. Because you're so sad and so locked away I can't bear it.'

She pulls her hand away. Is that how she seems? She pictures herself sitting primly in her black coat at her aunt's funeral, like a governess at a job interview, while children crawled under the table and a dog licked lentil soup from a pottery bowl. *I used to feel so at home there*, she thinks. *How did I get like this?*

Chapter 15

The Bat Skull

'Today is the longest day of the year,' Martin's mother told him. They were lying on their backs in the garden, in a nest they'd pressed into a patch of long grass. The sun had set, but the sky was a clear sweet violet, framed by grey feathers of nodding seed heads. Swifts were screaming across it, high and shrill as distant spacecraft.

'In the far north the sun doesn't set at all at this time of year,' she told him. 'It just sinks down to the horizon for a while, then rises again. And the night and day creatures are all out at the same time. Even this far south, if we wait long enough the bats will come out and start flying with the swifts.'

Martin tried to imagine a world where it never got dark, and a sky teeming with flying things, like the starlings outside the Ashmolean. He looked at his mother's bare brown arm pointing, at her big heavy fingers caked with dried mud from planting out sweet peas to train through the rose bushes. She smelt of sunshine and leaf mould.

'Swifts sleep and make love on the wing,' she was saying and he saw them in his mind, speeding belly-to-belly with their eyes closed, surfing high blue cirrus waves. 'They're built for flying so if they fall to the ground they can't get up again because their wings are so long.'

'So what happens to them?' He imagined them flailing and gasping like fish out of water. 'They die,' she said simply. 'They're like aliens from another planet. They can't survive in our world. Their feet are curved for gripping the sides of cliffs and tall buildings; they can't stand or walk on the ground. They can't even fold their wings like other birds.'

He thought about that: about a creature so perfectly adapted for what it does best that it dies when prevented from doing it.

They waited for the bats to emerge from the hole in the roof: three frantic black creatures, zipping through the overhanging branches.

'Pipistrelles,' she said, though he already knew what they were called.

'Pipistrelles,' he repeated, rolling the word around his mouth. Then again, 'Pipistrelles,' like an incantation, as if saying it would make the night last forever.

'Imagine being a bat,' she was saying. 'Being blind, but hearing where the trees are. Like they're aliens from a world where the sun never shines and every object casts a shadow of sound.'

They watched the bats for a while, diving like dolphins through shoals of dancing gnats.

Then: 'Can we have a Bat Day?' he asked, thinking back to the Rainbow Days when he was seven.

'And zoom around with our eyes closed and eat gnats?'

'I mean, pretend we're aliens and stay up all night until the bats go to bed.'

They slipped out through the back gate and wandered down to the river, then followed the towpath into the dark city. It was past midnight and there was no one about except a few Dog People and a student being sick under a lamp post.

'On my planet alcohol makes you drunk for a few hours then puts you quietly to sleep,' she said when they were safely out of earshot. 'It's full of vitamins and fruity goodness so when you wake up, instead of a headache, you're raring to go.'

'On my planet people eat blue food and drink the nectar from enormous cup-shaped flowers,' he said.

They walked slowly up Abingdon Road between pools of orange lamplight.

'On my planet,' he said, 'no one would be allowed to keep a dog as a pet, and there would be special sanctuaries where they'd roam free and form packs and live like wolves.'

'On my planet the weather's always warm and people make nests in trees or in caves by the beach,' she said.

'And no one goes to school but there's a library on every street corner with so many books they always have what you want and you never have to order anything on interlibrary loan.'

'Oh, yes. And every street would have its own café where neighbours take it in turn to cook for everyone – and where the men have to do the washing-up.' She nudged him, and he pushed her back. She was always complaining that he didn't do his share of the cleaning.

'On my planet all red fruit would be free, on prescription from the food doctor,' she went on, 'and no one would wear false eyelashes or high-heeled shoes. In fact it's such a perfect temperature all the time, people wouldn't wear clothes at all if they didn't want to. Just sandals to protect their feet from sharp stones and a hat to stop their noses going red in the sun.'

'On my planet the stones would talk and tell stories about what life was like millions of years ago.'

'And everyone would know how to play a musical instrument.'

'And there'd be no cars or pollution because we'd have a horse each and the roads would be dug up and replaced by grass for them to eat, with water troughs instead of zebra crossings.'

They'd reached the High Street now; he imagined it green, with horses tethered outside the police station.

'On my planet children could choose who they lived with,' he said.

She took his hand and swung it. 'You know there are some communes in Israel where children don't live with their parents at all. They're raised in nurseries all together. Imagine having fifty brothers and sisters and only seeing your parents at supper time? And in some parts of Africa the children are brought up by their grannies in the countryside while their mothers live miles away in the city. Some families share out their children like sweets, so every woman has the same number to help on the farm.'

They bought chips from a late-night van and sat in a punt under Magdalen Bridge to eat them. Water slapped against the jetty and the punt's tether clinked as they settled themselves on the wooden seat.

'Why did you only have one child?' Martin asked.

'Because you were such a horrible baby, I didn't think it would be right to bring another one into the world.'

'No, really.'

'Because it was such hard work looking after you, I vowed never to go through it again.'

'Mu-u-um! Be serious.'

'Well, lots of reasons really. I had a big long Bad Sad just after you were born and I thought if I got pregnant again that might make it worse. And I wasn't getting on very well with your father, because he thought I should go into a mental hospital and let his mother look after you.'

He was listening with his whole body. She'd never talked about this before.

'God, she was a real terror, your grandmother. She's the one who wanted you taken away from me, you know. Your father just went along with whatever she said. I realized that if the courts knew she'd be looking after you as well as him, there was no way I'd be allowed to keep you.'

She waited for him to digest this. The river rocked gently beneath them and a cyclist freewheeled quietly past on the towpath. The pub nearby had closed and the barman was patrolling the pavement for stray beer mugs.

Martin leant into her and she draped an arm around him.

'So those were the bad reasons I didn't have another baby,' she said. 'But the truth is I loved you so much, it never really occurred to me to have another one. I felt as though I'd been blessed enough.'

Martin thought of the swift's long dark wings flapping uselessly in the dust. He thought of a planet called Matala, where aliens lived in caves on a cliff face and where swifts landed and took off and never fell to the ground.

Chapter 16

The day after Easter, Sylvia's temperature dips. She calls Bennet and he manages to get on a flight that arrives the same evening.

She drives to Heraklion to pick him up, then dodges behind a pillar so she can watch him coming out through the baggage hall. He's half a head taller than everyone else, elegant and rumpled in his beige cotton jacket. *This is my husband*, she thinks as she watches him checking his watch, peering around for her, touching his forehead where the hair's receding. It's only nine o'clock England time but he looks pale and tired, like an over-exposed photograph of himself.

When they hug, he feels unfamiliar. Larger, somehow, than she remembers, and softer; a sofa when she is expecting a chair.

At the car, he puts out his hand for the keys.

'I'll drive if you like,' she says. 'I'm used to driving on the right now.'

'OK, if you're sure,' he says, concertinaing his long legs into the passenger seat. In minutes he's asleep, lolled sideways against the door, as she speeds along the night road with her window open, inhaling orange blossom and diesel fumes, wood smoke and fox musk, chasing the gibbous moon along the horizon.

He comes to as she parks in front of the taverna. 'Perfect timing, sleepyhead,' she whispers, leaning over and kissing his warm lips.

They make love with the light off and the shutters open. The moon turns the room into a monochrome photograph. As Bennet looms over her, she thinks of a red egg bumbling down her fallopian tube, swept by fronds of cilia. She thinks of cracking her egg against Aphrodite's the previous day, the surge of triumph when hers emerged unbroken. She thinks of a cardboard box full of framed photographs, of bright eyes and dark curls; of a flame flickering in a blue oil burner.

'Did you set up a meeting for us with the architect?' They're having breakfast outside the taverna in the sunshine. Swallows chatter on the telephone wire above their heads as Bennet dips crusty bread into the yellow eye of a fried egg.

'You can see the cottage from here,' says Sylvia. He sips coffee and peers obediently up the hillside. And there it is, as it always is, dishevelled and faded, nestling in the shade of the fig tree.

'You should get your artisan chappie to give it a lick of paint.'

'Actually, I'm going to paint it myself,' she says. 'When I can decide on the colour.'

'Ah, the human female and her aesthetic sensibilities. Talking of which, are there any sketches of the new house for me to mull over?'

'Better than that,' she says mysteriously. 'Come on, finish your breakfast. I want to show you something.'

This time he drives, and parks differently to the way she always does: closer to the gate, where the sun will roast it in a few hours' time. It doesn't matter – they're not staying very long – but she feels irritated that it hasn't been done properly.

'Close your eyes,' she says, leading him down the path towards the house. When he's standing in the middle of the little kitchen she tells him to open them again.

'Good grief! You have been busy.'

'Everything still needs painting, but I've put the furniture back exactly where it used to be to show you,' she says. 'And it all works. Even the cooker. I bought a new pipe for the gas rings and Martin took the tank to be refilled. There's a spare under the sleeping platform.'

She tugs him through to the bedroom and flings open the shutters. 'It was all in much better nick than it looked,' she goes on. 'All the lights work, and the water's on, and Martin's put new glass in the windows. And up here is where we'd sleep.' She's dragging him over to the sleeping platform, now completely reinstated with its little balustrade. 'There are two matching iron bedsteads outside waiting to be painted. I thought we could push them together and get a big double mosquito net.'

'This "we" you're referring to. It doesn't involve yours truly, does it?'

'Don't you like it?' He looks ungainly peering around the small rooms, like a tourist in a cultural museum.

'Well it's all perfectly charming and rustic, but my camping days are definitely over.'

Suddenly she sees it through his eyes: the patched doors and scabrous whitewash; the peeling shutters; the bare boards and cold-water plumbing.

'We'd only be here in the summer,' she says. 'But if the cold water's a problem we could easily fit an immersion for the shower.'

'There's that "we" again. The "we" I signed up to was going to build an elegant little villa with air conditioning and guaranteed bug-free sleeping arrangements.'

'I changed my mind.'

'Aha. Here's the "I" sneaking out of the woodwork.'

'I thought you'd be pleased.'

'Sylvie, the place is tiny. There's barely room to sleep a mouse, let alone swing the proverbial.'

'I've measured the platform, there's just enough room for two beds.'

'I'd bang my head on the ceiling every time I got up to go to the loo. Which, if I'm not mistaken, is a short hike away and has been occupied, until very recently, by a member of the great unwashed.'

'We'd be outside most of the time anyway.'

'If that's supposed to reassure me, may I remind you that a Bennet's preferred habitat is the interior of a cool bar.'

'I thought you liked rustic.'

'My darling girl, there is rustic and there's rustic. This is bordering on your actual primitive.'

'I thought that too, when I first saw it. But when I cleaned up the loo and tried the outside shower—'

'Outside shower? Now I know you're having me on.'

'No, it's round the side. I'll take you in a minute. But first I want to show you the secret room. You remember that cupboard you thought was full of rats? Well, look what we found when we unlocked the door.'

She leads him into the secret room. '*Voilà!*' she announces. 'The perfect darkroom.'

'Complete with grannie's silver plate and a cartload of table-cloths and napkins. God, what a monstrosity!'

'It's horrible isn't it? But what about the rest of it?' She puts her arms around his neck and looks up at him. 'Do you really hate it?'

'Well, hate is a very strong word,' he hedges, looking down at her.

'Dislike, then.'

'Let's just say it hasn't grown on me yet. But given time—'

'You'll dislike it even more.'

'Now you're putting words into my mouth.'

She sighs. 'I thought you'd love it.'

He looks at her. 'No you didn't. Otherwise you'd have told me about it ages ago.'

'I wanted to surprise you.'

'Now you're insulting my intelligence. You didn't tell me because you thought I'd be cross.'

'And are you?'

'Yes, of course. A bit. I thought this was something we were doing together. So it's a bit disconcerting to find you playing housie with one of the other boys.'

'He's not "one of the other boys", you dope. He's a builder. And it's not something I'm doing with him. It's something I'm doing on my own.'

157

There. She's said it. *It's my house. I want to do this by myself.* She has a sudden childish urge to squeeze her eyes shut and clamp her hands over her ears. She sneaks a look at his face.

He looks hurt, confused. She can see him marshalling his thoughts, trying not to be angry. There's something his chest does, something that's half a sigh, half a squaring of the shoulders. She's seen it a lot these last two years. She sees it again now.

'Right,' he says at last. 'If that's the way you want it. I suppose that's all this house business was ever about. Something for you to do. A place for you to recuperate.'

She's been holding her breath. Now she exhales slowly. 'I really love you, do you know that?'

'I should bloody well hope so.'

'And the house is going to be fab.'

'I don't doubt it for a second. I may even concede to spend the odd weekend here once in a while, provided I can recoup in an en suite in Chania.'

'You can help if you like,' she suggests with a grin.

'I might just do that. In an advisory capacity, of course. Make sure that hippy builder of yours doesn't try to take advantage.'

Martin arrives as she's demonstrating the new seat and the flush on the toilet.

'*Kalimera*,' says Bennet, proffering a hand to be shaken. 'Just flown in for a few days to see how the wife's getting on.'

'I've found you a fridge,' Martin says to Sylvia. 'It's a bit scratched but the seal's still good. It's on the trailer. I found it in an old house we're renovating in Kokkino Horio.'

'What's this, Sylvie?' asks Bennet. 'Surely we can run to a new fridge? Or is running a junkyard part of the revised plan?'

'Sorry.' Martin looks at Bennet, then turns back to Sylvia. 'I thought you were working with a tight budget? You can get a new one in Chania for about three hundred euros, but when we fixed up the cooker I thought—'

'It's fine. Thanks.' Sylvia shoots him an apologetic look. 'And

I am trying to keep costs down. I was just showing Bennet around the cottage and explaining things. He didn't realize how much work we'd been doing on it.'

'I believe I've got you to thank for this transformation,' Bennet says.

'Well, Sylvia did most of it. I just sorted out the platform and helped get rid of the rubbish.'

'What about that great monstrosity in the darkroom?'

'The sideboard? Have you had a good look at it? It's an amazing feat of workmanship. Those bird designs are hand-carved and the joints are all mitres and dovetails. It must have taken someone months to make.'

'Well it can't stay there,' says Bennet shortly. 'It completely dominates the room. And Sylvie needs the space for her film stuff, don't you sweet pea?'

'You'd never get it out without breaking it up first.'

'So? Break it up.'

'Sylvia didn't say—'

'Well, I'm saying,' says Bennet firmly. 'The only reason my wife hasn't insisted before is because she doesn't want to make a fuss.'

'It's OK—' Sylvia interrupts, feeling embarrassed. Why is he doing this?

'Look, I can't stop,' says Martin. 'I've got to be back on site in an hour. Shall I bring the fridge in or not?'

'Yes. Please,' Sylvia says quickly. 'Do you need some help?'

'Maybe you could grab hold of one end? It's one of those big ones. I thought you could use it as a larder too, when it gets hotter.'

'I'll do it,' says Bennet, shrugging off his jacket and draping it over a chair. 'Syl's not really dressed for lugging furniture.'

Sylvia can feel Martin surveying her white culottes and bolero. Her hair's blow-dried and glossy; her eyelashes darkened with mascara. She watches the two men manoeuvring the fridge off the trailer: Bennet in his loose grey shirt and chinos, saying 'All right, mate?' and 'Easy does it', and Martin, quiet and polite in his dusty work clothes.

She's struck by how slight Martin seems, almost skinny, beside Bennet's broad rangy figure. And how young, allowing the older man to take control as they carry the fridge down the path. She hasn't noticed before how supple Martin is; almost catlike, the way he insinuates his body between the fridge and the door frame as they take it into the kitchen.

'How much do we owe you?' asks Bennet, plugging it in and watching it judder quietly to life.

'I said I'd give the guy ten euros to take it away.'

Bennet feels for his wallet and extracts a crisp new note. 'Take twenty,' he says. 'And thanks for everything.'

'OK. I reckon I'm done here,' says Martin, to no one in particular. 'Good to meet you again,' he says to Bennet. Then, to Sylvia: 'You need to get a coat of primer on those door repairs before it rains again. I think Dimitri sells car enamel if you want to touch up the rust on the fridge, or you can use ordinary white gloss. Enjoy the house.'

'What was all that about him being cantankerous?' asks Bennet when he's gone. 'Seemed perfectly amenable to me. Practically tugging his forelock.'

'I expect I'm not masterful enough,' she says, watching the camper van bump away down the track.

'Well don't let him bugger off without getting rid of that sideboard.'

Bennet wants to make love after lunch, but Sylvia feels too embarrassed.

'Everyone will know what we're doing,' she says.

'So what? What else do couples do on their hols? What could be more natural than a man bonking his wife after a leisurely lunch in a rural taverna?'

But she can't get into it. She can hear Vasilios clearing a piece of waste ground under the window, hacking at the earth with his spade and chucking stones on to a heap. She can hear Aphrodite in the kitchen washing up, the chickens fussing in the yard.

Bennet's sucking her nipple very gently and one of his fingers is inching into her. He's lying next to her on one of the twin beds, pressing her against the wall. His leg is hooked over her body and his eyes are closed; his penis is slicking up and down against her hip.

She closes her eyes and tries to concentrate on what he's doing. The probing finger, the circling tongue. She can't stop thinking about the sideboard. About the man who made it; about how it might have got into the little room. She imagines a carpenter working away at it for years: reverently piling up the finished segments at the back of his workshop. Where would Kokona have got the money for something like that? Perhaps it was a gift from a grateful client? As Bennet positions himself to ease into her, she wonders what Kokona had done for this man, for his wife, for his daughter, to merit such an elaborate gift.

Sylvia sits in the passenger seat as Bennet drives to the airport. She's wearing her black linen skirt and a loose silk shirt. They've spent the last two days wandering around Chania, sitting in cafés, revisiting their favourite restaurants. It feels odd to be wearing normal clothes again, after weeks in baggy overalls. Her skirt feels tight and formal, as though it belongs to someone else: an older woman, perhaps; a solicitor. Her fingernails are broken and her legs need waxing; her hair's getting too long to blow-dry in its usual style.

'I need a haircut,' she says.

'And there was I thinking the ragamuffin look was intentional.'

'It's a shame you missed Easter.'

'Honey, you're the only bunny I need.'

'Do you think we managed to make a baby rabbit?'

'If not, put out a call for Super Buck next month and I'll swoop in again for another go.'

She holds on to him for a long time as they say goodbye. She wants to feel his tallness against her, to measure the precise level on his chest her chin comes to, the exact place his big hands rest on the small of her back.

Watching him going through passport control, she feels unsteady for a moment, as though a wall she's been leaning against has been removed. Blinking tears away, she wanders forlornly around the airport for a while, not ready to drive back yet.

She considers buying lunch upstairs in the airport restaurant, and looking out over the tarmac to watch him boarding. But the food looks dried out and uninviting when she gets there, so she drifts back downstairs and finds herself beside the row of car-hire kiosks in the arrivals hall. Leafing through the brochures, she stops at a photograph of a gleaming red scooter, a Peugeot Trekker with rugged little wheels.

Ten minutes later, she's surrendered the keys to her white Corsa and is fastening a crash helmet under her chin.

Leaning into the bends on the way back to the village, then swimming in the sea at dawn the next day, Sylvia feels like a selkie slipping back into its skin. Her black linen skirt is hanging in the wardrobe. Her blue overalls are waiting for her on the back of the door like an old friend.

'Where you been?' Dimitri asks truculently when she goes into the shop.

'Relaxing,' she says. 'With my husband from England. Now I am working again.'

'So what you want?'

'Paint,' she says, pointing to the frugal chart of gloss paints on the wall. 'I like that pale green.' Actually she picked out the shade days ago. She's decided to experiment with subtle mossy colours – muted greens and matt-varnished wood – to mirror the natural landscape.

'*Ochi*,' snarls Dimitri. 'No green. Green is finish. *Mono kokkino*.'

Kokkino is red; she knows that word now. 'What about that darker green?' she asks.

'*Ochi.*' He says it louder this time. '*Mono kokkino.*' Only red. '*Ligo kitrino. Ligo ble. Poli kokkino.*' A tiny bit of yellow and blue. And lots of red.

'Well, could you order the green for me?' she asks. 'The pale one, and that darker one as well?'

'Why you want green? Green is for *horta*, *anguria*. Not for *spiti*.'

'But if it's on the colour chart, you must be able to get it for me,' she argues, but he refuses to understand her. 'No green,' he says, folding penguin arms implacably over his vast chest. '*Kokkino. Kitrino. Ble.*' She knows he's lying. She knows he could get the green if he could be bothered. He's just pushing the red because no one else ever uses it.

She thinks ruefully of her abandoned Corsa, as a trip to a DIY store in Chania seems inevitable. She'll have to get a backpack of some kind if she's going to ferry paint tins back on the scooter. And it will probably take two or even three trips. Dimitri is watching her, his chin jutting mulishly from the folds of his neck.

She laughs suddenly. 'OK, *kokkino*,' she says. '*Poli.* And brushes. *Micro*, *megalo*, every size.'

She starts with the walls, with the bags of whitewash Martin delivered the previous week, and some fat old brushes she found when she cleared out the space under the sleeping platform. The paint goes on like grey yoghurt – thick and curdy, filling all the holes – then dries to an eye-aching white. It's heavy work, loading the brushes and spreading the gloop over the uneven walls: more like icing a cake than painting, and nothing like rolling emulsion on to a flat surface back in Newcastle.

By the end of the day the kitchen's finished and she's standing under the shower, watching milky water soak into the base of the vine. Her arms ache and her stomach's cramping with hunger.

I forgot to stop for lunch, she thinks. *Again.*

Then, a bit later: *Is this what Martin meant about me being so busy? Is this what I do to stop myself feeling sad?*

163

And she's aware, suddenly, that she's been half-expecting him to turn up all afternoon, that she hasn't seen him since he delivered the fridge to the house.

'Do you know where Martin is?' she asks Aphrodite that evening. She's taken to setting the tables for supper at the taverna, while the other woman finishes preparing the specials of the day.

'I haven't seen him since Easter,' says Aphrodite, stirring garlic soup. It's stuffed peppers this evening, squatting like green Buddhas in a wide metal tray, and *gouvetsi*, chunks of pork on a bed of rice-shaped pasta. 'Maybe someone else has something they want him to do. There is an English woman in Kalives he was working for before you. Maybe she wants him again.'

'He didn't say anything.' Sylvia feels obscurely irritated.

'Oh, Martin never tells where he is going,' says Aphrodite. 'He is like the Scarlet Pumpernickel. Now you see him, now you don't.'

'Scarlet Pimpernel,' laughs Sylvia, lining up cruet sets on a tray to put on the tables.

'One day he is there building your shelf, eating your moussaka. Then he is gone for three, four weeks.' Aphrodite shrugs. 'I think he likes to have secrets. He does not want people to know too much. Don't worry. He will be back.'

'I wasn't worried,' says Sylvia. 'It's just that I owe him some money for something.'

She doesn't owe him any money, she's sure of that. She went to the cashpoint in Vrisses on Easter Saturday and paid him everything she owed.

For the next week the whitewash occupies all her waking hours: churning it in the big bucket, ladling it into the small bucket, slurping it on to the walls and the ceilings – then getting down on her knees and scrubbing the splashes from the floors. By Saturday she's begun dreaming like the Sorcerer's Apprentice in Disney's *Fantasia*.

She'd intended to stop when she'd finished the insides of the rooms, but now the rain appears to have stopped for the summer, everyone in the village seems to be getting out their buckets and brushes to spruce up their houses.

So she carries on, propping Kokona's wooden ladder against the outside of the house and brushing down wasps' nests and gecko droppings, tipping and sloshing, until her shoulders ache and her arms are covered with small red weals from where splashes of caustic lime have eaten into her skin.

The work is exhausting, hypnotic, compulsive. There's always that last corner to finish; that uneven patch to recoat. She has to force herself to stop to eat, to wash, to go to the toilet. And she's so tired in the evenings that she can't be bothered to blow-dry her hair when she's washed it. It's too long now anyway, she tells herself, tying it back with the red ribbon Dimitri popped in with her white spirit the previous day.

When the whitewashing is finished, the house looks like a wedding cake: sweet and edible, with its crags and edges softened beneath a coating of white sugar.

As she glides through the dawn sea the next morning, she thinks of the tins of *kokkino* lined up waiting for her to start on the doors and windows, of the moment she's been looking forward to, when the bold splashes of scarlet sing out against the white.

So why does she feel like a piece of washing, limp and wrung out? Why does it all feel so hard, suddenly, the climb back up the cliff path; the five doors, the three sets of shutters; all those bright straight lines to paint?

Trudging back up the track, she feels the familiar dragging pain in her womb: her period starting, earlier than she expected; another red egg flushing out of her. And her mind begins dumbly picking over the past weeks, as it always does, counting up the cups of coffee and glasses of white wine, the whitewashing, the scooter, *mea culpa, mea culpa*, to work out what might have gone wrong this time.

'You need a day off,' pronounces Aphrodite, noticing her

listlessly forking through her scrambled eggs. 'I will telephone the beauty parlour in Chania that put all the bad ideas into my Maria's head. You will get your face done and your nails and buy chocolate in the big city. It will put you back to yourself.'

On the way back on the scooter, with smooth legs and pink toenails, Sylvia notices a sign to Kalives and swerves off the main road, on impulse, to see if she can find Martin. He's left a book open in her mind, with the corner of a page turned down, and she thinks it's time to close it.

Puttering down the narrow backstreets on the scooter, she feels her mood lighten. *This is fun*, she thinks, peering at neat veg plots and flower-filled courtyards; and begins taking cuttings and arranging plant pots in her mind, all the time looking out for the flash of red – around a corner, under a fig tree – that will betray the presence of Martin's camper van.

But it's not there; she's been round the village twice and she's sure of it. And finds herself feeling pleased – he's not with that other English woman after all – then amused at herself for feeling pleased. Then cross again that he's just disappeared without saying goodbye.

Remembering he'd mentioned a renovation in Kokkino Horio, she decides to ride out there, too, along the winding coast road, then loop back to Arkassa via Drapanos, where he'd said there was a new development of tourist villas. *If he thinks he can have secrets*, she says to herself with a grin, *he's got another think coming*.

The ride is exhilarating: lots of snaking bends to lean into, and a brisk wind off the sea to whip at her face. The scooter bucks over the uneven road, swerving neatly around cars and lorries. Until, when she brakes sharply to avoid colliding with a flock of sheep, the scooter skids on to its side and she comes off.

Dusting herself down afterwards, she thinks automatically: *Thank God I'm having a period. So that can't have dislodged any embryo.* Then, with a surge of anger: *Why can't I go out for a simple ride on the scooter without worrying about my uterus?*

166

At Kokkino she spends half an hour happily exploring the rambling clifftop village, and finds several old houses being reno- vated, with trucks and cement mixers, bricklayers and carpenters; but no sign of the red camper van. Sipping sweet coffee in a little *kafenion*, she plans out her route to Drapanos.

It's late afternoon now, so she knows the site will have closed for the day, but perhaps he's parked nearby. The site is easy to find: a raw wound of red earth on the outskirts of the village, with crude grey Lego shapes rising from it, and piles of blocks, pipes, sand. She pictures Martin working here among the Greek builders, barrowing sand and lifting planks, crushing empty tins of Fanta and iced tea and kicking them into the bushes.

Does he smoke when he's with them? she wonders, looking at the discarded cigarette butts and cartons littering the site. *Does he talk to them about plants feeling pain?*

When a couple of circuits of the village draw another blank, she gets out her map to decide on a route home. She's just remounting the scooter when she remembers what he said when she was looking for the key to the secret room: 'I just close my eyes and picture that person locking the door, then think where they would hide it.'

'OK,' she says quietly, closing her eyes. 'Where are you going to park this evening?'

She pictures him immediately, tugging the van's sliding door. shut and swinging himself up into the driver's seat. *You've found a shady spot off the main road*, she thinks, *and you're driving there now, because you want to be back before it gets dark. There's a good view of a valley, maybe even the sea, so it's quite high up. But with lots of vegetation to hide the van behind.*

She opens her eyes and looks around. But it's hopeless; the village is completely surrounded by likely-looking hills, and there were even more around Kokkino Horio and Kalami.

But you won't be in open countryside, she thinks suddenly. *You don't want people to think you're a vagrant. And you'll need water. So* – she's feeling confident again now – *you'll have asked around on the site if anyone knows of a disused house, where you could use the water, maybe pay something to cover the costs, maybe somewhere with an outside loo.*

But in a smaller village, away from where you're working, where you can hide away and feel private.

She consults the map again, the web of lanes between Drapanos and Kokkino Horio, and sees four small hillside villages caught like flies within it.

She finds the van an hour later, parked exactly as she'd pictured it: beneath a mulberry tree beside a semi-derelict cottage. She cuts the scooter's motor and props it against a stone wall, then takes off her crash helmet.

Now the hunt's over, she's not sure what to do. What will she say if he sees her? 'I was just passing,' when he's chosen such an obscure little village? 'I spotted the van,' when he's taken such pains to hide it from the road?

No, you mustn't see me, she thinks, wheeling the scooter into a ruined courtyard and hanging the helmet from the handlebars. She emerges cautiously and approaches on foot, treading stealthily on the grass at the edge of the path as though creeping up on a wild animal.

He's inside the van. The sliding door's open and she can hear him moving around inside; the chink of metal on metal, as though he's tidying his tools away; a heavy scraping, of something being pushed aside. His voice saying something. She stiffens – is someone with him? No, he's alone. She's sure of it. Now it's quiet. She strains her ears. Maybe he's changing, pulling a clean tee shirt from a drawer; maybe unrolling a sleeping bag.

She's never seen inside the van – the striped curtains are always closed and the door shut when he's parked at her place – but now she's itching to see the things he carries with him, how he's packed them all in his small space.

He comes out naked and barefoot, with a towel around his waist. There's no spare flesh on him and no chest hair; she can see the muscles move under his tawny skin, a suggestion of ribs. He walks around to the back of the little house where she imagines the washing arrangements are similar to those at Kokona's.

As soon as he's gone, she hurries over to the van and peers inside. She doesn't know what she was expecting inside the battered red exterior: a jumble of tools and clothes; a few Formica cupboards; dirty plates, beer bottles, cardboard boxes. Not this neat wood-panelled compartment – 'cabin' is the word that comes to mind – with its bench bed and fold-down table; its mosquito net knotted above its white pillow; its folding stools hanging flat to the wall; its brass hooks and corner shelves; its tiny sink; its kettle and pottery mugs. And books: yards of them, like a frieze all around the roof.

His work clothes are folded on his boots just inside the door and there's some kind of white dressing gown on the bed. The van smells of dust and toothpaste and wood shavings. It smells of fresh sweat. It smells of the figs and lemons in the bowl beside the sink.

Feeling oddly shaken, she backs hurriedly away. *Of course you'd have books*, she thinks. *If I'd thought about it for a second, I would have known you'd have books*.

But the frugal beauty of the little space disturbs her; the way it's been designed to contain everything essential and nothing superfluous. Like a testament. A reminder. A rebuke.

She retreats quickly, intending to go straight back to the scooter, but lingers instead behind a hedge of prickly pear and watches until he reappears and dries himself quickly in front of the van, then ducks inside and emerges dressed in the garment she'd taken for a dressing gown.

It's some kind of judo outfit, with a kimono-type jacket over baggy white trousers. *I knew you'd be into martial arts*, she crows to herself, as he bows to the wide flat space in front of the van and gives himself over to the slow orotund ballet of t'ai chi.

*

Painting the kitchen door the next day, sweeping long straight lines of lipstick red over the old wood, that image keeps coming back to her: of the supple white figure and the red van, the invisible sphere of air.

It becomes a habit with her, cruising around the countryside on the scooter when she's finished at the house for the day; as much a part of her routine as her dawn swim. As she putters down the lanes, she feels like a London cabbie learning the Knowledge, until she could find her way in her sleep if she had to, in the dark without headlights. And though she usually avoids the village where the camper van's parked, as the sun sinks lower in the sky and coats the countryside with honey, she does sometimes find herself heading in that direction.

Often he's there, and she watches him for a while: sharpening his chisels; washing his clothes in a yellow bucket; sitting on one of his folding stools and leaning back against an old wall with his eyes closed and the evening sun warm on his face.

Sometimes the van's gone and she takes the chance to prowl the empty site. She looks into the outside toilet, which is bigger and slightly newer than hers, with a shower head plumbed into one corner. She examines his razor and comb. He uses herbal shampoo with a built-in conditioner – for some reason this amuses her – and Johnson's baby soap. There's a new toilet brush beside the loo and a small mirror propped above the basin, but no shaving foam or aftershave; no deodorant.

You're a clean boy, but you don't like fuss, she thinks. *You like things to smell natural.*

He's rigged up a washing line, and a pair of jeans are pegged to it – waist 30, two sizes smaller than Bennet – with a thick work shirt and three faded black tees, four pairs of black socks and a navy-blue sweatshirt. No underpants.

Maybe they're white, she thinks, *and your mother taught you to wash them separately. But they'll be boxers, because you don't like things to feel tight on you*. Then, with a little smile: *Maybe you don't wear underpants.*

'Where do you go off every evening?' Aphrodite asks.

'Nowhere really. I just like riding around, getting the paint fumes out of my lungs and checking out places to photograph.'

'Did you find Martin?'

'What? Oh. No. I haven't been looking. But I've seen the site he said he was working on in Drapanos.'

'So, next time you are passing tell him I am still waiting for my bathroom shelves.'

She tracks him down the next day, arriving just as the site's closing up for the day.

'I was wondering when you'd turn up,' he says.

'What do you mean?' She can feel herself blushing.

'I've seen you driving around and I thought you might be looking for me.'

'Actually,' she says, 'it's Aphrodite who wants you. She told me to tell you she wants some shelves putting up in the bathroom.'

'And what about you?' He scans her face. 'How's it going? Are you ready for your blackout screens yet?'

'Nearly,' she says, avoiding his eyes. 'I wanted to get the place ready to move into first. I love being at Aphrodite's, but it gets expensive after a while.'

'Your husband didn't seem to think money was a problem.'

'Well, it isn't really. His new job pays well.'

'But you want it to be your house. And if he pays for things it won't be.'

'How did you know?' She looks up.

'Oh, I notice things.' He's smiling. 'That business with the fridge was a bit of a giveaway.'

'It's cleaned up beautifully, thanks. And it works like a dream, though there's not much in it at the moment.'

'What about mattresses? There's a place just off the Chania road that makes them, all different sizes. I'll fetch a couple back on the trailer if you like.'

'Actually, that would be brilliant, thank you.' She's grinning suddenly, excited by the idea of showing off what she's done to the house. 'That whitewash nearly killed me,' she says. 'But it's beginning to look like a proper house.'

'The mattresses are about sixty euros each, is that OK? I've seen cheaper in Chania but they're crap. If you measure up tomorrow, I'll go and get them in the afternoon.'

'What about Aphrodite's shelves?'

'Oh, she'll be OK. She only wants to keep tabs on me. She gets antsy if I disappear for too long.'

Sylvia's temperature does a sudden blip and she stares at the thermometer and calls Bennet after breakfast.

'Hi sweetie, how's the European periphery?'

'What are you doing this evening?'

'Dinner with Val. Out in the country somewhere. Her treat, she insists, though I'm sure it's my turn.'

'Can she drop you off at the airport instead?'

'Jeeze. It's a bit early isn't it?'

'My period was early, don't you remember? I warned you things might be a bit out of synch.'

'Damn. So you did. And like a dolt I forgot. Look, let me make a few calls and get back to you.'

'Is there a problem?'

'It's just that there's this Japanese laser beano at the RVI this weekend and they're wheeling me out to give the address tomorrow evening. Damn, damn, damn! I hate these things anyway.'

She can picture him in the hall, tie askew, running his hands through his hair.

'Don't worry if you can't manage it,' she says. 'If it's a short cycle there's probably not much point trying anyway. There won't have been enough time for the endometrium to develop.'

'Are you sure? It would really fuck things up here if I had to leave.'

'Yes. I'm sure,' she says. 'Say "hello" to Val for me and tell her to book her ticket soon. And tell her to phone me! I'm fed up with texting her and leaving messages.'

Switching off her mobile, Sylvia thinks of the red kite over Kalives. She imagines the wind tugging at it, and the string breaking suddenly, and its red shape zigzagging up into the blue, blue sky.

Chapter 17

The Cat Woman's Mirror

Recently Martin had been watching some of the Cat Women in Argyle Street: all living alone with one or two cats as pets. He hadn't really been aware of them before, because they came and went through their front doors. But recently he'd noticed them in their back gardens, calling to their cats and fussing over them.

The houses in the street were all joined together in a terrace, with long narrow gardens behind tall fences and hedges, backing on to the back lane and the wilderness running down to the river. Martin knew where all the gaps were in all the fences; he'd followed the route the foxes took through the gardens. He knew which trees were good to climb, which shrubs had the best footholds.

In the summer months he got up early to escape detection, but when the nights were longer it was easy to steal through the gardens, past dark ponds and rose beds, sandpits and swings. People didn't always bother to close the curtains at the backs of their houses, so he could see right into their lives, watch them moving from kitchen to bathroom to bedroom, like TV with the sound turned down.

At first he thought the Cat Women might be witches, and kept hoping he'd see them do witchy things. He'd read somewhere that you could be a witch without realizing; that you could cast spells in the night and wake up the next morning without remembering. The only evidence would be the dust on your feet from prowling in the shape of a hyena. But he'd never seen a Cat Woman with her shoes off; they even wore slippers to the bathroom. They seemed very clean, these women; he couldn't imagine them with dust on their feet.

One night he found a downstairs window open; without thinking he clambered through it into a dark kitchen. It smelt of cooking and perfume and cat food. The lino was smooth against his bare feet and the cat pushed through the cat flap and wound itself around his legs. The cat food was in a special bowl on a plastic mat.

He could hear the fridge humming; there was a little red light on the wall behind the cooker. The kettle was still warm and the remains of washing-up bubbles were popping in the sink.

The Cat Woman's handbag was on the table. Her gold watch was in a saucer beside the taps. Martin opened the handbag and felt inside. There was a fat purse there, with a card showing the Cat Woman's grave puckered face; and her name, Emily Jackson. There was a comb there, too, and a cheque book; an unopened pack of Handy Andys; an open pack of chewing gum and two biros; a lipstick in a gold case and a small round magnifying mirror with a handle.

Martin uncapped the lipstick and sniffed it. It was pink and perfumed and waxy. When he looked into the magnifying mirror his odd-coloured eyes looked back at him: huge and dark and serious. He imagined Emily Jackson's pinched mouth stretching itself open to apply the lipstick, her little lips rolling over one another like the mangle in the shed in their garden.

The next night he went back and slipped the magnifying mirror into his pocket. It felt as though he had a fragment of the Cat Woman with him.

After that, he went into night houses whenever he could: not just the Cat Women's houses; any house with an open window. He liked to stand there and feel the people asleep above his head. He liked the quiet sounds the houses made; their electric clocks clicking, their boilers bubbling. He liked their different smells.

One night he went into a toilet and pissed there, against the side of the bowl so it made no sound. The room smelt of soap. It was exciting, but he felt ashamed afterwards. He felt he had violated their territory by pissing there. Also he was afraid the people in the house would track him down by his scent. Though he knew humans didn't sniff each other like animals, he remembered how powerful human brains were, full of knowledge they didn't know they possessed.

When his mother questioned him he said he was out watching owls. And it was true in a way. There was a tawny owl perch in the big beech at the end of the street and he'd heard them calling and seen them flying silently out towards the river. Underneath the tree he'd found owl pellets crammed with beetle wings and the needle bones of shrews.

He knew it was wrong to hide in other people's gardens and break into their houses, but he didn't want to stop. It made him feel scared and excited; it made his dick go hard.

Sometimes he tiptoed through to a sitting room and sat on a sofa in front of a dark television. Or ate a mouthful of leftovers from the fridge. If it was leftovers, he reasoned, they didn't need it; and anyway it was never more than a mouthful. Eating what they'd been eating, like stealing the Cat Woman's mirror, was like taking a piece of them with him.

After a few weeks he started venturing upstairs. The air in the sleeping rooms made him giddy: the smells of hair and feet and toothpaste. Why didn't they wake up? He was certain he'd know immediately if there was someone in his bedroom. Sometimes he bent right over them and inhaled their fuggy breath, took a sip from a glass of water on a bedside table.

For some reason, he kept returning to Emily Jackson's house. There was something about her that intrigued him. Whenever he went there, things were exactly like the last time: the warm kettle and popping bubbles in the sink; the gold watch in the saucer; the handbag on the table. There were never any crumbs on the floor to stick to his bare feet. In the fridge there was always a packet of ham, a soft lettuce and some tomatoes; an open tin of cat food and a pint of semi-skimmed milk.

In the laundry basket on the landing there were always beige tights, plain white knickers and floral blouses in shades of pale blue and brown. Her duvet cover and curtains were made of similar fabric.

Emily Jackson kept her tea bags in a brown tin with 'tea' written on it and her coffee in a matching tin labelled 'coffee'. She collected her dry-cleaning every Saturday and polished her shoes every Sunday. At some point it occurred to Martin that she must have noticed that her mirror was missing.

Once she had a man to supper. In the fridge, the night before, was a pound of mince. There was a bottle of red wine beside the kettle. After the man had gone, she'd sat for ages at the kitchen table, surrounded by dirty dishes.

Why didn't she lock her window? He liked to think it was because she wanted him to keep visiting her house. Maybe it was her unconscious brain inviting him in. Maybe she wanted his fox feet on her clean lino; his garden hands on her soiled clothes.

He thought she might be sad, this Emily Jackson. He thought the man might have said something to upset her. When he was older, he thought, he'd find a woman like Emily Jackson and make her happy.

One night Martin realized he wasn't alone in the gardens. Perched in one of his favourite trees, he heard whispering in the back lane, then two figures scrambled over one of the gates about halfway down the terrace. They were trying to keep quiet, and they were wearing trainers, but Martin could hear them blundering through the bushes.

Parting the leaves, he watched them approach one of the houses and bend over by the back door. There was a quiet scratching sound and the crack of breaking glass, then they were opening the door and slipping inside. Minutes later they were out again and over the fence into the next garden.

Confident they couldn't see him, Martin settled down to monitor their progress up the street. They must have been watching the houses earlier because they avoided the two with dogs. He found himself tensing whenever they made a noise, expecting a bedroom light to flick on. It occurred to him that stealing from night houses was something he could do much better than them.

After a while he realized they were getting close to Emily Jackson's house. The thought of their muddy trainers on her clean floor made him feel sick. He pictured them grabbing her watch and rifling through her handbag. A moment later he was sprinting down the back lane, then along the footpath and on to Argyle Street.

Outside what he thought was her front door he hesitated. Was this really her house? He'd never looked at it properly from the front before. Then – yes, he recognized the curtains in the front room. Running to the door, he pressed on the bell and heard a weak little ding-dong in the hall. When nothing happened, he banged with his fists, then knelt and called her name through the letter box.

At last! A light in the upstairs window, and her pinched face peering down at him.

'Call nine-nine-nine!' he shouted. 'There are burglars in your back garden.'

For a second she was angry and he could tell that she didn't believe him, then he saw her face change and heard her feet on the stairs. The hall light came on and he heard her talking on the phone, then the door opened and she was pulling him into her house.

'They're sending a car,' she said, thrusting the mouthpiece at him. 'Tell them what you saw.'

Looking back, he realized that was when he should have run away.

The police arrived a moment later, crowding into Emily Jackson's narrow hall, then clumping up the stairs to look out of her bedroom window.

Martin started towards the door, intending to make a dash for it, but a tall policeman with a big nose and sloping chin, caught him by the shoulder.

'Not so fast, sonny. We'll need a statement from you.' He glanced at Martin's bare feet and scuffed knees. 'Let's start with what you're doing out at this time of night.'

He steered Martin into the kitchen where Emily Jackson sat shivering at the table in a padded dressing gown, with her handbag clutched to her chest.

'I was looking at the owls,' Martin said.

A policewoman in a stiff little hat was filling the kettle and putting some biscuits on a plate. The light seemed very bright. Martin was aware that his hair needed cutting and that he was wearing a four-day tee shirt.

'Where do you live?' asked Big Nose.

'Down near the end of the street,' Martin said vaguely. 'The house with the blue door.' (That was safe. There were at least five blue doors on Argyle Street.)

'Do your parents know you're out this late?'

Martin shook his head. 'Can I watch from upstairs?' he asked. He felt proud and excited to have been the cause of all this.

Big Nose laughed. 'Go on, then. Tell the officer in the bedroom that PC Dimbleby said it was OK.'

The upstairs policeman was looking out of the window and talking into a buzzing box on a wire attached to his belt. 'They're heading east,' he was saying. 'On a level with the school. There's a clump of fir trees.'

They caught the burglars easily, blocking off the back lane then advancing systematically through the gardens. A clumsy sprint and a scuffle and it was all over.

'Right, son, let's get you home.' Big Nose was waiting in the hall when Martin came downstairs. 'This racket will have woken your parents and they'll be wondering where you are. We'll come back tomorrow to take a statement.'

Martin started to say he'd go home by himself, but Big Nose put a heavy hand on his shoulder and steered him through the front door.

Outside two more policemen were progressing slowly down the street, knocking at each house, trying to find out who else had been burgled. Doors were opening, one by one, and oblongs of yellow light were falling out. Lights were on in all the upper windows. All the dogs were barking. Everyone was awake.

Mind racing, Martin set off slowly down the street. How could he keep Big Nose out of his house? 'My mum's been ill,' he tried. 'She took a sleeping pill last night. If I can slip in the back way, it won't wake her.'

'Sorry, son. Nice try. But I'm afraid we're going to have to wake her. I think she needs to know what you've been getting up to.'

Martin's house was the only one without a light on. The leaves of the towering privet hedge looked black in the orange of the streetlights. Ivy and clematis sprawled across the roof like a ragged blanket and hung down in swathes over the top windows.

'This is it,' he said. There were rolls of old carpet piled up against the front door and bits of litter in the branches of the privet hedge. He didn't dare look at Big Nose's face. 'We don't use this door,' he explained. 'The key doesn't work. We'll have to go round the back.'

'How long has your mother been ill, son?' asked Big Nose. His voice was quiet and controlled – different from the brisk friendly tone he'd used earlier.

Right up to the last moment Martin thought it might be all right. If they were quiet enough, maybe his mother wouldn't wake up. If they stayed in the kitchen, maybe Big Nose wouldn't notice the Jungle Room or the Swamp on the stairs.

But there was a light on when they got to the kitchen door; and his mother was standing at the sink in her nightdress, warming her big hands around the Peasant Cup.

When she saw the policeman, she tensed and looked around wildly for a moment, and Martin knew she was trying to work out a way to escape. Then her shoulders sagged, as though the air was leaking out of her body.

'I'm sorry, Mum,' said Martin.

She put out a hand to him. 'It's all right Marty. Something like this was bound to happen sometime.' She pulled him to her and hugged him tightly. 'Don't worry,' she whispered. 'We'll be OK.'

'There's been a burglary, ma'am,' said Big Nose. 'Your boy has been helping us catch the culprits.'

His mother looked up and smiled. 'Would you like a cup of herbal tea?' she asked.

The policeman asked his mother to pack a change of clothes, then drove them to the police station, where they waited for an ambulance to take them to the Littlemore Hospital 'for assessment'.

It was nearly light by the time they arrived and they were shown in to a big room with square red and beige chairs around the walls. There was a low table in the centre of the room, with a spider plant and three ashtrays on it.

A fat woman in a white cap brought them milk and tea and buttered toast with raspberry jam.

'It's Factory Tea,' Martin whispered. 'Are you going to drink it?'

'I suppose I'll have to,' his mother whispered back. 'I don't expect they serve Grasshopper in here.'

They ate slowly. The toast was soggy, but Martin liked it. The chairs were stuffed with yellow sponge that billowed out where the seams had split. They made a farting noise when you sat on them. Martin began to relax. Everyone was being so nice, and no one had tried to take him away. 'What's going to happen?' he asked. 'When will they let us go home?'

'I don't know, Marty. But you saw the way that policeman looked at the Swamp. I don't think they'll let us back home until the roof's fixed.'

'What'll happen to the animals?' He had a cat-mauled rabbit, three nestlings and a rat with a chewed tail in the Jungle Room. 'Will they let me go back and feed them?'

'I expect they'll send someone round to check on them,' she said. 'I expect they're used to making sure people's animals are looked after when they have to leave suddenly.'

Next afternoon an earnest young woman called Sue arrived to drive Martin to a place called Barnard House, just off the Banbury Road.

'Just for a few days, until we decide what to do with you,' she said, showing him how to fasten his seatbelt. 'Clunk, click, like on the telly.'

'Why can't I stay with Mum?'

'Your mother's been very ill,' said Sue, who had been introduced to him as 'your social worker'. 'She has to stay at the hospital while the doctors decide what kind of treatment to give her.'

'She treats herself,' he said. 'With Grasshopper Tea and t'ai chi. She hasn't had a big Bad Sad for ages.'

'What are they like, your mother's Bad Sads, Martin?' she asked in the same careful voice Big Nose had used when he'd seen the house. By the way she avoided looking at him, Martin could tell she was very interested in this.

'They're OK,' he said guardedly. 'She just goes a bit quiet, that's all.' Then, to distract her: 'Can we go to my house first and feed the animals?'

'Oh, don't worry about the animals. There are some people going to the house today. They'll make sure they're all right.'

Barnard House was a handsome old building zigzagged with green fire escapes. They rang the bell and went in via a boxy grey extension on the ground floor. A man wearing a brown jumper with beige lozenge shapes on the front appeared from a back room.

This is Mr McGillivray,' said Social Sue. 'He's in charge of the house.'

'Call me Jeff,' he said to Martin, holding out a small dry hand to be shaken. 'You're quite a hero, you know, catching those burglars like that.' He turned to Social Sue. '*The Mail* and *The Express* have been on the phone already. What shall I tell them?'

'No comment, I suppose. Someone in the office is writing a press release. If there's any problem, you'd better put them on to me.'

Call Me Jeff led Martin upstairs to a room with three beds and three chests of drawers.

'I've put you with two other boys, a bit younger than you,' he said. 'They'll be back from school at about four.' The sheets were thick and stiff and white, with 'Barn H' embroidered in the corner in red. There was a shaggy green rug on the brown lino. Behind the door hung two small tartan dressing gowns.

'Will I be going to school too?' Martin asked. He was beginning to feel excited. It was a bit like Matala, he thought, with all the boys in together. He wouldn't mind staying here for a few days.

'In the fullness of time, once you've settled in.' Call Me Jeff distributed Martin's few clothes in one of the chests of drawers. When they came down again the hall was full of the warm smell of frying onions.

There were ten boys and three girls living at Barnard House, Call Me Jeff told him, all aged somewhere between ten and sixteen; plus two 'youth workers' who took turns sleeping in a little room on the ground floor. 'And I have my own flat, up its own flight of stairs behind the office.'

There was a sitting room with a television, and a games room with a huge green table with a net, and a smaller glass-topped table with rows of little men on long sticks inside it. In the kitchen there was a massive silver cooker with six rings, and a sink so deep you could have a bath in it. A burly old woman called Ena, with threadbare two-tone brown hair, was ripping open a huge bag of frozen white chips.

Martin decided he liked the way the house smelt: of frying and boys' feet. And he liked Call Me Jeff. But the children, when they appeared, made him nervous. They seemed so big and loud, even the two younger boys he was sharing with. And spotty, especially the older boys. And rude, burping and swearing and shoving each other. At supper they were clumsy. Their hands seemed too heavy for their arms. They tipped out too much tomato ketchup and kept knocking their glasses and slopping their lemon squash on to the table.

'You're that wild boy, aren't you?' said the boy opposite, cramming a long chip into his wide mouth. 'You're in the papers.'

The newspapers had dubbed him the 'Wild Boy of Iffley Fields', and were saying he had some kind of zoo in his back room. 'What kind of animals do you have?' the children wanted to know.

'Just a few birds and wild rabbits.' Martin blushed as he felt their eyes on him.

'And you caught those burglars.' The boy – David – peered under the table, then glared accusingly at Martin. 'They said you didn't have any shoes.'

'I have got shoes, but I like going barefoot at night because it's quieter. You can sneak up on things better.'

They were impressed by this, he could tell. Their faces were softening and opening towards him. 'My name's Martin,' he said, and tried a smile.

A few days later Social Sue took him to see his mother at the Littlemore. There were three other women in the visiting room, sitting in a row against the wall, all smoking and tapping their cigarettes into an ashtray on a pole. They were all in their dressing gowns, even his mother.

He ran to hug her. But her arms, around him, felt leaden and she smelt odd: of cigarettes and coffee and some strange-smelling soap. He hugged her tighter, willing her arms to hug him back properly.

'Mum, please!' he said, as the arms dropped away like dead weights. 'If they think you're OK they'll let us go back home.'

But it was no good. As he released her, she sighed the kind of sigh that came all the way up from her feet and expelled every photon of light from her body.

'I don't think I can be OK in this place, Marty,' she said in a dull voice.

Chapter 18

Sylvia wakes with energy fizzing in her veins. She's got into a bit of a rut with the house; going there every day, sanding things down and painting them, but never quite completing any of the rooms. Now Martin's available again, she can get things finished. She realizes she's been waiting, stockpiling small jobs for him. If he comes for just two evenings, she'll be able to move in.

'Wow, that red is amazing,' he says, jumping down from the van. 'Blood on snow, like in *Snow White*.'

'Dimitri bullied me into it,' she says. 'I wanted pale green.' It's odd having him back in her house, actually talking to her, when she's spent so long watching him from a distance.

'The walls have come up really well, haven't they? And you hardly notice the repairs on the doors.' He places a brown hand on a whitewashed window sill. 'I can feel the place smiling.'

'The kitchen's nearly finished,' she says. 'If you could get those chairs back from that old man and put up some new hooks for those shelves, all I have left to do is the curtain for under the sink.'

He's touching everything in the room, running his hand over the table, the cupboard, the big fridge juddering in its corner. 'I thought you were going to strip everything down to the bare wood.'

'I was, but when I was saddled with the red, I just abandoned all attempt at subtlety.' She's sanded the table top and the top of the cupboard back to the golden wood, but painted everything else buttercup yellow: the fridge, the shelves, the cupboard doors, the chairs. 'It took three coats to cover all that mustard and turquoise.'

'You've done a really professional job too,' he says, squatting down to examine a table leg. 'Most people are crap at glossing. And the floor tiles look great, don't they?'

'I love the terracotta with that red and the yellow,' she's tumbling words out, relieved he approves. 'And I found a few bits of old pottery among all the other stuff. Four really ancient hand-painted plates and some jugs, and there were a couple of old bowls in the chicken house. I thought I'd go to Chania to see if I could find some more.'

She follows him through the cherry-red door to the bedroom. 'I left the old beams and the boards in here, but everything else was patched old and new, so I painted it.' She's used a rich bright blue for the wood in this room: the rickety wardrobe and the balustrade, the bedside table, the little flight of steps up to the platform. 'I did the beds blue, too,' she says. 'They're over there in bits, waiting to be reassembled. I tried doing it myself, but it needs two people to hold the ends up. And I need some hooks putting up for the mosquito net.'

'Blue's the colour of the unconscious,' he says. 'Did you know?'

'I'm going to get some rag rugs for the floor,' she chatters on; she can't stop. 'I saw some in that plastics shop in Kalives. And make some muslin curtains for the windows and door, so I can leave them open at night when it gets hotter.'

'It's lovely, Sylvia,' he says, turning to her with his open face. 'I was afraid you'd go for black and white, like your clothes.'

He pushes open another red door to the secret room.

'Apart from the walls and the window, I haven't done anything in here,' she says. 'It needs shelves by the sink, and some kind of workbench. And the blackout screens. And there's still our old friend to deal with.'

They stand side by side looking at the sideboard.

'You kept the light going,' he says quietly. 'I had a bet with myself that you'd let it go out.'

He sounds shaken, and she looks at him in surprise. It's never occurred to her to let it go out. Every day, the first thing she does when she arrives at the house is check the wick and top up the oil.

With the new mattresses and the beds assembled on the sleeping platform, the house feels subtly different: ready; waiting to be lived in.

'I need to buy sheets,' says Sylvia, lying down experimentally on one of the beds. There's a tiny window at eye level, framing a small square of lemon tree. 'This window's perfectly placed to look through when you're in this position.'

'It's designed to pull a breeze in when the door's open,' Martin says. 'All these old houses have them. Leonidas told me people used to hang pieces of meat around a building plot before starting on a new house. The one that stayed fresh longest showed where the coolest place was.'

'Did he do that in Drapanos?'

'You're joking. That's all off-the-peg stuff. Bulldoze the land-scape flat and plonk the houses down in rows like on a Monopoly board. Not stepped down the slopes or around the rocks like these old places.'

'It's strange to think of that old woman sleeping here.'

There'd been a tiny picture of the Virgin Mary in a pale blue plastic frame, and a wooden crucifix, tied with wire to the old bedstead. She's cleaned them and put them in the drawer of the blue bedside table. There's a hand-crocheted white mat she found on the top shelf in the wardrobe. She plans to wash it and set a jug full of red geraniums in the middle of it. She imagines waking up and looking out at her square of lemon tree, reaching into the drawer for her thermometer. Suddenly she can't wait to move in.

'My mother painted her bedroom blue,' he's saying. 'Well it was a kind of turquoise really, and she never finished it.'

'Why not?'

'Oh, she was always starting things, then running out of energy. The house was a mess.'

'God, I'm the exact opposite,' she says, sitting up and hugging her knees. 'I can never let go. Even if I absolutely hate a book, I have to go on to the last page.'

'But you get things done,' he says, stroking the top of the blue balustrade. 'I mean, look at this place.'

'You weren't here when I was doing the bloody whitewash. I was like a woman possessed.'

'Are you going to relax now?'

'I hope so. That's what I'm supposed to be here for.'

'To have a baby.' He's looking down at her; his mouth seems very soft.

'Yes.'

'But you've got to try not to think about it, because anxiety might interfere with fertility.' How does he know that?

'Actually the data's contradictory,' she says. 'But yes, something like that.' She sighs. 'Though I can't ever really stop thinking about it, because I have to take my temperature every morning – to check when I'm ovulating.'

'Why don't you just chuck the thermometer in the bin and use desire as a signal?' He's tugging on the balustrade, testing its strength.

'What do you mean?' The word 'desire' hangs between them.

He looks at her. 'Female sparrows don't need to take their temperature to know when they're ready to mate. You must have seen them. Full of lust, squatting down with their tails in the air and squawking until the males get the idea.'

She looks away. 'If you've been trying for a baby as long as I have, desire becomes a bit of an optional extra,' she says ruefully.

'But what if hormones are controlled by sexual desire?' He squats down so that his face is on a level with hers. 'If you're prepared to credit that hormones are affected by anxiety, why not by desire?'

'Because if that were the case I'd have had a baby ages ago.' She doesn't like the way the conversation is going. The closeness of his face is unnerving. Something happens to his eyes when he's arguing with her; they become very dark and open, as though drinking in her attention.

'Maybe you don't desire your husband enough,' he says.

She laughs shortly. 'I have to say this all seems a bit rich coming from someone who's banished desire from his life.'

'Being celibate doesn't stop you desiring someone,' he says matter-of-factly, vaulting suddenly over the balustrade and down from the platform.

'So what happened to her?' Sylvia asks, stepping more primly down to join him.

'Who?'

'Your mother. You were referring to her in the past tense.'

'She died when I was eighteen. And before you ask, I never really knew my father.'

'Oh, I'm sorry.'

'Sometimes I say they're in America, to stop people doing that thing.'

'What thing?'

'That "poor orphan Marty" thing you're doing. That "so that's why he's so weird" thing.'

'I don't think you're weird.'

'Yes you do. People like you always think I'm weird. The guys I work with don't give a fuck what I think about things. All they care about is whether I mix cement right and lay a level line of bricks.'

'How did she die?'

'Why do you want to know?'

'I don't know,' she says, bridling at his 'people like you'. 'Why does anyone want to know anything about someone else?'

'Because they want to hook them in in some way, usually,' he shrugs. 'Or because they want to have sex with them. Which probably amounts to the same thing.'

'God, you really are something!' Her hand tingles with the urge to slap him.

'That's why Aphrodite wants to know about me. It drives her crazy that she doesn't know where I live.'

'Why don't you just tell her?'

'Don't get me wrong. I really like Aphrodite. But she's like a spider in the middle of a web, with her little high-heeled feet on every strand feeling out for the vibrations. She likes to know where every one of her little flies is and what they're up to.'

'And you assume that means she fancies you.'

'I told you, most of the women I work for fancy me. It goes with the territory.'

'What about me?' She crosses her arms and faces him.

'Yes, I think you fancy me.'

'But?'

'You think I'm weird.' He grins.

'I think you're young,' she says tartly. 'I'm nearly old enough to be your mother – and, unlike some women, I don't go in for cradle-snatching.' She's surprised by the startled look in his eyes.

The next day she catches an early bus into Chania and comes back in a taxi, wondering why she hadn't thought to do this when she was worrying how to transport her tins of moss-green paint.

'I've just spent two hundred euros buying things for the house,' she tells Bennet when she phones that evening.

'Hurray! I was beginning to think you'd gone completely native. Cooking with cowpats and sleeping on a grass pallet.'

'I bought sheets and towels and a pink potty with a hinged lid for under the bed.'

'Glad to see you've got your priorities sorted out.'

'And a shiny red singing kettle and four puffy pillows. And an ironing board covered with little blue daisies. And an iron, and clothes pegs. And a yellow washing-up bowl. In fact I completely filled the taxi with various plastic items in garish primary colours.'

'That's my girl. What about an immersion heater for the shower?'

'I thought I'd see how long I can manage without. It's beginning to get really hot, so I can't see it being a problem for a while. And for washing up greasy things I can just heat water in the—'

'—shiny red singing kettle.'

'The sleeping platform looks wonderful. I'm going to spend my first night there tomorrow.'

'How's the temperature chart?'

'Steady. I'm expecting a blip in a week or so. How are the circulatory systems of the Arab World?'

'Bloody conveyor belt. I could sleep for a week.'

'I hope Val's keeping an eye on your nutrition.'

'If being forced to shell out a fortune for obscure veggie side dishes in posh restaurants is what you mean, then the answer is "yes".'

'She still hasn't called me, you know. Do you think she's pissed off with me about something?'

'What?' He sounds surprised. 'No. I mean, not as far as I know. Why?'

'It just seems odd, that's all. One minute she's planning a girlie holiday in Crete, next she seems to drop off the face of the earth.'

'I'll send her off to a travel agent tomorrow.'

'Tell her I'm working on a shortlist. She'll know what I mean.'

'What?'

'Give her my love.'

'Give you my love.'

Aphrodite gives her a lift up the hill with her luggage. 'Will you be scared up here on your own?'

'I'll be fine.' Sylvia gives her a hug.

'I will put clean sheets in your old room and leave the door open for if you are chased away by ghosts in the middle of the night.'

'Martin says they're all friendly. He claims we've scared all the baddies away.'

'Have you got towels? I can bring up more towels if you need. And the coffee, remember it must be like volcano lava when you take it off the flame. Have you got matches?'

'I've got everything. I've got too much. Look at all this stuff! I can't believe I've amassed all this clutter in just three months.'

'So, we will wave to each other every morning.'

'I'll come back to collect the scooter tomorrow.'

'And we will be friends now, yes? Not like the cook and the customer. Like two women with their troubles. We will visit and drink coffee and eat sweets.'

'I'm sure I've forgotten something.' Sylvia looks around distractedly at the hotchpotch of suitcases and carrier bags in the middle of the patio. She feels like a refugee on a railway platform.

'Let me make you a coffee while you put away your things.' Aphrodite takes the key from Sylvia's hand and unlocks the kitchen door.

When she leaves two hours later it's very quiet. Sylvia washes the cups and hangs them up on the new hooks she's attached to the old set of shelves.

I need a doormat, she thinks, wandering outside and sitting down on one of the old white plastic chairs. *And a bedside lamp. And I need to talk to Vasilios about looking after the vine*. She started a list as she was unpacking, but she's left it in the kitchen.

A movement draws her eyes down to the lower terrace, to the flat building plot, where two half-grown tabby kittens are stalking something invisible in the waving grass. Lying on her side in the shade, the tip of her tail flicking, a larger black cat is watching.

I should take some photos of the house, she thinks, *to compare with the 'before' shots*.

She gets up for her camera, but goes to the fridge instead. Inside is a Tupperware dish from Aphrodite – 'for your lonely supper' – and a shelf full of bottles of water. In the door is a bottle of ice-cold retsina.

She pours a glass and drifts from room to room, sipping. She thinks: *I have swept and scrubbed and painted every inch of this house.* It's a good thought, one that makes her feel at home.

Martin arrives as she's upending the Tupperware dish into one of Kokona's dented pans.

'It's June the twenty-first,' he says. 'The longest day, did you realize? Or the shortest night, depending on your state of mind.'

'Shortest night sounds good to me,' she says. 'I'm beginning to get a bit nervous.' She's absurdly pleased to see him, and finds she's been dreading the long first evening here on her own.

He's showered and put on clean clothes. His hair's damp; she can smell his herbal shampoo. Thinking about it, and his Johnson's baby soap, makes her smile.

'I wanted to make sure you were OK,' he says.

'I will be if you'll help me eat this. There's tons.'

'And I've brought you a house-warming present.' He hands her a small parcel wrapped in brown paper.

Inside is a tiny white Chinese bowl, with a blue fish painted on the inside. It's a crude mass-produced thing; the fish's tail is slightly smudged. But the way he's wrapped it, and the solemn way he's given it to her, makes her cup it in her hand as though it's precious.

'It's for the hungry ghosts,' he says, studying her face. 'You don't have to use it, but I thought—'

'No, no. I will,' she says. 'I want to. Thank you.'

'It might make you feel a bit less weird about moving in.'

They eat outside under the vine pergola watching the sun sink behind the Madares mountains. He shows her how to use the offering bowl, choosing small morsels of lamb and green beans and placing them separately on it.

'It's a gift, so it's important to choose the best bits,' he says, 'the bits you'd choose first for yourself. And do it at the beginning of the meal, when you're still hungry – not as an afterthought when you've eaten enough.' He watches her pinch off a soft chunk of bread and dip it in the gravy, then place it in the little bowl. 'You don't have to say anything, or even think about it,' he says. 'Just doing it is enough.'

Lights start to wink on in the village below and bats are swerving between the trees in the garden. Sylvia hasn't switched her own patio light on yet, but she can feel the eyes of the village on her: *There's that English woman, sitting outside Kokona's house at sunset with that young builder.*

'So what are you doing here?' she asks, pouring the last of the retsina into his glass.

'In the existential sense?' he asks, smiling in the semi-darkness. 'Or in the "what's a nice boy like me doing in a place like this" sense?'

'In the nice boy sense.'

'I used to come to Crete a lot when I was a kid. To a place in the south of the island. There were some friends we used to stay with.'

'What, so you came for a holiday and just stayed?'

'I'd been meaning to come back for ages, to scatter my mother's ashes. She really loved it here. It was the only place she really relaxed.'

'But she died, what? Eight, nine years ago?'

'Ten.'

'Sorry, do you mind me asking?'

'I just kept putting it off really. First I was getting my NVQ. Then going from one job to another, getting caught up. Involved with people. Then I realized I couldn't put it off any longer.'

'So why did you stay on afterwards?'

'Because I haven't done it yet.'

'What?'

'I didn't scatter the ashes. I went back to where we used to stay, in some caves overlooking the sea, but it was all completely different. They'd turned the place into some kind of heritage site and surrounded it with a wire fence.'

'Was it that hippy place? Where Donovan and Cat Stevens stayed?'

'That's the one. Peace and love, Indian beads, the whole thing. Apparently it used to be a Roman cemetery, so the Greeks turfed out the hippies and set up a kiosk where we used to have the big dining table. I had to pay two euros to go in.'

'So your mum was a hippy.'

'She wanted to go back there to live permanently. That's why she bought the camper van – well, it's my camper van now. She was going to drive overland from England and camp on the way.'

So the van was his mother's. 'Where are the ashes now?'

'In the van. I couldn't leave them in Matala, with all the ice-cream wrappers and beer cans. She'd have hated it.'

She thinks of the neat panelled alcoves in the van, trying to remember if she'd noticed an ornament that might hold a person's ashes. 'So what are you going to do?' she asks.

'I don't know. Work. Try to save some money. It cost a fortune in petrol to get here.'

'Don't you have to get home?'

'I'm not sure I believe in a place called home,' he says, looking out into the night. 'I think maybe we're supposed to be travellers. Like bushmen in the Kalahari, or Aborigines in Australia. Have you read *The Songlines*?'

She shakes her head, thinking of the neat frieze of books in the camper van.

'It's about how humans are meant to move from place to place, because we're genetically programmed to be hunter-gatherers. That we develop by moving, finding out things, interacting with our environment. That settling down, owning a house, is a kind of death.'

'Do you believe that?'

'I think we should tread lightly on the earth. It feels right to limit what I own to what I can carry in the van.'

'So you don't approve of second homes.' She thinks of her tall house in Newcastle, all the rooms in it, all the things.

'It depends. People in Botswana have two homes: one on the land where they grow their food, and one near the watering holes where they graze their cattle in the dry season. And they move between the two depending on the weather.'

'Like Brits flying off to the Canaries in January,' she jokes.

'That's just tourism,' he says. 'That's not about survival.'

'Is that why you live in your mum's camper van? Or is it just a hippy aversion to settling down?' She's been wondering about this, about why he's not married, not rooted, why he behaves like a man on the run.

'When my mother stopped travelling, she died,' he says quietly. 'I don't mean when she stopped travelling literally. I mean when she stopped trying, stopped thinking. I hate it when people get stuck. You see them plodding along in their muddy ruts. It makes me want to shake them.' He leans forwards suddenly. 'That's why I like you.'

'I thought I was just another "middle-class madam" with an aversion to germs,' she says, starting to pile up the plates.

'No, you're on a journey. Anyone can see that. This place, your photography, all your crazy fertility stuff.'

'Hey! A bit less of the crazy and a bit more of the helping clear the table.' They take the dirty things into the kitchen and she makes coffee and brings the cups back outside, while he fetches the little oil lamp from the secret room.

'How long have you been celibate?' she asks as he sits down again.

'Only a couple of years,' he says, 'but it's been good. You know ex-alcoholics go on about all the things they missed out on when they were drunk all the time? It's like that with sex. You'd never have let me sit here with you if you thought I was going to jump you at any moment.' He grins at her. The lamp flickers in his strange eyes.

'Celibacy sounds a bit like being married,' she says. 'I met Bennet at Cambridge and we've never been unfaithful to each other. It's as though we're in a lifeboat together, and everyone else is in the sea.'

'Safe, you mean.'

'More relieved I don't have to do all of that floundering about. All that will-he-won't-he, waiting-by-the-phone stuff. I like to know where I am. Plus loving and being loved, of course.'

'Of course.' She can hear the smile in his voice.

'So what made you get out of the water?'

'A woman I was having sex with tried to commit suicide.'

'God.' This isn't what she was expecting. 'Because she was in love with you?'

'That was part of it, yes. Though it was more about her weight problem and the way her bastard husband treated her. I was just the catalyst. I found her crushing paracetamol in a marble pestle and mortar.'

'Maybe she wanted you to find her.'

'No, she planned it for when she was going to be alone. And she knew you don't use paracetamol to make a gesture. That it fucks up your liver if you don't die. I can see the pestle in her hand, grinding away at the tablets; the sound it made. And that determined look on her face. She'd read somewhere that you start to vomit them up if you swallow them whole.'

'So you concluded you were a danger to women.'

'I thought I was helping her. You know, giving her a bit of self-esteem. She was a historian. Really clever, head of department. With beautiful breasts, and those chubby little arched feet some very fat women have.'

A tree frog starts up in the fig tree, ringing like a little bell in the darkness. A dark shape slinks along the path around the side of the house.

'Why are you telling me this?' she asks quietly.

'Because you need to know it.'

'So does Aphrodite. She's always going on about how secretive you are.'

He sighs. 'Wanting to know a thing and needing to know it aren't necessarily the same thing.'

'You know it can be really irritating when you talk in riddles,' she says.

'Some things make more sense when they're told indirectly. Like when a faint star looks brighter out of the corner of your eye.'

'See? There you go again.'

'OK,' he says, smiling again. 'I'm telling you because you pay attention. Because you kept that lamp burning, even though you didn't believe in it. Because you don't close a book until you've finished reading it.'

He leaves at ten o'clock. 'So people down at the *Petaluda* will see the headlights coming down the hill at a decent hour,' he says with a wink, swinging up into the driver's seat.

When he's gone, she sits for a while listening to the night noises: crickets churring over by the chicken house; tree frogs chiming across the valley; the nibbling of some rodent in the vine above her head; a quick rustle and pounce in the dry leaves out among the fruit trees.

She feels restless, excited, not at all ready for bed. But she goes through the motions anyway: washing and brushing her teeth in the Barbie toilet; putting on her nightdress and setting out her thermometer and temperature chart, her bottle of water.

Sitting on the blue bed with its crisp new white sheets, she picks up her mobile to call Bennet. But when she switches it on, the battery's dead.

She stares at it stupidly: neat and silver and inert, an artefact from another planet. She can picture the charger: still plugged into the socket in her room at the taverna.

It takes her a long time to get to sleep. She keeps thinking of the candle stub in the pocket of Kokona's apron, now burned along with the rest of her clothes; of the pitchfork exactly where she reached for it; the axe laid neatly as a knife across a plate; of the key on its secret hook under the stairs, now hanging beside the door to the third room.

She thinks of the third room itself, waiting for its new occupant, the empty room, like the spare room in her house in Newcastle. Of the evicted wild cats, out prowling somewhere else. The photographs in their frames, all those fierce smiles, stacked face-to-face out of sight in the sideboard.

She wakes briefly just before dawn, to the sound of her gate creaking open and shuffling footsteps on the patio. Behind her square of lemon tree a star shines in the dark blue sky. Later, when she gets up, she discovers a newspaper on the patio table, with four fat tomatoes and two cucumbers on it, still wet from the tap; and two small purple onions with crumbs of damp red earth on the roots. Beside them, wrapped in a twist of silver foil, is a fist of crumbly white goat's cheese.

'I suppose I could store things in it,' says Sylvia doubtfully, standing in front of the sideboard the next day. 'But it's much too high for a worktop.'

'I could make you a stool to stand on,' Martin offers.

'I'd break my neck the first day. It's too dark, even with the safelight on, to have things cluttering the floor. How about cutting off the legs?'

'I don't want to damage it. Anyway, surely even you can see that would ruin the proportions?'

'What proportions?' she asks hotly. 'And what do you mean "even me"?'

'It's obvious it was designed specifically to fit that space. It perfectly fulfilled its function for that old woman. You only think it's ugly because you don't have a use for it.'

'It's ugly because it's huge and over-elaborate and over-bearing.'

'It was made with love, and put to the use for which it was intended.'

'So?'

'So, it deserves to stay.'

'But what about my darkroom?'

'Work around it. Pretend it's a rock you can't move. Incorporate it into your plan.'

'My plan,' she says deliberately, 'is to get rid of it.'

'In Japan some people believe that certain objects earn the right not to be thrown away. Things like favourite hammers or worn-out jackets. They say "it has worked hard" and set up a special shrine for it. There's even a shrine called *hari-kuyo* for broken sewing needles.'

She stares at him. 'Where do you get this stuff?'

'That was in a book I found in a skip in Gloucester. Look, what about putting a short bit of workbench next to the sink, and a longer piece opposite? Like a sort of galley kitchen.'

'I suppose that might work,' she concedes.

'And you'd still have your shrine.'

'So it's a shrine now, is it?'

'What else would you call it?'

The weather changes overnight, rocketing to ninety-five degrees. Sylvia still goes for her morning swim, but the sea is warmer now, like a tongue on her skin. And she often goes in again at midday, too, with Aphrodite in her fuchsia bikini, in the brief hiatus between the tourists' late breakfasts and their long lunches at the *Petaluda*.

It's high season now; the cicadas start at sunrise and scream all day. The village is full of spanking new hire cars, revving and reversing down the narrow streets, parking at all angles. Sylvia keeps seeing blonde couples wandering the back lanes, plodding up the hills in shorts and strappy tops, leaning on her gate, peering rudely in at her neighbours, setting off over the rocks in search of the little pebbly beach. The taverna is crowded every evening: not just with tourists, but with young Greeks in fashionable clothes, home from Athens and Thessaloniki for the summer.

From setting the tables, Sylvia has graduated to serving and clearing at the weekends and finds her Greek suddenly improving as she moves among the tables taking orders and delivering them to the kitchen. She enjoys examining the faces of this sophisticated generation, noting a particular quirk of the eyebrow, a shape of the head, that identifies them as belonging to one or other of the families she recognizes in the village.

They are garrulous and expansive, these people, generous with their tips; in contrast to the tourists counting out their ten per cents. Totting up her booty at the end of the evening, Sylvia often discovers she has earned enough to live on for a week – though living costs little enough. Almost everything she eats arrives as a gift from one or other of her neighbours: figs, eggs, onions, potatoes.

'I wish I had something to give in return,' she says to Martin as she sets out a bowl of Greek salad one evening. 'I've got seven cucumbers in the fridge at the moment. I'm beginning to feel oppressed.'

'They don't expect it,' he says. 'Giving is such a part of the culture here, no one thinks to work out what they're owed. It's only in our society that we treat gifts as part of an exchange.'

Even though he's working at her house again, off and on, Sylvia still finds herself riding out to the place he lives. If the van's there she crouches behind a wall to watch him reading, doing t'ai chi, fiddling with the van's engine. Often he takes a shower and she gets a chance to peer inside the van again: at the wooden panelling and neat compartments, the toolboxes; everything put to the use for which it was intended.

Other times the van's missing, and she walks the site with her eyes on the ground, searching for traces of him. There: his bare footprints in the dust outside the shower room; specks of stubble peppering the basin; a knotted bin liner waiting to be disposed of.

Then one day he's gone. She knows it as soon as she gets there; by the way the gate has been closed and fastened instead of propped open. His things are gone from the bathroom too, and the washing line's been taken down.

She feels disturbed, as though a landmark in a familiar landscape has disappeared. He never mentioned he was moving. Yet he must have been planning this move for days: asking around, scouting out new places. She tries to remember where he said he was working. Vamos, she thinks it was, some last-minute work on the new bar before the opening in August.

She tracks him down more quickly this time, to a stately old two-storey house with a balcony overlooking an olive grove. The van's not there, but she recognizes his shirt on the washing line. *So you thought you could hide from me, did you?* she thinks with a smile.

By the end of the weekend the darkroom's ready and she's setting out the developing trays and poring over the instructions for the enlarger. It's much easier than she expected and soon it's plugged in and ready and she's carrying the oil burner into the bedroom, switching on the orange safelight and closing the blackout screens ready to start developing.

Taking out the first roll of film in the orange twilight of the little room, she feels as though she's snorkelling in orange water. The room seems airless, padded, muffled; like a tiny old-fashioned cinema. Her fingers inside the developing bag feel fat and clumsy.

It's one of the films she shot in Chania when they first arrived in March. When she takes it out of the developing tank and pins it up to dry, frame after frame of windows unspool before her eyes, all in negative. With their white openings and dark borders, they're like the title pages of biographies. The next roll is of empty boats bobbing on a white sea, the husks of other lives. And there's Bennet with his white lips and his glowing halo of receding hair; his black hat on the table beside him.

Hours pass as she works systematically through the familiar processes – developing, stopping, fixing, washing – until the first three are hanging up to dry like coiled chameleon tongues.

The third roll is almost all people in their carnival masks;

spooky in negative, with their white eyes staring. There are four of Bennet posing in his Pierrot, and one of her cat mask; and two badly framed shots the waiter took of them together. She remembers the crush of people in the streets, the toddlers passed overhead like balloons. The frisson of excitement when the Minotaur caught hold of her bare foot.

Then, unexpectedly, near the end of the roll, there's a shot of her asleep on the hotel bed: a white body swathed in a black sheet.

She positions it on the enlarger and examines it. How stiff she looks; her limbs neatly positioned even in sleep, her hair glossy white parentheses around her dark face. She's frowning slightly, as if she's annoyed at being photographed. One hand is clutching at the sheet. She looks as though she would wake quickly, this sleeping woman. That hand looks as if she doesn't dare to let go. As if she never dreams. Sylvia finds herself feeling sorry for her.

Her temperature dips the next day. Looking at the chart she feels oddly surprised. Is it only eight weeks since Bennet was here last? It feels like she's been living at the house for months.

'Look, sweet pea, I hope you don't mind, but I've booked us into that nice hotel in Chania,' says Bennet when he rings to tell her what flight he's on.

'Don't you want to see the house?' She feels thwarted, belittled; embarrassed for wanting so much to show it off to him.

'Of course I do. We can drive out there tomorrow afternoon. But I'm totally pooped and you told me yesterday it was in the nineties.'

'It's cooler at night. And you hardly notice the heat when you're inside. You just have to relax into it.'

'I've only got three days. There isn't time to relax into it. Sorry, sweetie. I can't face the rural idyll right now. Maybe later, when I can come for a bit longer, you can show me how to hunt wild boar and strain water through my hat.'

'Weed.'

'I knew you'd understand.'

When she goes to meet him it's like a film in reverse: taking off the crash helmet and surrendering the scooter keys to the hire people; picking up the car keys and placing them in Bennet's hand; pressing herself against his big rangy body, the top of her head under his chin, his hands on the small of her back; taking off her black linen dress and draping it carefully over the chair.

In the cool hotel room, on the white bed, she shows off her tan, placing her strong brown leg next to his hairy pale one.

'The guilty leg of the lotus eater,' he comments.

'Excuse me. That's the colour of good honest toil,' she retorts. 'I'm going to start on the garden now the house is finished, and I walk up and down the hill at least once a day to help out at the taverna, plus swimming twice a day. And working in the darkroom.'

'I don't suppose there was ever a chance that you'd actually relax?'

'This is the way I always relax: working hard, doing things I enjoy. If you stop moving you die.'

'What a weird thing to say.'

'You took a photo of me when I was sleeping,' she says in mock accusation.

'And stole your soul. Yes, I confess.'

'Except I've got the film.'

'Damn. And there was I thinking I had you in my power.' He rolls on top of her and pins her shoulders down with his hands.

'I looked sad,' she says, not resisting.

'You were sad,' he says, bringing his face down to hers.

She closes her eyes and lets him kiss her, lets his tongue into her mouth. It feels big and meaty. *He* feels big and meaty. She feels like a vegetarian eating a T-bone steak.

'I hired a motorbike after you went back last time,' she remarks when it's over, and he's rolled off her and has wedged the pillow under her buttocks.

'I thought you thought biking interfered with implantation.'

'I did,' she says. 'But I don't any more.'

Chapter 19

The Pepper-Salt Pot

Two days later Social Sue visited Barnard House and told Martin she couldn't take him to see his mother for a few days. 'She's a bit poorly,' she explained in a walking-on-eggshells voice. 'Doctor Storr says she can't have any visitors until she's feeling a bit brighter.'

Dr Storr was the psychiatrist at the Littlemore, who had interviewed Martin when he'd first arrived: a kind, broad man with a mane of fluffy grey hair brushed back from a domed forehead. Martin had thought he looked very clever; he'd imagined a big brain sparking away behind that expanse of forehead. Sorting things out and storing them away. Storing his mother in the hospital with the mad people and him with the herd of Lost Boys in the Barn.

Martin knew what 'a bit poorly' meant. It meant rocking backwards and forwards and staring at the floor. It meant not washing for weeks and forgetting to go to the toilet. It meant cup after cup of tea ignored, and going cold, and poured away.

His mother used to say, afterwards, that even though she'd never looked at him or said anything, she had been aware of him bringing her tea. That the Peasant Cup on the floor in front of her had been like an anchor holding her steady.

Now Martin thought that if she had the Peasant Cup, she might get better sooner.

He slipped out a few days later; after lunch, when Ena went home for a rest and Call Me Jeff got out the *Guardian* crossword and closed the door of the office.

He walked quickly, avoiding people's eyes. It was easy to find the way. Oxford was like a starfish with six arms. Banbury Road was one arm. All he had to do was walk down that long arm to the centre, then find the arm that was Iffley Road and set out along that until he reached the turning for Argyle Street.

When he got there he hardly recognized the house. The hedge at the front had been cut and the rubbish removed from the garden, leaving a square of black earth with white roots snaking across it. The creepers were gone from the roof and walls; the bricks were peppered with little pale dots and bits of broken stem from where the ivy had been ripped away. Upstairs the windows looked naked and vulnerable without their trailing green curtains. Downstairs someone had nailed planks of wood over the bay window so he couldn't see inside.

He walked slowly up the path like a sleepwalker and touched the door with his fingertips. There was a new lock, a shiny brass one. The pinkish flesh of the old door grinned out where the chisel had bitten in.

Would the back have a new lock too? In panic, Martin ran along the road and down the side passage to the back lane. The big back gate was bolted from the inside, but he scrambled over it, then stopped and stared.

The back was even more shorn and naked than the front. And there was scaffolding up to the roof and a patch of paler new tiles where the hole used to be. The downstairs windows were boarded up and a few limp tendrils of clematis hung down from the scaffolding poles. The plastic awning outside the Jungle Room had gone and the overhanging branches had been cut back to white stumps.

Had someone else taken over their house? There was a heap of smoking charred wood on the t'ai chi lawn, surrounded by a wide swathe of scorched grass.

Heart thudding, Martin approached the kitchen door. The glass part was boarded up, but the lock hadn't been changed. And the Yellowy-Grey Stone, under which they kept the spare key, was still in its place under the lilac tree. In a moment he was inside.

It was dark downstairs, because the windows were covered, and the lights didn't work. He felt his way to the fuse box and switched the power back on.

The house had been ransacked. In the kitchen the chairs were missing and the shelves were bare; the pantry and cupboards were empty. And the Jungle Room had been completely stripped: no rabbits or nestlings; no sluggy rug or mousey sofa; no carpet or curtains. Just three big wooden crates in the middle of the room.

Martin made his way slowly upstairs, past the pink window and on to the landing. The house seemed huge and his feet echoed on the bare floorboards. The magazine bricks were gone and pale oblongs on the walls showed where his mother's bright room photos had been taken down. In the toilet bowl upstairs was a sodden cigarette butt and a spreading brown stain.

Martin pictured it all suddenly, how it must have been: the men in checked shirts and dusty workboots, sitting on the stairs and pouring tea from a flask. Grinding out their cigarettes on the floor, then getting up to carry on ripping things down and clearing things out.

He went into his old bedroom. The bed was still there but the bedclothes were missing. The wardrobe was there too, but four empty metal hangers clinked together when he opened the door.

Back in the kitchen he started to rummage through one of the wooden crates under the table. There was a label on it, where someone had written 'kitchen' in blue felt tip. It seemed to be full of balled-up newspaper, but when he investigated one ball he found it was actually the Birthday Candlestick with its sprawl of yellow wax. Someone had packed all their belongings into wooden crates.

The next bundle he opened was the Pepper-Salt Pot. His mother had always kept the salt in the pepper pot because it sprinkled better. 'In the old days,' she'd told him, 'people were afraid to sprinkle salt, because they believed the Devil was attracted to the spilt grains. That's why they tipped it through a single hole, so it could be poured into a tidy heap.'

'Do you believe in the Devil?' he'd asked. There had been a few grains on the blue Formica and he'd eyed them nervously.

His mother had laughed. 'I think the Devil's just an excuse people use for behaving badly,' she'd said, licking a finger and blotting up the grains. 'He's something they can blame for not controlling their evil impulses.'

'So you're not worried about spilling the salt?'

'Do I look worried?' she'd asked, sprinkling more salt and licking it from the flat of her fingertip. 'Anyway I like this little pot. It's real crystal and the lid's sterling silver. It was in a box of old things belonging to my grandmother, so it's an heirloom.'

'What's an air-loom?'

'A machine the gods use to weave wind-threads into clouds,' she'd said. 'The thread comes in three colours. White, grey and blue. Ouch!' He was laughing, bashing at her hand with his spoon.

'Tell me the truth,' he'd said and she'd relented.

'An heirloom is something you pass down to your children, and their children, when you die. In the old days it was often an actual weaving loom. These days it can be anything valuable.'

A sprinkling of salt had spilt out into the paper. Martin tipped it into his palm and licked it up. Then he wrapped the Pepper-Salt Pot back up again and put it into his pocket.

About halfway down the crate he found his Man Spoon in a clump of cutlery, and put that in his pocket too. Then, near the top of the second crate, he found the Peasant Cup.

He gave it to Social Sue the next day.

'Put it somewhere she can see it,' he said, thrusting it at her before she'd even got her coat off. 'Please. Tell the nurses. It won't look like she's noticing, but she is.'

'Where did you get it?'

'I went back to the house. Someone's mended the roof and packed up all our things. Do we have to move out?' He'd been worrying about this all night.

'It was very messy, Martin. And we're not allowed to let children live in messy houses, so it had to be cleaned up. As soon as your mother's better, you can go back there.' But there was something about the careful way she said this, as though she was reading it, that made him suspicious.

'Is your mum a loony?' asked the boy with freckles and crooked teeth who shared his room.

'No, she just gets sad sometimes. When she's left alone, she always gets better.'

'So why's she in a loony bin?'

'They want to try out some pills on her. If they work, then we're going back home.'

'What if they don't work?'

'Then my dad will take me to live with him.'

Martin hadn't meant to say that. The words just slipped out like they'd been waiting there. Afterwards the thought ballooned out to fill his head.

There'd been no mention of his father since Dr Storr had asked about him that first day at the Littlemore. But now Martin started wondering whether they were trying to track him down.

When he thought of his father he pictured a big man in a long green coat on a white stallion. He thought perhaps his father had a fishing rod, like Karl's in Matala. And a camper van full of cunning cupboards and tools, like Jan the carpenter's.

He decided to ask Social Sue about it.

'The police did manage to contact your father,' she said in her careful-eggshells voice. 'He was still living in Chislehurst, so it was quite straightforward.'

There was a buzzing in Martin's ears. Though the words made sense, he felt he couldn't put them together.

'He's remarried and has two more children now, but he says when you're ready he'd love to meet you.'

Martin was staring at Social Sue's mouth. 'I thought I'd wait a while before I mentioned it,' she was saying. 'What with everything else that's been happening. But since you asked —' She had the remains of a cold sore in one corner, which kept splitting and bleeding. She was dabbing at it with a hanky.

It was too much to take in. His father in a house in Chislehurst with two children. Martin's feet felt too big. His tongue wouldn't work properly.

'Does he have a horse?' he asked.

*

The next week he went to school for the first time in his life. Call Me Jeff took him to the clothes cupboard and they went through all the old bits of grey uniform there to find things to fit him.

Social Sue took him in on Monday morning and handed him over to a woman with thick glasses and a red cardigan, who asked him to read bits from lots of different books and do sums, and joined-up writing, then gave him some sheets of paper with funny quizzes on them.

'Very good!' she pronounced as he finished the last one. 'Your mother's obviously a born teacher. There'll be a few things they've done that you won't recognize, but you're way ahead in the main subjects. I'll pop you straight into Form One with Mrs Appleby and come back to check on you next week. OK?'

Mrs Appleby had a pink face and dyed black hair with white roots. She smelt of cigarettes and her voice was deep and hoarse. She sat him at the front so she could check on what he was doing.

Everyone seemed to know he was the Wild Boy, but there were two other Barn kids in his class, so it wasn't too bad. And the lessons were a bit boring, really. Copying things from the blackboard, waiting for ages while the slow kids finished, then answering questions by reading one page in a simple book.

Martin had never thought of himself as clever before, because he'd only had his mother to compare himself to. Now, watching the other children hesitate and chew their pencils, he thought: *I can do this. Easy-peasy lemon-squeezy*, as his mother would say.

Some days were like beads on a necklace: small and round and regular; one after another; all the same pale colour. Other days were like brooches, with big gaudy stones crammed into intricate settings. Time behaved differently on a brooch day. It hesitated and swelled up and glowed. It looped out and curled back on itself. Brooch days made big bumps in the memory. They were bright and hard and sharp and you never forgot them.

A brooch day was worth a whole necklace of small beads. Moving into Barnard House had been a brooch day; going to school; seeing his old house shorn and bare. Martin felt like a year had passed since the night he climbed up a tree in Argyle Street and watched two men blundering through the gardens below. He felt he'd been transported into another life.

He used to be a boy who lived alone with his mother in a cluttered, rustling house. Now he thought he might be becoming a boy who lived with his father in a normal house with an aquarium in the sitting room.

By the time Social Sue took him to the Littlemore again, Martin had had twenty-six brooch days in a row. But his mother was in the middle of a long necklace of mud-coloured beads.

She was dressed this time, but her hair was lank. And she was like her hair: limp and stale and greasy. She seemed fatter, he thought. But it was hard to tell, because her body was so saggy, as though all the bones had been removed.

She smiled at him but didn't get up; just raised one big hand, then let it fall back on to her knee. 'The pills make me so stupid and sleepy,' she said, apologizing. 'The air feels like cotton wool.'

Martin's air felt like sea spray and limes. He started to tell her about Dave and Peter, who shared his room, and Rob the youth worker who played cards with him; and Call Me Jeff and Red Cardie and Mrs Appleby. His mother put on a bright face, but it started to slip after a few minutes, and her eyes drifted off. Then she forgot to say things like 'Really?' and 'Wow!' to keep him going, so he eventually stopped talking and just sat there beside her until Social Sue opened the door and said it was time to go.

Every time he was alone, Martin thought of his father. He looked up Chislehurst on Call Me Jeff's road atlas.

'That's where the Rolling Stones come from,' says Call Me Jeff. 'Dead posh. Full of Rolls-Royces and swimming pools.'

Martin saw that there was a railway station there and he traced the black wiggly line from page to page of the atlas until it reached a big station called Charing Cross.

'How long would it take to get from Chislehurst to here?' he asked.

'Depends how you went,' said Call Me Jeff. 'By car maybe two and a half, three hours. By train a bit less, if you were lucky with your connections.' Then: 'I hope you're not considering another unauthorized absence. We let it go last time, because you were new. Next time we won't be quite so soft on you.'

Martin smiled sheepishly and closed the atlas. But the route was burned into his brain. Oxford to Paddington. Paddington to Charing Cross. Charing Cross to Chislehurst. He could hear the trains rattling over the tracks; then back again, like a spell: Chislehurst to Charing Cross, Charing Cross to Paddington, Paddington to Oxford.

He chanted it to himself in bed that night, imagining fields and houses rushing by; hearing rattling tracks, galloping hooves; conjuring his father on a train coming to get him.

The next day, when he came back from school, Call Me Jeff intercepted him in the hall and took him into his office.

'I had a call from your father this morning,' he said. 'He's asked if he can come here to visit you.'

Chapter 20

After Bennet goes home, Sylvia spends the next three mornings in the darkroom. She's working through the remaining rolls of undeveloped film: views of the house looking up from the taverna; views of the village looking down from the kitchen; of the kitchen itself as Kokona had arranged it; of the secret room as she had first seen it; the ghostly gallery of faces; the sideboard and its contents.

Viewing the contact sheets with her magnifying glass, she's amazed at some of the shots she's taken. There are photographs here she doesn't even remember: two girls' faces, identical to each other, in separate frames; an elaborate girl doll in a crinoline holding a smaller girl doll in her arms. The photographs show shafts of light blowing through the window like milk dust, then solidifying in flat shapes like white paper. She imagines swarms of photons bombarding the film and expiring, burning their energy into it.

She keeps coming back to the picture of herself asleep. Something about it disturbs her. Is this how she is when she's not aware of herself? Stiff and straight; slightly anxious, slightly impatient. Not a hair out of place. One hand clutching at the sheet. Is this how Bennet sees her?

On the fourth morning she emerges, blinking, into the sunlight to discover Martin sitting quietly on the patio.

'How long have you been here?'

'Not long. I knocked but you didn't hear, and I didn't dare open the door in case I ruined something crucial.'

'What time is it? What day is it? God, I've been in there for ages.' The thought of him sitting out here waiting, while she's been so engrossed, makes her feel like a blind woman in a bright room full of silent people, thinking she's alone.

'Do the screens work?' he asks.

'Like a dream. I'm completely cut off in there. It's like a decontamination chamber.' She stretches to ease her shoulders. 'I've been looking at the contacts, deciding what to print up.'

'Can I see?' He follows her back into the darkroom and she closes the door. They stand together in the cool orange twilight. She can feel heat radiating from his body.

'It's like all the colour's been sucked out of the room,' he comments. 'It's weird, isn't it, that things aren't really the colour they seem? That colour is a sort of light an object reflects, like a mirror.' He starts leafing through the contact sheets.

'I don't remember taking half of those shots,' she says.

'Maybe you didn't.'

'Here we go,' she says, bracing herself. 'Let me guess. I was channelling the ghost of Kokona and she forced me to take them.'

'Do you think so?' He grins at her. 'Actually I was going to suggest something much less interesting. That maybe looking through the camera allowed the right hemisphere of your brain a bit more freedom than usual, and that your non-verbal self took the photos.'

'So I'm a multiple personality now, am I?'

'We all are.' He's serious again. 'It's inevitable. There's no way we can be aware of everything that's going on in our brains at any one time. The Sylvia you think you are is just one tiny facet of who you really are.'

'I think it's just because I'm an inexperienced photographer. I keep thinking what you see is what you get. But it's not like that with photography. Light acts on film in a completely different way to light hitting the retina, then being processed by the brain. You have to learn to see light as light, before the brain interprets it.'

'Writing with light,' he says.

'What?'

'*Photos* and *graphie*, they're the Greek words for light and writing.'

'Look at this one. I thought I was taking a picture of the incense burner, see? But it's come out with this sword of light cutting straight across it, so all you're aware of is this little doll on the far right. There are lots like that, where the light shifts the focus of the picture.'

'I think you must have been aware of those things at some level, though. I think you wanted to show the doll. I guess the trick is to stop your dominant self interfering.'

What he's saying makes sense – though she hates to admit it. There had been something wordless and instinctual about her concentration while she was taking these photos. 'I took them all the same morning; one after another. Not thinking, just looking through the viewfinder.'

'What about this one?' He's holding a large print she's made of herself asleep.

'Oh, Bennet took that. So it's his right hemisphere you have to blame.'

'You look so vulnerable,' he says, touching a finger to a curve of glossy hair.

'I think I look rather tense – and a bit cross.'

'Is that how your husband thinks of you? As someone who needs looking after?' He's still holding the photo.

'I suppose so, yes. He's been really worried about me recently. I went a bit mad after the second miscarriage. Nothing too florid, I wasn't hearing voices or anything, but he thought I should—'

'I don't like it,' he says.

'Why not?'

'It shows too much.' His voice sounds strange: low and strangled, as if his throat has closed on it. 'It makes me want to wake you up. I want to uncurl your fingers from the sheet.'

'It's only a photo, Martin.'

'He shouldn't have taken it,' he says. He sounds as though he's going to cry. 'You look dead.'

216

'Don't be silly.'

'You shouldn't do things to people when they're asleep.'

After he's gone she looks at the photo again. Now he's said it, she can see she does look dead: the colourless face, the body covered with a sheet; a cadaver in the autopsy room waiting to be dissected.

She'd had a glass of wine with lunch and had felt drowsy, she remembers. They had just made love. She remembers she'd been looking at the ceiling while Bennet was inside her, thinking of her knees bent either side of him, her feet slipping on the sheet as he moved against her. There was a smear of blood on the ceiling, where someone had squashed a mosquito. *I remember wondering what my face looked like when I was having an orgasm,* she thinks. *I was wondering why pain and pleasure did the same things to the muscles of the face.*

She thinks: *I look dead because the picture's in black and white.*

That evening she drives into Chania on the scooter to look for a photography shop. It takes her a long time: lots of bumping along cobbled backstreets, lots of laboured conversations with pale-faced young men behind glass counters loaded with lenses and flashguns. But eventually she finds what she's looking for: a shop run by an old man who remembers how to tint photographs and stocks all the old pigments.

'You must to use some small things for the baby ears to put the colour,' he tells her, taking bottles from a wooden drawer in an old cabinet.

'Q-tips?' she asks, miming a small screwing movement.

'*Neh, oraya.* And put it quickly or the face will come like a *kukla.*' He smiles, the eager smile of someone discussing a passion. 'You will try. Little, little. *Ligo, ligo.* You will see.'

And she does, as soon as she gets home, poring over the kitchen table until the small hours. First on a piece of blank photographic paper, mixing the tints, seeing how they penetrate the shiny surface; then taking the print of herself and smearing smudges of rose on the sleeping cheeks, streaks of brown on the glossy dark hair.

The effect is crude and garish, like make-up on a boarding-house landlady. So she tries again, early next morning, on a print of Bennet sitting in the café. And again, on the photo of the two of them together. But they all look comical, jangling, like dames in drag.

Frustrated, she goes back into the darkroom and starts opening the doors in the sideboard, dragging out the stacks of old framed portraits she's stored there and bringing them into the bright kitchen.

Laying them out on the table, she sees at once that she's been going about it the wrong way. She's been tinting every feature, trying to make them look natural, when all she needs to do is highlight particular bits of each photograph – a pair of full lips, perhaps, the blue pool of a dress – leaving the rest black-and-white. It's not the complete face that she needs to enliven, but some key fragment that will act as a password to the person.

'Can I photograph you cooking?' she asks Aphrodite the next morning.

'Yes of course. I thought you will never ask. But I must put lipstick first and take this off.' She starts untying her flowery apron.

'No, please. Leave it on. The green bits match your leggings. I want to try something.'

'But I want to be glamorous. Not a sweating old lady stuffing *kolokithakia* flowers.'

Sylvia laughs, looking at the other woman's signature gold sandals and hoop earrings. 'Silly. You always look glamorous. Anyway it's not for a proper portrait. I need some photos of faces to experiment with. I've tracked down some of those paints photographers used to colour their pictures years ago, and I want to try them out. But I've discovered that most of my photos are of buildings.'

'OK, but you must take Maria too. And Vasilios in the garden. Then I will have my complete happy family.'

'It seems so easy when you look at the old photos, but there's a real skill to it. Right, try to ignore me. Just carry on doing what you were doing.'

'Years ago there was a man from Episkopi who used to come to the villages,' says Aphrodite, picking up the grater to shred cucumber for tzatziki. 'Every month on the same day, he comes to the *kafenion* and people invite him in their homes. Some women put on their wedding dresses, five, ten years after the wedding, sometimes even after the husband has died, so he will make a picture of them.'

'I found that photo of you with the yellow ribbon,' says Sylvia, moving around the kitchen with the camera to her eye, testing out different angles. 'You were looking very mischievous.'

'Kokona chose that photo. I wanted her to have another one, but she said that one had the most life in it.'

'Why did you give it to her?' She's been wondering about this for weeks.

'She helped me once, when Vasilios was in the hospital and I came back to the village.' The plump face, framed by the camera, winces at the memory. 'I was young, and Maria was just a baby. I was angry and a bit crazy. I forgot I had a husband.'

'Why didn't you give her a picture of Maria?'

'Because it is not Maria who needs the help, it is me.'

'I don't understand.'

'Kokona, she always has her way of doing things. If she says she needs this photograph, we give her this photograph.'

'But how did she help you?'

'You have to understand,' Aphrodite sighs. 'It was not easy to find a doctor in the villages in those times. There were not so many cars and buses. And if you are a woman everyone wants to know why you are going to Chania, to Heraklion. So if you need help, it is easier to look for it where you are.'

'So she was a kind of healer.' Sylvia thinks of the crumbling bundles of dried leaves, the incense burner, the yellowed envelopes of seeds.

'Yes, you can say that. She makes medicines. She listens to you tell your troubles. She knows the old ways of managing women's things. People say that she is not modern, but they still go to her in the middle of the night.'

'And you went to her.'

'Yes, that one time. I went to her.'

Back at the house Sylvia takes the framed photographs out again and looks at them. Though there are one or two boys, they are mostly girls; all different ages, from tiny babies to gawky pre-teens with thickening eyebrows. She thinks she recognizes some of the faces, as young ghosts inhabiting the bodies of older people: in the queue for the bus to Chania, in the grocer's shop buying feta and *psomi*, parking a truck outside the *kafenion*.

She imagines their younger selves, thirty, forty years earlier, walking up the hill in the darkness, in the small hours, and knocking quietly on Kokona's turquoise door.

On an impulse she prints up a photograph of the secret room as she discovered it when she unlocked the door all those weeks ago: with the bed against the wall, the stool beside the bed; the pillows dented and felted with cat fur. She imagines the oil lamp burning on the sideboard and the candles lit; a young woman lying on the bed; an old woman sitting beside her.

She shivers suddenly. *What happened in here?* So many people, so many photographs. So many children with life in them.

It takes days before she makes the colours do what she intends. Days of printing up black-and-white photos in the monochrome twilight then bringing them out and laying them on the yellow table in the bright kitchen to tease colour into them. It reminds her of the tissue samples at the histology lab: how they all start out the same, brown and featureless in the formalin; brain and bone, liver and lung. And how the stains seek out the features and

220

make them reveal themselves: the nuclei and cell membranes, the cilia, the organelles; make them blossom blue, red, purple, green on the slides.

'But these are wonderful,' declares Aphrodite, when Sylvia shows her the few prints she's happy with. 'We are looking our true selves. I will frame them for the taverna.'

'No!' Sylvia is horrified. 'I'm just starting to get the hang of it. Give me a few weeks and I'll do you some better ones.'

But the other woman insists, snatching them up and bearing them off to a framer in Rethymnon that afternoon. The next day there they are, hanging behind the till: Aphrodite with a wicked smile on her lips, tasting lentil soup from a ladle; Maria, solemn and shy, with a tray of glasses; and Vasilios picking green beans, staring sorrowfully at the camera in his hat.

'They're really good, you know,' says Martin when he sees them. 'The lentils look even more lentilly than real life. And the way you've done the cheeks really brings out her dimples. You've got a real talent for this.'

'Is that me you're talking about, or my inarticulate alter ego?' she says, pleased.

'They're both you, Sylvia,' he says patiently.

'Make one of Martin too,' says Aphrodite. 'Then when he disappears, we will remember his face.'

'Would you mind?' Sylvia asks. 'I need some more shots to practise on. Maybe of you working somewhere, so I can try out the tints on different textures. Stone and wood; brick, metal; that kind of thing.'

'You're really serious about this, aren't you?'

'Oh, I'm just playing about really.' Why is she blushing? 'I don't expect it will come to anything.'

'But you want it to, don't you?' he insists. 'You're really getting into it.'

Is she? She considers this with surprise for a moment.

'Does that mean you'll do it?' she says.

★

He takes her to Kefalas, where he's building a garden wall for the English woman Aphrodite had mentioned.

'She's in London sorting out her divorce,' he explains, fishing a key out of his pocket and unlocking the garage door. 'I promised I'd get it sorted for when she gets back.' He hoists a bag of cement on to his shoulders and carries it outside. 'So she can get on with the garden. Take her mind off it.'

'Was that her idea or yours?'

'She's been wanting it done for ages, but she's had to spend all her money on lawyers.'

He's doing it for nothing, she realizes, *but he doesn't want to say so*. 'Why are you always helping people?' she asks, framing him slitting the bag open with a pocketknife.

'There's an angel on my left shoulder writing down all my sins, and another on my right writing down all my good deeds. If they cancel each other out I'll go to heaven when I die.'

'No, really.'

'Yes, really. Plus Rebecca's a nice lady who doesn't deserve all this shit she's going through.' He shovels sand from a heap, and mixes it with some of the cement.

'How did your mother die?'

'You mean, am I trying to atone for her death by helping women of a certain age with their DIY?'

She smiles. 'Are you?'

She photographs him stirring sand and cement together with his spade: yellow and grey, coarse and fine, like dry cake ingredients.

'She died from choking on her own vomit when she was drunk,' he says. 'Does that answer your question?'

'Christ.' She lowers the camera; her eyes watch the spade chopping and churning. 'Did you find her?'

'Her boyfriend found her when she didn't turn up for her driving lesson.' He takes a bucket to the garden tap and starts to fill it. 'He was teaching her to drive so she could take the van

222

through Europe. The coroner's report said she'd been drinking on and off for days.'

She photographs him lifting the bucket, the water slopping over the side and staining the dry concrete. 'Where were you when all this was happening?'

'Breaking into a house in Woodstock, nicking two hundred quid and a platinum card from a guy with a BMW.' He puts the bucket down and checks to see her reaction. 'I did it to see if I could. Then after she died, I just kept on doing it.'

She lowers the camera again and stares into his two-tone eyes. Her arms feel heavy. The sun's very hot on the top of her head.

'Most robbers nick things from people in their own community,' he says. 'Did you know that? You're much more likely to be done over if you're poor. But I always chose rich people and I never made a mess.'

'So that's all right then.'

'I'm not saying it's all right. I'm just saying it could have been worse. I was eighteen and my mum had just died, for fuck's sake.'

'Did you get caught?' Her mind's racing, trying to keep up with what he's saying.

'Only stupid criminals get caught. Even if there's an alarm, you can be in and out before the plods have stubbed out their fags. But I preferred to rob people when they were at home. It's easier to get in and they don't bother to set the alarm.'

That's how he knows so much about locks, she's thinking. Then, feeling sweat break out on her lip: *He could have broken into my house at any time and I'd never have known.*

'Don't worry,' he says, reading her face. 'I gave it up years ago, when I realized I got more satisfaction earning money than stealing it. If it had been harder, I'd probably still be out there nicking things. But it was such a doddle I got bored.'

She's picturing him standing on an expensive carpet in the middle of the night, feeling for a wallet in a jacket pocket. 'I don't think I've ever stolen anything in my life,' she says.

'Because it was wrong or because you were scared?'

'Both, probably. I was a terrible little goody-goody at school.'

'And your mum drove you there in her small car, but you came home by bus.' He makes a hollow in the sand-cement heap and tips water into it. 'And you had riding lessons and did A levels and went to the dentist, and your dad picked you up from the disco in his big car on a Saturday night.'

'So?' she says. 'What's wrong with that?'

'I used to really hate kids like you,' he says. 'With your school blazers and Sunday lunch all set out in your proper dining rooms.'

'I don't know why you're trying to make me feel guilty. It's you who was the juvenile delinquent.'

She watches him mixing the cement, adding water, slicing and turning, until it's the consistency of mashed potato.

'She wasn't an alcoholic, you know,' he says. 'Drinking was just one of the ways she used to get through her depressions. That's what I meant about her giving up. When I was little, she tried to cure herself. Read up about it, tried t'ai chi and different herbs and things. It didn't always work, and she had some really bad downers, but we got through it.'

'Why didn't she go to a psychiatrist? There are some really good drugs she could have had.'

'Because she was scared I'd be taken into care if people found out how ill she was.'

'But what about you? Coping with a depressed mother.'

'I didn't mind. I was used to it. And it was better than later, when she did go to hospital. And they filled her full of Zispin. She'd tried all those years to manage without, but when they put me in the children's home she just gave up.'

The mortar's mixed and he starts laying bricks, spooning up chunks of grey mash with a flat trowel and dolloping them on to the unfinished wall. 'I think it's better to feel something than to feel nothing,' he says.

Sylvia watches him moving fluidly along the wall: picking up a brick, dolloping mortar, placing it, tamping it, scraping off the excess. She thinks of the young boy and his mother. She tries to imagine his first night in the children's home. She doesn't even know what a children's home might look like. She feels as though she's been doing a jigsaw with all the wrong pieces.

She develops the photos of Martin that evening. She tells Aphrodite she's ill. She doesn't want the noise and colour of the taverna. She doesn't want Aphrodite's questions. She doesn't want to smile and take orders and be charming with the customers. She wants this quiet monochrome space, and the familiar ritual of dipping and washing, dipping and washing, of waiting and rinsing and hanging up to dry.

Selecting the frames to print, and enlarging them, she feels furtive. It's the same feeling she gets when she's watching him in his secret campsites. Excited. Guilty. As though she's stealing something.

A lot of the pictures are close-ups: of his hand clenched on the bucket handle, the sinews of his forearm like ropes; of his back bending to shovel sand, the gap between his tee shirt and jeans, the knobs of his backbone, the long ridges of muscle either side; of his face squinting at her in the sunshine, the damp hair on his forehead, the stubble shading the sharp angle of his jawline.

She thinks of him pushing up a window and hoisting himself silently over the sill. His jeans have a faded patch to one side of the crotch. The hairs on his forearm are fine and silky. There is a small scar on the side of his nose, faint white lines in the tan at the corners of his eyes.

She finds herself looking for a long time at a photograph of his neck. It's very slender and smooth, almost girlish. Wisps of hair escaped from his ponytail lie like seaweed against his skin. She can see the shadow of his artery, can almost hear the blood pulsing there in the hollow below his ear.

What would it smell like, that hollow place? Of wood shavings and cement dust. Of herbal conditioning shampoo.

A knock on the door makes her start guiltily and shuffle the print under some others of bricks and cement. It's Martin, smelling of baby soap, in a clean shirt.

'I'm on a roof tomorrow,' he says, 'if you want to photograph some tiles.'

'I think I've got enough to be going on with for a while, but thanks.'

'Sorry about earlier. I didn't mean to freak you out.'

'You didn't freak me out.'

He sighs. 'Why won't you admit it?'

'You think I'm such a frail little flower, don't you?' she shoots back. 'That I've led such a sheltered life.'

'I don't think all those dead babies count as a sheltered life,' he says quietly.

'OK, then,' she admits. 'Yes, it did freak me out a bit. All that stuff about stealing. Being taken into care.'

'I wanted you to know about me.'

He's standing right next to her, not quite touching. She's aware of the hairs of his forearm, nearly brushing her bare arm.

'When I was a kid I used to have this thing about being invisible,' he says. 'When people have an incomplete picture of you, it's as though a part of you doesn't exist.' He reaches past her and picks up the pile of prints.

'I thought you said every picture was incomplete. That we only ever show a fraction of ourselves.' She wants to snatch the photos away from him. Her cheeks are hot. She can feel herself sweating.

'I did. But some parts are more important than others.' He's leafing slowly through the prints. 'Is this how you see me?'

'Yes, I suppose so. Why?'

'You've made me look beautiful.'

She nearly says, *You are beautiful.* Instead she says: 'Thank you.'

'We went into hiding,' he says, as though the words are being forced out of him. 'Me and Mum. Dad was going to divorce her when she went loony, and get custody of me. So she emptied their savings account and bought a house in Oxford, and she hid me there for years until the police found out and she was sectioned.'

After supper that night she calls Bennet.

'You know Martin?' she says.

'No. If I recall right, it's you who knows Martin. A mite too well, if I may hazard an opinion.'

'What do you mean?'

'I mean he sees a damn sight more of you than I do.'

'Well, it turns out he's that wild boy in Oxford. It was all over the papers in the eighties. They discovered this boy living with his mad mother in a derelict house with loads of dying animals.'

'Are you serious?'

'He says the animals were dying because no one would let him go back and feed them and the tabloids got hold of some pictures.'

'I'm not sure I like the sound of this, Sylvie. A feral child wielding a screwdriver in the vicinity of my nearest and dearest.'

'Ex-feral child. And he wasn't feral anyway. Just a bit eccentric. Apparently it was all much more normal than it seemed. They made a big thing about him not going to school, as if he was Jungle Boy. But his mother had been teaching him from library books and when they tested him he turned out to be way ahead for his age.'

'Well I don't want him working for you any more. And I want you to get some new locks fitted on the doors, toot sweet. People like that can be dangerous.'

'He's not working for me any more. And it was all ages ago. If you'd spent any time with him you'd know there was nothing to worry about.'

'So how much time *are* you spending with him?'

'I've been taking photos of him to try out that hand-tinting technique I was telling you about. And before you start getting all suspicious, I've been taking pictures of practically anyone who'll let me and spending a fortune on solution and paper.'

'As long as he doesn't start getting ideas. Woman on her own.

Hubby miles away. Any red-blooded man would be tempted.'

'Actually, the results are quite good. Aphrodite's framed some and hung them in the taverna and people have started asking me to do commissions.'

'I always thought he was a bit weird. Never trust a man with a ponytail.'

'Honestly, B, he was just a kid brought up by a hippy-dippy mother who happened to get in the news. You can check him out yourself next time you're here.'

'I've got the twenty-eighth of July pencilled in. Does that still look likely?'

'I think so. My cycle seems to have settled down to being here now.'

'I hope you're not getting too settled.' His voice is serious suddenly.

'What do you mean?'

'I mean I miss you, sweet pea. I don't think I'm cut out for the bachelor life. I need you to keep me on the straight and narrow.'

'Why? What have you been up to? Gambling on the Internet? Downloading kiddie-porn?'

'Call me old-fashioned, but I think a man and his wife should live together. Less suspicion, less trouble all round.'

Sylvia likes getting up in the morning in the village. She likes waking at dawn and looking out at her square of lemon tree. She likes stretching naked under the mosquito net, and feeling the cool air on her skin. She likes lying back with the thermometer in her mouth, then pulling on her shorts and trainers and jogging down the hill to the sea.

She particularly likes the sea at this time of day, the way its skin looks, scaled with ripples like a fish, the way it nuzzles the rocks. And she likes walking back up the hill in the pink sunshine, to shower the salt off under the sky, and spoon yoghurt and peel purple figs and watch her coffee erupt in the little jug like brown lava. And set out her offering for the hungry ghosts.

And she likes not talking to anyone. People nod quietly if they meet her before seven; they're immersed in their own daily rituals too. She likes washing her cup and bowl and placing them on the old marble drainer, and taking the oil burner out of the darkroom, where she puts it last thing every night. She likes checking the wick and topping up the oil, then setting it down carefully on a shelf in the bedroom. *The changing of the guard*, she calls it to herself, though she doesn't know what's being guarded.

Then one morning she notices that the oil hasn't burned as low as usual. *Perhaps I filled it higher yesterday*, she thinks, though she knows she hasn't. Filling it to exactly the same level is one of the small pleasures of the process; so it will burn down not quite to the bottom every night. That's how she knows, with a bolt of hot certainty, that the only other person who would have topped up the oil in her lamp is Martin. But he hasn't been near the house for days.

She finds him in Kefalas piling half-bricks into a plastic sack.

'You've been in my house,' she blurts out without saying hello.

'You've been in my van,' he counters, straightening up and facing her.

'What do you mean?' She can hear her voice faltering.

'Fresh tyre marks on the track. Footprints by the washing line. You've been stalking me for weeks.'

'Why didn't you say something?'

'Because I didn't mind. I liked you looking at me.'

'Why did you break into my house?'

'I wanted to watch you sleeping.' His voice is very soft.

'Why?'

'I wanted to see if you were still clutching at the sheet.'

'And was I?'

'No. You were splayed out like a starfish.'

She's silent. She feels like an oyster with its shell prised open. 'I wasn't wearing a nightdress.'

'No.'

229

'I saw you coming out of the shower once.'

'I know. I wanted you to see me.'

Sylvia's temperature dips the next morning. She stares at the thermometer as though it's a lie detector and she's been caught out in some kind of deception.

Her scalp prickles with sweat as she remembers. Martin knows she's been watching him. He's known about it for weeks. He's been displaying himself to her, like a whore in a peep show. The thought makes her cringe with shame. What must he think of her?

She sits on the edge of her blue bed, trying to work out when the innocent challenge to discover where he lived turned into this furtive obsession. *It was when I saw you doing t'ai chi*, she thinks. *When I realized how beautiful you were. I wanted to see you naked.*

Now he's seen her naked too.

'All the decent hotels in Crete seem to be full of vacationing Athenians,' Bennet reports when he phones back. 'So it looks like I'll be sweating it out in the village this time.'

'I'll buy a fan on the way to the airport,' says Sylvia, feeling dismayed.

'Goodie. Make sure there's lots of black lace and tassels. And don't forget your seven veils.'

'An electric fan. To set up in the bedroom,' she says tiredly. Why does he have to make a joke out of everything? She'd been hoping to get away from the village for a few days; put some time, some tarmac, between herself and Martin.

The fact that they have been watching one another has shaken her. It's as though they've been meeting secretly. As though she has become two people who know nothing about one another.

She stares at her face in the pink-framed mirror. 'I have been stalking a man ten years younger than I am,' she says aloud, as though in the confessional box. 'I have been photographing him and staring at his naked body. What kind of woman have I become?'

The face stares back at her: eyes luminous, skin flushed, hair shaggy and shiny and sun-streaked. *I look like a fertile woman*, she thinks.

Nothing has happened, she thinks as she speeds along the coast road to the airport. *I'm just curious about him. Like Aphrodite is. Like that woman in Kefalas. I've just been observing him, like a detective tracking a criminal.*

And he's been observing me, she thinks.

She hangs on to Bennet when he hugs her. She wants to press herself on to him, as though she's the limpet and he is the rock.

On the way home they share fish soup and a jug of rough rosé at a tiny restaurant on the harbour at Rethymnon, and crumble dry bagels into the water for the fish. Bennet tells her about a new research project he's starting at the hospital, and about how house prices are rocketing in their part of Newcastle. They discuss whether they should sell up and look for somewhere outside the city, on the coast maybe. They talk about where they should spend Christmas and New Year; about how selfish her mother is and how his parents get more right wing every year.

Sipping her wine, Sylvia feels calmer. She feels like a crumpled letter being smoothed out and folded and slipped back into its envelope. In the car she leans back against the headrest and lets herself be driven.

But as they drive up the hill towards the house, her body stiffens. Martin's red camper van is parked beside her gate and he's sitting on the patio reading a book.

'What on earth's he doing here?' asks Bennet.

'I don't know. Wait here a sec and I'll get rid of him.'

She gets out of the car quickly and slams the door.

Martin gets up and comes to meet her. 'I wanted to make sure you were all right,' he says, scanning her face.

'Bennet's in the car,' she says awkwardly. 'He's going to be here for a few days.'

'I won't stay. I just wanted to see you.' He's still looking at her, at her forehead, her eyebrows, her lips, as though burning her on to his retina.

'What's up, sweet pea?' It's Bennet, carrying his bag on to the patio. 'Sylvie? Is something wrong?'

'Nothing,' she says. 'The blackout screens needed a bit of adjusting, that's all. He can come back another day, can't you?'

'Hello, sir.' Martin shakes Bennet by the hand. 'What do you think of the house?'

'Perfectly charming. I was particularly taken with the pink loo last time I was here. And I hear the new darkroom's just the business.'

Sylvia is struck again by the contrast between the two men: by Martin's litheness, Bennet's broadness.

'You should see the photos Sylvia's been doing,' Martin's saying. 'Some of them are extraordinary. She's got a really good eye.'

'Glad you approve,' says Bennet sarcastically.

Martin winces. 'OK then, I'll get off. Enjoy your stay. Bye Sylvia.'

'There was no need to be rude,' Sylvia says when he's gone.

'Does he often do that?'

'Often do what?'

'Lie in wait for you.'

'Don't be silly,' she says, carrying his bag into the bedroom. 'He's just conscientious. And I'm normally in at this time of day.'

'Come off it. I saw the way he was staring at you. The guy's obviously nuts about you.'

'He's ten years younger than I am.'

'So? Maybe he likes older women. Come on, pour me a cold beer and let's christen that marriage bed.'

'I thought you wanted to see the photos,' she stalls. Seeing Martin has left her feeling jittery.

'First things first, my sweet. Beer and skittles, then art.'

'What about a shower?'

'I'm working up to that. Maybe after the skittles.'

When they're kissing she feels she can't breathe. Her breasts are flattened against his chest and her hair's caught under his shoulder. Her skin sticks to him wherever he touches. Like masking tape. Like flypaper. She wants to heave him off her. He's Brer Rabbit and she is the tar baby, and she wants to hurl him into the briar patch.

She stares up at the knotted mosquito net, swinging gently in the breeze from the new fan and thinks of Martin looking down at her. She thinks of how she must have looked, sleeping naked with her legs apart, a brown starfish on a white beach. She thinks of his eyes intent on her, of his hand quietly unzipping his jeans. There's his flat belly, shockingly white from being hidden from the sun; the neat line of hair bisecting it. *No underpants*, she thinks, as the hand follows the line of black hair and burrows into the thatch at its base, as it edges out his swollen penis. Then lets it go. And he's just standing there with his legs apart and his penis out, its wet eye watching her as she sleeps.

'That was surprisingly quick and satisfying,' comments Bennet afterwards, reaching for the tissues. 'If this is what the bucolic life does for you, then I'm all for it.'

'And you didn't bang your head once.'

'No. So far, this accommodation's suiting me fine.'

'Do you feel up to braving the shower yet?'

'As long as you promise to hold my hand.'

'Great darkroom, shame about the sideboard,' Bennet remarks when she shows him inside the secret room.

'I hardly notice it any more.'

'It would be a lot easier not to notice if it wasn't there. Why don't I get rid of it for you? A few whacks with a hammer and—'

'No!' It's out before she can stop it. 'I mean, Martin persuaded me to keep it.'

His face hardens. 'Since when does some hippy builder's opinion count for anything?'

'He reckons it was designed for that space.'

'Remind me who is working for who in this arrangement.'

'For heaven's sake, B. It's only a sideboard,' she says crossly. 'And actually I thought he had a point. You should have seen this room when we opened it. It was like a cross between a chapel and clinic, with the sideboard as the altar.'

'Hence the votive candle.'

'That's the Easter light I told you about. I'm supposed to keep it burning until Good Friday next year.'

'Saints preserve us. You'll be sacrificing poor wee baa-lambs next. Obviously the sooner I get you away from this place the better.' He moves to her workbench. 'Right, let's see these photos everyone's talking about.'

'There are tons,' she says, relieved by the change of subject, 'but these are the ones I like best.'

She spreads out a small sheaf of tinted prints. 'That's the wife of Dimitri who runs the shop. He asked me to do a portrait for her birthday. And this is Aphrodite, of course. And Georgia, that woman down the hill with the chickens. And Nicos with his war medals. He's that old guy from the *kafenion*.'

'Very tasteful,' he comments. 'Very arty. The tints give them quite a surreal look, don't they? I rather like it.'

'It took me ages to work out how to do it. I thought maybe I could try taking them to a gallery when I get home or—'

'My wife, the photographer. Yes, I can see it all now.'

'I don't mean give up my job at the lab. Well, not straight away. I just wondered—'

'What are these?' He's put the tinted photos down and is thumbing through the other piles of prints.

'Oh, they're those pics of Martin I was telling you about,' she says, keeping her voice even. 'I was doing some studies of texture. Seeing how it reacted with the tints.'

'So I see.' He picks out the print of Martin's back, with the tee shirt riding up.

'What do you mean?'

'Texture my arse. What's the name of that guy who took pictures of nude black men? I expect he said it was all about texture too.'

'Robert Mapplethorpe. But that's not what these are about.'

'Give me a bit of credit, Syl,' he says. 'Some of these are positively pornographic.'

'I don't agree,' she says, trying not to sound rattled.

'He's a pretty boy. You're bound to find him attractive.'

'He's a bloody builder, for God's sake!' She feels backed into a corner.

'And your point is?'

'Will you please stop? I'm married to you. We've just made love. We're trying to have a baby together.'

He subsides suddenly, like a burst balloon. 'God, I'm so sorry, sweet pea,' he says contritely. 'Don't take any notice of me. It's being apart for so long. I've been imagining things. Val's been feeding me all kinds of horror stories.'

'Well, you shouldn't let her wind you up,' says Sylvia, shuffling the photos back into a neat heap. Her back's sweating. *But nothing's happened*, she thinks. She feels like she's just crossed a very deep valley on a very rickety bridge.

They walk down the hill to the *Petaluda* for supper. It's packed, but Aphrodite's saved them a table outside. The lute player is setting up in the corner and parties of people are pushing their tables together and shouting for wine.

Bennet sits down and picks up the menu. Sylvia stays standing. 'What do you want to start with?' she asks. 'Beer? Ouzo? Olives?'

'What's this, are you a waitress now as well?'

'Only when it's busy. Wait, I'll just find out what the specials are.'

She escapes to the kitchen, grateful for the distraction. The conversation about Martin has left her exhausted. And Bennet's right about the photos. As soon as he pointed it out, she could see how erotic they were: all those close-ups of Martin's skin, his hands, the muscles under his jeans.

She pours Bennet's ouzo and sets it on a tray with a jug of water, then makes her way back to their table. 'I've ordered the *kleftiko*,' she says. 'With *horta* and lemon potatoes. Do you mind? They're rushed off their feet, so I thought I should get our order in quickly.'

'I didn't realize you knew so many people,' he says as she sits down. 'I felt quite the johnny foreigner watching you jabbering away in Greek to all and sundry.'

'I was just explaining why I wasn't working this evening. But I might help out a bit later, if that's OK with you. There's a huge group booked in for ten o'clock.'

'I see your photos have pride of place,' he comments.

'Aphrodite was just telling me there are four more people wanting commissions. Everyone's sons and daughters are back home for the holidays and they all seem to have money to spend.'

'Come home, Sylvie,' he says suddenly, leaning across the table and grabbing her hand.

'What?'

'The house here is finished. You're obviously not depressed any more. It's time to come home.'

'I can't leave now. I'm just getting into my photography.'

'I'll organize you another darkroom in Newcastle,' he says.

'But I don't have to be back at work until November.' She feels dismayed and aggrieved, as though he's trying to make her leave the cinema in the middle of the movie.

'I need you with me. The house is like a morgue without you and this flying superstud act is beginning to wear a bit thin.'

'But I'm not ready to come home yet,' she says. 'We agreed six months. Time to completely recover, you said.'

'It's that Martin bloke, isn't it?' His face sets solid, accusing.

236

'No!' She bangs the table with her hand. 'Stop going on about him. It's nothing to do with him. It's all the things we talked about. The clean air and the food. Swimming at dawn. My square of lemon tree. Taking photos people like enough to pay for and hang on their walls.'

Keeping the light burning, she thinks.

'The guy's besotted with you. It's written all over his face.'

'Why do you assume there has to be a man involved?' she asks angrily. 'Why can't you believe that I might have some other reasons for wanting to be here?'

'Come home, Sylvie,' he says. 'Before it goes any further.'

'Before *what* goes any further? Can you hear yourself? You sound like a bloody soap opera.'

'I can get on the mobile now to book you a ticket.'

'My photos are really good, you know,' she says angrily. 'Why can't we talk about that? Why can't we talk about what I'm going to do with my life?'

'Come home and we'll talk about anything you want.'

'I'll go and get the food,' she says wearily, standing up. 'Let's discuss this again in the morning.'

By the time she gets back with their *kleftiko*, a litre jug of red wine has appeared on their table, courtesy of one of her regulars, and Bennet is well down his second glass.

'My beautiful talented wifie,' he announces, toasting her. 'An angel in the kitchen, a queen in the darkroom, a whore in the bedroom.'

'Less of the whore,' she says, relieved at his change of mood.

'I love you,' he says, topping up his glass. 'I have been crass and stupid and there is no health in me.'

'It's because we're just grabbing little chunks of time. Why don't you come for a proper holiday?'

'What about lover-boy?'

'*What?*'

'Sorry, sorry.' He holds his hands up to fend her off. 'Yes, a good idea. I will. I want to. Put all this behind us.'

The food's delicious, and he eats greedily, dipping bread in the lamb juices and forking up great dripping mouthfuls of *horta*. A second litre jug appears and he starts on that too. Sylvia sips her wine slowly and moves the food around her plate, wondering how she's going to steer him back up the hill. At least we won't have to have sex again, she thinks as he drains his glass and orders a Metaxa.

They zigzag up the hill to the house, with Bennet draped like a greatcoat over her shoulders, nuzzling her ear and telling her that he's a big bad hubby, that she's his ickle wickle wifie, and that they will be together for ever and ever, amen.

She wakes in the small hours to the sound of banging and splintering wood coming from the darkroom. Pulling on her nightdress she runs to push open the door.

The safelight's on and Bennet's standing naked in the middle of the room, swinging Kokona's axe at the sideboard.

'What on earth's going on?' she gasps.

'What does it look like?' he pants. 'I'm getting rid of your lover's pet sideboard.'

'He's not my lover,' she says helplessly as he swings wildly at one of the carved doors.

'Pull the other one, sweetheart. It plays "I Believe".' He swings again and the door splits in two.

'What can I do to convince you? Look, I'll tear up all the photos of him and burn the negatives.'

'Val was right,' he shouts in time with the axe blows. 'She said you'd be at it as well.'

Sylvia stares at him as the import of what he's said sinks in. 'What do you mean "as well"?' she says coldly.

'Ah.' He lowers the axe.

'Have you been having an affair with Val?'

'You left me on my own,' he says, genitals hanging, the axe dangling from his hand.

'So it's my fault, is it?'

'I'm sorry, Syl. I didn't mean it to happen.' He swipes vaguely at the splintered wood with an orange foot, trying to tidy it into a heap.

'So that's why she never answered my calls,' says Sylvia. 'She was too busy in bed with my husband.' The axe, the genitals dangling, the orange monochrome, make her feel unreal.

'I'm a bad bad man,' he's saying.

'Give me the axe.' She holds out her hand. She feels numb. She feels a hundred years old. 'Oh, don't worry,' she says as he flinches. 'I'm not going to hurt you.'

'I need you, Sylvie,' he says.

'Go back to bed.'

'Does that mean you forgive me?'

'It means you're drunk and I'm exhausted and I don't want to hear any more of your pathetic crap.'

Chapter 21

The Brown's Matchbook

Martin's father was coming on Sunday afternoon. Martin couldn't eat anything. He kept wanting to go to the toilet, even though he'd been six times since breakfast.

His father arrived early, but Martin had been ready for hours, lurking on the landing and looking out of the window above the front door. He saw a long sleek grey car turn into the driveway and a man in a mossy tweed jacket get out. The man had a bald patch, like a monk's, at the back of his head and longish sandy-grey curls. He stood for a moment, then walked towards the front door.

'Paul Miller,' he announced to Call Me Jeff as they shook hands in the hall, 'I made better time than I expected. The M40 was clear practically all the way from the Westway.'

Coming slowly down the stairs, Martin thought there had been a mistake. This man was too small and he was wearing the wrong kind of jacket.

'Hello, Martin,' said the man, holding out a freckled hand. Martin looked at the hand and a jolt went through him. He remembered the ring on the man's little finger. He knew that there was writing on the inside of the ring and that the skin underneath it was white. He knew that the man had a long scar at the base of his thumb as though someone had tried to cut it off.

He looked up at the man's face. It was fatter than he remembered and the sideburns were gone, but the eyes were still blue and smiley.

Martin's whole body felt hot and numb. 'I polished my shoes,' he said, then blushed and looked down.

'So did I,' said the man. He was wearing heavy brown shoes with a pattern of little holes in the leather. They looked old and comfortable. They looked like they'd been polished many times.

'How old are your shoes?' Martin asked.

'About the same age as you are,' said his father. 'I bought them for your christening, a few weeks after you were born.'

They drove into the centre of Oxford, then parked and walked around. Martin wanted to ask if he should call him 'Dad' or 'Mr Miller'. He wanted to ask how he'd felt when his wife and son had disappeared. He wanted to ask what he'd done to try to find them.

He wanted to ask when his father was taking him home to Chislehurst.

Instead they talked about Martin's new school and whether he had any hobbies. And what the other Barn kids were like and if he had a best friend. And what his favourite TV programme was and what football team he supported.

In a big noisy restaurant called Brown's his father ordered a perfumy tea called Earl Grey and lit a cigarette from a red-and-white packet. Martin had a chocolate milkshake. The sweet thick liquid filled his mouth and throat. After one swallow he'd had enough, but he kept drinking.

The things they weren't talking about burned in his chest and made it hard for him to concentrate. His brain kept getting snagged on them, like a dangling sleeve on a nail. He kept noticing things about his father: his smell of dogs and aftershave and pub doorways; the little nick in his chin from shaving; the way the corduroy of his trousers was looser and slightly paler at the knees.

His father was looking at him oddly, blowing out blue smoke and rolling the end of his cigarette along the edge of the ashtray.

'It's good to see you, son,' he said. 'Maybe we can do this again soon.'

And he reached into his jacket and took out his wallet. 'Here,' he said, handing Martin a twenty-pound note. 'Don't spend it all at once.'

*

Afterwards the boys were all talking about his father's car and debating whether Jags or Daimlers were best.

'Your dad must be loaded,' they said. 'Did he give you any money?' they asked. Then: 'When's he coming back for you?'

Martin didn't answer. He felt like a blocked drain; as though his head and throat were clogged with something solid but the rest of him was empty. He was hungry but he felt sick. He'd packed a suitcase in his mind, but there was nowhere to take it.

He went to Call Me Jeff's office to ask when his father was coming back to get him. The office was empty, but in the in-tray was a letter with 'Paul and Helen Miller' printed at the top in curly green writing. And underneath, an address in Chislehurst, Kent.

He chose a Saturday afternoon, when the boys were allowed to go off wandering in the city centre. He had the address on a brown envelope and the twenty-pound note in the pocket of his jeans. He reckoned it would be past six before anyone wondered where he was.

He was lucky with his connections and Call Me Jeff was right: in less than three hours he was alighting from the train at Chislehurst, where a woman with a tartan bag on wheels and an Alsatian dog offered him a lift to his father's house.

'It's hopeless waiting for a taxi here on a Saturday. They're all ferrying people home from Bromley with their shopping,' she said, peering down the leafy road outside the station. 'My hubby will be here in two ticks.'

They dropped him at the gate of a long white house set back from the road. There were two cars in the drive – the grey Daimler and a mustard-coloured Mini – and a swing seat on the front lawn with a stripy blue awning.

The sitting-room window was open; he could hear football on the TV and someone clattering about in the kitchen. Just as he was plucking up courage to ring the bell, the front door opened and a pudgy blonde woman with pink lipstick came out.

'Is Mr Miller in?' asked Martin.

'Paul!' The woman went to the open window. 'There's a boy here for you. I think he's bob-a-job. Sorry—' smiling at Martin and brandishing a fan of white envelopes. 'I've got to catch the post. Paul! Door! And keep an eye on Sarah. I'll be back in a minute.'

A moment later his father was standing in front of him.

'Good God!' His features all expanded suddenly, as though something had exploded inside his head. 'What on earth are you doing here?' Then, collecting himself: 'Does the home know where you are? Come inside and tell me how you tracked me down.'

Everything in the kitchen seemed gold: the bare floorboards and cupboards; the wooden table and chairs; the two little girls eating scrambled eggs on toast.

'Are you hungry?' asked his father. 'I can put on some toast and open a tin of beans. I'd offer you eggs, but the girls say my scrambled eggs taste like rubber.'

The girls looked up and smiled shyly. They were very pretty: curly and pink with dimpled elbows.

They're my stepsisters, Martin thought. *Half of their genes and half of mine are the same.* He looked for some signs of similarity, but couldn't find any. He had big feet and long legs like his mother. His hair was dark chestnut-brown; his arms wiry and tanned.

There was a holiday photo pinned to a cork noticeboard, with the two girls and their parents in it: all smiling the same white smile; all with the same sunburned cheeks and bleached curls. They looked like a complete set of something; like matching plates, or cups and saucers. And he was from a different set altogether.

While his father telephoned Call Me Jeff to explain where Martin was, the girls took him to see their ponies. They were in a field at the back of the house, with a new wooden stable in the corner. Sarah, the smaller girl, was chatty. She kept calling him 'Martin' and tugging on his hand. Her pony was a fat white Shetland with tiny hooves and pale eyelashes. The other pony, a slim chestnut, belonged to the bigger girl, Kate.

They showed Martin where the pony nuts were kept and let him feed them; he could feel the ponies' soft noses whiffling them up from his palm. There was a row of coloured rosettes on the wall in the stable; it smelt of wood and hay and leather.

Martin stroked the rough ginger whorl on the chestnut's forehead and ached with envy.

When they came back inside, his father's new wife Helen was back and they'd obviously been talking about him.

'I'll have to call you Bob,' she grinned, 'because I mistook you for a bob-a-job boy.' She was a laughy, talky sort of woman, with stumpy hands. 'The home says you can stay tonight and Paul will drive you back tomorrow. Come on, I'll show you where you're going to sleep. I hope you don't mind mauve flowers. It's where my mother stays when she comes to visit.'

He stayed up to eat with them after the girls had gone to bed. It was some kind of red chicken stew from a heavy orange pot, ladled on to thick brown Peasant-Cup plates, with baked potatoes. Martin wanted to talk about when he was coming to live with them. He knew there was another spare room upstairs, full of wooden crates and suitcases. But the talk was the same as in Oxford: just questions about school and friends and hobbies.

Later, Martin lay awake listening to Helen and his father getting ready for bed: water running and the toilet flushing; lights being switched off. He was wearing a blue tee shirt of his father's as a nightshirt. The puffy duvet on his bed smelt of perfume and there was a glass dish of rose petals on the window sill.

When he was sure they were all asleep, he slipped out of bed and crept downstairs. The washing machine was swooshing in the kitchen and Helen's handbag was beside her chair in the sitting room. He opened a door in the hall and found an ironing board and box of brushes and shoe polish. Behind another door was a dark waterfall of coats. He opened a third door and found himself in a room he hadn't seen before. It was lit by the ghostly green light of an aquarium, full of flicking fish bright as boiled sweets. And next to it, a small, still tank full of pale branching coral.

A jigsaw piece dropped into a space in his mind. He remembered that quiet bubbling sound. He remembered the coral, and the swaying branches that turned out to be sea horses. He remembered them hoovering up food particles through their tiny snouts.

In the flickering light from the tanks, he lay down on the carpet and felt the sleeping house surround him: solid and warm and satisfying as a completed jigsaw.

All the way back to Oxford in the car, he was waiting for his father to talk about coming back to fetch him. He was thinking he could unpack one of the wooden crates at Argyle Street and fill it with his own stuff. He was thinking, if they put it in sideways, the crate would just squeeze on to the back seat of the Daimler.

Instead his father kept talking about 'when your mother's better' and 'visits' and 'phoning from the station'. When they arrived, he gave Martin another twenty-pound note, then went into Call Me Jeff's office and closed the door behind him.

Martin's punishment was no puddings and no TV for a week, but he didn't care. He had his father's telephone number on a Brown's matchbook in his pocket.

After his brooch day in Chislehurst, Martin's life was a long string of plain beads. Every morning, when Call Me Jeff gave out the mail at breakfast, he expected a letter telling him when his father was coming to fetch him. There was a flowery notelet from Helen one day, saying how nice it had been to see him and signed 'with love from us all', but nothing else.

Social Sue visited and told him that his mother was 'stabilizing', but that she wasn't ready to see him quite yet. Afterwards he looked up 'stabilizing' in Call Me Jeff's dictionary, and found it meant calming and balancing, after a storm or upset: nothing to do with horses at all. But he couldn't shift the image of his mother as a rangy brown mare in a bridle, reined in tight, with the bit cutting into the corners of her soft mouth and her eyes rolling with alarm.

He found himself comparing this image with his memory of Helen Miller: pink and busy and efficient. They were like the two little figures foretelling the weather on the cuckoo clock in their kitchen at Argyle Street: 'bright and sunny' or 'cloudy with showers'. When one was out, the other was in, and vice versa; one or the other, and nothing in between. Martin felt he was waiting for the sun to come out.

One day it occurred to him that Call Me Jeff might have been hiding his father's letters, as a further punishment for his trip to Chislehurst, so he decided to telephone from a phone box in Banbury Road. He held the receiver hard against his ear and pictured the cream phone ringing in the golden kitchen. But there was no answer. He tried again, an hour later; and again in the evening. And again the next day.

Two days later he received a postcard of a donkey in a straw hat from Corfu, telling him they were having a wonderful time, the girls had been riding on the beach every day, it was very hot, the sea was warm, they sent their love.

Martin recognized Helen's writing, but this time his father had signed it too: 'and Paul'.

Looking at those two words, scrawled so casually on what must have been a stack of postcards prepared by Helen, a fist clenched in Martin's chest. The fist unclenched for a moment, then clenched again and stayed clenched. And it was like a rock had been dropped into his stomach. He wasn't going to live in Chislehurst. He had never been going to live in Chislehurst. Paul and Helen and Katy and Sarah were bright and sunny, but Martin was cloudy with showers.

A month later his mother came out of hospital. She was paler and fatter than he remembered, and she had a new pair of jeans and an unfamiliar jumper on. But her hair was glossy and her arms, when she hugged him, stayed around him for ages, and squeezed and squeezed as though she was pressing him back into her body.

Social Sue took them shopping in Tesco then back to the house in Argyle Street, where she dumped two carrier bags of groceries in the kitchen, and propped a little white card with her telephone number on it on the clean mantelpiece of what used to be the Jungle Room.

Martin and his mother prowled around the house. Their feet made too much noise on the bare staircase. Nothing rustled or flickered and there was too much light coming in through the naked windows.

Back in the kitchen, they stood looking out at the shorn garden.

'I feel like we should be talking in whispers,' said his mother.

Martin nodded. 'I feel people are looking in all the time.'

'We could get some curtains, I suppose,' she said. 'Or blinds. Your father's given me some money to spend on the house.'

Martin had told her about his father coming to Oxford, but not about his trip to Chislehurst. 'Best not to,' Social Sue had advised. 'No need to worry your mother about your gallivantings at this stage.'

'The grass has started to grow back,' he said after a pause. 'But the trees will take ages.'

Martin thought of the Rainbow Days and the Bat Day. He thought of the way the old house had used to merge into the wilderness, through the Jungle Room and the secret corridor of overhanging foliage. He felt they'd been stranded on an island by a sea of neatness. He could see the swing in the neighbour's garden over a row of tidy shrubs, and the roof of the school to the left of the pruned apple tree.

'The people next door can see right into our garden,' he said. He thought of the Cat Women and the Dog People reading about the Wild Boy of Iffley Fields in their newspapers. He thought: *I can never go barefoot or follow the foxes again*.

'At least the Swamp's gone,' said his mother eventually.

'And the frogs. And the slugs,' he agreed.

'I'd got rather fond of the slugs,' she said with a sigh. Then: 'I suppose we should start unpacking our things.'

Neither of them moved.

Then she said: 'What do you think, Marty? Shall we leave them all packed and move them to a different house?'

Chapter 22

Bennet's overnight bag is waiting on the patio. At Sylvia's insistence he's changed to an earlier flight. She wants her house back to herself. She wants to pull it around her like a blanket and huddle inside it for hours with no one looking. But that will have to wait. Right now, rage is gusting out of her, blowing away all her guilt about Martin. *Nothing happened*, she thinks, plonking breakfast things on the outside table. *It was just a fantasy*, allowing cups to clatter and crash. *It was* nothing *compared with this*.

'Come on, Sylvie,' says Bennet, pleading for her to calm down, sit down.

'But she smokes!' says Sylvia, dolloping yoghurt into his bowl. 'You've always said you hate that.'

'It wouldn't have happened if you'd been at home.'

'And you're just a poor red-blooded male who needs his oats, is that it?'

'It was just sex. It was uncomplicated.'

'If you like knee-tremblers in the Bigg Market. The last man she fucked was a porter at the university, for God's sake.'

'So?'

'So what about love? What about trust? What about fucking Aids?' She dumps a spoonful of honey on to the yoghurt and pushes it over to him.

'We were careful.'

'Oh I love your idea of careful. Get pissed and spill the beans as soon as you see me.'

'Would you rather I hadn't told you? Val was all for keeping it secret.'

'Bully for her. I can just see you two sitting up in bed discussing what to do about poor little Sylvia.'

'We didn't want to hurt you.'

'Oh that's priceless,' she says, slopping his coffee into the saucer. ' "Poor Sylvia's just had two miscarriages and she's gone a bit loopy. Let's have a little think. What can we do to make sure she's not hurt any more? Oh, yes, we'll have sex but we'll make sure she doesn't find out." '

'You told me to go out with her.'

'Why do you keep trying to make this my fault?'

'Of course it's not your fault. I take complete responsibility. But—'

'But what?' She rounds on him, eyes blazing.

'Well, you have to admit you've been a bit difficult to live with recently.'

'A bit "complicated" do you mean?'

'All those food obsessions. All the rules about what we should and shouldn't do to increase our fertility. Endless discussions about hormones and pollution. Then there was that mad bout of ice-bathing.'

'I didn't realize I'd become such a bore.'

'You used to be so funny and energetic. Full of plans. Then everything got so serious and grim.'

'Having a baby is serious,' she says, slumping down opposite him suddenly, as though a current's been switched off.

'I could see you were trying to snap out of it,' he says gently, 'to stop me worrying. But you were like the light bulb in a fridge. Whenever I opened the door, there you'd be with your bloody "I'm all right" smile. But I knew as soon as I stopped looking you'd be on the Internet obsessing again.'

'That's what I'm like, Bennet,' she says, and her head feels too heavy for her neck. 'That's what I've always been like. I can't just mope. I have to do something.'

On the way to the airport he keeps the windows closed and the air conditioner blasting cold air. She stares out at the sea, at hedges of dusty pink oleander, at watermelons heaped up like green boulders by the side of the road. She's trying to calm down, but her hands keep forming themselves into fists in her lap.

'One mistake, Sylvie,' he's saying. 'That's not much compared to a lifetime's commitment.'

'I was under the impression it was quite a lot of "mistakes",' she retorts. 'At least twice a week since March.'

'Please, don't let this ruin everything.'

'It's up to me, is it? To "come to terms with it" and "save the marriage"?'

'I'll tell her it's over.'

'Is that supposed to make me feel better?'

'What about your Jungle Boy?'

'They were *photos*, Bennet,' she spits at him. 'Photos. Not sex. Not sperm and saliva. Not "pass the tissues, sweetie" and after-sex cigarettes.'

'They were *erotic* photos,' says Bennet, warming to his theme. 'Of a guy who clearly fancies the arse off you.'

'Oh, didn't I mention? He's celibate. So even if he does fancy me, he'd never do anything about it.'

'Celibate?' he snorts. 'Like bloody Jesus Christ? There's a line if ever I heard one.'

'It's true,' she says, suddenly weary. 'Ask Aphrodite. Ask anyone on the island. He hasn't been to bed with anyone for years. But that's irrelevant, because *I* wouldn't do anything about it. Even if I did fancy him. Because I'm married and marriage means not having sex with other people. Though apparently the terms of the contract have been changed in my absence.'

'They haven't. I love you. Please, try to forgive me.'

'I don't know if I can,' she says, subsiding back against the headrest. This is what it's been like: anger blazing through her like fire catching a sheet of newspaper, then exhausting itself, leaving her flat and fragmented and spent. By the time they reach the airport, and step out into the thundering white mid-morning heat, it's built up again.

'Look, it's ridiculous for me to be leaving like this,' he says, hanging back, not wanting to join the check-in queue. 'It's not too late to get you a seat. Come home with me.'

'Why? So I can imagine her in my house, imagine her head on my pillow? I take it you did use our bed?'

He looks abashed. 'Only a few times.'

'Oh, that's all right then,' witheringly. 'Only a few times.'

'Please, we need to talk this through.' He's got his hands on either shoulder; he's trying to make her look at him.

'No, *you* need to talk this through,' she snaps, shrugging him off. 'I need to be as far away from you as possible.'

'Let me change my ticket. We'll find a hotel. We'll sort this out.'

'Get on your plane, Bennet.' Again, the blaze burning out; the flat grey aftermath.

'What are you going to do?'

'I don't know.'

'I love you.'

'Goodbye, Bennet.'

When he's gone she locks herself into the disabled toilet in the arrivals hall and slumps down on the closed seat. Leaning back against the cool cistern, she waits for the tears to come. *My husband's unfaithful*, she thinks. But her eyes stay hot and dry. She stares at two drowsy mosquitoes bobbing weightlessly against the wall. She's all bone; all knuckle and knee, as though her flesh has solidified.

I'm in shock, she thinks, unlocking the door and walking across to the car-hire kiosks.

Back at the village, she can't face going straight back to the house. She doesn't want to see the dirty breakfast things piled up by the sink, with all her hurt stuck to them. She parks the scooter and wanders down to the sea, thinking she might find a place to swim naked. But there are three sets of blonde tourists sunning themselves on the rocks when she gets there, so she trudges back up the path again.

'"Who is Sylvia? What is she?"' It's Vasilios, watching her over the fence. He's standing over a pile of small plant pots on a table in the shade of the mulberry tree.

'*Kalimera*,' says Sylvia, pushing open the gate. 'What are you doing?' She loves Vasilios's garden, its green smell, its shaggy ordered rows.

'A plant does not speak, but it does bear witness,' he says, handing her a pot to fill with earth. 'A plant marks the seasons with you. It tells you that you are surviving.' He peers at her from under his hat. 'You plant the seed, then you see the flower. And you remember the seed and the self that planted it. You see how much comes from light and water and air. You marvel at how these simple ingredients can produce such a miracle of colour.'

It's soothing work: placing small stones in the bottom of each little pot, then cupping reddish soil in her hands and tipping it in. '"One is nearer God's heart in a garden than anywhere else on earth,"' she quotes.

'Ah, the Creator. The Omnipotent. The Omnipresent.'

'You weren't at the church on Easter Saturday,' she says.

'My wife prefers me to stay away.' He smiles briefly. 'She doesn't want people to speculate. It's easier if I am out here with my hat on.'

'Do you pray?'

'I am praying now. Everything we do is a prayer.'

'What *are* we doing?' she asks.

'Planting geranium cuttings. "Clones", I think, is the correct term. You take a piece of the mother and in a few weeks there will be an identical new daughter. Though of course it will be different in many respects from the mother, due to the vagaries of light and water and air.' He picks up a plastic bag and empties it out on to the bench. It's full of luscious green geranium cuttings. The scent of bruised leaf rises from them like steam. 'Actually, I was making a small collection for your new house. There is one of every colour, but you will not know them apart until they flower.'

Without looking at her, he begins stripping off the lower leaves of the cuttings.

'Thank you,' she says thickly, her throat suddenly full of tears.

'Once rooted, the geranium is a forgiving plant,' he says, inserting them gently into the earth. 'You may neglect it for several weeks before it rebukes you. But you must water it eventually or it will die.'

She fishes for a tissue and blows her nose.

'There is much comfort to be had from a plant,' he says.

'Is there?'

'Believe it and it will be so.'

She leaves the scooter and carries the little pots up the hill in her crash helmet, carefully nestled together like a clutch of eggs. Arranging them in the shade of the vine, righting the cuttings that have tipped sideways, softens her arrival home and makes it easier to face the breakfast things, the tousled bed, the great splintered wounds in the sideboard.

She tidies up quickly, clearing, sweeping, ripping off sheets and bundling wet towels into the big plastic washing bowl. An hour later, dripping with sweat, she's standing under the shower, under the sky. And it's now that the tears come at last. Now, when she's tidied him away and there's nothing left to do: hot hiccoughing sobs that bend her double until she's retching, kneeling on the concrete, watching water and tears run away to the roots of the vine.

I should eat something, she thinks as her empty stomach contracts. *I should drink some water. It's ninety-five degrees and I haven't had anything all day.*

Perhaps I'm ill, she thinks, slipping on her white nightdress and lying down on the freshly made bed. The thought consoles her slightly. She rolls on to her side and stares out at her square of lemon tree. It's four o'clock and people are beginning to emerge from their siestas. Unknotting the mosquito net and arranging the folds around her, she can hear Georgia calling to her chickens, the *thud, thud* of Sophia picking *kolokithakia* and dropping them into a bowl. She feels flat and heavy, wrung out like a wet towel.

It's past nine in the evening when she wakes up. For a long moment, she just lies there looking at the stars prickling between the leaves of the lemon tree. Then she remembers: *Bennet was just here. He's been having an affair.* Her fortress, her place of safety, has been broken into.

Immediately the anger ignites again and catapults her out of bed. She wants to bite, but not swallow. She wants to tear things. She wants to punch the wall and make her knuckles bleed.

She opens the fridge and looks vaguely at its contents, thinking again: *I must eat.* She takes out cheese and a fat red tomato and slices bread for a sandwich; then slides it all into the bin. She goes back to the fridge and gulps cold water straight from the bottle. She eats half a peach, sitting on the patio in the dark, then hurls the rest down into the garden.

The night is hot and airless; enveloping her like a black blanket. Sweat trickles from her armpits and down her back and mosquitoes are humming around her damp ankles. She goes to the fridge again and takes out a glistening bottle of white wine.

'Bad Sylvia,' she says aloud into the darkness, feeling the cold wine splash into her empty stomach. 'Shouldn't drink when you're ovulating.' Then, viciously: 'Fuck it. Fuck my fucking hormones. Fuck the lot of them. Fuck everything.'

After the storm, the tears come again: silent, wet tears. She's crying for the woman Bennet found so difficult to live with: sleeping Sylvia, with her little frown and anxious mouth, her curves of glossy dark hair, her fingers gripping like clothes pegs on to the folds of a white sheet.

Towards the end of her first glass of wine, she stops crying. By the end of the second, she's feeling angry again. But it's a different kind of anger now: tipsy; reckless. She's restless and sweaty, longing for a breeze to raise the damp hair from the nape of her neck.

'Sylvia,' she says to herself. 'What you need is a ride on the scooter.'

Giggling drunkenly, she pulls on her trainers and ties a scarf around the waist of her nightdress. Her crash helmet's crumbed with damp soil, so she leaves it behind. In ten minutes she's riding out of the village with the night wind in her hair and her nightdress billowing behind her like a sail.

She doesn't ask herself where she's going, but she arrives there anyway: at the red camper van under the walnut tree with the folding chairs outside and the sliding door open.

She cuts the engine and dismounts. Her ears feel hollow suddenly, full of silence. The nightdress collapses around her. She's aware of the heat again, of air slowing down and sinking, heavy as treacle.

He's on the bed asleep, one arm curved like a fast bowler on the pillow above his head. The sheet's a spilt milkshake on the floor. His pale legs are tangled in the mosquito net, like a selkie caught without its skin. The net drifts slightly with each in-breath; he looks as though he's underwater.

She tugs off her trainers and climbs barefoot into the van. She crouches beside the bed. His body seems to fill the small space: a lung in a cage of ribs. When he breathes in, the van seems to contract. When he breathes out, it expands again. She can feel the air lapping at her skin.

She finds herself inhaling as he breathes out, trying to catch the scent of his breath. Crouching closer, she topples forwards and grabs the net to steady herself. His eyes flick open immediately.

'Sylvia! What's wrong?'

Now he's awake, she's confused. All she wanted to do, she realizes, is crouch beside him and breathe in as he breathes out. 'I didn't mean to wake you,' she says.

'Don't be silly.' He's knotting the net, retrieving the sheet from the floor.

'I'm sorry,' she says, but it comes out sounding strange. Like a giggle, or a sob. Then, when she sees the calm warmth in his eyes: 'Can you hold me?'

'Of course,' he says. 'Let me move over.' He rolls on his side and raises the sheet like a white shell for her to slip into.

He's naked, brown to the waist. His penis is very hard, very straight. He doesn't press it against her, but she can feel it nudging her hip as she lies down beside him. His smell fills her lungs: sweat and damp hair and citronella. She feels like a mouth flooding with saliva.

'Where's Bennet?' he's asking.

'Gone,' she says. 'I sent him packing.' The words feel furry on her tongue.

'Have you been drinking?'

'Just a bit. To help me screw my courage to the sticky place.' She giggles and corrects herself. 'Sticking-place.' Then: 'You're sticky.'

'We both are. It's a hot night.'

'I was like flypaper yesterday,' she says, burying her face against his shoulder. 'And Bennet was a fly sticking to me. But I flicked him off and he's flicked right off back to Newcastle.' She giggles again.

'Did you have a row?' He's stroking her back through her nightdress, long soothing movements.

'He took an axe to the sideboard,' she says and his hand stops. 'He said if you need a thing doing you have to do it for yourself.'

'Did he hurt you?'

'He thinks you're in love with me.' She looks at him, but it's too dark to see the expression on his face.

'I am in love with you,' he says simply. 'I've loved you ever since – God, I don't know. Ever since I saw you scrubbing those bloody tiles. Ever since you closed your eyes and worked out where Kokona's key was.'

She closes her eyes now and tilts her mouth to be kissed, then opens them again in confusion when nothing happens.

'I told Bennet you were celibate,' she says. 'But he said you were just spinning me a line.'

'It's not a line, Sylvia.'

'But you want me.'

'Yes. I want you.' He sighs.

'So?' She unties the scarf and pulls off her nightdress, pressing the length of her body against him. All her attention is riveted on where the flesh of her belly is moulding itself around the shape of his penis.

For a moment his whole body strains against her, then he's pulling away. 'There are so many reasons why this is not a good idea,' he says.

She worms a hand down between their bodies to touch him, but he grabs her wrist and drags it away from his penis. 'Reason one,' he says, fingers digging into her. 'I don't do this any more. Reason two: you're married. Reason three: you've just had a blazing row with your husband. Reason four: you're fertile.'

'I'm not married any more,' she retorts, trying to wrench her hand out of his grasp.

'What do you mean?' He lets her go suddenly.

'He's been screwing my best friend to the sticky place.'

'Has he left you?'

'He wants me to put it behind me,' she snorts. 'I said he should put it behind him and shove it right up.'

'So you want revenge,' he says quietly.

'I want a baby,' she says, caressing his boyish chest. 'You could give me a baby. Young sperm are much friskier than old ones.'

Again he takes her hand off him. 'Look, I'm not going to have sex with you tonight,' he says firmly, 'so there's no point trying to persuade me.'

The effect is like a bucket of cold water. Sylvia sits up suddenly and wrenches up the sheet to her shoulders. 'It's because I'm older, isn't it?'

'No it's not because you're older.' He sighs again. 'It's because you're upset and a bit drunk and not in control of what you're doing.'

'But I've been in control all my bloody life,' she pouts. 'I'm tired of being in control.'

'If you only knew how much I want to give you a baby.'

'So, kiss me.'

She sinks back down beside him and squirms on to her side until she's facing him on the pillow again. His breathing is shallow and his lips are slightly open. She's careful not to let her body touch his at any point, but she's aware of the space between them, like a fire door straining to close itself.

She shuts her eyes and tastes the air on the pillow, the smell of his lips, the sweat between his eyebrows. He's a fish on a line and she's reeling him in with her breath. When his lips touch hers at last, and his mouth opens and allows her tongue inside, she feels a gasp somewhere deep in her lungs, and a dropping away, like Alice tumbling slowly down the rabbit hole.

His tongue is turning in her mouth like a key, that parts her legs and slides her under him and rotates her pelvis until she's against him and nudging at him and enfolding him, until something shifts – her legs, his buttocks – and he's suddenly, shockingly, inside her.

For a second they're breathless, motionless, glued to each other. Then he pushes her roughly away and sits up.

'I can't do this,' he says.

'What?' She feels raw now his body's gone, as though a sticking plaster has been ripped off.

'It's not right. I'm not right.' He hunches away from her, wrapping his arms around his knees.

'If it's too fast, we can slow down.'

'It's not that. It's me.' His fists are clenched. He's banging his head against the side of the van as he speaks. 'You have to go. You don't know what I'm like.'

'Stop it. You're scaring me.'

'My mother—' He stops himself. 'There's things I haven't told you.'

'So, tell me.'

'I should never have let you in. Please, just leave me alone.'

'Are you sending me away?' She can't believe it.

'Just go.'

She wakes late with a hangover and it all comes back to her: Bennet's infidelity, her drunken ride to Martin's van.

There are too many thoughts to fit into her head. She makes peppermint tea and sits on the patio, sipping. The thought of swallowing anything solid makes her feel nauseous.

She thinks: *Three days ago I had two houses, two men who loved me, two lives to live. Now I'm not sure what I have.* She thinks: *I'm back where I started six weeks ago, a refugee on the platform with my luggage.*

When she focuses her thoughts on Bennet, the same image comes into her mind over and over: of their white bed in their white bedroom, and Val's cigarette stubbed out in the black Japanese bowl on her bedside table. Bennet would open the window, of course, and wash the bowl. But she would always know the cigarette had been there.

She can't, *won't*, think about what they're doing in her ebony bed, under her Egyptian cotton duvet cover. Her tightrope would snap if she went there, and she'd hurtle down to somewhere bottomless and terrifying. This one image is all she can face: her perfect little Japanese bowl, with the cigarette stubbed out in it. It's all she needs to concentrate her anger. Anger is good. Anger is strong. Anger is better than pain.

When she tires of contemplating that image, and the sharpness of her disgust starts to fade, she turns her mind towards Martin's face as he pushed her away from him. The horror frozen there for a second, as if she was the dead head of the Medusa.

At that moment it was easy to think he was psychotic: a gun with a trigger and no safety catch. That he'd killed his mother in a frenzy and burned her body. Could any child survive his strange upbringing without damage?

Then she thinks of kissing him, of tasting inside that mouth she's pored over in photographs. He tasted of sleep and toothpaste, of garlic and olive oil. She thinks of herself melting into him, like sugar in coffee, welling up like lava. Then she thinks of his hard fingers on her wrist, the humiliation when he forced her hand away, how he crushed the bones there, as if he didn't know his own strength.

Then, when the hot shame of that memory cools, back to the Japanese bowl, where she finds her anger has renewed itself and is as honed and sharp as ever.

And so it goes on all morning: anger and shame, shame and anger, as the adrenaline surges through her bloodstream, dilating her pupils and opening her capillaries, making her heart race and her muscles tense. Until she feels she has been running for hours along a hot hard road. Until she is sick and tired of the inside of her head and longs for it all to dissolve in the brain-emptying balm of tears.

But through it all, an insistent faint refrain in the background, she keeps thinking: *Martin loves me*. Like the Easter light guttering.

The light! She's forgotten to top up the oil. She leaps to her feet and rushes into the darkroom. She catches it just in time.

From that familiar action, she progresses to others. She washes her hair and irons her favourite shorts. She puts on moisturizer. She plucks a few stray hairs from her eyebrows. She waters the geranium cuttings, just a little, as Vasilios instructed.

She walks down the hill for a fresh *meso-psomi*, a half-loaf, then climbs back again and spreads two thick slices with butter and honey. And cuts off a corner for the hungry ghosts, and eats the rest, and feels the starches churn in her stomach, and feels better, and looks around at her small neat world.

It's five o'clock and the fierce heat of the day is starting to abate. She switches on her mobile. There are six text messages:

four from Bennet, one from Val, one from her mother. She switches it off again without reading them.

Martin will be at home now, she thinks. *It's his time for t'ai chi, when he's showered and it's cooler, before he starts wondering what to do about supper.* She thinks of the white figure against the red background; his body and his blood.

Then another image comes: of a fat woman with shapely feet crushing paracetamol with a marble pestle. And she thinks: *The last woman you made love to wanted to kill herself afterwards.* Then: *I was ovulating. I was drunk. I was angry. You were trying to protect me.*

And a final image comes, and stays: of him holding the photograph of herself asleep, and caressing the glossy curve of her hair; and wanting to uncurl her clutching fingers from the sheet.

Are you as wrung out and traumatized as I am? she wonders. Immediately she asks the question, she knows the answer. Without thinking twice, she locks up the house and starts up the scooter.

He's not there. Apart from a stain of water on the cement floor in the shower room, it's as though he's never been there.

She drives to Kefalas, though she knows the wall's finished. Then to Kalami, on the coast, where he was digging a swimming pool; then the three tiny hamlets inland, and the new bar in Vamos where he sometimes has a Mythos after work. But there's no sign of him anywhere.

I'll try in the morning, she thinks, heading for home. And the thought anchors her through the long evening serving at the taverna, and Aphrodite's curious looks, and the long night afterwards.

But next morning she can't find him either: at the sites in Drapanos, in Kalives, in Kokkino Horio. No one has seen him; no one knew he was moving; no one knows where he might be.

You've gone to ground, she thinks. *To lick your wounds.*

Chapter 23

The Horsehair Plait

The clenched fist in Martin's chest never really unclenched completely. By the time he was fifteen, it had become a predatory creature, stalking and sniffing for danger.

At seven he'd been a wild chestnut colt. Now he was a wary, angry fox.

His mother had sold the big house in Argyle Street and bought a smaller house on the outskirts of Kidlington, four miles from Oxford. It was a squarish oldish semi with a garden backing on to farmland. She'd hired a taxi to lug home rush matting for the floor and reed blinds for the windows, so it smelt like a stable and was bathed in a continuous golden twilight. 'We'll be like Mary and Joseph in Bethlehem,' she said.

She planted jasmine and clematis and something called mile-a-minute in the garden and soon the trees and fences were draped with green tendrils and the house was shielded from neighbourly eyes.

Martin had expected her to start t'ai chi again, and mowed a t'ai-chi-shaped space with the new turquoise electric lawnmower. But she said the movements made her legs ache and, anyway, the pills she was taking meant she didn't need to do t'ai chi any more.

She'd found a job as a part-time barmaid at a pub in the centre of Kidlington and had started taking classes in homeopathy, with the aim, so she said, of 'putting up a brass plaque and opening for business' when she qualified.

In most ways she was the same as before. The new house was still a patchwork of colours, and the rooms were strewn with clothes and books and cardboard boxes, as though someone was sorting things for a jumble sale. But she cooked now: big untidy stews full of herbs and foreign vegetables. And there was enough money to get things mended when they broke down, and Official People checking to make sure that they were.

Social Sue had moved to Manchester and been replaced by Not-so-Social Beth, a psychiatric social worker from the Littlemore with cropped hennaed hair and Doc Martens. She called once a week to make sure Martin and his mother were going to school and taking their pills, respectively. And under cover of 'getting out the milk' for a cup of tea, she always had a quick peek in the fridge to see what they were eating.

It was all almost normal, and in most ways a big improvement on their occult existence in Argyle Street. But, just as something had clenched in Martin, something had unclenched in his mother. Where she had once been alert and wily, she had become rather casual and careless. She got drunk and cycled home without lights. She skipped her homeopathy classes and forgot to do her homework. Now the worst had happened – and had been endured, and survived – the needles and nudges of anxiety had gone from her life. And it was as though she'd been heaving a long sigh of relief ever since.

Martin couldn't get used to this bland mother, who shrugged her shoulders too often and said 'it doesn't matter' about things that used to matter so much. He thought she should stop taking the pills and start drinking Grasshopper Tea again.

'You were fine, weren't you? Before you went into hospital.'

'Not really,' she said. 'Not all the time. And it was such hard work, Marty, living like that. It was hard for you, too. Don't you remember? Never knowing what kind of mood I'd be in; having to look after yourself when I couldn't get up.'

'I didn't mind. Anyway I'm older now. I know how much a tin-opener's supposed to cost.'

'I can't face it again, Marty. Please don't make me.'

He couldn't stand it when she went all pathetic little-girlie. She'd never been like this before she went into the Littlemore: wanting him to tell her that it was all right to stop trying. That it was all right to come home pissed every night from the pub job she'd taken on 'for a few months' four years ago when they'd first moved to Kidlington, 'while I decide what I'm going to do with my life now I'm better'.

That it was all right to sleep with Dan and Brian and the other nondescript Neanderthals she met at the pub. He'd heard them talking to her, about football and the Labour Party, stupid TV programmes. As if she never read anything, as if she was pug ordinary.

On her own with him she was so clever and creative; so amazing, even when she was drugged up; so unbelievably fucking beautiful.

When he saw them with their arms around her he wanted to kick something. Chi tingled in his feet like lightning. He wanted them dead as trees: felled and blackened and split open.

He stole from their jackets: cigarette lighters and coins; the occasional five-pound note. Once he took a credit card and dropped it in the street outside the house. It was easy-peasy lemon-squeezy to nick their stuff.

School was easy-peasy too. Without trying he was near the top of his class. The only reason he didn't make more of an effort was because he didn't want to be noticed. After ten years of being invisible, he didn't like to draw attention to himself. He preferred to lurk on the outskirts of excellence: a fox passing as a retriever.

He was lean and good at sports, but they bored him. Team games reminded him of the Dog People's dogs: tame and obedient; chasing a stick and bringing it back. He'd started learning martial arts instead, at the Old Fire Station in Oxford.

It started with the t'ai chi class he went to, to encourage his mother to take it up again. He liked the fact that the exercises were slow-motion fighting moves. He liked controlling his body's power and its anger. He liked feeling it coiled tight, like a spring inside him.

The teacher took another class in tae kwon do, and Martin started going to that too, and practising in bare feet in the tai-chi-shaped space in the garden. He tied his hair back in a ponytail and his body became hard and graceful. He could have slammed his fist right through the front door if he'd wanted to.

Some of the other boys at his school went to the classes too, but they didn't practise enough, so he always outshone them. It made them wary of him, which he liked, and meant they didn't give him a hard time about the books he carried everywhere in a small black rucksack, along with the front-door key of the house in Argyle Street and the little magnifying mirror from Emily Jackson's handbag.

Boys his age were like bluebottles, he thought: blundering into things and buzzing too loudly. Poking their big noses into anything to do with shit. Martin preferred the girls, some of them: the serious ones with small breasts and neat hair who sat at the front of the classroom at school. He steered clear of the others, though he knew they fancied him. They were too sauntery and fleshy for him. He didn't like the way they smelt, of chewing gum and perfume. He didn't like their lacy push-up bras and purple nail varnish.

He didn't like thinking about them when he masturbated, but he couldn't help it. When they smiled at him sideways the way they did, it was as though they were slipping a bit of themselves into his head, a seed which grew and grew as his dick thickened, and wouldn't go until he'd whacked his sperm out of it.

Martin read all the time. In summer he read on his stomach in the middle of his t'ai-chi-shaped space. In winter he stretched out on his bed with a tartan rug wrapped around him.

Right now he was reading *Grassblade Jungle*, about how insects live, and *A Wizard of Earthsea* about a man haunted by the Shadow he conjures. He was also reading *Tools for Conviviality*, about how society mirrors the machines it uses, and *The Heart of the Hunter*, about Bushmen surviving on next to nothing in the Kalahari Desert.

Every book was a coat he tried on to see if it fitted him.

He was looking for a book about a boy, raised in isolation by his mentally ill mother, whose father rejected him. A boy who used to believe he was two boys: one who lived in a cluttered rainbow house, and another who lived in a bare house with an aquarium in the living room. A bright boy who didn't get on with other children his age. A boy who stole from his mother's lovers and liked to roam the fields on his own at night. An alien boy; a reincarnated boy; part human, part horse, part fox.

He was reading *The Psychopathology of Everyday Life* about how accidents were really the intentional acts of the unconscious. And *Totem and Taboo* about how love and hate were really the same thing.

It was the week before the week before Christmas and the frozen ruts dug into Martin's feet like barnacles. His mother had sent him across the fields to the petrol station for mince pies. It was the only place that would be open at this time on a Sunday.

'I'll make some brandy butter to go with them,' she said, rummaging under the sink. 'Provided I can find the icing sugar.' The brandy was already on the table, of course. She never had any trouble finding that. It was a full bottle of Courvoisier with the foil still on.

Martin jabbed his heel into a frozen puddle, making it craze like smashed specs. She tried not to drink when he was watching. Always, somehow, got him out of the way. Hands jammed deep into his pockets, he hunched along in his duffel coat. He was thinking he should have put on a jumper too. His hands were freezing and the wind was worming cold fingers between the toggles through to his tee shirt.

It was getting dark and he saw a yellow light wink on in the tack room of the stable block in the middle field. He thought of the three horses in their blankets inside; the big chestnut mare and the bay and black geldings; of their kind eyes and velvet lips. They belonged to a shouty woman in a headscarf and her two subdued lanky daughters, who cantered them over five stripy jumps at the weekends.

On the way back half an hour later, he stopped and leant on the gate. The tack-room light was off now, and Shouty Scarf's blue Cortina estate had gone. Mr Kipling's Deep-Filled Mince Pies were under his arm and his hands pulsed with cold. He imagined slipping his palms under the mane of the chestnut mare and warming them on the bright skin of her neck.

Once he'd thought it, the need filled his throat. Putting down the mince pies he vaulted over the gate.

The horses whickered when they heard his footsteps and shifted and stamped in the dark. Unbolting the mare's door, he slipped inside her stall. It was pitch-black. At once he was engulfed by her thick brown smell. Holding out his frozen hands like a blind man, he moved towards her; touching a shoulder, then the rough blanket on her back.

She snorted. He imagined her head jerking upwards, her eyes looking for him in the darkness. Under her mane it was just as he expected: warm and pulsing with blood. He pushed his nose against her skin and breathed in, thinking of Mongol nomads who drank the living blood of their horses; and Masai herdsmen, who ate only the milk and blood of their cattle. There was a concrete mounting block in the yard outside. Martin pushed the door open and tugged the mare's mane to lead her over to it.

He'd never ridden before, but the mare was gentle and well trained and seemed to know what he wanted her to do. She walked him around the edge of the field a few times, then, when he squeezed with his knees, broke into a slow trot.

He wrapped a twist of red mane around his hand and leant forward, trying to ease his groin against her jolting spine. In a minute or two he got the knack, and sat up straighter to urge her into a canter. Her back was moving under him and with him; his legs had fused with her flanks. Their warm breath left a wake of white in the air behind them. He felt he had been waiting for this moment all his life.

He was discovered, of course, after less than a week. Shouty Scarf noticed that the mare's hooves were packed with mud and fresh grass when she came to saddle her the following Saturday, and she came back that night and caught him unbuckling the mare's blanket.

The police let him off with a caution, but Not-so-Social Beth decided he was 'at risk' and sent him to the Isis Centre in Little Clarendon Street in the New Year 'to talk things through' with a pillowy soft-spoken counsellor called Claire Reece.

Claire wanted to know all about his feelings. 'What did you feel when you were galloping around that dark field?' 'What did you feel when your mother went to bed for nineteen days?' 'What did you feel when you realized your father didn't want you to live with him?'

To begin with Martin was polite but evasive. It was none of her business what he felt. But by the third session, he'd become intrigued by the process of using words to beat a path through the wilderness. And he liked Careful Claire, with her long brown plait and intelligent grey eyes. He liked the slim silver chain around her neck and the drapy layery clothes she wore. He liked the way she seemed to care about seven-year-old Martin in his lair by the school, and eleven-year-old Martin at the police station with his mother.

Telling her some things made his throat ache and his nose run. When she pushed a pack of tissues towards him, he realized she expected him to cry. And after some clumsy hiccoughing, he discovered that crying was like riding: a headlong exhilarating gallop that left him calm and wrung out and sated.

Careful Claire drank clear tea with a slice of lemon in it. She had a tiny dimple in her left cheek. He thought she didn't wear a bra. He wondered what it would be like to kiss the corner of her mouth.

'What do you feel about the girls at your school, Martin?' she asked. He liked the way she said 'Martin'. It made him feel visible. He was a country and she was a cartographer, naming his cities, making a map of his mind.

'They're OK, I suppose,' he said. But he knew this wasn't what she was asking. She wanted to know whether he wanted to have sex with them. But he didn't want to tell her about the girls he liked and the ones he didn't; and what happened in his mind when he masturbated.

He didn't want to talk about the copies of *Hustler* and *Men Only* the other boys brought to school. He didn't want to say what he felt about all those shocking red cunts. That it bothered him to think that, deep down, they were all the same: the girls he liked and the ones he didn't; the Cat Women and Dog Women; Social Sue and Not-so-Social Beth. Careful Claire.

He wondered what she'd look like with her long brown plait unravelled. He wondered whether she shaved under her arms. He wondered what it smelt like in her armpits.

One morning he went to the Isis Centre early, when he knew she wouldn't be there. The receptionist hadn't even arrived yet. There was an open black bin liner in the middle of the waiting room and the

268

cleaner was still hoovering in the hall. He slipped into Careful Claire's room and closed the door quietly behind him.

The room looked strange: full of early-morning sun. By the time his session started the sun had moved round past the window. He began to go over to her chair, then hesitated. There was a blue tissue crumpled by the waste bin, and wads more inside. His back teeth clenched suddenly: who else had been crying in this room?

He approached her chair and looked down at the soft dents in the embossed seat-cushion. Those dents had been made by her bum. The thought sent a hot shock through him, and he knelt and placed his hands there to touch the ghost of her heat. He wondered what was beneath the fabric; iron springs, perhaps, and the matted tails of dead horses. Wasn't that what they used to stuff these old chairs with?

He pressed his hands down, investigating, feeling springs tilt and twang, compressing. In less than an hour it would be her bum making them do this. Closing his eyes, he swayed forwards and sniffed the chair fabric. Then he was searching every inch of it, trying to pick up the scent of her.

His dick thickened and he put an angry hand down and squeezed hard, like he'd read about, to make it go away: the fox in him, the horse. Why was it always like this with women? Clever or stupid, old or young, why was *this* what he always ended up thinking about? The red folds they all had under their clothes; the hot hole that made them all alike?

Chapter 24

Bennet keeps phoning, filling up Sylvia's voicemail with messages. She listens to the first few, then erases the rest and switches her phone off. He sends flowers, an ungainly bunch of exotic blooms, delivered by van to the *Petaluda* in the middle of the evening rush. He telephones the taverna, worried about her, and infuriates her by asking Aphrodite to intervene.

Aphrodite's been like a kitten with a ball of wool ever since: batting at it, chasing it, pouncing and tangling herself in it.

'You have to speak to him sometime.' They are laying the tables for the evening, topping up oil and vinegar in the cruets.

'Why?'

'Because he loves you. This is obvious.'

'He should have thought about that before.'

'Men do not think about these things before,' Aphrodite says, tipping a heavy trickle of green oil. 'They only think of the thing in front of their noses. Anyway, he says it was the first time he has been unfaithful to you.'

'It's the first time we've been apart for more than a week since we met. What does that tell you about the strength of his commitment?'

'But he has sent flowers!'

'Obviously he finds it easier to track down an international florist than keep his trousers on for a few months.' She's still angry; it comes in waves, like a fever she can't shake off.

'What shall I say if he telephones again?'

'Tell him to leave me alone. Tell him I'll call him if I have anything to say to him.'

'And where is Martin?'

'What's Martin got to do with it?'

'I thought maybe your Bennet is jealous about Martin. And this is why he is playing around.'

'Don't you start! Martin did some work for me, that's all. Now he's doing some work for someone else. End of story.' Sylvia can feel herself blushing.

'So he has disappeared again.' Aphrodite nods in a satisfied way. 'Whenever life becomes difficult he always disappears.'

For the first week, she goes searching for Martin every evening, setting off at around six and cruising the lanes until the light fades. To begin with she drives in random loops through the countryside, but when all her early hunches fail, she becomes more systematic, marking out specific quadrants on the map and trawling them exhaustively one by one.

It's absorbing and calming, this search for him, like the fingering of *komboloi*. It stops her thinking about Bennet, about Newcastle, about her marriage, her future. It plants her in this landscape, in a kind of timeless present, moving along the network of roads and tracks, like a red blood cell in a capillary.

Her period comes, a day early, surprising her with a whoosh of blood that soaks straight through to her shorts. Rinsing them out, she thinks: *What if Martin hadn't stopped me? What if I'd conceived? What if I'd been pregnant with his child?*

The thought stays with her. *What would a future with Martin be like?* She spreads the thought out on the table and looks at it.

They could take it in turns looking after the baby. He'd go out to work in the mornings, to some site or other; she'd travel the villages doing portraits in the afternoons, maybe set up a little photographic studio. Put in heating, hot water. Maybe build an extension. She could work in the taverna for extra cash in the summer. They could get some chickens. Re-establish Kokona's vegetable plot. It would be a future of work shirts and concrete dust; dirt under the fingernails; pictures on the walls. Hungry ghosts.

She considers it, this future, this stamp of the butterfly's foot. Another world. Another planet. Planet Martin.

Is it any better or worse than the future she'd planned with Bennet, in their lofty Newcastle terrace, with its attic conversion, its view of the allotments and the Great North Road? Working part-time at the lab; a nanny for the baby. A second home in Crete. Shopping at Sainsbury's. Christmas with the in-laws. Savings accounts, ISAs, pension plans.

She thinks of her mother's pursed mouth as she dabbed calamine lotion on to flea-bitten ankles. She thinks of a kitten's tongue rasping at her earlobe and a purr like a bee in her head. She thinks: *I don't have to be like this*.

She thinks of an old woman with a long white plait and a house by the sea. She thinks of a photographer with a cat and a motorbike and a garden full of vegetables.

She thinks: *Who is Sylvia?* She thinks: *I can be anyone I like*.

By the end of the third week, when she's searched almost every lane and track on the Apokoronas peninsula, it dawns on her that Martin may have left the area, may have travelled south to Sfakia or Paleochora; or back to Matala, to the caves he told her about; that he may have left the island altogether.

She doesn't give up, though; simply widens her search to take in the area around the resort of Georgioupoli, where three new estate agents have opened recently. The surrounding villages are scarred with new building sites following a Channel Four series set there about buying a house in Crete.

Why would anyone want to live here? she wonders, bumping along the beach road of the crowded resort. It smells of chips and drains and hot cars. You can have Full English Breakfast at ten different tavernas. The sand is packed with oiled bodies basking in plantations of beach umbrellas. The sea is sheened with suntan lotion.

It's odd seeing people on holiday; jam-packing their two weeks with sunshine and bizarre cocktails. Burning their shoulders on the first day; buying garish sarongs and diamante flip-flops;

overeating; oversleeping; smearing moisturizers and peering at their skin. Living here makes holidaying seem like an aberration, like an allergic reaction to work that takes two weeks to abate.

She remembers her holiday with Bennet back in March, how Crete seemed like a cake cut into fourteen thin slices that had to be eked out before they returned to their normal life back in England. She thinks: *This could be my normal life.*

All through August, she's had more photo commissions than she can manage and finds herself driving into Chania once a week for supplies. She's decided on a fixed rate for the photos, enough to cover costs and give her a reasonable profit. But she always waives the fee for people she owes favours to: Dimitri at the shop; Spiros and the two Sophias; Georgia, Costas. She gets these portraits framed herself, so that they are proper gifts. It's good to be able to offer something in return for all the things they've given her over the months.

Her days are full of village faces: photographing them, developing them, tinting them.

She spends her mornings sitting in people's houses, sipping jolts of sweet coffee and nibbling sesame shortbread, while her clients shift furniture around for the photograph and fuss with their clothes and hair.

Sometimes they ask for group pictures, but she always refuses. Part of the pleasure for her is posing the single portraits: studying one person at a time; the way they sit and smile, the way they fiddle with their wedding rings. She likes to experiment with light sources, looking for the angle, the play of shadows that focuses attention on the personality she's studying. Then watch them swim to the surface of the developing trays in the darkroom.

The photo sessions can take hours: of chatting and sitting, trying different chairs, different occupations for their hands, until the person relaxes and allows their face to open. The trick is to stop them fixing their expressions into a self-conscious mask. Often she'll click the shutter twenty or thirty times before even loading the film, until they get used to her leaning on the table with the viewfinder to her eye, or crouching at their feet, moving the reflector around.

It gives the audience time to get bored, too, and drift away. Because there's always a room full of curious visitors when she arrives, who stiffen up her subjects' features every time they start to relax.

It's at the end of the sessions that she takes her best shots, sometimes just the last three frames on a roll of film, when the second cup of coffee has been drunk and it's just the two of them in the quiet room, and the hens clucking, the canary trilling on the balcony outside.

Sometimes they tell her surprising things. 'My father had a fight with my brother before he died and left him only the donkey in his will as a punishment'; 'I was engaged to the priest before he was a priest'; 'My son lives in Sydney with another man'; 'I was a dancer in Thessaloniki before I got married, but everyone thinks I was a receptionist'; 'I had ten children, but only three survived'.

Once or twice she finds herself photographing women she recognizes as 'Kokona's children'; middle-aged women, mostly, sitting portraits for birthday or anniversary presents. And she thinks, looking at their cushiony bodies and lived-in faces, of the young women they were thirty years ago, with light legs and glowing skin, making their way up the hill to Kokona in the small hours.

It's at the end of the day that her own thoughts crowd in, when she's finished at the taverna and sits on the patio in her nightdress, sipping peppermint tea and staring down at the lights of the village. When she thinks of her body, preparing for another ovulation, her womb building up layers of red cushion, another month passing when she isn't conceiving, isn't becoming a mother. As though she's a passenger on the wrong platform with a different ticket, and that train, that life, is passing her by.

Sometimes she switches on her mobile and counts Bennet's

messages, and smiles grimly as she erases them, one by one. And thinks of him sending them, sitting over a cappuccino in an Italian café, or in a pub somewhere with the football on widescreen, and the *Guardian* folded small on the crossword page. And wants to hurt him; puncture him somehow, quash the confident bigness of him. It's all she can do: press *delete, delete, delete.*

'But he is a good husband, your doctor,' says Aphrodite, returning to one of her favourite subjects.

'Provided you leave faithfulness out of the equation,' says Sylvia. They're sunning themselves on the hot rocks after their swim: Aphrodite in a purple two-piece encrusted with silver embroidery, Sylvia in one of her neat black bikinis.

'But these men are hard to find. Handsome men with good jobs. Good family men. They are the bulls of the herd.'

'He went to bed with my best friend,' Sylvia objects, stretching out her legs and inspecting them. The skin on the calves seems thin and papery; the epidermis thinning; the juicy plumpness of youth drying up. *Would I be more fertile if I was fatter?* she wonders. *But I couldn't bear all that mess; rolls around my waist, a double chin, sagging bum spreading out.*

'In a marriage there are always things to forgive.' Aphrodite smoothes oil on to her chubby arms. 'In my marriage there is the hammer and the cars; the silent hat in the garden. But Vasilios is a forgiving man too.'

'What do you mean?'

'I have not always been a good wife.' Aphrodite lowers her voice, though there's no one to hear. 'There was a time when I made a very big mistake. There was a man from Episkopi. He was not even educated!' She shakes her head at her own folly. 'He was a man of *kremithia* and *karpouzia*, with a van. You have seen them here, coming around, selling things. Chairs, tables, *psaria, domates*. I was still breastfeeding Maria; my stomach was still fat from being pregnant.'

'And you had an affair.'

'Yes, we were lovers for more than one year. Then just last summer – I will tell you this, because we are two women together with our troubles. Last year, I was a very silly woman with Martin.'

'You went to bed with Martin?' Sylvia feels blood thud into the backs of her eyes. She can see corpuscles swimming across her field of vision.

'No, of course not! He will not even kiss me. But I fell in love with him a little, I think. I was thinking about his hands very much, and his hair. I think when you are in love, you notice these things. It is the same with Maria. Since Martin was here she does not even look at another boy.'

'But nothing happened.' Sylvia finds she's holding her breath. She lets it out very slowly so that the other woman won't notice.

'No. Nothing happened. But if he is willing, who knows? With Nicos I was crazy. We were making love in the van, with the onions on the back and the dog tied under the tree.' She laughs, almost proud of herself. 'I didn't care. I didn't think. And of course there were the consequences.'

'What kind of consequences?'

'What do you think? When a man and woman make love? Anyway, I told Vasilios. Not at that time. Later, when I had been to Kokona and it was all finished and I wasn't crazy any more.'

'And he forgave you.'

'Yes. And do you know something? Now I will never leave him. Never. Because of that big piece of forgiving.'

Sylvia thinks of the quiet man in the garden; the clutch of geraniums in her crash helmet. 'He's an unusual man.'

'Your Bennet, too. I remember you telling me when you are first here. About his big American motorbike. His work in that terrible place in Africa.'

'The refugee camp. Yes. But that was ages ago. He's not like that now.'

He'd had thick hair then, a heavy wedge of pale curls that he hacked at himself; strong thighs from balancing the Harley. She met him when he was just back from Zimbabwe: sun-browned and impassioned, showing slides at a student meeting to raise money for Oxfam. Or Amnesty. Something Third Worldly. She remembers how powerful he seemed, big and shaggy and brown, pacing the stage like a lion, talking about the conditions in the camps, the injuries he'd seen; about torture and human rights.

He'd approached her afterwards and handed her a plastic cup of warm wine.

'I'm not always like that,' he'd said.

'Like what?'

'Angry young man. Staring eyes.'

'Oh?' she'd said, bemused. 'What else are you like?'

'Studious and reliable. Tweeds and brogues. Sherry and cream tea.'

'Not together, I hope.' She'd smiled; she'd liked leaning against the wall looking up at him.

'But I do have one confession to make,' he'd said ruefully.

'Which is?'

'I'm afraid I do own an unfeasibly large motorbike.'

He'd told her later that when he first saw her, setting out the chairs, handing out leaflets, he'd wanted to whisk her off on the Harley right then. 'You were so unruffled,' he'd said. 'I wanted to ruffle you good and proper.'

She examines the image in her mind. Typical Bennet: always charming, always in charge. 'Ideal husband and father material,' her mother had commented approvingly when she'd first met him. He stood up when she entered the room, held the door, pulled out her chair, held her coat.

'A woman could get lazy with you around,' her mother had told him.

Though she daren't dig around in the earth to check, Sylvia thinks most of the geranium cuttings have taken. A few rotted and keeled over in the first week, but the rest have all produced new leaves, like tiny green fans opening.

'I'll need to plant you out soon,' she says to them as she feeds them their regular trickle of water. 'Where would you like to go?'

She surveys the parched garden. It glares back at her: bleached and neglected, studded with thirsty-looking fruit trees. In England she'd know exactly what to do, but the seasons are different here. *Did Kokona water them?* she wonders. *Or do they hibernate in the summer?*

Later that afternoon, when the heat abates, she takes Kokona's scythe and begins slashing at the grass around the patio. It's surprisingly easy, once she's got the knack, and soon she's cleared most of the top terrace and is raking up blonde hay into a big rustling heap.

Over the next few days, she clears the rest of the garden. Not properly: not rooting out nettles and couch grass; not hacking back brambles. Just enough to see what's there, what used to be there, what might be nurtured back into life. She thinks: *It could take years to get this garden how I want it to be.* The thought comforts her. It makes her feel rooted.

She discovers six knotted rose bushes and a sparse-looking jasmine on the level nearest the house. And in one corner, near the kitchen, there's the wizened skeleton of a rosemary bush, and desiccated clumps of mint and angelica, oregano and thyme, that give off sudden puffs of herby perfume as she rakes over them. Between the fruit trees on the lower levels are dusty rugs of some kind of flowering succulent, and bushes of multicoloured lantana; toppling stands of prickly pear. And right at the bottom, on the big flat vegetable plot where they'd planned to build their new house: a pomegranate sapling, bowed down by rosy fruit, and a clump of stately blue artichoke flowers; sprawls of purslane and drooping tussocks of *horta*.

Then, what's this? Beside the big flat boulder she sat on all those weeks ago, where she planned to site the kitchen of the new house, her rake hits a double row of white stones set in the ground.

*

One lunchtime, four weeks after she sent him packing, Bennet turns up at the house. She's been developing film all morning and her head's aching slightly. She's just sitting down outside with a glass of cold water when a car parks beside her gate and out he gets.

She blinks. It's so unexpected to see him there, she thinks for a second that she might be imagining him.

'*Kalimera*,' he says. 'Or is it *kalispera* at this time of day?'

'*Kalimera*,' she supplies automatically.

'If the mountain won't come to Mohammed, Mohammed reckoned he'd better schlep along to the mountain.'

'What are you doing here?'

'I found a note in my palmtop that said "Ovulation, Crete".'

'Why didn't you call?'

'If you'd bothered to listen to your messages, you'd have discovered that I did. Several times. Possibly more than several. Probably even bordering on many.'

'I keep forgetting to charge the phone,' she lies.

'Well I'm here now. Aren't you going to offer me a beer?'

'I don't have any beer,' she says. 'I hate beer. Will coffee do?'

'Thanks,' he says, sitting down opposite her. 'Anything with a kick. That drive was horrendous. Scads of Brits driving open-top jeeps in the middle of the road.'

'This is ridiculous,' she says crossly. 'You can't just turn up unannounced.' But she can feel a smile budding at the corners of her mouth; she should have predicted he'd try something like this.

'I thought a big gesture was needed. And as flowers didn't seem to do the trick, I thought I'd do the Man of Mystery thing and parachute in with a box of Milk Tray.'

'Is that what this is about?'

'I love you, Sylvie,' he says. 'I miss you. I want us to be together, forsaking all others, until death us do part.'

'It's not that easy.'

'I know. And I'm quite prepared to do penance. Hot coals, sackcloth and ashes, you name it. I just wanted to let you know I'm in this for the long haul. If you'll have me.'

'I don't know,' she says, getting up to make his coffee. 'I'm still angry.'

'So you should be.'

'But these last weeks —'

'Have been hell.'

'Have been – interesting. Being in limbo. Not knowing what to do. In a way you've done me a favour. It was time I thought about things. About me. About us.'

'Now you're worrying me.'

Sylvia spoons coffee and sugar. 'Did she use the Japanese bowl as an ashtray?' she asks.

'What?'

'Val. My perfect bowl. The one we bought in Osaka.'

'Of course not. I'd never let her smoke in the bedroom.'

'Oh,' she says. 'Right.'

'Why?'

'It was bugging me.'

'I gave the sheets to Oxfam, if that helps,' he offers.

'It's just too soon, B. I'm nowhere near ready to forgive you.'

'Val's fucked off to do an epilepsy consultancy in the States.'

'I don't care about Val.'

'Can I take off my jacket?' He tries a lopsided smile.

'When are you flying back?'

'Tonight if you send me away with a flea in my ear. Monday if you're prepared to put up with me for a few days.'

'I wish you hadn't come,' she sighs, but it's only half true. She's glad to see him; pleased he's made the effort. But she's not ready to make a decision about their marriage.

'I had to come. Surely you can see that.'

'I was managing not to think about it.'

'Is that good or bad?'

'More surprising than anything, I suppose.'

'Can I stay until Monday?'

'No.'

After Bennet's gone, she feels disoriented and fuzzy, as though she's been watching old movies on the sofa all day and someone's just switched the TV off.

They'd had lunch on the patio, then sat over coffee. Then, when the heat started to abate, he suggested they went for a walk. Not down into the village, but up the hill behind the house, and over the other side, wandering through olive groves and sheep pastures, with the cicadas screaming and blue-tailed lizards darting across the path.

After four hours of wrangling – he arguing, pleading; she oddly calm and implacable – there was nothing left to say. So they said nothing: just meandered companionably side by side, kicking through fallen olive leaves.

Sylvia had looked down at their feet, bare and dusty-toed in their matching Birkenstocks. They'd bought them together on a trip to London the previous year. They'd agreed that it was naff to choose the same design, the same colour, but neither had been prepared to give way and buy something else.

'What does this say about us?' she'd said ruefully as they left the shop.

'That we're perfectly suited,' he'd said, putting an arm around her and squeezing.

'Perfectly boring, you mean. Give it a few more years and we'll be wearing matching cardies and finishing each other's sentences.'

'Sounds all right to me,' he'd said.

Climbing on to the scooter as usual that evening, it occurs to her suddenly that Martin might have been watching her over the last four weeks: noting where she's been searching and predicting her next move; that he might have been staying at several sites and shifting between them, to make sure she kept missing him.

Perhaps she's been looking in the right places all along, but he's been covering his tracks to outfox her?

As with Kokona's key, she succeeds with her first try. There: he'd scattered the floor of the toilet with dry leaves, but when she lifts the pan lid, there's fresh water in the bowl. And there, the grass where the van must have parked has been scuffed upright again, but the scars on the overhanging branches, where he's cut them back, are still clammy and white.

After three hours she's found three sites, three remote old hillside cottages with commanding views of the surrounding countryside. That night, pouring hot water on to her peppermint tea bag, she allows herself a little shudder of excitement. Tomorrow, if she's right, she'll find him.

She decides to get up before dawn and visit all three sites in quick succession, before he's left for wherever it is he's working at the moment. Once again, she succeeds with her first try, spotting the telltale glint of chrome through a screen of rustling bamboo.

Her heart seems too big for her chest suddenly and her hands start to sweat. The sun hasn't risen yet and everything seems blueish and soft-focus: the scabby whitewash on the old house, the stones on the track, the haze of jasmine flowers over the front door.

A scrawny cat is pawing at something on the ground in front of the van and there's a faint smell of charcoal. *You barbecued last night*, she thinks. She creeps nearer to check, and yes, there's the circle of stones and the ashes, the greasy grille propped against the wheel of the van.

The sound of movement inside the van makes her retreat behind the bamboo thicket. Then there he is, jumping down from the open door of the van in the blue light: lithe and boyish and naked – and completely bald.

The shock of his shaved head makes her cry out and he turns immediately.

'You've shaved your head,' she says.

'I'm atoning for my sins,' he says, not bothering to cover his body.

'It gave me a shock.'

'You weren't meant to see.'

'No. Sorry,' she says. 'I wanted to apologize. But I couldn't find you.'

'I didn't want to be found.' He's stretching in the dawn light, then squatting and flexing his legs one after the other.

'What are you doing?' Without his hair he seems alien; from another culture, another planet.

'I'm going through a process.'

'What kind of process?' He looks like an Indian brave or a Tibetan monk; someone tribal; someone who might dance or paint his body; who might go into a trance.

'Look, I'm sorry. I can't talk to you now.' He speaks politely, but there's a touch of desperation in his voice. 'Please, could you just leave me alone?'

'I felt responsible,' she tries. 'That night, I wasn't thinking.'

'It's nothing to do with you,' he says rotating his head, then pulling it from side to side with his hands to stretch his neck. 'It's my karma. My sins to atone.' She can't stop staring at his naked scalp. She wants to touch it. It's very smooth, very brown. He must have shaved it weeks ago.

'We have every kind of animal in us,' he's saying. 'Did you know that? The human embryo starts out as a fish, then it becomes an amphibian, then a bird, then a dog. Except it would be a wild dog, of course, a wolf or a fox. Or a wildcat.'

'Ontogeny repeats phylogeny,' she says.

'Yes!' His grin blazes at her suddenly. 'I used to think I was possessed by the spirit of a wild horse.'

'Why a horse?'

'I don't know. Because of my hair. Because of my hooves. When I was eighteen I could punch them right through a door.'

'Is that why you shaved your head?' She doesn't like the way he's talking: disconnected, as though he's on drugs.

'I used to dream that my mother was a brown mare. She was one of those women with long legs and big hands. She always wished they were smaller, but they were exactly right for the way she was.'

'I thought maybe you'd gone back to Matala,' she says, trying to change the subject.

'She's with me all the time, you know,' he says. 'In my head. In the van. In my fucking hands. Look at them—' He holds them out towards her. 'These are her hands.'

'It's understandable that you can't—' she begins.

He laughs bitterly. 'It's not understandable.'

'Why did you shave your head?' she asks again.

'Maybe I liked the look of it,' he says, sitting down on the step of the van. 'Maybe I had lice. Maybe it's an outward sign of inward grace.'

'It makes you look younger.' She's beginning to feel nervous. He's stopped making sense. 'Where are you working? I tried everywhere.'

'I'm not working any more. I told you. I'm going through a process.' His knees are apart, his genitals dangling dark between them.

'What about money?'

'What about it?'

'It's been a month. How are you managing?'

'As the birds do, mother; as the lilies of the field. Hunting and gathering.'

'I was going to ask you to come and look at the sideboard,' she says, trying to steer him into a normal conversation. 'To see if it can be mended. Or if I should just throw it away.'

'I'm making a box,' he says. 'It's going to be a good box. I should have made it years ago, but I kept putting it off.'

'Can I see?'

'It's over there,' he says, pointing towards a heap of logs.

'Where?'

'It's not finished yet,' he says and bursts into laughter.

'Martin—' She puts a hand on his knee and he freezes as though he's been shot. 'What's going on?'

He stares in silence at her hand, and his whole body seems to cave in.

'Please,' he whispers brokenly. 'Don't touch me.'

Tears are pouring down his face and splashing on to his bare thighs. 'I have to be alone,' he says. 'I have to finish the box.'

Chapter 25

The Silver Toe Rings

Martin soon found another horse to ride, in a different field on the other side of the main road. He told Careful Claire about it, but not about the next one, a flighty chestnut gelding near Kidlington Airport. And by the time he was on to the next – out towards Woodstock, where the rich people lived – he was eighteen and his sessions at the Isis Centre had come to an end.

His latest night ride was one of two horses that belonged to a sturdy blonde family in a pseudy-Tudy gabled house, with a BMW and a Land Rover in the drive. One was a big placid piebald with soup-plate hooves; the one Martin rode was a sharp-witted black thoroughbred, who nipped him when his back was turned, but was keen and responsive when mounted.

He cycled there at night on the silver ten-speed his mother had bought him for his eighteenth birthday. He'd wanted a motorbike, but she'd said if he couldn't be bothered to sit his A levels, she couldn't be bothered to fork out the money for a 'noisy little Yamaha for you to break your neck on'.

They seemed to fight quite a lot these days. Randomly, it seemed to Martin, and inconsistently; about things he thought they'd thrashed out ages ago. It was as though she sometimes jolted awake from her cheerful carelessness, and was filled with dismay at the position in which she found herself at the age of forty-three: working in a dead-end job and living with a dropout son in a semi in a garden city.

But in between, when she was sober, they were as close as ever: going for long walks together, making picnics, debating, poring over books.

'Why can't we be like this all the time?' she asked one morning, in the middle of a late breakfast of pancakes and a long discussion about Jungian archetypes.

'Because I'm eighteen and you're a drunken slut,' he said affably. He was standing bare-chested in his white t'ai chi trousers at the cooker, tossing his third pancake. She was in a blue towelling dressing gown, spooning honey and Greek yoghurt on to her second.

'If I stop drinking, will you stop being eighteen?' She was just out of the shower and her wet hair was slicked back from her face. She looked young and fresh and beautiful.

'How old would you like me to be?'

'You were lovely when you were eight,' she mused. 'And I expect you'll be lovely again when you're twenty-eight.'

'Isn't there anything you like about me now?'

'Well you make a pretty mean pancake, I'll grant you that. In fact you're generally quite handy around the house. And you can string three sentences together, which is more than most males of your age. And you wash regularly and your feet don't smell and you haven't got anyone pregnant yet – as far as I know.'

'But?'

'You know all the buts, Marty. Going off at night God knows where. Dropping out of school. Forgetting to sign on. Loafing around all day with your nose in a book.'

He sat down at the table and reached for the honey. 'We talked about that, and you agreed.'

'I know,' she sighed. 'And Illich is right. You're probably better off educating yourself. But I worry about what will happen when you want to apply for a job and they turn you down because you don't have maths A level.'

'I'll lie,' he said. 'No one's going to ask to see a certificate. And I'm hardly likely to apply for something where I'll be integrating functions all day.'

'Perish the thought,' she said. 'Sounds disgusting.' Then, sighing: 'I don't know why I get so het up about these things. I should just be grateful to have such a clever, sane, thoughtful, handsome son.'

'My point precisely,' he said, licking his plate then going back to the cooker.

'And you're careful about Aids.'

'Never go anywhere without a condom in my pocket.' He ladled the last of the batter and tilted it expertly around the smoking pan.

'That was scrummy,' she said, leaning back and patting her stomach. 'I won't need to eat again for a week.' Her dressing gown was gaping at the throat and her hair had separated into glossy black coils. She looked like a sated cat stretching in the sun.

'So, will you be dragging back tonight?' he asks.

'I wish you wouldn't call it that.' 'Dragging back' was his term for when she brought one of her men home for the night, a dismissive reference to the Neanderthal habit of hauling a mate back to the cave by their hair.

'Well? Will you?' It came out more belligerently than he intended.

'I'm not sure,' she said. But he could tell by the way she was sitting up and pulling shut her dressing gown – as though he'd seen too much – that she would be.

He stayed out all night when she dragged back. That way he didn't have to smell whoever it was in the toilet or see him bleary on the landing first thing, with one of their clean towels wrapped around his waist. He hated to think of their hands on her. Their tongues. On her. In her. His beautiful mother. He hated the way it made his dick hard.

'It's up to you,' he shrugged when his mother objected. 'I don't want to interfere with your sex life, but you can't expect me to sit with my hands over my ears while you get stoned and keep me awake half the night bonking.'

First he went riding on the black mare, then he bought a bag of chips in the centre of Woodstock and caught the night bus into Oxford to go dancing.

He loved dancing and from his reflection in the disco mirrors he knew he was good at it. Like riding and t'ai chi, dancing inhabited his body and moved it automatically. By now he knew the regulars at the three main discos, and some of the kids from his old school went there sometimes; but he preferred to dance by himself. In the pulsing dark caverns, with their jungle lights, he didn't mind being looked at and made space for. These were anonymous theatrical places, like the cosmetics department at Debenhams, where people were like caricatures of themselves; where they ogled and performed, and smeared the samples, but rarely spoke or made a purchase.

What he liked best was dancing when he was stoned. There was often a spliff being handed round and the bouncers didn't seem to care. After a few tokes the music buffeted him like seawater and he could feel the rushing lights skate across his skin like caresses.

These were the nights when, with a tube of KY and a packet of three in his jacket, he'd look for an ugly girl to go home with.

He'd begun having sex with ugly girls when he'd felt sorry for a fat redhead left sitting at a table full of half-empty lager glasses one night. It had been slow-dance clinch-time and her prettier friends had all been tongue-kissing a group of students on the dance floor.

Initially he'd asked her to dance to irritate the friends, who'd been eyeing him up earlier that night. But she'd felt so soft and eager pressed against him, and smelt so good – of lemons and marshmallows – that his dick was hard in an instant and he'd found himself bending to kiss her grateful upturned face. And her breath had been sweet, and she'd tasted good too: of lager-blackcurrant and the salty sweat from her upper lip.

Her name was Sally and she was living with three other nurses in a flat on the Cowley Road. She'd made him tea in the small kitchen, then asked shyly if he'd like to see her room. At every stage he monitored his responses, watching for the moment when he would get up and go. But she was so needy and nice, he couldn't bring himself to leave. And later, in bed, she was so clumsy and tentative, he found himself being more tender than he ever was with the pretty girls he usually went to bed with. And discovered a deep satisfaction in gentling her, and pleasuring her, and feeling her grow graceful and sensual as the animal in her responded to his hands and tongue.

Afterwards, near dawn, as they sat up in bed in the darkness eating buttered toast, he'd explained that he wasn't looking for a girlfriend and wouldn't be asking for her telephone number.

She'd sighed: 'I knew you wouldn't. Girls like me don't have boyfriends like you. But you were so nice, I thought maybe you did like me a bit.'

'I do like you,' he'd said truthfully. 'And I loved making love to you. But I don't want to be "Sally and Martin in the same breath" with anyone.'

'I wish you'd told me earlier,' she said in a small voice.

'Sorry.' He felt terrible. What he'd meant as a kind gesture had ended up hurting her. 'Would you have turned me down if I had?'

'I don't know,' she said thoughtfully. Then, with a shy smile: 'Probably not. It was wonderful. No one's ever made love to me like that, as though they really liked my body. And it was worth it just to see the looks on their faces when we walked out of the disco together.' She wiped her buttery mouth with the back of a plump freckled hand. 'And I can always make up some story when they ask if I'm seeing you again.'

'At least you know,' he said sheepishly.

'But next time' – now she was severe – 'you should tell the girl before you put on the condom. Then she can decide for herself if she still wants to go through with it.'

So that's what he did now. And after a while, he found he preferred making love to ugly girls. Because, usually, they were friendlier and more interesting than the pretty ones; and less mannered and unnatural in bed. And he admired them, the lively clever ones he chose, for their bravery and gusto. And began, eventually, to appreciate the look of a big nose or thin lips, and the feel of a huge bottom or bony chest under his hands. And some became friends – though never 'girlfriends' – and some he went to bed with more than once. But in the end, in the dark, they all felt just the same.

It was around this time that his mother started to talk about going back to Matala. She'd finally got around to renewing her passport, and had got one for him too. She was smiling in her photo, with her dark hair up in an unruly sort of chignon. Martin looked serious and glum in his.

'Wouldn't it be wonderful if it was like it used to be?' she said.

Martin wasn't sure. What had been OK back then seemed rather hokey in 1994. He thought of Rachel and Greg and Karl in their forties, still camping out in the caves, smoking dope and talking politics; and it seemed more like a retreat than a revolution.

'If I had a few months in Matala I'm sure I could get my head together,' said his mother. This had become her standard response whenever he quizzed her gently about her abandoned homeopathy course or suggested she tried reducing the dosage of her medication.

She wanted to buy a camper van and drive it overland to Crete with him. One of the men at the pub was selling an old red one and had promised her first refusal once he'd put in a new gearbox. 'It's a bit rough on the inside,' she said. 'But there's a little fridge that works and a sink with taps, and a cooker. I could paint it and re-cover the cushions. It would be like a gypsy caravan.'

She kept talking about getting driving lessons, and taking an experimental trip to France to get used to driving on the other side of the road.

Martin didn't say anything. Ten years ago it would have seemed like a wonderful adventure. But now it just made him feel sad. Had she even written to Rachel and Greg? He didn't think so. They probably weren't even there any more. Anyway there was no point arguing. He doubted she'd get around to booking the driving lessons, let alone passing the test. And even if she did, she'd be banned within a week for drink-driving.

But there was a part of him that wondered if his mother might be right. Perhaps a voyage to Planet Matala would galvanize her into recovering her old self. If she was away from the pub and the Neanderthals, if she gave up boozing and started meditating again, maybe she'd emerge from the good-humoured fog she'd been in for the last seven years.

So he watched, silently willing her on, as the camper van appeared in the street outside the house and the Yellow Pages were unearthed and opened at 'D'. And helped her sort through all the paint pots in the garage for appropriate Mediterranean hues, and pull the velour Age Concern curtain off the treadle sewing machine and lug it downstairs for her fucking cushion covers.

And soon, despite himself, he got caught up in her fantasy. And began thinking again of Karl's small green tent under the pine trees; and Big Jan's cunning wooden compartments and sharp chisels. So that when she finally embarked on her course of driving lessons, he'd signed up for building classes at the Poly and had used his saved allowance from his father to buy a set of carpentry tools.

Their eyes would meet sometimes – him poring over a geometry textbook, her pulling the gathers in a pair of camper-van curtains – and they'd find themselves grinning stupidly at each other.

And that's the way it continued, more or less according to plan, until his mother failed her driving test.

Martin was sitting at the kitchen table reading the *Guardian* when she came in and slumped in the chair opposite.

'I didn't deserve to pass,' she said. 'My three-point turn was a five-pointer and I stalled twice on the hill start. Then I got half the Highway Code questions wrong.'

'When can you take it again?'

'They can't fit me in again until July. But by then it will be too hot to drive through Europe.'

Martin didn't say, 'Why didn't you book it earlier?' but he wanted to. She'd been putting off the test for months. He didn't say, 'Why didn't you practise more?' but he thought it. Her current Cro-Magnon, Pete, had offered to take her out in his Fiesta every evening last week, but she'd kept making excuses.

What he did say is: 'Why don't we fly to Crete for a few weeks anyway to check it out? Then we could drive back in September when you've passed your test and it's cooler. Or early next year.'

'Oh, I don't know,' she said in a dull voice. 'Maybe I'm just not cut out to be a driver.'

Martin wanted to slap her. Instead he got up and put on the kettle. 'Factory or Grasshopper?' he asked, trying to keep his voice level.

'Factory, please. And three packets of chocolate digestives.' He looked at her; she was smiling at him. 'Fucking examiner. Called me "Miss Stevens" and wouldn't laugh at any of my jokes.'

'It's not the Comedy Store, Mum.' Now he was exasperated. 'He's not there to test your one-liners.'

'Still, it wouldn't have hurt him to crack a smile or two.'

She'd put on her Smart Shirt Dress for the test, and put her hair up, but an escaped black tendril was hanging down on one side. A wave of tenderness engulfed him and swept away his irritation. She'd been trying so hard recently. He shouldn't be so critical.

'Was it truly awful?' he asked.

'Incontrovertibly dire and humiliating,' she said. 'He made me feel like a naughty schoolgirl. But it's my own fault. I should have practised more. I'll have to call Pete to confess. Then I'll phone and rebook the bloody test.'

While she was on the phone, Martin went up to his room and lay down on his bed. He was more disappointed than he'd expected about the postponement of their trip to Crete.

His mother's idea of using the journey as a chance to reassess her life had struck a chord for him too. He didn't want to spend his life on the dole, but he didn't want a 'career' either. He hated the thought of doing just one thing. It seemed criminal to develop one power and allow the others to atrophy. A vague plan had been forming in his mind: to learn a trade to pay his way while he continued his self-directed reading. On Planet Matala it made sense for a philosopher to work as a builder too.

He tuned his ears to downstairs and heard his mother go out. To meet Cro-Magnon Pete, probably, for a bit of liquid commiseration. So she'd be dragging back tonight and he'd have to make himself scarce.

Martin sighed. It was too wet to go riding and he didn't feel like dancing. Reaching under his pillow, he took out a little screw of silver foil. Perhaps some dope would put him in the mood.

He preferred eating it to smoking it; the effects seemed more organic, less superimposed. He liked tracing the slow way his senses unfurled as the drug percolated into his bloodstream. He'd been reading about shamanism and recording his dreams; exploring the conviction he'd had for as long as he could remember, that at some preconscious level he was a horse. He'd been wondering if it was possible for a person to turn into a spirit creature. He'd been thinking that not believing a thing didn't mean it wasn't true.

The dope took ages to hit, and he fell asleep waiting. When he woke up it was dark and he was in the middle of a dream in which his hands and feet had turned into hooves. He sat up and peered at the clock. It was past two and the house was silent; no grunts or murmurs from across the landing.

His feet echoed on the bare boards as he clip-clopped downstairs; he could hear his hair swishing past his ears and his hands didn't seem to work properly. The dope must have been stronger than he'd thought. A sound reached him from the sitting room, a sobbing sound, and he shouldered open the door.

His mother was kneeling on the hearthrug in the dark, with two empty wine bottles overturned beside her. There was a broken glass in the fireplace, and wads of bloodstained toilet paper scattered around.

His first thought was that she'd cut her wrists, and he bent his knees and lowered himself to see. His head felt long and heavy. His hair was falling over his eyes.

'I cut my foot,' she was saying. 'There's blood on my skirt and it won't come out.'

'Go to bed, Mum,' he said. His voice sounded funny, like in a slowed-down film.

'I'm forty-three,' she said and started crying again.

Her face looked smaller than it should, then loomed larger suddenly, red and wet. She'd started saying something else, but the words were coming out in the wrong order so he couldn't make sense of them. And now she seemed angry with him. Her hands, with little finger feathers, were flapping in front of his face and her red mouth was moving, spitting syllables out. He could feel them on his face, hear all the spitty bits, but they wouldn't stick together to make words. Now he was closer, he could smell her breath: so much pain in it. He could see the tears on her cheeks shining, and the saliva on her teeth. Beautiful, the way the light was glinting on it. Like she had a mouth full of diamonds. Or glass; shards of glass she was spitting out at him.

She wanted him to say something, but his tongue seemed to have swollen and was pressing against the insides of his teeth. When he tried to swallow, he could feel it sliding backwards to the top of his throat, then forwards again; like a slimy belt of brown seaweed being sucked in and out by the waves.

His arms felt awkward, stiff as grasshoppers' knees. It felt unnatural to be on just two legs, flailing his front hooves like dead stones. He wanted to drop forwards and put them on the ground and stand solid: four-square, with his belly under him, away from her splintery voice and flappy fingers.

Didn't she realize how dangerous he was? How his hooves would cut crescents in her flesh if he kicked her? He stared at her through eyeballs that had sunk deep into their sockets. He could see his nose stretching out in front of him, and the flare of his nostrils. He could see his nostrils clearly, opening and closing as her word-splinters hit them.

His teeth were grinding together; his ears were flat to his head. Why was she shouting at him? The words were stinging his cheeks. They were stabbing into his eyes, making his ears bleed. They made him want to rear up and tower over her, and come down on her with his stone fists, and make her just – shut – the – fuck – up.

A second later, a minute, an hour later, she was standing up and backing away from him and crashing out of the room. He could hear her sobbing as she stumbled up the stairs and into the bathroom.

Something had happened but he didn't know what it was. And he was too stoned to find out.

He clip-clopped carefully into the kitchen and put some bread in the toaster. He opened the door and looked out. It was still raining and shards of glass were shattering into puddle mirrors. When he stepped outside they needled into his shoulders and the top of his head. The night garden smelt of moss and snails.

He came back inside and ate four slices of toast and peanut butter, very slowly, and drank a mug of Factory with two sugars. After a while his hands started behaving normally and he could feel his toes at the end of his long feet. Blotting up crumbs with his finger, he tried to focus on what had just happened in the sitting room.

She'd been crying and begging him to stop looking at her; then she'd started shouting, flailing at his face. He remembered being scared she'd blind him. Then what? He had an image of her head jerking sideways and her hair slewing round in slow motion. Christ, he must have punched the side of her head.

A moment later he was sprinting up the stairs three at a time and flinging open her bedroom door. She was lying on her back on the bed in just her bra, with blood caked in one nostril and a wad of toilet paper in her hand. The Smart Shirt Dress was in a heap on the floor and there was a long smear of blood on the duvet from the cut in her foot.

Was she dead? Panic sank him to his knees, but when he brought his face close, her breath stank of cheap wine. Just a nosebleed then, he thought with relief. He tried to wake her, to apologize, but she was out cold. Her hair was a tangled mat on the pillow and her mouth was slightly open.

He hadn't seen her naked since they were in Matala and the sight was both familiar and shocking. He'd forgotten how long her pubic hair was: trailing like seaweed tendrils. There was a mole beneath her left breast. 'My witch's nipple', she used to call it.

The streetlight shining through her reed blinds striped her skin with black and orange. She was a camouflaged creature, a human tiger, and he was the Ethiopian in Kipling's story: black and invisible in the shadow of the neem tree. There was another smear of blood on her calf and silver toe rings on her long bare feet. Why was she wearing them under her clothes?

Then he understood, and an aching love bloomed in his belly and filled his chest. She'd put them on to remind her of Matala and bring her good luck for the driving test.

It occurred to him that he should roll her over in case she vomited and choked in her sleep. And maybe try to clean up some of the blood.

He fetched a damp flannel from the bathroom and wiped the blood from her face and leg, then examined the wound on her foot and put a plaster on it.

Rolling her on to her side, he unhooked her bra. Her arm was lifeless and a smoke of alcohol rose from her skin as he eased the arm through the loose strap and let her breasts fall out in a soft jumble. He tried to tug the rest of the bra out from under her other arm but it wouldn't come, so he rolled her on to her back again.

Her legs had lolled apart and she looked splayed now, like a photo in *Penthouse*. Or dead, as though she'd jumped from a high-rise and landed on her back. She looked like the cover of a crime thriller.

Picking up a heavy foot, he put her legs together. He thought: *My fingerprints are all over her.* He thought: *If I were an Ethiopian, and my black skin was still wet, she'd be covered with leopard markings.* He thought: *She's like a swift that has fallen from the sky and can't get airborne again.*

The silver toe rings reminded him of the rings ornithologists clipped on to a bird they'd captured to track its migration. The image troubled him, so he pulled them off and put them in his pocket. He thought: *I wish I could make her happy.*

Hauling her into a sitting position, he tried to get her under the duvet. Her head lolled on his shoulder and her arms hung like pendulum weights either side of his body. He could smell the fox scent of her armpits and the hay scent of her hair. He could feel her breasts pressing against his chest. He could smell the horse smell between her legs. He thought: *She is the only woman I want.* He thought: *She is my Best Beloved.*

He looked at her face all the time he was pushing into her. Her eyelids didn't flicker and her breathing stayed steady. There were grey smudges under her eyes. She looked peaceful and unconcerned. She was tight and dry, and he had to edge in slowly with little wriggling thrusts. His pushing moved her whole body up and down on the bed and rocked her head slightly on the pillow.

It was like stealing Emily Jackson's mirror in the middle of the night. It was like watching pipistrelles dive for gnats in the summer garden. It was like pissing outside a lair to mark his territory. It was like racing the black mare through the grounds at Blenheim Palace. It was the most natural and most terrible thing he had ever done.

And as the way eased open and he kicked into a canter, he thought of all the ugly girls and all the pretty girls he'd had sex with; of all the kind girls and the vain ones; all the clever and sad women he'd ever known; of Careful Claire and Social Sue and the others. And as the canter spurred to a gallop, he thought that inside they really were all the same.

Chapter 26

Three weeks later, as Sylvia is setting out her tinting bottles on the kitchen table, Martin appears at the door. He hovers on the threshold like a feral cat: drawn by the smell of the chicken, but with a paw raised ready for flight.

She's shocked by how he looks: gaunt and wild-eyed; very bald; very brown. Like a vagrant; like one of the Albanians she's seen on the backs of lorries being ferried from one building site to another; sleeping rough, in dormitories, in tents, wherever the work is.

'Hello,' he says.

'Hello.' She starts towards him, but he puts his hands up to ward her off.

'What about this sideboard then?' His voice sounds rusty from disuse.

'How are you?' His ribs are showing through his tee shirt. He smells like sour milk.

'Can you pay me in advance?' he asks abruptly, then tries to soften it with a stiff smile.

'Of course.' *It's OK*, she wants to say. *You're safe with me*. She aims for normality instead. 'Are you hungry? I was just going to make a sandwich.'

'I'm fine. Is it OK if I start now?' He's edgy. She can see he doesn't want to sit down.

'Yes. I'm not working in there today.'

She follows him through into the darkroom, where he takes down the screens and pushes open the shutters to let the sun in.

'You put the photos back up,' he says. He seems stunned, backing away from the row of faces on the wall.

'Yes. I've got rather fond of them. And Bennet smashed up the cupboard they were in, so—' She shrugs.

'You said they were spooky.'

'I think they are, a bit. But I'm used to them now. And I've been photographing some of them as grown-ups, so I like seeing how they were as children. Before they settled into the people they were going to be.' She's talking fast, trying to fill up the air between them.

He picks up a splintered piece of cupboard door.

'He used the axe,' she explains.

'You said.'

'What do you think?'

'I think he lacks respect.' He runs his fingers over a bit of broken carving, the jagged edge of a bird's wing.

'Most of the drawers are OK. It's just the top, and that side panel. And the cupboard doors.'

'He's hacked right through the carvings.' His voice is shocked. 'How could someone do something like that?'

'He thought they were ugly.'

'So is a rhinoceros,' he says. 'So is a vulture. But they don't deserve to be destroyed.'

'Can you fix it?'

'I thought you wanted to get rid of it too.' He meets her eyes.

'Yes, well. It's grown on me.'

He sighs then, and his body seems to relax slightly. 'I can try glueing the bits of carving together, and fixing ply to the back,' he says in something approaching his normal voice. 'But there'll be gaps. Some of it's just splinters. The best thing would be to start again. Try to match it.'

'Carve new doors you mean?'

'There's probably enough of both doors to see what the original design was.'

'It seems like an awful lot of trouble.'

'The top's completely fucked too, but it's an easier job to replace that. The main problem will be getting the wood.'

300

'How much will it cost?'

'If I can find some old wood the right size it would be cheaper, but if I have to get new oak it'll cost a fortune. I'd probably have to send off to Athens or something for it. And get some more tools. Oak's a bugger to carve.'

'I'll make Bennet pay for it,' she says grimly. 'Serve him right.'

'If he's paying I'm not doing it,' he snaps. 'I work for you, not him.'

'I don't think I can afford it.'

'I'll try to find some old wood, then we'll talk about it.'

'But it'll take ages, won't it? If you're going to carve new doors.'

'Are you in a hurry?' His face takes on that wary feral look again.

'I was thinking about you.'

'Maybe I want to do it.'

'OK,' she says, and his body relaxes again.

She makes him a sandwich anyway, cramming ham, cheese and tomato between doorsteps of fresh bread. He bites into it and seems to swallow without chewing.

'When did you last eat?' She puts a bottle of water on the table and watches him upend it into his mouth. His neck's thin, the tendons like blades.

'I'm not sure,' he says with his mouth full. 'Ten, twelve days ago? When I last saw you.'

'Have you been fasting?' There's something about his appearance – the shaved head, the wild expression – that makes her worry he's in the middle of some kind of breakdown.

'I wanted to concentrate.'

'Did you finish your box?' She sits down opposite him and takes a bite of her own sandwich, then pinches a corner off for the hungry ghosts.

'Yes. That's what I've been doing.'

'All this time?'

'I wanted to start with a complete tree trunk then find the box inside it. There were loads of olives felled after that snow last winter, but it took a while finding something thick enough.'

'Can I see it?'

He rams the last of his sandwich into his mouth and goes to the camper van.

The box is the size and shape of a shoebox: honey-coloured and covered with the dense swirls typical of slow-growing olive wood. When he puts it into her hands, it's warm to the touch, as though it's been basking in the sun. There's a tiny brass lock and a key, which she turns. 'It's beautiful,' she says, lifting the lid and inhaling the sweet oily scent of the interior.

'You can make a bad box or a good box, and they will both hold your things,' he says. 'But only the good box will make you smile when you open it.'

'What are you going to keep in it?'

'I haven't decided yet.'

He eats two more sandwiches and drinks a litre of Mythos, while she works on at the kitchen table with her tints. She doesn't look at him. She doesn't ask any more questions. She just refills his plate every time he empties it, as though he's a wild animal she's taming.

'I lied to you,' he says eventually. 'I have decided what the box is for.'

'You don't have to tell me.'

'I want to. There are some things from when I was a boy. Things that remind me of how I used to be. With my mother. My father. I've been carrying them around pretty much all my life.' He pauses and she looks up. He's edgy again, fidgeting with the crumbs on his plate. 'Like a caddis fly larva, you know? Those creatures that make cases for themselves out of bits of pebble and shell they find at the bottom of the stream.' She nods.

'I'll show you if you like,' he says after a pause. 'They're in an old tin I found in a skip when I was little.'

She nods again, and he hurries out. In a moment he's back with a big tartan tin pockmarked with rust. There are two

Highland terriers on the lid, one black and one white, and a border of red ribbon.

'"Crawford's Shortbread Selection",' she reads. 'My gran used to keep her Christmas cake in a tin just like this.'

'I really liked the dogs,' he says. 'I used to keep it buried in a den I had, in the woods. But it's falling to bits now.'

'Are you going to open it?'

'I've never shown it to anyone before. Not even Mum.' He prises the lid off. 'They're silly things really,' he says, holding the tin on his lap and hunching over so she can't see.

'You don't think so,' she says.

'No.' He leans back and she peers in. Inside is a collection of perhaps ten, twelve, grubby oddments, crumbed with bits of rust. 'Each one's a chapter of my life,' he says, stirring through them and picking out an old-fashioned navy-blue passport. 'This is my mother,' he says, handing it to her.

She opens it. 'Theresa Elizabeth,' she reads. 'She looks so young. A real Sixties' Chick.' The face staring back at her is very pretty, almost beautiful, with long wavy dark hair and eyes ringed with kohl.

'That was taken just after I was born,' he says. 'It's got my details in the back. And these are my first proper shoes.'

She picks them up and examines them. She can see the marks of his toes inside, a curved row of brownish dents. A little boy: she can see him suddenly. There are creases across the front, and scuffed toes, where he must have been kneeling, or crawling on the floor. And one of the laces is frayed at the end. She can imagine his two-year-old fingers fumbling with the laces; can almost hear him sighing his frustration as bigger hands tie them for him.

'She never talked about my father,' he's saying. 'For years it was just me and her, her and me, in the same breath. Together all the time. As if he never existed.'

Sylvia puts down the shoes and picks up an ugly brown mug, the kind that used to be sold in Habitat in the seventies.

'That was her favourite mug. She called it the Peasant Cup, because it was sort of rough and peasanty. When she was depressed, I'd make tea in it for her and put it where she could see it. She couldn't always look at me when she was like that, so it worked as a kind of transitional object. A comforter.'

'Aren't you angry with her? For keeping you locked away?'

'Of course not.' He seems surprised. 'She had to, or they'd have sectioned her and put me with him.'

'Would that have been so bad? Being brought up by your father?' Sylvia keeps thinking of the row of toe marks in the little blue shoes; of the two-year-old boy they belonged to.

'When I was little I had all these vague memories of him, from before they split up. I had this idea that there was a big empty house somewhere, with him in it. And a fish tank. I found out later that he was a kind of small-scale property developer. You know, chuck out the swirly carpets, slap on the woodchip, sell for a profit. He must have taken me to some of the houses. He used to keep tropical fish, so they were in my memory too.'

'Did you ever meet him again?'

'When there was all that Wild Boy palaver in the papers, he contacted social services. But by then he'd married someone else and had a new family. He used to visit me in the children's home and take me out.' He ferrets in the tin and hands her a rust-stained matchbook. 'We always went to this place. A big noisy restaurant in Oxford. And we always had the same thing. Steak and Guinness pie twice. Chocolate milkshake for me, bottle of house red for him.' He takes back the matchbook and drops it into the tin. 'That was when Mum was in the Littlemore – the loony bin in Oxford.'

'Why didn't you go and live with him?'

'He didn't want me.' He shrugs. 'Anyway, he wasn't really my type.'

'He might have been if your mum hadn't hidden you away.' Sylvia's getting heated; she can't help it. She keeps thinking of the boy she read about in the papers; the mad mother; the filthy house and dead animals. 'You'd have been a different "type" if she'd let you stay with him instead of her.'

'He's rich now,' he says. 'Two cars, gravel drive, horses, the lot.'

'Maybe your mother just wanted you to herself.'

'No, it wasn't like that,' he says patiently, as if she couldn't possibly understand.

'How do you know?' she persists. She wants to shake him.

'Because she wasn't like that.'

'Oh? And what was she like?'

'Wonderful. Funny, clever, beautiful.' He reaches for the passport and opens it again. 'You can't really see it from that photo. She had velvety-dark eyes and a mane of long black hair she'd tie up all anyhow. But it always looked great. Kind of ringlety. Gypsyish. All the guys in Matala fell for her. But it wasn't just the way she looked, it was the way she thought about things. She never took anything for granted. She was always saying "how do you know?" and "let's find out".'

He drops the passport back in the tin. 'We stayed up all night once, so we could watch the bats going back to roost. That's why she didn't want me with my dad,' he says, looking at Sylvia. 'She wanted me to have those kinds of experiences and she knew he couldn't give them to me. She didn't want me turning out ordinary and boring.'

'So what was she doing with him if he was so boring?' Sylvia's surprised by how angry she feels.

He shrugs. 'I never asked. She was young and she got pregnant. He was safe. It was the thing to do, I suppose.'

'I don't think she was wonderful at all,' she says. 'I think she was a sick and selfish woman.'

'You're wrong. You didn't know her. She wanted the best for me.'

'And locking you up with a mentally ill woman was best for you, was it?'

'She wasn't depressed all the time.'

'A child shouldn't have to look after his mother.'

'Why not? In the Third World kids of five, six, are out earning a living. Cooking, minding their brothers and sisters.'

'This isn't the Third World.'

'So?' Now he's getting heated too. 'Kids are like monkeys. They're far brighter and tougher than people realize. They grow up early, then keep on developing. Our society disables them. Prevents them from taking responsibility.'

'I keep thinking of you making tea for her in that mug. And her not looking at you.'

'I was used to it. It wasn't a big deal.'

'You shouldn't have had to get used to it, Martin. If she'd thought about you for a second—'

He rounds on her. 'She gave me years of her life. Years. Not some mean little allotment of hours squashed between nannies and playschool. I've seen what most middle-class mothers are like. Going on about how unhealthy TV is, then switching it on the minute they come in because they can't stand being with their kids.'

'Maybe she gave you too much.'

'What do you mean by that?' he snaps back, and she knows she's said too much.

'It just sounds rather intense, that's all,' she says, backing off.

'We were fine,' he says doggedly. 'We looked after each other.'

She dips into the tin. 'There's a key in here,' she says after a while. 'Did you know?'

'That's the key to the front door of the house I told you about. The one we were hiding in. The place was so damp the door swelled and wouldn't open any more. I should have kept the back-door key really, because that was the door we used. But this one was like the key to the whole front-door world of cars and schools and hospitals. I suppose I didn't want it to disappear.'

'What about this?' A palm-sized piece of rock.

'The Yellowy-Grey Stone.' He laughs. 'She was always on at me to release it back into the wild. You see? That's what I mean about her.'

'And what are these? Toe rings?'

'She wore them in Matala,' he says shortly, taking the tin away from her and putting the lid back on.

'The chapters seem to stop when she died,' Sylvia says quietly, as he cradles the rusty tin in his lap again. Then, getting up to clear the plates: 'Look, I've got to go to the taverna now. You can stay here if you like. Or come with me and show yourself to Aphrodite. She'll have spotted the van, so there's no escape.'

'I don't want to see Aphrodite.' That wary look again. 'I don't want to see anyone.' *Except you*, say his strange-coloured eyes.

'OK,' she says. 'But what shall I tell her? How shall I explain the shaved head? Someone's bound to have seen you.'

'Tell her I was trying to stay cool. Tell her it's none of her fucking business.'

'You scared me, you know,' she says quietly.

'I know. Sorry. It was a place I had to go. You weren't supposed to see.'

'Will you be here when I get back?'

'I don't think so.'

'But you won't disappear again.'

'No.'

Sylvia tells Aphrodite that Martin's been off work with some kind of fever; that's why he shaved his head. All evening, while she's serving people at the taverna, she keeps glancing up the hill, to the red camper van parked beside her gate. It starts off red, then darkens as the sun sets, until all she can see is a black outline against the sky.

She doesn't see him drive away, but at some point between ten and eleven, the black shape disappears.

Something relaxes in her belly when she sees the stars there, where the dark shape had been; something that has been holding itself tense all evening, thinking he might stay.

*

He comes back the next evening with some long dark planks on the trailer.

'They're not wide enough, so I'll have to glue them,' he says. 'But they're the best I could find. Once they're finished you won't notice the joins.' He smells different; fresher.

'Do you mind working outside?' she asks. 'Only I need the screens shut tomorrow and—'

'And the mess. And the dust,' he smiles. 'Your equipment. I know.'

'I'm not as bad as I used to be.'

'I remember. "There are over a hundred different kinds of bacteria in human excrement,"' he mimics.

'Well there are,' she says, spooning coffee and sugar into the little jug and motioning him to sit down.

'You know it's the clothes that stink, not the person, if you don't wash. After a while the skin's bacteria stabilize and keep the surface clean. The dirt just drops off when the surface cells are shed.'

'What about hair?'

'It goes sort of lank and silky. But if Elaine Morgan's right we'd have spent most of our time in and out of water anyway when we were evolving. It's soap that's the problem, not water per se. People are always trying to get rid of the smells of their own bodies.'

'But you wash.'

'Yes, but not because I'm ashamed of the way I smell. Sweat only stinks if you're unhealthy or scared, when it's full of toxins.'

'"The skin is the largest organ in the human body. Its functions include excretion, protection, perception and thermo-regulation."'

'Sorry. I keep forgetting you know all this stuff.'

'That doesn't mean I approve of BO.'

'That day we were unloading the stuff for the platform. When it was raining and your clothes were soaked. God, the smell coming off you! I wanted to bury my face in your armpit.'

'Did you?' She stirs the coffee, watching tiny bubbles start to form on the surface.

'It was the most erotic thing I've ever smelt.'

'I couldn't wait to get in the shower.' She feels hot. She can feel his eyes on her. She pours the coffee and hands him his cup.

'I can smell when you're ovulating, too,' he says.

'You're joking.'

'I don't know why you're so surprised. If the human nose can identify the year a wine was bottled, it ought to be able to detect when a woman needs a shag. There's so much we could be aware of if we only open our minds.'

'What does it smell like?'

'Salty. Slightly fishy.'

'Oh.' She pours iced water into two tall glasses and brings them to the table. 'It sounds horrible.'

'It makes me want to touch you,' he says, looking at her.

She sits down and sips her coffee. It burns her tongue. 'I'm not ovulating now,' she says.

'I know. I still want to touch you.'

He reaches out his hand and runs his fingers along her forearm. She feels a shudder in her belly; a sting between her legs.

'You could stay,' she says. Her arm feels hot, then cold, where he's touching it. 'Tonight, I mean.'

'I can't.' He pulls his hand away abruptly.

'But you want to.'

'Oh yes,' he gets up suddenly, scraping the chair over the tiles. 'The horse in me wants to. The dog. This things wants to.' He grabs the bulge in his jeans and seems to twist it viciously.

'Stop it!' she cries. 'You'll injure yourself.'

'I have to,' he says through gritted teeth. 'I mustn't—'

'We don't have to do anything. You could sleep in the other bed.'

'I might hurt you.'

'You won't.'

'You don't know me.' There are tears in his voice.

'I know enough to know you won't hurt me.'

She hears the camper van start up and drive away. He's drunk some of the water, but hasn't touched the coffee. Sylvia gets up and pours it all down the sink. Her heart's thudding; her lungs feel as though they can't fill with air, as though her heart's swollen in her chest. When he touched her, it was like switching on Christmas tree lights. There's just a muddle of dead wires and empty glass, then an explosion of light.

She cooks chicken with pasta, then puts it in the fridge without eating it. She drinks two glasses of Costas's barrel wine and stares out into the night.

He loves me, she thinks. *He wants me. But there's something stopping him. Something more than his celibacy. Something that frightens him.*

She thinks about his den in the woods, the rusty tin hidden there. She thinks of his hand grabbing his crotch, as though he wanted to rip his penis off. She thinks of his white legs, his tight buttocks inside his jeans. She thinks: *Could he smell my desire?*

'Sylvia.'

She wakes up and he's there. She can see him through the mosquito net: a blurred figure in jeans and a white tee shirt, squatting down beside the bed.

'What time is it?' She sits up; pulls the sheet up to her neck.

'Late. Early. I don't know.' He seems nervous, distracted.

'Do you want to lie down?' She pulls the net aside and reaches out.

'Don't touch me.' He backs away, and she lets the net fall. 'I haven't come to make love to you.'

'Why are you here then?'

'I have to talk to you.'

'Couldn't it wait until the morning?'

'No. That's what I kept asking myself. But if I don't tell you now I don't know if I ever will.'

'Tell me what?'

'About my mother. About how she died.'

'You told me.'

'I didn't tell you everything. I didn't tell you the bad part. I mean, it was all bad. It was awful. Disgusting. Humiliating. A degrading way to die. But I didn't tell you the really bad part.'

'You're scaring me.' His voice seems slightly out of focus, muffled by the folds of the net.

'You have to know. If we're going to touch each other.'

'Are we going to touch each other?'

'I'm tired of fumbling in the dark, Sylvia. I'm tired of false pretences.'

'Let's sit outside,' she says, pulling on her nightdress. As she slips out from under the net, he comes into focus.

'OK. Good,' he says, relieved. 'Away from the bed.'

'Yes.'

Sylvia makes peppermint tea for them both and they sit either side of the patio table looking down at the lights of the village.

'I love sitting here,' she says. 'Sometimes I get rooted here for hours when I should be in bed. Just looking out at the night. Listening to the rustles, the owls, the tree frogs, the cats off hunting somewhere.'

'There was one night she got drunk,' he says, not looking at her. 'She'd failed her driving test because she hadn't been practising and she was crying. I was pissed off with her because it was so bloody typical of the way she was at that time: fucking about with these no-hopers, not sticking at anything.

'Anyway, I went off to my room and got stoned and the next thing I knew I was back in the sitting room and we were fighting. I mean really fighting, hitting each other.' He stares at his hands as though they belonged to someone else. 'I can't remember why. The dope was really strong and I suppose I must have lost it.'

'You killed her,' she whispers. Her throat seems to have closed up.

'No. Worse than that.'

'What could be worse than that?' The air seems too thin. It won't fill her lungs.

'I fucked her.' He says it quietly, deliberately, like a heavy weight sinking steadily to the bottom of a deep pool. 'Not right then. Later. I had something to eat and tried to clear my head, then I started worrying I might have hurt her. She was in her bedroom passed out with blood all over her face. But she was fine. I undressed her, checked her breathing, washed the blood away. Then I fucked her.'

'You didn't mean to.' She doesn't want it to be true. 'You were stoned.'

'I did mean to,' he insists. 'I made sure she was unconscious, then I just did it.'

'Why?'

'I don't know.' He's shaking his head. 'I was eighteen. I was full of testosterone. I was angry. And she had this awful boyfriend.' His hands close into fists. 'And she was so fucking *beautiful*.'

'You raped her.'

'I loved her. I was *in* love with her. I was jealous. I didn't know what else to do with her.'

'You could have left her alone,' Sylvia says coldly. Her heart seems to be beating in slow motion.

'Yes.'

'Then what?' She can hear a mosquito humming in her ear. Her ear feels a long way away from her head.

'I cleaned her up and went to bed.'

'As if nothing had happened.'

'Except she found out.'

'How?'

'I don't know. A trickle down her leg when she got up. The smell of semen. I could tell by the way she looked at me the next morning. Really shocked and hurt.'

'She was drunk.' Again, she doesn't want it to be true. She

wants to find chinks in his version of events. Some redeeming fact. Anything to reduce the enormity of it. 'She could have thought it was her boyfriend. Or someone else. An intruder.'

'She knew it was me.'

'Wasn't she angry?'

'I don't know. I went out. I couldn't face her. Then when I got back she was drinking again. Just sitting in the kitchen with the bottles lined up on the table. Deliberately, meaning to get drunk.'

'Didn't she say anything?'

'She said "sorry",' he says, his voice thick with tears. 'She kept saying it, over and over: "Sorry, sorry, sorry, sorry".'

He weeps for a long time, sitting straight up in the chair in the darkness, not bothering to wipe his eyes.

'Three days later she was dead.'

'So you did kill her,' she says.

'Yes.'

'I've lost you, haven't I?' he says later, when he's dried his eyes and blown his nose and she's fetched a jumper to wrap around her shoulders.

'You never had me.'

'But you wanted me,' he says. 'You wanted to see what it would be like. You wanted to try.'

'I suppose so. Yes, maybe.' She can't look at him.

'But not any more.'

'What you did – I can't even begin—'

'No.'

'I don't know how to think about it.'

They sit in silence with the table between them.

'Can you leave now, please?' she says.

She can't remember going to bed. She just remembers lying awake staring at the square of lemon tree, at the stars slowly moving through the leaves. And thinking of the boy, Martin,

unzipping his jeans. The lolling weight of the woman's unconscious limbs; his secret push in and his rush of release. And the
woman, Theresa, waking up and stumbling to the toilet. The hot
trickle; her fingers investigating, expecting blood. Her shrug of
puzzlement, then the slow creep of understanding.

As soon as she's dressed the next morning, she phones Bennet.
She wants to hear his big voice. She wants to hear Newcastle in
the background: the washing machine churning; the hum of the
Great North Road; the murmur of Radio Four. She wants to be
transported to his world for a while.

'I miss you,' she says.

'Good.'

'I can't come home yet.'

'I've bought a new Black and Decker.'

'Do you love your mother?'

'Does Mark Thatcher love Maggie?'

'Seriously.'

'I suppose so, in a bemused kind of way. I mean she's so
unreconstructed. All her golf cronies and charity dos. And those
weird hats she goes in for.'

'What about when you were little?'

'The same really. She was always a bit remote and jolly. Not
the huggy type.'

'So you never fancied her.'

He snorts down the phone. 'You are joking, I hope. Though I
did go through a phase of wearing her underwear.'

'*What?*'

'I thought you'd like that.'

'You used to wear your mum's knickers?'

'Only the soiled ones. I used to fish them out of the washing
basket when she was out and wank in them.'

'Jesus, Bennet.' She laughs; it comes out like a gasp.

'She had a surprisingly raunchy taste in undies for a woman
of her political persuasion. God knows what I looked like in

them,' he chuckles. 'Great hairy thighs, testicles oozing out the sides.'

'How old were you?' She feels slightly giddy; tilted unexpectedly back into Martin's transgressive world.

'Fifteen, sixteen. Maybe older. I'm getting hard now just thinking about it.'

'You're disgusting,' she says, but she's smiling.

'That's testosterone for you.'

'Are all teenage boys perverts?' She finds the idea almost reassuring.

'My dear girl, I could tell you tales that would make your toenails curl.'

'What's the Black and Decker for?'

'Your new darkroom.'

'Oh.'

'I love you, Sylvie.'

'I'm still angry about Val.'

'Of course you are.'

She isn't, though. All that seems very petty suddenly. Her spectrum of what's forgivable, what's moral or immoral, has expanded way beyond his infidelity.

'Bye, Bennet,' she says.

Talking to Bennet is like tuning into a different radio channel. Something playing loud classical music, clever-Dick quiz shows, belligerent interviews with politicians. As soon as she clicks off the phone she's back in her little whitewashed kitchen with its yellow cupboard and terracotta tiles. Back on Planet Martin, with its shocking blurred boundaries, its disturbing philosophy, its exhilarating beauty.

The two mugs are upside down on the drainer. There's a cricket hiding under the drying-up cloth and a gecko prowling the ceiling for flies.

She keeps thinking of him unzipping his jeans. Did he take them off? Pull them down? The thought makes her feel swollen and itchy between her legs; wet. The wetness makes her angry. His zip being pulled down, the inert legs rolled apart: she doesn't want her head full of these images; she doesn't want them attached to her arousal.

It's as though he's handed her a live coal that's burning her hand. She didn't ask for it, but he gave it to her anyway. And now she can't put it down.

When she arrives at the camper van, he's sitting on one of the folding chairs with his hands on his knees. The folding table is open beside him; the second chair on the other side of it.

He looks calm. He looks as though he's waiting for her. He looks as though he's been sitting there all night.

The sight of him sitting calmly like that, when she is in such a turmoil, makes her even angrier.

'What do you want from me?' she says, dumping her crash helmet on the table.

'I just wanted you to listen.'

'I don't want it, Martin,' she says. 'I don't want my head full of what you did.'

'There's more. Something I didn't tell you.'

'I don't want to know!' She puts her hands over her ears and glares at him.

He just looks at her. Patiently. Like a guide dog waiting outside the supermarket. Until she takes her hands off her ears and sits down on the other chair.

'When I was doing it,' he says. 'It didn't feel wrong.'

'It must have.'

'It didn't. It felt natural. It felt like the right thing to do. The only thing to do.'

'To fuck your mother?'

'To make love to the only woman I loved.'

'She was unconscious.'

'I wanted to be part of her.'

'You wanted to get your rocks off.'

'It's the same thing. Loving someone. Desiring her. Wanting to ejaculate into her. We're animals, Sylvia. What else can we do? My DNA, her DNA. Trying to put them together.'

'She was your *mother*.'

'She was my wife.'

'She was your mother, Martin.'

'I felt like she was my wife.'

Sylvia looks at her feet. There's a line of large black ants passing in front of her, carrying what looks like grass seed. They've cleared a path three inches wide from the corner of the house to a hole under a stone near the outside tap.

'Why did she say "sorry"?' she asks after a while.

'I don't know. That's what I keep asking myself,' he says. 'To begin with I thought it was about her bloody driving test. It was this big thing, right? She'd been talking about it for ages. She'd learn to drive, then we'd take the van to Matala together. She'd get off anti-depressants, I'd get some casual work. We'd live happily ever after.'

'But she failed the test.'

'It was hopeless. She was so flaky by then. So I thought she was saying sorry for that. And for getting drunk again. But it didn't really make sense as a reason if she knew what I'd done to her.'

'How can you be sure she knew?' she asks again.

'It was in her eyes. She looked so injured. So ashamed. Of herself. Of me.'

'But you'd hit her.'

'I thought about that. But she'd have said something if it had just been that. Made a joke, or told me off. This was different. It was eating her up.'

She knows he's right. She's thought about it; she can't stop thinking about it.

'Maybe she knew you loved her like that. Like a husband,' she says. 'Maybe she thought it was her fault, for not letting you stay with your dad.'

'I didn't want to stay with him.'

'She could have made you,' she insists. 'If she'd loved you enough.'

'She did love me.'

'You thought she was your *wife*, Martin.'

'Yes.'

'You were obsessed with her. For years she was the only woman you knew.'

'I had girlfriends.' He's weeping again; head hanging, tears dripping on to his knees.

'The ugly girls, you mean? The ones you never committed to?'

'I didn't want to hurt anyone.'

'You didn't want to *love* anyone,' she says.

She can see the two of them together: the woman, still young, still beautiful. Like Rapunzel in the tower, locked away where no one else can see her. And the little boy with blue shoes, locked away with her. Growing taller, stronger. Passionate. Unable to look away.

'I think that's why she said "sorry",' she says slowly, thinking it through again. 'I think she understood why you did it. That "sorry" means she blamed herself. Don't you see? It means she forgave you.'

Sylvia leads him into the camper van and he curls on the bed in the foetus position: shoulders curved inwards, arms bent, knees up.

She locates the matches and makes herself a shot of sweet coffee, then takes it outside and sits watching the sun move across the sky while he sleeps.

It's a beautiful spot he's found, surrounded by grey crags and olive trees. There's some kind of hawk wheeling high in the sky, mewing like a cat. He always chooses such lovely places.

'Sylvia?' he calls.

She gets up and goes over to the open door. 'Yes?'

'You're still here,' he says, and his eyes close again.

Two, three hours later, when she's opening the tiny fridge to look for something to eat, he wakes again.

'Hello,' he says, sitting up.

'Hello.'

'She forgave me.'

'Yes.' She smiles at him. 'I think so.'

'I can't tell you what it feels like, waking up to that thought.'

'I could be wrong.'

'No. It's the only thing that makes sense. She didn't mean to die. She was just drinking until she'd got used to the idea. Then she was going to take the bottles to be recycled and book a new driving test. Pull herself together.'

'How do you know?'

'I just know.'

She looks at him. 'Why aren't I more shocked?'

'You were.'

'It was a bad thing you did.'

'I know.'

'But you were so young. You didn't mean it. You just got carried away.'

'No, you're wrong. Sylvia,' he says seriously. 'I did mean it. Don't make me into this innocent little puppy creature. I knew exactly what I was doing. She was my woman, my territory. And I was mounting her. Putting my scent on her, swamping the semen of my rivals.'

'God,' she says with an intake of breath, 'you really have a way with words sometimes.' She doesn't like these images. She prefers the confused boy, the blue lace-ups, the sleeping beauty.

'I was a male animal, Sylvia. I'm still a male animal.'

'But you loved her too.'

'Yes.'

'That's why she forgave you.'

'Yes.'

'What are you going to do?'

'Take you to Aphrodite's for lunch.'

She laughs. 'Are you serious?'

'I'm starving. Aren't you?'

'You know what she'll think.'

'Well she'll be wrong then, won't she? I'm still celibate and you're still a faithful wife.' He gets out of bed and quickly strips off his clothes. 'I'm going to have a shower. Don't go away, will you?'

He comes back streaming with water with a towel knotted around his waist. He looks like an athlete. He looks like a warrior. He looks like the most beautiful thing she has ever seen.

He tugs her to her feet and kisses her suddenly, a strong shocking kiss, with his tongue right inside her mouth, his dripping arms pinioning her, his chest soaking through her dress. She can feel his penis hardening, pressing through the towel. She can feel the hot blood draining from her head, from her feet.

'I thought you wanted lunch,' she says when he releases her.

'I do,' he says, picking up his jeans.

'So what was all that about?'

'It was about wanting to fuck you.'

'So why don't you?' The itch is back, worming its way between her legs.

'God, if you only knew how much I want to,' he says. 'But it's too soon. There's been too much to take in. I want you to be sure.'

All afternoon they know they're going to make love. At Aphrodite's, eating stuffed zucchini flowers and *kleftiko*, ordering more bread, more tzatziki, more retsina. Clearing the table for her and washing up. Joking with her about his shaved head, about his disappearing acts, flattering and teasing her out of her suspicions.

Then later, up at the house, piecing the damaged sideboard together: a giant jigsaw in the dappled shade of the pergola, with the first of the autumn vine leaves thudding down like yellow petals around them.

He's in shorts, with his tee shirt off. She's in a loose dress with no bra. They're both barefoot, crouching on the concrete, concentrating on the broken bits of carving.

She's trying not to look at him, but she can feel him beside her. She knows he's naked under his shorts. She can smell his sweat as he reaches past her for a new piece of carving. Biscuity, like a horse. She can feel her breasts inside her dress.

They're talking about what they're doing.

'Can you see the other half of this lizard anywhere?'

'Here's the rest of that bunch of grapes.'

By six o'clock they're finished. The top and side panel, and the two carved doors, gaping with jagged wounds, have been reassembled, and there's a pile of unidentifiable shards to one side.

'Are you hungry again yet?' she asks, sitting back on her knees.

'Are you?'

'I don't know.' She wants him to kiss her again. She wants it so much, her mouth is watering.

'Shall we make some food while you think about it?'

'OK.'

'Whether you want to make love, I mean. How you feel about what I did.'

'OK.'

Together they make a Greek salad. He washes purslane and tomatoes under the single cold tap; she peels cucumber and slices onion.

'Have you thought about it yet?' he asks, placing two taut ripe tomatoes on the chopping board for her.

'No,' she says. 'Well, sort of. I can't work out what I think. If you give it labels it seems so terrible.'

'Rape. Incest.'

'Yes. But when I try to imagine how it was. How you were, what she was like afterwards, those labels kind of melt away. And it all goes blurred.' She cuts into one of the tomatoes; the flesh is sweet and pink as watermelon.

'A court would convict me,' he says. 'I was old enough and there was no way she consented.'

'I know. But that's not the point.'

'Isn't it?'

She looks up. 'You said once that it's the act that's important, not what you believe when you're doing it.'

'Yes.'

'But I don't think that's right. I think they both matter. What you do and what you believe.'

'"*And*, not *or*, must be the law."'

'What?'

'A little rhyme a poet once taught me. In our society people like things to be black or white. Either or. Good or bad, dead or alive, Christian or atheist. When usually it's much more complicated than that. And, not or.'

'Lots of greys,' she says, jumbling the vegetables in a big bowl.

'And reds,' he says. 'Greens. Blues.'

'I think it was a bad thing to fuck your mother,' she says. 'I mean, God! The words just hit me between the eyes every time I think about it. But then I think, taken in context, it wasn't such a terrible sin. I mean, compared with systematic torture, child abuse, genocide.'

'Wasn't it?' He sits down suddenly and puts his head in his hands.

'You tell me. It doesn't matter what I think. What do you think?'

He raises his head and looks at her. 'I think her ghost is waiting for me to do something, but I don't know what it is. I think bringing her ashes to Crete was part of it. And making the olive-wood box, for some reason. And telling you, I had to do that. Get it out of here —' banging his chest. 'Let daylight get to it. But there's something else too.'

'You still haven't scattered her ashes,' she reminds him.

'Maybe that's it. But I don't think so.'

'What about supper? Perhaps she wants you to have supper.'

322

He smiles at her and reaches a hand across the table. 'I really love you, you know.'

'Are you still hungry?' she asks, putting her hand in his and squeezing it.

'I don't know,' he says. 'My mouth's confused. It wants to taste you again. Beneath your tongue and in that dip at the base of your throat. And under your breasts, where it's damp.'

'I want to smell your neck,' she says.

They go into the bedroom and take off their clothes. She arranges the net over the bed and lies down inside the gauzy white tent with the sheet over her.

'Why are you hiding?' he says, looking down at her. He's brown to the waist, then pale, as though he's wading in water. He's smiling; he's excited. His penis is erect.

'You're so young,' she says.

'And you're so old, is that it? You think I won't like your body.'

'Something like that.'

'Sylvia, have you any idea how much I desire you? Not bits of you. Breasts, buttocks, skin. You. Sylvia. The mole on your cheek. The lines at the corner of your mouth. Look at me. Look how hard I am. I can't wait to find out what the rest of you is like.'

She lets him pull the sheet back and lie down beside her, then she closes her eyes as he moves his body very slowly against her until they're facing each other, belly to belly, thigh to thigh. Then she's moving her leg over his so she's open, and stroking down his lean back with her hand: over the ridges of muscle there, the knobs of backbone, feeling how hard he is, every part of him, and every part tensed towards her, wanting her.

She can taste his breath against her mouth: ragged breath, cucumber breath. She feels her lips, her cunt, swelling and parting. She feels warm and wet and red, as if all she has to do is open her eyes and look at him and he'll be inside her.

She opens her eyes.

★

She wakes to find him slipping out of bed and reaching for his clothes.

'Where are you going?'

'Moving the van. I can't leave it outside all night.'

'Why not?'

'Think about it. People want to think you're a respectable married woman. They probably suspect something's going on between us, but as long as I don't stay the night they can't be certain. Trust me, it's not worth the hassle.'

'Don't you mind?'

'Of course I mind.' He crouches beside her and grabs hold of her shoulders. 'I want to live with you. I want to give you a baby. I want everyone to know we're together.'

'But I'm a respectable married woman,' she says. She feels drowsy, rumpled. There's a slight ache in her vagina.

'So I'll have to wait.' He pulls on his sandals and vaults over the balustrade.

'Wait for what?'

'For you to decide!' he calls, sprinting out through the door.

He's back early the next morning with bread warm from the bakery in Vamos. They break hunks off and douse it in butter and honey, then go back to bed and lick butter off each other's chin.

'Did you take your temperature when you woke up?' he asks, wrapping his arms around her.

'It's all right,' she says. 'I'm still safe.'

'I don't want you to be safe.'

'I thought you could tell by the smell.'

'I was teasing you.'

'Were you?'

He grins. 'No.'

Later he follows her into the darkroom where she has a roll of film to develop, and stands behind her kissing her neck and pressing against her like a cat as she tries to concentrate with her hands in the developing bag.

'Sorry. I can't stop,' he says. 'I want to eat you alive like one of those wasp larvae. I want to climb right inside your caterpillar skin.'

'How revolting,' she says, pushing him away. 'Now go and stand over there until I've finished this.'

'The children's faces look so strange in this orange light, don't they?' he says, looking at the row of framed portraits. 'As though they're in another room, looking out through a row of little windows.'

'I've been talking to Aphrodite,' she says. 'Trying to find out what used to happen in here.'

'Did she tell you anything?'

'Not in so many words. And I didn't like to ask directly, but I think she might have had an abortion. Or maybe a miscarriage. I couldn't work it out. But she definitely had an affair, and I'm pretty sure she was pregnant. And she said that was why she went to see Kokona.'

'And gave her this photo.' He stands in front of it.

'She said Kokona chose it especially, because it had so much life in it.'

'So you think the old woman was doing abortions.'

'I don't know,' she says hesitating. 'Maybe. But she was delivering babies too. I do know that. People used to call her to their houses when they were in labour. As far as I could tell they really liked her, and whenever I pass there are always fresh flowers on her grave. Then I spoke to an old woman last week who said Kokona had given her a baby.'

'Given? Not "helped with"?'

'No. That's the exact word she used. *Thoro*. Like a gift from heaven.'

'So she was involved in some kind of fertility treatment too. Which means the photos could be all the babies she brought into the world.'

325

'I thought of that. But then why would Aphrodite's photo be there?'

'What about all the toys we found on the sideboard? Do you remember? All the little dolls and cars. And the sweets.'

'The kind of thing you'd put on a child's grave,' she says, looking at him in the orange light.

'Phew. I see what you mean.'

'Then last week I found this row of white stones in the garden.'

'You think she buried them here?'

'Maybe. I don't know. She didn't have the equipment you'd need to suck out a foetus. So all she could have done was get the process started somehow and wait until it happened, maybe days later. And there wouldn't necessarily have been a foetus to bury. An early miscarriage is more like a really heavy period.'

'So the photos are what?'

'Aphrodite said they were a kind of payment, but I don't think she knew really.'

'I knew they were important,' he says, staring at them. 'When you wanted to take them down, it felt like a desecration.'

She goes over to him and puts her arms around him. He feels so lithe and alive; like a lizard, a monkey, pressed against her.

'I'm glad you put them back up again,' he says.

'Yes.'

Sylvia lies back against the pillow and sighs. She feels bloated with sex, reeling with it. Her legs feel heavy and her fingers are sticky, as though she's eaten too many figs.

'I wonder whether Kokona would have been able to help me have a baby,' she muses. 'With all those herbs, or whatever else it was that she did. Incantations. Spells.'

'I think it's more likely to have been ordinary Christian-type prayer,' he says. 'With the incense burner and all those icons.' He's circling her nipple with his finger, watching it pucker.

'I probably destroyed a unique cure for infertility when I burned all those dusty old bunches,' she says.

'You never know. Maybe the prayers were the important thing. Maybe you have to call the spirit of a child to you in some way.'

She laughs. 'You never give up do you?'

'That woman said Kokona gave her a baby.'

'Haven't you ever heard of the placebo effect?'

'That's just science trying to label it out of existence. Most people would call it magic. A miracle. But even if it was a placebo effect, that's still amazing.' He sits up suddenly. 'Think about it. You say a prayer and your mind somehow instructs your body to cure itself. Conceive a baby. Have a miscarriage. Whatever.'

'Do you think that's what happened with those women?'

'Unless you ask someone directly, we'll never know. But Kokona doesn't sound like the bent coat hanger type, does she? So maybe it was all done with prayer and the laying on of hands.'

'Maybe it was all a series of coincidences. There are such things as spontaneous abortions, you know. Something like twenty per cent of pregnancies end in miscarriage.'

'I wish you weren't such a cynic,' he sighs, batting her gently with the back of his hand. 'Your life would be so much richer and more satisfying.'

'I'm quite satisfied enough for the moment,' she says, smiling up at him.

'I don't think it matters what she did. All that matters is that it was done with respect. That she never forgot they were real babies she was dealing with, real lives and deaths.'

'What do you mean?'

'Len Williams says the defining characteristic of human beings is that we bury our dead with ceremony. No other creature does that.'

'And who is Len Williams when he's at home?' she asks lazily.

'Father of the more famous John. Williams. The guitarist.'

'Don't tell me. You found one of his books on a skip.'

'In an attic actually. The lodger of one of my clients left it behind. Anyway this Williams guy founded the Spanish Guitar

Centre in London, then gave it all up to live in some kind of commune in Cornwall raising woolly monkeys.'

'God, I've been there!' she says. 'The Woolly Monkey Sanctuary. My aunt took me years ago. It was amazing.'

'See? That proves it.' He grins at her.

'I think I spoke to him. A gaunt old man in a checked shirt. Like an emaciated Freud.'

'Bald head, white beard? That's the guy.'

'The monkeys were wonderful. They've got these leathery black hands and feet, like little long-fingered gloves, and prehensile tails.' She remembers a tiny baby, dangling upside down by its tail from a tree branch, grappling at its mother's head with its spidery fingers. 'It looks like they're locked in, but they can escape any time. But they don't even think about it, because they don't want to leave the rest of the troop.'

'Well this Williams guy reckons it's our sense of an afterlife that makes us human. Our belief in a spirit world, however you define it. Souls. Ancestors. Ghosts.'

'So I'm not human, then, according to your Mr Williams.'

'Why do you keep doing that?' He frowns at her.

'What?'

'Pretending you don't believe.'

'Because I don't.'

'You put the photos back up, Sylvia. You kept the light burning. You kept the dolls.'

'That was your idea,' she objects.

'I didn't make you do any of it.'

She rolls over on her side and pulls the sheet over her shoulders. 'I've been thinking about my miscarriages,' she says quietly. 'I mean, of course they're always there somewhere at the back of my mind. But recently, ever since I found those stones in the garden, I keep thinking about how they —'

'How they died?' Very gently.

'Yes.'

328

'Because they were alive.'

'Yes.' She can feel tears seeping out of her. 'One was a boy. They analysed the remains from the D and C. I don't know about the other one. I just flushed it away.'

'Oh, Sylvia,' he sighs, gathering her into his monkey arms.

'And the triplets.'

'What triplets?'

'The IVF babies. Peter, Paul and Mary, Bennet called them.' She's smiling through her tears. 'And the other three we didn't even give names to.'

'It's OK.' He's nuzzling her hair, stroking her back.

'No it isn't OK. I let them go, just like that. I let them be taken away.'

'They were dead, Sylvia.'

'But they were alive first. That's what I didn't want to think about. They were alive. Then they were dead. And I let them be taken away.'

'I've got to go back to Newcastle,' she says after supper that evening.

'I know.' His eyes are glowing in the candlelight. His face looks open, ironed out, clear.

'Not because of Bennet. Because of the babies.'

'I know,' he says again.

'Because ghosts stay in one place, don't they? If they exist.'

'Yes. As far as anyone knows, they seem to be rooted in the place where they died, or were buried. Sometimes in a place they loved. A house, a tree, a garden.'

'Like an image on photographic paper?' she smiles.

'God, you really went for me when I first suggested that!'

'I still don't believe,' she says, taking his hand and kissing it.

'Yes you do. Some part of you does.'

'I love you,' she says.

'I know.'

'I'll leave the key, so you can keep the lamp burning.'
'OK.'
'Only if you want to.'
'I want to.'

Chapter 27

The Olive-Wood Box

Martin stands in the road and watches until Sylvia's out of sight down the hill. Then he walks on to the patio and watches for her to appear in the village below, a tiny figure in a white crash helmet on a scarlet scooter. He hears her toot the horn and raise her hand as she passes the taverna, then the distant two-tone revving of the engine as she throttles down around the bend and heads off towards the main road.

He keeps watching as she appears and disappears around the bends in the road, the engine growing fainter and fainter, until all he can hear is the screaming of the cicadas and the mew of a hawk floating high on the updraft of hot air from the valley.

Only then does he drag his eyes, all his senses, away from her.

Sylvia.

He feels as though his skin has been peeled away. His jeans, he can feel them chafing between his legs. He can feel the lining of the zip against his dick; the seams running down the sides of his thighs. He can feel his tee shirt, the damp under the arms, the slight pull on the hairs there.

She licked his armpit, diving her pink tongue into the white hollow; her tongue that tastes of peppermint and honey.

He's getting hard again. He can smell her on his fingers, around his mouth. He's a fox. His brain is all nose. This morning he wanted to crawl up inside her, face first; he wanted to push his nose right into her clean little bumhole. She stopped him. She was embarrassed. But she won't always be.

She wants to wash everything, to shower everything off, but she won't always want to.

He doesn't know what to do with himself. Chi is singing in his fingers, in his lips. He can almost see the energy sparking along the surface of his skin. He's radioactive, a charge wanting to discharge. He wants to run. He wants to laugh.

He paces around the little house touching her things: her neat things in their proper places. The damp towel over the balustrade; the folded white cotton knickers and the folded black ones. The ironing board on its special hooks at the side of the wardrobe. She'd asked him to fix the hooks there, and the little blue shelf above it for the iron, its flex neatly coiled, the special plastic jug for filling the iron.

'Stop laughing,' she'd said when he'd smiled at the little shelf she'd painted ready for him, all sanded down and primed properly, and the metal shelf supports she'd painted to match. 'I can't help being a perfectionist. I've always been like this.'

He loves her energy, that look she gets on her face when she's squaring up to some task.

He loves her little hands, her narrow fingers, the half-moons at the base of her pink nails. So confident, those hands, so precise. And her wrists, all the small bones in there, the blue veins like seaweed under the skin. And stronger than they look, those slender wrists. That's another thing about her—

There are so many things about her.

He opens the washing basket – how typical that she'd have a washing basket, just for her little bits of washing, just so there'd be something round and wheat-coloured in that little alcove beside the door that needs something round and wheat-coloured in it. As though it was meant to be there. That's another thing about her, her artistry with ordinary things, the way she arranges them to feed the eye.

And another thing, the smell of her at the end of the day, when the sun's been on her skin, and the soap smell and moisturizers have worn off. He takes out the nightdress she shoved into the basket before she left and buries his face in it, and inhales over and over until he's dizzy and there are tears in his eyes because he is so fucking *happy* he could shout.

*

He's parked the van by the gate where anyone can see it. He wants everyone to see it. He wants Aphrodite and Maria to see it.

They can't say anything about him staying there because they know she's away. But when she comes back, the whole village will know. When they see the van's still parked there.

It doesn't take him long to move in. He sets up his folding table in the bedroom and places her blue oil lamp in the middle of it. He fetches the olive-wood box and the tartan tin and places them either side of the lamp. He drapes his t'ai chi things over the balustrade, puts his razor in the pink toilet and his soap and shampoo by the shower.

Then he goes back to the van for his mother's ashes. They're in the oven – he's never really known what to do with an oven – in the big ornate silver tin where he used to keep his dope stash and skins.

'Come on,' he says as he carries it into the house. 'We're going to stay here for a while.'

He puts the tin on the folding table and squats down beside it for a moment. 'Will you be all right here? The lamp will be on all the time and the van's just outside. I'll be sleeping over on that platform. How about if I get out the Peasant Cup to make you feel at home?'

He rummages in the rusty biscuit tin and places the Peasant Cup next to the silver tin. Then he takes out the passport and stands it up nearby, and uses the Yellowy-Grey Stone to prop it open on the photograph page.

'What am I going to do with you, Miss Theresa Elizabeth?' he sighs.

He'd tried taking her to Matala again a month ago, that time he'd run away from Sylvia. When she'd come to him in the middle of the night, drunk and angry, and had kissed him and wriggled under him, until he was suddenly inside her, without trying, just like that.

Just like that. Just like that.

With his mother in the same room.

And that same sweet winey taste in her mouth, that same alcohol sheen on her skin. That same red place, that same wet place, that same urge in him to gallop and gallop and gallop. And Theresa Elizabeth lolling there unconscious at the back of his eyes.

After he'd sent Sylvia away he would have whipped himself, if he'd had a flail. He would have hammered a nail through the palm of his hand. But he'd shaved his head instead and promised his mother he would keep it that way until he'd done whatever it was she wanted him to do.

His plan was to camp just outside Matala village and wait until it was dark, then sneak over the fence to the caves. He was going to climb around the headland, out of sight of the cocktail bars and beach umbrellas, to the flat rock where he used to fish with Karl. And empty the silver tin there. She'd said he'd come to her on the sea wind. He thought he'd let the sea wind take her away.

But he'd turned the van round before he was even halfway there. It wasn't right, he knew it. She'd never stay there. Or at Argyle Street, where a music teacher and a statistician had moved in, and the garden was all gravel and decking. Or at the Kidlington house, where a retired coach driver had rotovated and planted potatoes.

When he goes to fetch his food from the van, he finds Smelly Spiros dithering at the gate asking where Sylvia is, wondering if it's OK to come in.

'The lady doesn't like me,' he confides in Greek. 'Because I live with the goats.'

'She likes things to be clean,' Martin explains.

Martin is fond of Smelly Spiros. He likes his growly voice and his smell of rancid meat, goat dung and woodsmoke. He likes to see him shambling around in his loose shoes and flappy raincoat, talking to the feral cats he feeds. He visits him sometimes in his odd half-a-house, to see if he needs any jobs doing, and they sit together on the bench outside and don't say very much.

'I've put a lock on the toilet,' Martin says apologetically. Then, seeing the old man peering hesitantly down the path: 'Would you like some coffee?'

'Is it OK?' Spiros asks.

'It's fine. Don't worry. You are welcome. Come and see what the lady has been doing to Kokona's house.'

At the patio Spiros stops short and stares at the fractured wooden carvings laid out on the concrete.

'What are you doing?' he asks, obviously distressed. 'This belongs to Kokona.'

'Someone broke it, so I am mending it.'

'You have put this bit in the wrong place,' he says, picking up a piece. 'They are not feathers; they are fish scales.' He kneels down stiffly and moves the pieces around, then nods and grunts with satisfaction.

'It took me two years to make this. I still have the tools, but my hands are no good for this careful work any more.' He displays wide trembling hands. 'It was a gift for Kokona. She liked it very much.'

'Why did you make it for her?'

'Kokona was always kind to me. When the boys threw eggs at my house, she was angry with them. She cooked *spanakopita* and *koulourakia* for me. She gave me medicine when I was sick.'

He creaks to his feet and eases himself down on to one of the patio chairs.

'You loved her.' Martin looks at the old man.

'Yes, always. Since we were children. But she was clever and I was not clever. I think very slowly. My feet are clumsy. People would have laughed at us.'

He leans down and points to another section of carving. 'That bunch of grapes is wrong. The leaf is on the wrong side.' Then, when Martin has corrected it: 'I could never come to her house when she was there, because people would talk. So I fitted it at Easter when she was staying with her sister in Vrisses. It was a surprise for when she came back.'

He sits back and sighs. 'I made it from my sleeping platform, my beams. I didn't have any money. So I made it from the wood of my house.'

In the darkroom a few days later Martin finds a photograph of Bennet Man. He's in a smart café with bamboo chairs and glass tables, with a Greek coffee at his elbow and a posh white hat on the table beside it. He imagines Sylvia looking through the camera and framing him slightly to the left, so that she can fit the hat in the photo too.

He takes the photo through to the kitchen so he can see it in daylight. If he didn't want to kill him, he would quite like Bennet Man. There's something benign and bearlike about him. Martin looks at his rival, sizing him up: his obvious wealth, his wide chest, his big brain. No Cro-Magnon Pete here; this is a proper man, a worthy opponent.

There's the sound of shuffling feet and Smelly Spiros appears in the doorway, his brown smell arriving a moment later. He's visiting every day now to check on the repairs to the sideboard.

'So, this is the husband,' he says, lowering himself into a chair and picking up the photo.

'Yes.'

'You must not be here when he comes back. He won't like it if he finds you staying in his house.'

'It's not his house,' says Martin, lighting the gas for coffee. 'It belongs to the lady, to Sylvia.'

'But the lady is married to this husband. So it's not good for you to be here in her house when she gets back.'

'I think maybe the lady will be coming back alone.'

'But you are not sure.'

'No, I'm not sure.'

They look together at the photo.

'He is a big man,' comments Spiros.

'Yes.'

'I think he must have a big house in England. And a big car.'

'Yes.'

'Do you have a house in England?'

'No. My mother had a house, but she died and strangers are living there now.'

'So where is your house now?'

'I don't have a house. I live in my van.'

'Why?'

'I like to move around. See different places, different people.'

'But you have to come home sometimes,' says the old man. 'In the summer, when I was a boy, I took the goats to find grass in the mountains. It was nice to sleep under the stars and shoot rabbits and light a fire. But after one, two days I was always hungry for home. Even when I went out on the fishing boat, after one day I was ready to come home. Even the fishermen, the loudest men, the strongest, used to stare at the horizon, for the outline of the land, and dream of their mothers, their wives.'

This is a big speech for Spiros and he's quiet for a long time afterwards. Martin sets his usual *gleeko* coffee on the table and a glass of cold water. The old man closes his thick brown fingers around the tiny cup handle and sucks noisily, then takes a big gulp of the water. When he's finished he looks at Martin.

'If you don't have a home, what do you dream of when you are away from home?' he asks.

'I don't know,' says Martin.

'Maybe you don't dream like other people,' says Spiros.

Martin does dream, though. Big hungry dreams where Sylvia's right there in the bed with him, opening her mouth, clambering up him and on to him as though she's a lizard, he's a tree. He wakes with a grin on his face and his dick hard as a chisel, and just lies there, gazing out at her square of lemon tree, feeling he's going to burst.

He's sure it must show. When he strides down the hill with his toolbag over his shoulder – because the air is so fucking *green* and he's too hyped-up to drive – he's sure people must notice, must scent something about him, though he washes every day, a musk rising out of him, that says he's in rut, he's in love.

He's sure Aphrodite suspects something. The way she stands appraising him as he works on her shelves, with her arms folded under her plump little breasts, pushing them up at him in her lacy low-cut bra.

'So, you are staying with Sylvia,' she says, fishing for more.

'Just house-sitting while she's away.'

'Don't you think she is too old for you?'

'How old is too old, Aphrodite?' He bats her away with a teasing smile. 'Are you too old for me?'

This makes her sashay to the mirror, she can't help it, and fluff up her curls; then clippety-clip down to the kitchen to fetch him a Mythos. But it's Maria, all breathless and pink, full of this silly hairdressing course she wants to do, who brings the beer back up for him.

With Aphrodite it's simple. She fancies him and she likes to flirt. It's like dancing when you both know the steps, and it always ends when the music stops. But Maria's on a helter-skelter; she's launched herself and she doesn't know how to stop. Even though he's told her – 'Maria, I don't want you' – she doesn't believe it. She thinks if she can just love him harder, and longer, eventually she'll wear him down. If she can just get him to look at her, then he'll see how gorgeous she is. If she can just get him to kiss her, she'll turn him into her prince.

Now she's asking if he'll teach her to drive.

'I'm going to need a van for my business,' she's saying. 'For when I'm qualified. So I can go house to house.'

And she's so wide-eyed, so passionate, so sure he won't refuse, that it's hard to say 'no'. But he does, and sees her flush with humiliation, and tries to make her understand – again – why he won't be her boyfriend.

'I'm too old for you.'

'I thought you say it is not important what age someone is. It is the soul that is important. The heart.'

'We don't have anything to say to each other. You don't read –'

'I do.'

'I mean proper books. Not just magazines.'

'We don't have books in our house. But I want to read books. Give me your books to read.'

'They're in English, Maria,' he sighs. 'Difficult English.'

'You think I'm stupid.' Now she's hurt. Her mouth has gone small.

'No, I don't think you're stupid,' he explains patiently. 'I just think you're more interested in hairstyles and fashion than in philosophy or anthropology.'

'But I'm young,' she says. 'All young girls are like me.' She grins at him suddenly. 'You don't know how I will turn out when I am mature.'

He smiles back. She's right. He has no idea what she'll be like in a few years' time.

'I will have books in my hairdressing van,' she declares. 'And you will look at me and wish you were with me.'

*

338

Every day Smelly Spiros comes to watch him work on the sideboard. He shambles on to the patio and sits quietly in the sunshine until Martin stops to make coffee. Then he sucks up his sweet shot of brown liquid, drains his glass of water and shambles off back down the hill to his half-a-house.

Some days he'll light up the half-cigarette he's been saving and tap the ash carefully into his hand, then wipe the hand on to his trousers. Some days he'll say something. Some days not. When he does say something, Martin always tries to answer him properly.

'Where is your mother buried?' is one of the things he says one day.

'Nowhere. She wasn't buried. Her body was burned.'

'Why?'

'So she would be small enough to carry with me. I needed time to decide where to bury her.'

'When you find that place you will have to stop travelling, or you will leave her behind.'

'Yes. I suppose I will.' Martin hasn't thought about this before. But Spiros is right. He can't just abandon her somewhere and move on.

Then he thinks: *I've been doing this all wrong. I shouldn't be finding a place for her. I should be finding a place for me.*

'I need to buy a piece of land,' he says aloud. 'A place to think about when I'm away. A place to go back to.'

'I have a lot of land,' says Spiros, waving his wide hand vaguely towards the back of the house, where the hill scrambles higher before stumbling into the next valley. 'It's just goat land, with rocks and caves and olive trees, and no flat places for vegetables. Only cats live there, and lizards. It's the land my brothers didn't want.'

'Could I get the van there?'

'Yes, there is a road. And a well with sweet water. You can see right across the valley to the sea.'

Martin looks at the old man. He's thinking: *I could find a cave with a view of the sea.* He's thinking: *I could grow a house out of the rocks.* Something that feels like a balloon is inflating in his chest. He's thinking: *I could bury the silver tin and the olive-wood box.*

Chapter 28

Bennet's car is parked outside the house when Sylvia arrives back in Newcastle, and the lights seem to be on in all the rooms. She's got her front-door key in her bag, but she rings the doorbell instead. She feels like a visitor. It doesn't feel like she lives here any more.

'Sylvia!' His smile is huge; it seems to fill the hall. He's wearing navy overalls and there's a smudge of something white on his chin.

'I changed my ticket,' she says, edging past him.

'Why didn't you call?'

'I don't know. I wanted to think.'

'Where's your luggage?' He peers vaguely into the porch.

'That's what I mean.'

'Oh. Right.' His face falls. 'You're not staying.'

'No, but there are some things I have to do. And I wanted to see you.'

'See away.' He strikes a pose and rotates his body in front of her. 'I give you Ironmongery Man!'

'What's going on? What's that smell?'

'Screwing and glueing. Once I finished the darkroom, I found I couldn't stop. Amazingly addictive this DIY lark. So I've started on the attic.'

'Shouldn't you be at the clinic, lasering the Arab World?'

'The Arab World is *finito*. I've traded in my laser for a bradawl. When you threw me out I just couldn't drum up the enthusiasm any more. The zeros kept accumulating in the deposit account, but with you hunkered down in your hovel there didn't seem much point trying to be a filthy capitalist pig.'

She hangs up her coat and follows him into the kitchen. There's a box of paint tins on the floor; bin bags stuffed with bits of wood by the back door.

'You see how it is? Leave a man on his own for a few months and all hell breaks loose.' Half a pizza, still in its carton, is on the table, along with three half-drunk mugs of tea and an empty bottle of red wine. The sink is full of paintbrushes.

'Coffee?' he offers. 'Wine? Slap in the face with a wet fish?'

She moves a pile of ironing from a chair and sits down. 'Peppermint tea if there is any.'

He fills the kettle. 'That research grant came through, by the way. So I'm not entirely a born-again artisan. But I thought if you ever did forgive me, we should spend a bit more time together.'

'Bennet—' she begins.

'I know. This is just a visit. You haven't decided. I don't expect you to fall into my arms straight away. But this isn't just about you. It's about me, too.'

'You look smaller,' she says.

'Downsized, you mean?'

'Ha ha. No. Thinner, I suppose. Younger.'

'Do you want to see what I've been up to?'

She follows him upstairs, treading warily on a dust sheet. The banisters are smeary, caked with grey dust.

'It was your sink that got me started on the attic, really,' he's saying. 'The plumber said while he was messing around with the pipework it made sense to get the ducts up for the bathroom on the next floor. Then I got an architect in to talk about staircases. Next thing I knew your darkroom was cut in half and there was a bloody great hole in the ceiling.'

There's a ladder where the door used to be; through the hole she can see where he's begun fixing tongue and groove between the rafters. The landing carpet's gone and there are sheets of plasterboard propped against the wall.

'You weren't here to consult, but I remembered we said we might go for the Shaker look up there. Hence the panelling. I thought I'd leave you to decide on the colour.'

'I can't believe the mess you've made of the landing. Molly Maids must be having nightmares.'

'The challenge is good for them. They get paid far too much for what they do. I'm getting some proper chaps in to do the stairs and the Veluxes in the attic, but I thought I could probably manage the rest myself.'

She's thinking: *God, what a mess he's making*. She's thinking: *I should be cross, but I'm not*.

'Take a look in the darkroom.'

She pushes open the resited door, and switches on a light. There's a proper dog-leg lobby just inside and then a second door: close-fitting, covered with black felt. Inside is everything she could ever need: state-of-the-art enlarger, shelving, sink unit, cupboards. Even wires and pegs to hang up the prints.

'Well? Do you like it? I got some photographer bloke from the university to advise me. He was quite jealous when he saw the final result.'

'God, Bennet. It's wonderful! I can't believe you've done all this.'

'Not bad, is it?' he says, looking pleased. Then, after a pause: 'Sorry about the sideboard.'

'That's OK,' she says. 'I've asked Martin to mend it.'

'Oh. Right.'

'He's found some matching wood.'

'I went a bit loopy back there.' He looks embarrassed.

'It's OK, honestly. It'll be fine.'

'But you still want me to make up the spare bed.' It's a statement rather than a question.

'Yes,' she says.

He phones out for a Chinese takeaway and they eat it out of the cartons, by candlelight, at the kitchen table.

'Sorry there's nothing in the fridge.'

'It's fine. It's nice to eat something without olive oil for a change.'

'Good to see you're drinking sensibly again,' he says as she pours more Pinot Grigio.

'I came back because of the babies,' she says, laying down her chopsticks and looking at him.

'Right.'

'You always say "right" when you're not sure about something.'

'OK then. What do you mean?'

'The miscarriages. The IVF babies. I don't think I mourned them properly when they died.'

'You didn't want to talk about it,' he says quietly, toying with a hunk of sweet-and-sour chicken.

'I know.'

'So I didn't push it.'

'Did you want to?'

'In a way. I was probably nearly as cut up about it as you were. But I was relieved, too, that you were being so brave. You know the Bennets – stiff uppers, soft soles.'

'But I wasn't, though. Being brave, I mean. I was being cowardly. I was treating them like clumps of cells, so it would be easier to cope with.' She takes a sip of wine and looks at him. 'You remember when you named the first IVF batch?'

'The singing trio.'

'I really hated you doing that. I didn't want to think of them as babies.'

'I named the second batch too.'

'You never said.'

'No. Well.'

'What did you call them?'

'Mary, Mungo and Midge.'

She explodes with laughter. 'Oh, I do love you.'

'Do you?'

She sighs. 'Yes. That's what makes everything so complicated.'

'Ah, complicated,' he says. 'Yes. Love will do that.'

'Have you still got the photos?'

'They're in my wallet.'

'Can I see them?'

They're just as she remembers: grainy, blobby, monochrome; like an illustration for rock cakes from an old cookery book. On the back he's written their names, in inverted commas, and the date.

'Where are they now, do you think?' she asks.

'Somewhere in the North Sea, I expect. Isn't that where all our effluent ends up eventually?'

'I didn't mean that.'

'Oh. Right.'

'There you go again.' She smiles at him.

'You're referring to their noncorporeal essences.'

'Something like that.'

'I didn't think you believed in all that "unexplained" guff.'

'Do you?'

'I suppose I must do, really, mustn't I? Why else am I carrying the little buggers' photos around with me?'

She looks at them again. 'People used to think the soul sort of swooped in at quickening, when you feel the baby move for the first time. But right-to-lifers say it's when the sperm enters the egg.'

'What's the legal time limit for abortion these days? Twenty-four weeks? Presumably some erudite committee's decided that's when a foetus qualifies for its human rights.'

'What do you think?'

'Has to be conception, doesn't it? Or it doesn't make any sense.' He pauses; catches a dribble of wax from the candle on his finger. 'Not that any of it makes any sense really.'

'Maybe it seeps in gradually,' she says. 'And we become more and more ourselves as we grow older.'

'When I was in Africa someone told me that some parents

don't name their kiddies until they're six months old. Presumably so it doesn't hurt so much if they die before then.'

'That's what I was doing, wasn't it?' They look at each other, then she giggles. 'I can't believe you called them Mary, Mungo and Midge.'

'There was the boy, too.'

'The second miscarriage.'

'I called him Stephen.'

'Your middle name.'

'Yes. I thought maybe he'd have looked a bit like me. What with me being his father and all.'

'What about the other one?'

'She was there for such a short time, I never got round to it. I mean, you started bleeding almost as soon as you found out you were pregnant.'

'She?'

'Well, yes, I suppose I've always thought of that one as a girl. Because she was so much a part of you and we never really saw her. I mean, with Stephen there was the scan and the histology results. And with the others, we had the photos. But with her – well, she just slipped away all by herself.'

'Into the North Sea.'

'Yes.'

'Do you ever think about the others? The leftover embryos at the IVF Unit? The ones they froze?'

'No.' He seems surprised. 'We signed a form.'

'I know. That's one of the reasons I came back. I want to find out what happened to them.'

He hands her a clean towel as she goes into the bathroom. 'I did manage to keep on top of the washing,' he says. 'So I'm not a complete caveman.'

'You know when you smashed up the sideboard,' she says, hugging the towel to her chest, 'because you thought there was something going on between me and Martin?'

'Look, I'm really sorry about that. I was so racked with guilt myself, I didn't know what—'

'Well there was.'

'What?'

'Something going on, I mean. Not then, not when you accused me of it. At that point it was just an attraction. But later, after you told me about Val. When you went back to Newcastle. Well, it went further.'

'Oh. Right.' He looks at his feet, then at her face. 'Do you love him?'

'Yes, I think so.'

'But you love me too.'

'Yes.'

'What are you going to do about it?'

'I don't know.'

Sylvia goes to the hospital the next day. She dresses in her work clothes because she doesn't want to be fobbed off. She wants the people she deals with to think she speaks their language, that she belongs to their world. If she approaches them as a patient, she's afraid they'll be defensive.

At the IVF Unit the receptionist assumes she's come to arrange another IVF attempt.

'No, not yet,' Sylvia smiles. 'I'm not ready to go through all that again quite yet. But I was wondering what happened to the rest of my embryos. You know, the ones that were frozen.'

'Didn't you sign a research consent form?'

'Oh, yes. But I was curious about the process.' She makes her voice disinterested, professional. 'Do you keep a record of what happens to them?'

She knows they do. They have to keep a record of everything in this department. There have been too many IVF mix-ups to risk leaving anything unlabelled. There's bound to be a batch number, a date, a technician's signature.

'I should ask Professor Drury,' the receptionist says doubtfully.

'Only we don't usually give out that kind of information. It's on the consent form, the kind of research they might be used for.'

'Did they go to the Stem Cell Unit?'

'Well I suppose it's no great secret. Yes, they get everything we don't use these days.'

At the Stem Cell Unit, she finds out the name of the consultant in charge, then she hangs about in the corridor until he emerges. She follows him to the doctors' canteen and sits down opposite him.

'I'm Mrs Bennet,' she begins. 'From Histology. I had a couple of IVF attempts last year and I wanted to find out about my embryos. The leftover ones that came to the Stem Cell Unit.'

'What did you want to know? Only we don't normally—'

'I wanted to see if I could get them back.' She sees him stiffen.

'Didn't you sign a consent form?'

'Yes, but I've changed my mind.'

'May I ask why?'

'The ones you succeed with, the ones that you turn into cell lines, they become immortal, right?'

'Yes. Once we create a cell line, it will go on pretty much indefinitely producing new cells with the potential to become any kind of tissue. That's what makes them so valuable to us.' He's choosing his words carefully, watching for her reaction.

'Is that what happened to my embryos?'

'Not necessarily. It's a very complicated process, and we're not always successful. We go through hundreds of embryos for every single cell line we manage to produce.'

'So they might all be dead.'

'That's certainly the most likely scenario, I'm afraid.'

'But one might have been turned into one of these immortal cell lines.'

'It's possible, yes.'

'Can you find out? Only I don't like the idea of my babies being turned into cell factories.' She sees him flinch at the phrase. 'Or anyone's baby, for that matter.'

'There are ethics committees for this kind of debate, Mrs Bennet,' he says.

'So we don't have to think about it, you mean?' She wants to argue with him, but he won't be drawn.

'They're alive at the moment, you realize,' he says. 'The cell lines I mean.'

'Yes.'

'So if, for the sake of argument, one of your embryos has been developed into a cell line, and we give it back to you, it will die. You do realize that, don't you? It will be like switching off the life-support machine of a terminal patient.'

'But I'll be releasing it back into the wild.'

'What?'

'It doesn't matter.'

'Do you have the batch number from the IVF Unit?'

'No, they won't tell me without your authorization.'

'OK. Let me think about it.'

A letter arrives from the hospital the next day.

She searches in vain for the ivory letter opener, then gives up and rips it open with a steak knife.

'He didn't waste any time,' comments Bennet, dunking a paintbrush in white spirit.

' "Dear Mrs Bennet," ' she reads, ' "It was interesting to meet you yesterday. Unfortunately," blah blah. "Forces beyond my control," blah, blah. Bastard.'

'You didn't really expect him to risk one of his precious cell lines, did you?'

'I wanted to know.'

'They're gone, Sylvie. You heard what the man said.'

'But one of them might still be alive. Maybe more than one. It's horrible, B, what happens to them. They take out the middle of the blastocyst, the bit that's the baby, and put it on to a bed of feeder cells, like an artificial placenta. And that makes them reproduce themselves over and over forever. Then they take the new clones and use them to manufacture nerve cells, or blood, muscle, whatever.'

'It's only horrible if you think of them as babies.'

'But that's the whole point. How would you feel if it was Mary, Mungo or Midge? Or Peter, or Paul, or Mary? The ones they're experimenting on are no different. They're just the ones you didn't give names to.'

'So, what now?'

She smiles. 'Two Marys. Did you realize?'

'So what? It's a name I'm particularly fond of.'

'It's your mother's name.'

'Well, they did have one quarter of her chromosomes.'

'I suppose so. God, Grannie Bennet. What a prospect.'

'So, are you going to give up?'

'I don't know.'

'I could try to pull rank if you like.' She stares at him. 'They're my babies too, you know. Or had you forgotten?'

Yes, she realizes, she had forgotten. She's been so caught up with her desire for a baby, with her cycles, her obsessions, she'd forgotten they were part of him too.

'Let me make a few phone calls,' he says, going into the sitting room and closing the door.

'What happened?' she says when he emerges a few minutes later.

'He's going to look into it. Obviously had no idea I was the father.'

'It's outrageous that you being a consultant should make a difference.'

'Fortunate for us, however. Though I doubt if it will come to anything.'

'Why are you doing this, Bennet? I don't expect it will do much for your reputation.'

'Boring though it may seem, I still love you. And, pending a better theory of life and death, I'm prepared to go along with whatever it is you want to do.'

349

'Mary Warnock,' she says.

'Excuse me?'

'Another Mary.'

'Oh. Right.'

The consultant telephones the following afternoon and asks to speak to Mr Bennet. Sylvia calls him down from the attic, where he's sanding purlins, and he gallops downstairs beige with wood-dust.

'Bennet here,' he barks. Then, after a pause: 'Just as well, really. Thanks for looking, mate. Much appreciated.' He puts the phone down and turns to Sylvia. 'He says he's checked their records and none of our embryos survived.'

'So that's it.'

'Yes.'

'Do you believe him?'

'Apart from storming the place and demanding to see for ourselves, I think that's as far as we can take it.'

Sylvia sits up late after Bennet has gone to bed. She feels unsettled; as though she's forgotten something, though the surfaces are all wiped and the dishwasher's chuntering away.

She's spent the afternoon cleaning the kitchen and preparing supper. Trying to feel at home with the bleached wood and white walls, the black and white tiles; the silver cutlery his parents gave them as a wedding present; the lovely spacious elegance of everything. And she does, sitting there listening to Bennet running water upstairs, flushing the loo, closing the bedroom door. And the radiators ticking as the central heating switches itself off for the night.

Normally she'd go to the computer at this time of the evening, to see if anything new had been published about infertility. Now, though, she just wants to sit and wonder what it is she's forgotten. If she has forgotten anything.

She can sense something at the edge of her mind, and thinks

of what Martin said about faint stars that you can't see if you look at them directly. *That's because the centre of the retina is full of cones*, she thinks. *For distinguishing colour. But the perimeter is mostly rods, for perceiving light and dark. Shades of grey.*

She takes out the IVF photos and looks at them, and smiles again at what Bennet had written on the back.

You deserve a funeral, she thinks. *And your brothers and sisters. Stephen. Sylvia. But there's nothing to bury.*

She closes her eyes for a moment and pictures Kokona's key; and an axe laid across a heap of logs, like a knife across a plate; a door opening and a row of photos on a wall like windows to another world. All the children looking out.

She finds the photo of Bennet easily. She'd organized all their childhood snaps into albums soon after they were married, and they're shelved in a neat row in the sitting room. The one she chooses is of him on his seventh birthday: full of life, standing astride a new bicycle with the sun in his eyes, obviously itching to career off on it.

'Hello, Stephen,' she says.

But when she looks through her own childhood photos, she can't find anything she likes. *I look so stiff and self-conscious*, she thinks. Then, sighing: *That's because they were all taken by my mother.*

Then she remembers the photo her aunt took of her in Devon, that was with her letters and the 'When I Grow Up' list. A minute later she's laying it on the table. It's the grin she wants: the bright triumph of it. *I could have become anyone*, she thinks. Then: *I still can.*

She remembers how much her teeth were chattering that day, how her skin was stinging from the wind-whipped sand.

'Hello, Sylvia,' she says, smiling at the shivering girl in the rainbow beach towel.